FALL PREY

FALL PREY

THE ATTACK

DALLAS MASSEY

.   .   .   .   .

Book Cover Design by ebooklaunch.com

DEDICATION

To Dillon Massey, my brother in Heaven, and Beau Massey,
my brother on Earth

ACKNOWLEDGEMENTS

I thank everyone who encouraged me to finally take up writing and helped me to develop, edit and breathe life into my story.

I thank God for granting me the time and the ability to write, my mom, Cindy Rambo, Beth Ann Porter, a librarian and long-time family friend, Marilyn Holt, my cousin and mentor, and my editor, Caroline Giammanco. I would also like to thank all those who provided me with additional motivation, and my dad, Steve Massey, who kept me up watching *Blade* all those nights, whether he remembers it or not.

TABLE OF CONTENTS

"It was meet that we should make merry, and be glad: for this thy brother was dead, and is alive again; and was lost, and is found."

—Luke 15:32, KJV

Chapter I

The Unforgiving Blade

Jerrick snapped to attention, startled by the sound of leaves crushed underfoot somewhere in the redwood forest. He scanned the dense coverage of trees on the hill, searching for the source of the noise through his gun scope. The sun sank ever lower in the sky, barely visible despite the late afternoon, its red-purple light concealed by the thick foliage. The giant, darkened shadows of the forest's mighty trees stretched over the landscape as the twilight continued its advance.

Jerrick's heart raced as his eyes passed over the cover points before him. He was one of several human security guards responsible for the vampire camp behind him and the first to blame should an attack occur. Jerrick swung his assault rifle back and forth, expecting an entire company of Legion soldiers to suddenly emerge and mow him down in a hail of gunfire.

Only his vampire overlords could hope to survive a full assault. They would leave their expendable human underlings to deal with their attackers as they made their escape.

Jerrick knew he couldn't allow the panic to control him.

He countered its effects by taking several deep breaths, forcing himself to relax. Jerrick let his weapon fall back across his chest, finding nothing of concern within the wood's heavily foliaged thickets. A squirrel was likely responsible for the noise, as the forest held a plethora of wildlife within its realm.

"Oh, well…" Jerrick muttered to himself, his anxiety dwindled into boredom. He almost wished there actually was a company of Legion soldiers lurking somewhere nearby.

Any action was preferable to the monotony of a late afternoon watch.

Jerrick's shift began at noon and lasted until dusk. He saw virtually nothing during his time on duty. Vaylat, the appointed leader, preferred the humans to keep watch during the day. He believed them good for little else, as their physical inferiority allowed the vampires to rest while they awaited the night.

Jerrick looked back at the camp and cringed. The thought of Vaylat made his skin crawl.

The guy was a creep, even among vampires.

Jerrick stood near the base of a massive redwood some distance from the camp perimeter, out of sight and earshot of the vampires. Despite his loyalty to Atropos, he cared little for his overlords. As far as he was concerned, he could never stay far enough away from them.

Completing yet another quick scan of the dark, leaf-littered forest, Jerrick looked down at his modest attire. Except for his bulletproof vest, he wore simple street clothes, and not good ones, with multiple holes perforating his t-shirt and jeans. The vampires hadn't even bothered to supply him with a helmet, and his baseball cap offered no protection.

Jerrick's weapon bore testament to their apathy, even more so than his clothing did. The gun was an old, worn to pieces AK-47, the stock kept together by too much duct tape. He dreaded what might happen should he fire it. Regardless, Jerrick refused to let his inadequacies affect him.

He knew it would be worth it one day.

God-like strength and immortality were the eventual rewards for his undying loyalty.

Jerrick snapped out of his daydream and raised his weapon to his eye, his finger on the trigger when he heard the sound of more leaves underfoot.

Four figures emerged from behind one of the redwoods some distance away, obscured beneath the trees' shadow. Two walked out in front with their wrists bound, and two others followed, their weapons trained on their captives.

Jerrick had let himself lose track of time, and the sun dipped ever lower in the sky.

"Oh, sorry," said Jerrick as he lowered his weapon.

He recognized the approaching figures, though he waited until he saw the bloody red shears painted on the helmets of the two gun wielders just to be sure. Both were human Atropos soldiers, albeit better equipped than Jerrick, provided with helmets and modern firearms.

The soldiers had left the camp for the woods near the middle of Jerrick's watch to forage for their masters. They now returned with what appeared to be a pair of unwary, frightened campers, both of whom were unable to cry out due to the gags in their mouths. The two, a man and woman, looked toward Jerrick as they walked. Their posture grew tense when they saw him, both terrified yet with no idea as to what was truly in store for them.

"Hold it!" Jerrick commanded. He knew the old song and dance was merely a formality, another means by which their masters exercised control. He enjoyed it regardless, as it was one of the few times when he could enforce his own will.

"Not another one..." muttered one of the Atropos soldiers, a woman, her face just visible under the trees' shade.

"What was that?" asked Jerrick, a smug grin on his face as he relished yet another opportunity to exercise control.

All looked up at him with irritated glances, both captors and captives. The female soldier shook her head though remained silent.

"That's what I thought," Jerrick let his smirk fade away. "State your business!" he demanded.

"We have returned with two captives, just as requested," said the female soldier, obviously the one in charge. Her taunt, rigid posture suggested she wished to do Jerrick harm.

"Excellent," Jerrick's smirk returned. "Did they give you any trouble?" he indicated towards the prisoners with his firearm.

"No trouble at all," the woman gave him an awkward smile, perturbed by Jerrick's need to start a conversation.

The sound of crushed leaves met the female soldier's words. The group turned around and looked for the source of the noise, growing tense.

Jerrick raised his weapon to find naught but tree bark and foliage in his crosshairs.

"Uh..." Jerrick grasped for his throat.

He fell to his knees and dropped his weapon, blood gushing from his wound as a blade slid out from his tender flesh.

"Uh…" Jerrick gurgled blood in his mouth. He tried to cry out and found himself unable to do so, his voice box decimated by the assassin's weapon.

Jerrick could only watch as the dark wraith moved onto the two soldiers, hungry for more blood.

The blade sang as it cut through the soldier's throats. The blackened steel glistened in the dwindling sunlight as its impossibly sharp edge sliced through flesh and bone.

Jerrick's vision grew dim, but he saw that the weapon seemed to be part of the assailant. Its arm became the blade, and the sword a dark projection of its bloodlust.

The assailant swept past the soldiers like a shadow-spun whirlwind. The severed heads fell to the ground, and the spent corpses collapsed as torrents of bright blood spewed from their necks.

"Uh… Uh…" Jerrick kept his hand clenched to his throat and looked down at the ever-growing pool of his own blood. The viscous fluid was almost gelatinous upon the dense grass.

Jerrick felt a sudden burst of rage and hated Atropos for forcing him outside the camp. He hated himself for proclaiming allegiance to such heartless curs. He found it strange he should experience such a strong emotion now so close to death.

The assailant turned toward Jerrick, somehow able to sense the small amount of life left within him, able to hear his weak moans and gasps for breath. It sped toward him, its blade still shimmering in the low light as its straight edge took on a wicked curve.

The shadow creature was upon the dying guard in a heartbeat, the phantom reaper back to claim its prize. The obsidian blade tore into his throat once more.

Jerrick's vision cut to black as it severed his spinal cord, his head falling to the ground.

* * *

"Stay still," said Cyrus as he turned toward the bound prisoners.

The last guard's headless body lay prostrate upon the ground as his blood slowly flowed down the hill.

"We're here to help," he told them.

Cyrus spread his arms wide to reassure the rescued captives and allowed his blade-arm to grow into a rippling, bubbling black mass. The individual nanobots composing the weapon actively cleaned its surface as they swarmed. The fluid blood flowed off the prosthesis as it transformed back into a forearm and hand.

No matter his intentions, Cyrus presented a startling sight. He was a menacing creature with a beastly grin, the upper portion of his face concealed under his helmet, his strange, black body armor drenched in blood.

The prisoners remained cemented to the ground, eyes wide, their faces flushed with fear. They stood there for a brief moment before turning to run away from him.

"Oh, come on," Cyrus released a mirthful sigh. "And after what I just did for you."

"Just stay cool," Sergeant Laveau spoke in a low tone. He emerged from the bushes, with Elysia following him.

The Legion soldier raised a hand to stop the fleeing man. Both the sergeant and Elysia had decided against helmets. This allowed the freed prisoners to make eye contact, helping to convince them of their security.

"Stay calm," Laveau continued in a whisper.

He caught the man's female companion in a bear hug as she made to run past him, surprisingly agile despite her awkwardly bound wrists.

"You really are safe now," the sergeant reassured them.

"You'll be alright," said Elysia, remaining near Laveau. She gave the freed prisoners a brilliant smile, helping to provide a calming presence.

"You have a knife on you, Elysia?" asked Laveau. He craned his neck to look at her, his arms wrapped around the still struggling woman.

"Never leave home without at least a dozen," said Elysia as she pulled a long knife from her cloak.

The male prisoner began to back away, his fear renewed when he saw the glistening blade.

"Don't freak out," Laveau told him. "She's gonna cut you loose."

"I guess I'll leave you to it," said Cyrus, though he didn't expect an answer. He was sure they would find what he was about to do more than a little unsettling.

"Nope," said Cyrus to himself as he squatted down to inspect his latest kill. He let the deceased man's still warm hand fall back to the ground after giving it a quick sniff.

"No good," said Cyrus, shaking his head as he went over the remaining corpses. He leaned down and briefly went over the second body, considering giving it a kick. "That's unfortunate," Cyrus sighed as he took a whiff of the last body.

He clenched his stomach, finding his morning meal of raw beef long since vanished away.

Three guards and not a single vampire among them.

"Come on," Laveau gave Cyrus a flat look as he hissed at him. He released the prisoner from his grasp. The woman had grown calm after watching Elysia cut her companion's bonds.

"Why you got to do that?" Laveau's voice remained severe. "You know we have food for you back at base camp. You need to hide the bodies. You made the kills, so clean them up!" he threw a hand up in frustration.

"I was going to do that next. I just thought it would be better to forage off the enemy," said Cyrus. He gave the sergeant a fanged smile, unable to look him in the eye due to his helmet's visor. "I don't see a reason to dig into the Legion's food stocks when there's vampires around."

"There's more than enough raw meat for you back at the camp." Laveau let out a heavy sigh, and exasperation filled his overly expressive eyes. The sergeant was a man with a smug, arrogant face, and this aura was further exaggerated by his spiky, gelled-up hair. "Besides that, it's cannibalism. I don't care if they're vampires or not."

"Well, I suppose if the Legion's good for it." Cyrus shrugged. "I've eaten plenty of unsavory things already."

"Well, you won't be eating anymore of them if I can help it." The sergeant swung his gun strap around his back and took his shotgun in hand. "Now, are you going to hide these bodies, or do I need to provide some encouragement?" "Will do," said Cyrus with a nod. He retained his good mood, though he felt he had forgotten something. "Sir," his delayed response came at last, the word feeling unnatural in his mouth.

"Have you finished with the prisoner's bonds?" asked Laveau as he turned away from Cyrus to give Elysia an overenthusiastic smile.

Cyrus rolled his eyes as he picked up one of the victim's heads by the hair and made for the nearest bush. He had only known the sergeant for a few days and was already tired of his "ladies' man" antics.

"Yes, sir," said Elysia as she returned her knife to its sheath, her back to the freed prisoners. "Would you like me to remove the tape from their mouths?"

"No, not yet. We're too close to the vampire camp to risk them screaming," Laveau moved in close to speak to her. "You go on ahead and take the refugees back to the outpost. We need to move as quickly as possible before the vamps are onto us. I'll stay out here and help the kres... er... Cyrus, clean up."

"Yes, sir," Elysia saluted, always ready to follow orders with all too much fervor.

Cyrus shook his head as he dragged a headless body away, the blood trailing over grass and dried leaves. He never held it against her, as he knew Elysia's willingness to follow commands stemmed from her super-soldier genome. The kresnik tossed the body into the thorny bush with its head, leaving it there as he went for another.

"I'm sending you back to the Legion outpost with Elysia here," Laveau pointed toward her as he addressed the prisoners, now turned refugees. "Do not attempt to escape. If you do, she will be forced to eliminate you using whatever means she deems necessary. Understood?"

The two nodded in vigorous agreement as they eyed the sergeant's automatic shotgun.

"Good. The outpost is that way," said Laveau as he pointed past them. "We will meet you back there shortly, Elysia."

"Yes, sir," said Elysia. She turned to the refugees, taking each by the elbow to lead them into the woods.

The sergeant remained where he stood and watched as the three moved into the shadows, waiting until they were safely out of earshot.

"We were all told not to attack," growled Laveau. He rushed at Cyrus, intending to shove him.

Cyrus dropped the body he was moving and rose up to his full height. He snarled at the sergeant, causing him to stop in his tracks.

"I didn't have a choice," Cyrus spat, extending his organic arm for emphasis. "Do you really expect me to just sit there while the bloodsuckers march more victims into camp?"

"Absolutely," Laveau answered without hesitation, giving Cyrus an exaggerated frown. "Those were the orders, and we are expected to follow them. Failure to do so jeopardizes the mission and could blow the whole operation. We were to scout out the vampire camp and return with intel so we can attack. Now tell me, how are we supposed to make a successful, coordinated attack when the enemy is already onto us?"

"I stand by my actions, sergeant," Cyrus hissed the last words, causing Laveau to take a step back. "Human life is always more important than the success of the mission. We're no better than Atropos if we lose sight of that."

Laveau was ready to fly into a tirade, sweat starting to condense on his forehead.

"Remember, sergeant, our orders are to remain quiet, lest we reveal our position," Cyrus taunted mischievously.

"I don't have time for this," said the sergeant. His face shone red as he gave Cyrus a look that could kill. "I'll see you back at the outpost," Laveau suddenly turned to leave, his steps heavy as he reeled in his anger.

"Aren't you going to help me clean this up?" asked Cyrus, though he felt he already knew the sergeant's answer. "I've got one more body and two more heads."

"I already told you," huffed Laveau as he turned back. "You make the mess, you clean it up." He pointed an accusatory finger at him before he proceeded back into the forest.

"Should have expected as much," Cyrus muttered to himself. He flung the second body into the bush with the first and went back for the third. "And there we go," Cyrus whispered, throwing the last body down beside the others.

He went back for the remaining heads and then carelessly tossed them into the brush, one after the other. Done with his task, Cyrus made for the woods at a leisurely pace. He was in no hurry to return to the outpost, sure he was in for a tongue-lashing from at least one of the Legion's many officers.

Cyrus swaggered through the forest with the confidence of a jungle cat. He acted unaware of how minuscule he looked underneath the giant redwoods; the claws of his feet retracted so that he barely made a sound even over the dry, leafy ground.

The sun was barely visible through the trees now, and the forest grew dark.

Cyrus's vision slowly changed to acclimate to the lack of light as the yellow and blue wavelengths gave way to black and white. He had no reason to fear the wood, unlike the other human soldiers. His night vision and his array of weapons made him the most dangerous creature around.

The dark purple sky faded to black as Cyrus neared the outpost. The birds cried out their last while they prepared to rest for the night, their songs seemingly a warning of impending doom. The sounds of the camp grew louder as Cyrus approached, allowing him to use the noise to guide him. The kresnik stopped as he squinted to see through the trees.

Cyrus scanned the ridge until he found the outpost's high, wooden search tower, the structure illuminated by the surrounding lights. His eyes fell back on what lay ahead, landing on Laveau, the sergeant still several hundred yards out in front of him. The kresnik remained where he stood for several moments as he contemplated his entry into the camp, his thoughts causing his carefree attitude to vanish.

Cyrus burst into a sprint, hoping to catch Laveau. The kresnik was on the sergeant in seconds, careful to move off to the side so he couldn't see him. He took a position behind a formidable-looking bush as he prepared to enter the camp at just the right moment.

"What happened, sergeant?" Captain Dunkirk asked Laveau as he strode into the camp.

The captain was a tall, redheaded woman with a long braid.

Dunkirk removed her helmet so she could better chastise the sergeant. "I already have the intel from Elysia. It was only a scouting mission. I told you directly, you are not to engage the enemy, regardless if they have taken prisoners or not!" The Amazon jabbed Laveau with an extended finger. "It's only a matter of time before they find their dead! They'll have fled their position before we have a chance at them! You may have wrecked the whole mission."

Dunkirk stopped when two luminous yellow eyes appeared just over Laveau's shoulder.

"It was my fault," said Cyrus as he emerged from the woods, carrying his helmet in the crook of his good arm.

The whole camp went silent when they saw him upon the ridge.

The kresnik was a monster to most of them despite his loyalty to the Legion. He was their bioengineered answer to the growing vampire threat.

Cyrus smiled at the captain, his hairy, lion-like face and glistening fangs offsetting his true demeanor. "I saw the captives, and I just couldn't help myself. The filthy vamps would have drunk them dry before we got back. What was I supposed to do? I'm not really a soldier. What do you expect?"

"You jeopardized…" the captain started as she attempted to muster her courage.

"Can somebody tell me why we have gained two refugees?" asked a man's voice, deep and raspy, suggesting the speaker hadn't fully completed puberty.

Commander Griffin emerged from the mass of soldiers gathered around the camp's search tower. A man in his late 20s, his was hair long and white as snow.

"Talk to Sergeant Laveau and the kresnik, sir," the captain spoke the last words with a degree of disdain. "I told the sergeant not to cause a ruckus, and now here they are with refugees!" Dunkirk threw both hands up in frustration and let her firearm slide off to the side.

Cyrus glared at her and snarled.

The captain's eyes went wide with fear, her rant finished.

"Sergeant?" the commander turned to Laveau.

"I failed to retain control of Blackthorn, sir," said Laveau as he gave him a weary look. "He spotted the prisoners and took off. At that point, all I could do was let him do this thing." He paused and shook his head. "Surely you can understand, sir. He is difficult to control." He nodded toward Cyrus, speaking in a hushed tone.

"Yes, I suppose I should have expected as much." Griffin's steely grey eyes remained steady. "We are dealing with a civilian made into an anti-vampire predator, nearly against his will. You saw how he was in the mountain lab. We wouldn't have any control over him at all without those new nano-implants. Can we really expect such a turnaround in a week?"

"Sir?" The captain began again.

"Listen up!" Commander Griffin turned away from them and stepped toward the gathered troops. "The agenda has been changed! Due to events beyond my control, our initial scouting mission has resulted in a technical failure. In all likelihood, the enemy knows of our presence. We need to make our move now before they have a chance to escape." His voice softened as he explained the situation.

He received blinking stares from his soldiers, having failed to generate urgency.

"Suit up and ship out!" Griffin raised his fist up in the air.

The clearing below exploded into a flurry of activity upon hearing his command.

"But we'll be attacking at night, sir!" Dunkirk shouted in protest, her rant re-ignited.

"I'm fully aware of that, captain." Griffin looked her in the face, calming the storm in her eyes. "We have no choice but to attack immediately. We cannot chance their escape even if we are catching them at a time when they hold the advantage."

"Yes, sir…" Dunkirk trailed off. The commander's gaze had a hypnotizing effect on her, finally convincing her to relax.

Cyrus's stomach raged, nearly causing him to drop his helmet as he moved to clench his gut with his free prosthetic hand. "Could I possibly grab a snack before we move out, commander?" He looked toward Griffin, the desperate need in his eyes concealed by his visor.

"Corporal Spiro!" the commander turned away from Cyrus.

He spotted the soldier responsible for providing the kresnik with fresh meat as he emerged from the swarm of personnel. Elysia moved right behind him.

"I was just about to go looking for you," Commander Griffen told Spiro. "Cyrus has grown hungry. Could you attend to his needs, please?"

"I have already been informed of his needs, sir," replied the short, mustachioed man, as he indicated toward Elysia with his head. "Catch!" he exclaimed, casually tossing Cyrus the red, bloody bundle.

Cyrus caught Spiro's offering with the TAPSAW, the kresnik's prosthesis becoming a two-pronged fork to impale the meaty mass. "Leg of lamb," the kresnik proclaimed as he dug his fangs into it, blood dripping from his mouth.

"Should we really feed him before engaging with the enemy, sir?" Dunkirk turned to Griffin, her helmet returned to her head, a teasing smile on her face. "I figure it would be better to have him at his leanest and meanest for the vamps."

Cyrus looked up from his meal as he felt eyes upon him.

Laveau glared at him while he leaned against the base of the nearest redwood.

"It is far worse to have a hungry kresnik with a gurgling stomach than one that has been fed," said the commander without expression. "The mission does require some degree of stealth after all."

Their small congregation of officers and two genetically enhanced bioweapons remained at the top of the ridge. They watched the frantic shadows of hurried soldiers beneath the tower lights as the personnel prepared for the battle at hand.

"Form up!" Commander Griffin shouted at the soldiers below, breaking the silence amongst those standing around him. "Form up! We will have a quick briefing before we move out!" He continued his orders as he strode back down toward the camp.

Cyrus continued to gorge on the leg of lamb as he and the others followed after.

Chapter II

Family Portraits

Commander Michael Greaves made his way through the sparsely lit hallway, a certain weariness to his step. The passing soldiers and lab personnel failed to notice his obvious fatigue and greeted him with a series of salutes, further hindering his pace. Greaves was the highest-ranking officer at the base and was almost regarded as a celebrity. A tall, sinewy African American man of around middle age, he commanded a one thousand soldier strong battalion. Greaves wore his usual black tank top, blue jeans, and cowboy boots, always preferring to go casual despite his rank.

The District V commander's exhaustion was due to the rollercoaster of the previous week, punctuated by one of his force's highest highs. Greaves's soldiers had played a central role in eliminating Atropos's head scientist, a vampire who called himself The Surgeon. However, their achievement came when they were right at the brink, torn from the clutches of what might have been a humiliating, bloody defeat. They lost personnel by the hundreds, and their new kresnik weapon was nearly a part of that number.

They won through blind providence alone.

The Surgeon's own experimental cyborg broke free to destroy its creator and tormentor. The Legion would justify their losses through the beast's capture, along with the other items they already took from their foe's laboratory.

"What you got for me, doc?" Greaves asked Dr. Kaisar as he stepped into the base morgue.

The commander walked a vast, sprawling room, the space laid out like a hybrid gymnasium and laboratory.

"I thought it might be pertinent to show you some of our district's portion of The Surgeon's recovered assets," said Kaisar as he closed the door behind Greaves. An aged man with thinning, wispy white hair, the doctor was equal in rank to the commander.

Over two hundred steel examination tables stood before them, the bodies of slain vampires laying atop them. The corpses had sustained heavy damage and most of the dead monsters still wore their black body armor. All were beheaded and torn asunder by bullets or kresnik fangs and claws.

Large, red-skinned, hairless orangutan-like animals occupied the rest of the tablespace, these making up the majority of the recovered bodies. Another of the Legion's spoils of war, these experimental specimens were taken from The Surgeon's mountain lab.

A multitude of lab staff surrounded the corpses and further filled the boundlessly large room. Most of the scientists worked on dissecting the creatures while leaving some of the more heavily damaged ones alone.

"Due to the seclusion of The Surgeon's facility, we were able to recover nearly all of the bodies, there being no need to dispose of them as we do in our more visible operations," Kaisar noted. "The examinations have led to some very interesting findings already. All of it thanks to your success on the battlefield, commander."

"If only you could tell it to our dead soldiers." Greaves shook his head as he kept his pain at a distance. He had other matters to attend to, and his position offered him little opportunity to grieve.

"You come up with a name for them yet?" asked Greaves as he walked up to one of the tables. He grasped the specimen's wrist, examining its arm.

"*Homo exsanguinarius*," Kaisar spoke slowly, careful to enunciate as he stepped around to the other side of the specimen. "Though for a more pronounceable option, some of my staff like to call them blood monkeys. Kind of a lewd bunch, my staff."

"Couldn't have come up with anything better myself," said Greaves as he let the arm flop back onto the table surface. "I suppose the reason the vamps created these things is self-explanatory."

"Yes, we picked through most of the data taken from The Surgeon's computers, and it seems what we found coincides nicely with what was initially proposed," said Kaisar as he slapped a gloved hand of confirmation down on the creature's bare shoulder. "Atropos created *Homo exsanguinarius* as an alternative vampiric food source, presumably as a means to reduce their dependency on humans."

"Makes sense, the way Atropos runs." Greaves nodded vigorously. "Hopefully, us takin' their blood monkeys will help keep them from expandin' like they've always wanted. The way things seem to go for us, though, I'll wager takin' The Surgeon's lab experiments will probably come back to bite us. They'll have no way to feed and sustain their population in the future. Their numbers do always end up growin' no matter what."

"I see your reasoning, Commander, though I doubt even they could supplant their human food source quickly enough to reduce the number of human attacks and abductions. Realistically, it would have probably been a while before Atropos did something about their dependency on humans. It may even be good for us in the end. If the vampires did manage to find an alternative food source, wouldn't we all be out of a job?" asked Kaisar. The doctor crossed his arms, a sly smile running across his wrinkled, bespectacled face.

"I reckon it will just depend on how good their alternative tastes." Greaves placed a hand under his chin, thinking. "The vamps have had enough chances to go for cadavers, and they still go after the living. That, and with their tendency to view us as dirt, I doubt some collection of blood monkeys would stop 'em from feedin' on us."

"My thoughts exactly, Commander. Though I would assume the slow production rate is the real limiting factor."

"Just out of curiosity though, Doc, what were they tryin' to do here exactly?" Greaves pointed at the specimen. "What would make the vamps prefer these things over 'blood bag flesh'?"

"Well, I can't say anything for the taste," Kaisar smirked, "but *Homo exsanguinarius* possesses several attributes that make it preferable to Homo sapiens. For example, they are substantially larger than us, which means they produce more blood and meat. They also seem to have an enhanced ability to reproduce blood cells, regenerating their blood mass much faster after 'donation' than any human possibly could. They have a high muscle mass, their tissues also regenerating much faster than our own. Their capacity to regrow muscle is unlike anything ever observed in a mammal. A whole muscle group could be amputated and then fully regenerate in less than a month. With this capacity, they wouldn't ever have to kill the animal for its meat. *Homo exsanguinarius* is essentially the vampire version of a meat 'tree.'"

"The vamps do like their torture," said Greaves as he shook his head. "That's quite a lot, though. They do anything else?"

"They have all the other features that you might expect from the ultimate blood donor." Kaisar grabbed the specimen's left wrist, holding up its arm for Greaves to see. "They have very little hair, and their translucent skin makes the blood vessels more accessible. Obviously, that's the reason the skin looks red, all the blood made visible," he said as he placed the arm back on the table.

"Looking at their brain scans and some of their other features, they display an all-around sensory depression, such that they have inferior sight, hearing, and sense of smell. They also have very small brains for their size. I would say they're about as intelligent as a beef cow," Kaiser shrugged.

"If they got all that goin' for 'em, then why don't the vamps go ahead and switch over?" Greaves frowned, his eyes concealed under his sunglasses. "I'd think at least the smarter vamps would see the sense in it, even if the blood monkeys don't taste as good as we do."

"Sterility is the reason they can't switch over." Kaisar shook his head and tried not to laugh. "*Homo exsanguinarius* is an extremely hybridized creature. Its genome contains sequences from humans, vampires, nearly all the rest of the primate order, and even a few novel, patented genes. Atropos effectively overshot their goals. All those genetic additions led to an inability to reproduce. They could create more through the use of artificial wombs, though I doubt Atropos has the capacity to birth a sufficient enough supply to fully replace human flesh and blood. As I've insinuated, this was likely still one of their earliest attempts at creating a human substitute. And, as much as they seem to want to punish humankind, there's not much pressure for a switch over."

"Dang stupid lab vamps." Greaves gave the doctor a broad grin. "Put all this effort into makin' these blood monkeys only to have it all undone by one bloodsucker with a big mouth."

"I assume you're referring to our new vampire informant?" Kaisar took off his glasses, wiping the lenses on his sleeve. "You forced all the information out of him?"

"That's the usual method," said the commander with a frown. "Still, seems like our vamp rat would have some kind of loyalty to his own kind. Puts one heck of a damper on any chances of the ol' organization expandin' their numbers, judgin' by what we have here. Our canary went out and made himself number one on Atropos's kill list. He's just lucky he's in here under our protection. Maybe he's just like the rest of 'um and likes human flesh over blood monkey."

"Yes, it all does seem rather suspect, though it's not my department to have a reliable opinion on something like that."

"That's all you got for me, Doc?" asked Greaves. He remembered all the paperwork sitting on his desk.

"I have nothing else to tell you." Kaisar pushed his glasses back up on his nose.

"I'll leave you to it," said the commander as he turned to leave.

The sound of his boots on the concrete floor echoed throughout the laboratory.

* * *

"Uh…" Captain Kilgore sighed. He slowly closed the door behind him as he stepped outside the interview room and into the barren, polished concrete hallway. The officer wore a set of body armor and only his head remained uncovered, a shock of thinning, red hair growing upon his crown.

"I take it the interview didn't go well, sir?" asked Lieutenant Tarango as he turned to speak to Kilgore. The short, Hispanic man wore body armor as well, though he felt it unnecessary given the situation.

"Not at all," Kilgore replied.

He latched the door lock behind him, the mechanism nearly sliding into place on its own.

"Well, did you get anything out of her?" Tarango tried to sound hopeful, though he expected a dismal answer.

Both officers turned to face the one-way window in front of them, able to view their captive interviewee as they talked. Their subject was a young girl around six years old. She was adorned in a simple dress with blue floral patterns, her skin like porcelain. Her pitch-black hair concealed both her eyes and her artwork. The child never looked up, always intent on the picture she drew.

"Couldn't really get her to talk, as usual. Maybe she just doesn't like me, I don't know," Kilgore said with a shrug.

"Did you at least get a name this time?"

"Sure did. Nearly forgot about it, been in there so long," said the captain. He placed an open palm on his forehead and slid it back through his hair. "She said her name was Asellia or Azalea or something like that. Said it right after I asked her, near the beginning of the interview. I couldn't get her to tell me anything else after that. She went right back to drawing. I doubt we'll get any kind of last name out of her either, with her being raised by vamps. Stupid bloodsuckers and their one-name nonsense…"

"She still singing all of those nursery rhymes?"

"Yeah," said Kilgore as he stared at the girl through the window. "About the only words she speaks. Honestly, it's one of the creepiest things I've ever seen, even counting all of the crazy things the real vamps do. Really favors the more violent ones too. Three blind mice, Humpty Dumpty, stuff like that."

"What's so creepy about nursery rhymes, sir?" Tarango's eyes were full of mirth, though his voice remained level. "I know Greaves said the same thing about her when he interviewed her the first time. Do you both have repressed childhood memories you might want to tell me about?"

"Not at all." Kilgore's smile was brief. "The rhymes aren't creepy by themselves. It's the way she sings them, all airy and whispery."

"Do you think maybe she saw it off of a movie or something, sir?"

"Possibly…" Kilgore thought for a moment. "Who knows? She's a human child raised by vampires. Who knows what kind of things she's seen."

"What about her drawings?" asked Tarango, nodding to the papers in Kilgore's left hand.

"Could be the most informative things we've gotten out of her." Kilgore looked down at the pictures. "Some real messed up stuff, just as you might expect." The captain handed Tarango the first of the drawings.

"What's so messed up about this?" asked the lieutenant. He frowned as he scrutinized the papers. "It's just a picture of her family, all nine of them, standing outside the house. Every kid on the planet draws this stuff."

"Does this look normal to you?" Kilgore showed the lieutenant the next picture, frustrated by his unwillingness to believe.

The drawing depicted a loving family gathered for dinner. It would have been a pleasant image if not for the bloody, dissected corpse that lay on the table and the fact that each family member held a hatchet or knife.

"There's also this." Kilgore handed Tarango a drawing of the vampires as they drained one of their victims. They had suspended the corpse upside down, a bucket placed below to collect the blood.

"This is probably the worst one." The captain gave him a drawing of the vampire coven attacking another victim in a back alley; the body drowned in a pool of blood.

"Here's the last one." Kilgore held up the last drawing for Tarango to see. It was a picture of the girl's family playing croquet in the backyard, seemingly ordinary until one realized the balls were human heads.

"Yeah, most of them are pretty messed up, sir." Tarango stared at the drawing, taken aback only for a moment. "Though I can't say I'm surprised she's been exposed to stuff like that."

"Yeah, me neither." Kilgore took back the rest of the papers. "Run-of-the-mill stuff when you're talking vamps. Unfortunately, none of these drawings help us much. Doesn't tell us whose custody we ought to release her into. I think it's easier to deal with plain ol' bloodsuckers. Bullets take out all the hassle." He patted the pistol holstered at his side.

"Doesn't give us anything on Atropos either," said Tarango with a frown.

"Not at all." Kilgore balled his gloved hand into a fist and rested it against the wall. "That was really a heck of a lot to expect. We did go into the house under the assumption that those vamps had almost nothing to do with Atropos. They certainly never acted like they did when we had them under surveillance." The captain stopped as a thought surged through his head. "Whatever happened with the kids we recovered from the mountain lab? Have we sent them home yet?"

"Not yet, sir," said Tarango. "They're in Room 2 right now. Went in when you were in Room 1 with Asellia. You're a captain. Why are you asking me?" The lieutenant crossed his arms.

"Pff..." Kilgore nearly snorted. "Greaves hardly tells me anything, especially when it comes to recovered victims. Likes to handle stuff like that himself. I don't usually care for being kept in the dark, but it does keep me from having to fill out the paperwork." He stopped and looked down the hall at the door to Room 2. "Who's interviewing them today? I was pretty sure Greaves was through with them for the time being."

"They are being interviewed by the child psychologist right now, sir." Tarango smiled. "Real attractive blonde in a pants-suit. Not what I expected."

"Any word on the caseworker?"

"Should be along any moment, sir," said Tarango as he looked at his watch.

Both men glanced up to find a tall woman in high heels walking toward them. She wore a simple grey wrap dress and glasses with lenses so thick it seemed she looked through magnifying glasses.

"Well, speak of the devil..." Kilgore muttered. He took a careful look behind his back and then quickly but casually re-positioned himself in front of the one-way window, blocking the woman's view of the child inside the room.

"Hello, gentlemen," the woman greeted them. She shook Kilgore's hand. "I'm Nicole Ashleigh, caseworker for the Williams children. I'm here to retrieve them," she said as she moved to shake Tarango's hand. "I have walked the length of this place looking for them. Would either of you know where they might be found?"

"They are in Interview Room 2, right down the hall that way." Captain Kilgore pointed down the corridor. "They are with the psychologist now. She should be almost finished with them. If you'll just have a seat over there, she will be with you shortly."

"Thank you very much, sir." She gave them a brief smile and then turned to walk back down the hallway, pleased to have received the information.

"I take it she hasn't been briefed on our operations, sir?" Tarango turned toward the captain, his voice kept low.

"That was the plan," Kilgore responded in kind. "This will be the first and only time Ms. Ashleigh will walk these halls. Greaves saw no reason to waste time on a complete briefing. The Surgeon barely touched them, and they are healthy. Priority dictates that we move them out of here as soon as possible."

"Understood, sir."

Both men looked back down the hallway to find the caseworker sitting in a chair near Room 2, now engrossed in what they presumed was the children's case file.

"If she only knew what they have actually been through..." said Tarango. He stopped, feeling he missed something. "What's going to keep those kids from telling her about it?"

"Everything she needs to know about the children is in that file," said Kilgore with a nod toward the woman. "Greaves made sure to put something in there about them having a tendency to tell fibs. Fantastic as their stories are, I doubt she would ever believe them."

"What exactly did Greaves put in that file, sir?"

"The commander made sure to make things sound as realistic as possible. Said the kids' parents were killed in a home invasion and that the kids were kidnapped. After that, the home invader, who was also a drug cook, held the children captive in his home, possibly using them as guinea pigs for the drugs he made."

"Sounds a little weird, sir." Tarango frowned. "Not much of an improvement either, still really dark."

"Greaves didn't want to get too creative. Wanted to keep it as close to the real story as possible." Kilgore yawned the last few words. He raised an arm above his head to stretch, somehow bored by the topic. "I don't think what he put in there matters a whole lot, so long as he excluded all the vampires."

"I suppose so." Lieutenant Tarango nodded in agreement as another idea formed in his head. "Did the commander at least tell those kids to try not to say anything about the vampires? I can't imagine that we would want to send them out into the civilian world only for everyone to think they were insane."

"They will be provided with counseling services after they

leave the base." Kilgore shrugged. "There may not be much we can do to keep them from developing some kind of psychosis. Suppose they'll just try to convince them that everything they saw was a hallucination from all the drugs they were on."

"If that's all we can do..." Tarango muttered, ending the conversation.

The men looked down the hallway as the door to Room 2 slowly opened. Two children stepped out, one a girl of about seven, the other a boy around five.

"Oh, hello," said the caseworker as she quickly closed her case folder and went to greet the children. Though her tone remained level, her voice echoed through the barren hallway, audible to all. "You must be Imani and Isaac." She kneeled down to speak to them. "I'm Ms. Ashleigh, your caseworker. I'm here to take you home, to your grandparents' house."

"Yay!" the little boy exclaimed with his arms raised above his head. "We're going to see grandma!"

His sister remained stationary when she looked over at him, shaking her head and rolling her eyes.

"Where's this psychologist?" Captain Kilgore asked Tarango, careful to make sure the caseworker didn't hear.

"I assume she is still in there. Probably just finishing her notes or something."

A young, blonde woman in a tight-fitting pants suit stepped out of the interview room just as the lieutenant spoke the words.

Both of the officers' jaws dropped when they saw her.

She was a vision of loveliness. Her gold hair shone like the sun. Her eyes blazed like piercing sapphires, and her body was like a dream.

"Wow... Somebody's going to be the talk of the base." Kilgore casually pulled his sunglasses from his collar and slid them over his eyes. "Could we not find someone less... flashy?" He was sure to keep his voice down so only Lieutenant Tarango heard.

"Dr. Richmond comes highly recommended, sir." Tarango gave him a broad grin. "One of the best child psychologists around, or at least that's what she says. Her appearance is just an added bonus."

"Well, I suppose so long as she's one of the best." Kilgore

tried not to smile too much. "I assume she must be pretty intelligent. I'm impressed Greaves got her to believe everything. Generally, the brainier types won't really go for it."

"You must be the children's caseworker," said the psychologist, her voice and smile exaggerated as she moved to shake the other woman's hand. "I was told you would be taking the children home to their grandparents?"

"Yes, that is correct, thank you." The caseworker gave her a strange look as she tried not to frown.

The children stood to either side of her, though they never attempted to interact with the blonde woman.

"I'm afraid I don't have time to speak to you at length. The facility director, Mr. Greaves, I believe that was his name, was very clear about leaving with the children as soon as possible."

"I'm aware of Mr. Greaves's request," said the blonde woman, acting as though it were the most incredible thing she had ever heard.

"Well, children, it's time to go," said the caseworker as she placed a hand on each of the children's shoulders. "You sounded ready to go."

"We sure are!" Isaac proclaimed as Imani nodded in vigorous agreement.

"I guess we'll be leaving then. Say goodbye to Dr. Richmond." The caseworker nudged the children forward slightly, encouraging them to speak.

"Goodbye, Dr. Richmond." They said the insincere words in unison just before the situation grew awkward.

The caseworker led the children away from Dr. Richmond, letting them leave things at that. They turned the corner into the adjoining hallway, their footsteps growing steadily softer as they departed.

The psychologist remained where she stood and removed a compact from her purse, opening it up to review her reflection. Content with her appearance, she put the mirror away then walked down the hallway toward the officers as though she were a model on the catwalk.

"Hello, I'm Dr. Heather Richmond." She gave the officers the same over-done smile as she shook each of their hands. "I assume the other child is in Room 1. That's the room behind you, correct?"

Tarango could only stand beside his commanding officer, smiling like a child on the first day of kindergarten.

"Yes, it's this room right here," said Kilgore, remaining professional. He made no attempt to move and kept Dr. Richmond from reaching the door. "Commander Greaves has briefed you on the specifics regarding this child?" he asked.

"I have been extensively briefed on the child, her condition, her previous situation, everything the commander could give me," said Richmond as she moved toward the interview room door once more.

"There have been a few new developments since then," said the captain as he blocked her way. He watched the psychologist's smile finally break due to her frustration. "The girl told me her name was Asellia, and she drew these pictures." Kilgore handed Dr. Richmond the drawings. "She doesn't really talk at all and seems to only want to sing nursery rhymes."

"Hmm…" the doctor examined the drawings.

A squeamish look formed on her face when she moved onto the second paper in the pile.

"Very interesting," she muttered as she scrutinized the last two drawings, playing off her initial reaction as though it were nothing. "Thank you for your help, Captain Kilgore." She looked up at him, the fake smile returning. "These drawings may provide an opportunity to reach her."

"Would you like for us to join you in the interview room?" asked Kilgore before she could try for the door yet again. "It may not be a good idea for you to go in there without some kind of protection."

He put a hand on the showy Desert Eagle pistol at his waist.

Richmond frowned, misinterpreting the meaning of the captain's words. "I really thought more of the men around here. I'm not some poor, defenseless damsel in distress that needs a big, brave man to protect her." She pouted the last words, causing Tarango to look as though he might fall over. "I'm a grown woman, and I can take care of myself. I also find it very inappropriate to bring a gun near a child for a simple interview. It is entirely unnecessary and sends the wrong message. How do you expect me to glean any additional information from little Asellia in such an environment?"

"I'm sorry, doctor," said Kilgore as he tried to defuse the situation. "You may have misunderstood my meaning. Asellia was only recently rescued from a coven of vampires, and, though she shows no signs of having contracted the virus, there's still a slight possibility she might be dangerous."

"Well, thanks for the apology." Dr. Richmond sounded as though she hadn't believed it, however. "I have been thoroughly briefed on the specifics of vampirism. As I understand it, the disease usually manifests after only a few days. Asellia has been in your custody for over a week and has likely lived among victims of vampirism her whole life. In all likelihood, she would have developed the disease years ago. She is clearly immune."

"That may be." Kilgore tried his best to sound civil. "All I know is that I've been hunting vamps for a while now, and I've seen some crazy things. I probably need a psyche eval more than the kid does. You have to be ready for anything. Trust me, you'll want to have a firearm nearby."

"I'll take my chances, Captain Kilgore." She glared as she prepared to push him out of the way.

"Suit yourself," said Kilgore. He made a dramatic step to the side as he extended his arm to usher her toward the door. "You're the one with the Ph.D." He stopped abruptly, only just catching himself before he said something derogatory.

"Thank you." Richmond's smile returned for a brief moment. "You may observe the interview through the one-way window. Should I experience any trouble I won't hesitate to call out for you." She rolled her eyes and made for the door. She opened it and then shut it carefully, sure to conceal her dissipating anger.

The door locked automatically, and the sound echoed throughout the hallway.

"Dang, that cat has got some nasty claws," said Lieutenant Tarango, the door safely closed. "Don't let her looks fool you." He turned to look at the doctor through the one-way window.

"You bet," said Kilgore as he joined him in front of the window. "You know, we might need to update some of our protocol. Far as I know, we don't have anything on dealing with uninfected humans who merely live in close association with vamps. Let's hope we didn't make a mistake. Greaves will have our heads if something happens to her."

"Why should he?" Tarango frowned at the captain. "You heard her. She's a grown woman."

* * *

"Hello, Asellia," Dr. Richmond spoke to the girl at the other end of the stainless steel table as she entered the barren brick interview room.

The locking door behind her caused her to take a quick look back.

Asellia remained seated as before, entirely engrossed in her drawing. She never looked up as she leaned over the table; her eyes kept concealed under her hair.

"I'm Dr. Heather Richmond, and I'm here to help you." Richmond gave Asellia one of her biggest, broadest smiles, hoping she might respond. She took a seat at the other end of the table and placed her purse beside her on the floor.

"A-tisket, a-tasket, a red and yellow basket," the girl sang in a whisper, ignoring Dr. Richmond as she continued to draw.

"Captain Kilgore told me you love to sing nursery rhymes. That's one of my favorites too."

"A-tisket, a-tasket, I might blow a gasket," Asellia's voice became a quiet hiss.

She placed the crayon she was using back into the box at her side and took out another, this one crimson red.

"Now, there's no reason to be that way, Asellia," said the doctor, only just catching the threat. "I really am here only to help." She moved to take the girl's hand from across the table but decided against it right before she made contact with her skin.

"A-tisket, a-tasket, a red and yellow basket." Asellia's tone returned to normal, her eyes focused on her drawing.

"That's better," said Richmond, letting up on her over-done grin. "Captain Kilgore says you are quite the little artist." She placed the drawings she carried onto the table and spread them across its surface. "He let me look at some of your artwork, and I must say I'm very impressed. Would you care to talk about some of these drawings with me?"

"I wrote a letter to my mom," Asellia continued in her singsong whisper and placed her red crayon on the table. She held up her drawing, turned so Dr. Richmond couldn't see it.

"Did you now?" Richmond asked with uncertainty, unsure if Asellia was speaking to her.

"But on the way, I dropped it." Asellia continued the rhyme. She placed her artwork back on the table and began again with the red crayon.

"What do you mean?"

"I dropped it, I dropped it. But on the way, I dropped it," sang Asellia as she began to color in what she drew, her soft strokes now a frantic scribble.

"Oh, yes, that's right. Sorry, I forgot the rhyme." Dr. Richmond's smile returned, this one genuine, mirroring her embarrassment. "It has been so long since I sang it," she said as she shook her head.

"A little boy he picked it up and put it in his pocket."

Asellia abruptly stopped her scribbling and slid the crimson red crayon back into the box. "Would you like to see my picture, Dr. Richmond?" she asked in a whisper. She pushed the drawing toward the doctor, all while she kept her eyes down, glued to the table.

"I would love to see it."

Richmond's fake smile vanished when she looked down at the drawing.

It was a picture of the interview room. It showed Asellia as she crouched over the blonde-haired body lying on the floor, the walls and floor covered in crimson.

"I had a little dog that said bow-wow!" Asellia began a part of the rhyme unfamiliar to the doctor. "I had a little cat that said meow-meow!"

"Why would you want to draw something like this?" Richmond rose from her seat, aghast and angered, nearly forgetting she spoke to a child.

"Shan't bite you, shan't bite you, shan't bite you," Asellia's soft voice changed into a threatening hiss. She snapped to attention and pushed her chair backward, out from under the table.

"Why would you want to do this to me?" the doctor asked, confused, suddenly feeling hurt.

"Shall bite you!" Asellia glared up at Dr. Richmond.

Her eyes glowed an otherworldly, ghostly blue.

Asellia jumped onto the table and flung herself at the doctor. She leveled her to the ground in an emotionless, stone-cold rage-frenzy, intent on searing agony.

"Open the door, lieutenant!" Captain Kilgore roared from the outside.

"I can't, sir!" Tarango cried out in desperation. He drove his shoulder into the door, struggling with the doorknob. "The door is jammed!"

"Help me!" Dr. Richmond cried out in panic. She found the child impossibly strong and was unable to push her off, her own blood splattering the walls and floor.

"I dropped it! I dropped it! I dropped it!" Asellia screamed as she repeatedly slashed at the doctor's face. Her assault was relentless, her talon-sharp fingernails stained crimson.

"Dang you, Lieutenant!" Captain Kilgore chastised his underling as he pulled his Desert Eagle from its holster.

He emptied his magazine into the one-way window, the bulletproof glass cracking only where his rounds struck it.

"Help me!" The doctor screamed without ceasing, her face soaked red with her own blood, the gashes wide and deep.

The window shattered when Lieutenant Tarango kicked it in with his steel-toed boot.

Shards of glass went flying everywhere.

"Shoot her!" Tarango cried out to the captain.

"And by the way, I lost it!" Asellia ended the rhyme.

She drove her fangs into Richmond's throat as the bullets flew all around her.

Chapter III

Wolves to Slaughter

Anoura leaned down toward the ground, stretching her back while she remained seated on her spot on the log.

"Did you hear that?" she asked, believing she heard a distant noise.

Anoura was on edge, her narrow escape from The Surgeon's mountain lab nearly a week ago still fresh on her mind. Injured by The Surgeon's experiment, she had managed to limp out through the laboratory's back way before the Legion's full sweep of the area.

Anoura had reached the outside only to find herself abandoned amongst the impossibly rocky terrain. She crossed the mountain range on her own, her injuries painful, though quickly healing as she progressed. She knew she needed to reconnect with some agent of Atropos but had little idea where she was going.

Just as Anoura considered turning back to search for a more urbanized area, she caught the scent of a large gathering of her own kind. She stumbled into Vaylat's camp just three days ago. The lost vampire automatically enlisted into the Atropos-sanctioned company assigned to recover The Surgeon's escaped experiment.

Anoura rose from the log on which she sat and tried for a better perspective, ready for The Surgeon's monster to emerge from the trees in full fury at any moment. Her eyes darted back to the campfire area in front of her. The setting sun, bright even through her sunglasses, made her search difficult. The massive redwoods that lined the perimeter of their camp helped offset the light, though they kept the vampires concealed.

It all did little to soothe Anoura's anxiety.

"I don't hear anything," said Frater, Anoura's fellow vampire standing up from where he crouched in front of her.

He leaned on his impossibly long rifle as though it were a walking stick and looked off in the distance. The man was freakishly tall. Though of medium build, the shadow of his elongated form stretched over the ground, illuminated beneath the trees in the light of their red campfire lamp.

"Lotsa noises in the woods," said Fischer as he waved for him to sit back down with a clawed hand. "Every little noise you hear can't be the Legion about to come down on our heads."

The two men dressed in black body armor. Their dark sunglasses protected their eyes from the sun, and their faces were concealed underneath black cowls. Where Frater was tall, Fischer was relatively short and rather weasel-like in appearance. The two were obviously related despite their sizes, likely brothers, their movements and manner of speech so similar it was undeniable.

"You don't know the Legion the way I do." Anoura shook her head.

She was unwilling to take her seat and felt awkward in her new wardrobe. She wore black body armor and a cowl just like the others. Anoura found her new defensive shell clunky and restrictive. She hated that it hampered her usually smooth, quick vampiric movements.

"Be pretty ballsy for 'em to attack us in our own camp." Frater returned to his spot beside his brother.

He sat on the ground and rested his back against the log. He placed his rifle across his lap and stretched out, extending his long, spider-like legs so that his feet nearly touched the glass of their campfire lamp. With two AK-47s strapped to his back in addition to his primary firearm, the soldier kept himself overly armed for a vampire.

Anoura only knew Frater for a short time yet was convinced of his skills as a sharpshooter. He just acted like a man who knew what he was doing.

"It would, but I don't think it's wise to assume they wouldn't," said Anoura. She remained standing, her flabbergasted frown concealed under her own cowl. "After the run-in with that... the Legion's new vampire killer in The Surgeon's lab, I'm certain

31

they're capable of almost anything."

"Didn't The Surgeon kill that thing?" Fischer looked up at her and almost laughed when he spoke, as though he barely believed his own words. "You know before the other monster, his own experiment, broke loose and killed him? I thought The Surgeon cut off that Legion hunter's head with his plasma sword." He motioned across his throat with his skinning knife, a gesture made even more menacing with his face concealed.

Where Frater trusted in his guns, Fischer preferred the ice-cold steel of a cruel blade. He possessed nearly every type of knife imaginable and carried weapons of all kinds. Most of his blades he held in the bandolier strapped across his chest.

"What?" Anoura exclaimed, frustrated by Fischer's ignorance. "I don't know where you got your information from, but I was there! The Surgeon cut its arm off but left it alive!" Her temper simmering, she clenched her own AK-47.

The weapon felt unnatural in her clawed hands.

"Well, there you go then." Frater shrugged, not at all put off by her movements. "That thing won't be a threat to us no more."

Anoura tensed and briefly entertained the thought of opening fire, though she knew it would only serve as an outlet for her frustrations. Machine gun rounds were little more than bee stings to a vampire.

"Look sharp," said Fischer as he rose to his feet. He nodded toward the tent some distance behind Anoura, motioning for the other two to do likewise. "His majesty, the king has decided to grace us with his presence." His wicked grin was obvious, even under his cowl.

Anoura nearly allowed herself to smile, shaking her head.

Vaylat, the leader of their search party, emerged from the tent, his form illuminated under the cover of the trees by the rows of red-glowing lanterns hung overhead.

He wasn't happy.

Vaylat's step was quick but heavy as he made for the center of camp. His movements looked all the more ridiculous given his attire. Their fearless leader appeared to have walked out of Victorian-era England. The vampire was decked out in a black, double-breasted vest and breeches, his frock coat flowing nearly to his ankles.

Anoura had known Vaylat for only a few days, but as far as she could tell, Fischer's assessment was an accurate one. The man was a prima donna and constantly snapped at his followers over the most minor details.

Anoura stood up and turned toward Vaylat's large, elaborate, black-cloth tent, intent on the looming spectacle.

"Where are my hunting parties?" Vaylat demanded of no one in particular.

He approached the line of corpses hanging upside-down from a wire strung overhead, blood buckets resting beneath the bodies. Vaylat had ordered his soldiers to hang up the corpses, the victims tied, gagged, and then yanked upwards by their feet, their jugular veins sliced open with a box cutter.

"We'll be dry before nightfall!" Vaylat raged and kicked the nearest bucket with a booted foot.

The metal struck the nearest tree with a loud clank, splattering only a limited amount of blood.

"I will not be forced to eat flesh!"

Vaylat was a strict hematophage, as he drank only blood and abstained from flesh entirely. He was a purist and forced his ideas on those who served under him. He believed that even living Atropos vampires should behave like their literary counterparts.

"I'm sure they will be back soon, Master." A timid voice tried to console him as the slightly built figure ran after Vaylat. "I'm certain there is more than enough left for you," said Manavi, Vaylat's servant. She picked up one of the blood buckets and poured its viscous contents into another, filling it up.

Where Vaylat never appeared in anything less than formal wear, Manavi dressed as though she were unaware of the invention of the washing machine. Her simple dress, once white, now remained stained by dirt, grass, and blood. It seemed her master didn't allow her to bathe, leaving her blonde hair matted and her dead white vampiric skin marred with grime.

"Leave the blood buckets alone, Manavi," hissed Vaylat as he moved his long, black hair out of his face. "The blood is far too curdled to drink now." He turned away from the clothesline of hanging bodies and stomped back toward his tent.

"Yes, sir," said Manavi. She dropped the bucket to follow her master, always the loyal servant.

Anoura grimaced under her cowl. She was more than tired of her superior's antics, feeling his actions reflected poorly on their organization as a whole. She deplored the way Vaylat treated them all, especially Manavi.

"I will have blood!" Vaylat snapped as he turned back to shriek at them all. "The price will be paid by Atropos!"

He raised his nose toward the sky to smell the air as he sought the nearest human soldier.

"Stupid blood-drinker," Fischer muttered so only Anoura and Frater could hear.

"Be way less cranky if he would have a bite of flesh every once in a while," said Frater with a solemn nod.

"Your blood!" Vaylat pointed a long, clawed finger toward the guard who stood beside the entrance to his tent. He glared at the man through his red-lensed sunglasses. "Yours is the blood I will have!" He rushed the guard, the man having little time to turn and run before the vampire was upon him.

"Ahh!" The man screamed as Vaylat knocked him to the ground, his AK-47 falling from his grasp.

"Not again," Anoura frowned and turned to Fischer and Frater. "Soon we'll be entirely out of human soldiers."

"Manavi!" Vaylat screeched. He turned toward his servant, a booted foot planted firmly on his victim's back to pin him to the ground. "Bring a length of rope to bind him!"

"Yes, master!" shouted Manavi as she ran for the tent. The speed of her actions suggested she was afraid she might be next, vampire though she was.

"You don't have to do this, sir!" The guard cried out in desperation as he struggled to stand up from the ground, but Vaylat was too strong for him. "The hunting parties will be back soon!"

"I have little choice given the situation," said Vaylat with a marked lack of regret. He looked down at the doomed man and shook his head. "It is unfortunate that I must terminate your employment, but the circumstances are simply beyond my control. Might I suggest taking your grievance up with HR?"

"Let me up!" the man's voice grew higher as tears formed in

his eyes. "If you could just wait until the hunting parties come back!"

"Shut up, blood bag!" spat Vaylat as he pressed down on the small of the man's back with the heel of his boot, threatening to break the vertebrae. "Shut up, or I'll snap your spine right here!" He sneered and a psychotic grin formed on his face. "Don't forget to bring a gag, Manavi!"

"You!" Vaylat pointed toward Anoura and her companions. "Fischer, is it? Come here, I need someone with a blade. There is no need to dirty my claws on this filthy blood bag."

"Yes, sir!" A knife materialized in Fischer's hand as he responded. "Here you are, sir," he extended his Bowie knife. The vampire leaped over Anoura's sitting log and sprinted toward Vaylat and Manavi.

"No, you keep it," said Vaylat. He stopped him with an open palm, an exasperated look on his face. "You will do the cutting. I already told you, I will not sully my own claws!"

"Yes, sir," nodded Fischer as he shoved the blade back into the belt around his chest and moved off to the side for the moment.

"Hurry up, Manavi!" Vaylat snapped.

His servant emerged from the tent immediately and went to tie the man's hands behind his back.

"Make sure his bonds stay tight," Vaylat instructed. "I don't want this one to come untied and fall before he's drained," he removed his foot from the man's back.

"You there!"

Vaylat turned toward a gathering of vampire soldiers standing on the other side of his tent.

"Help Manavi string him up!"

The downed guardsman gasped, his screams of protests silenced when Manavi stuffed a bloody rag into his mouth.

"Get up, blood bag scum!" Manavi kicked the man lying on the ground.

She grabbed him by the back of his armor vest and hoisted him back onto his feet, strong as any other vampire despite her small frame. She relished whatever opportunity she had to lash out at her human underlings. Her actions were nearly as sadistic as her master's.

"The corpse-line is full!" Vaylat shouted at the incoming vampires. "Hang him from the branch over there." He pointed toward a low-hanging bow near the edge of the camp.

"Come on!" Manavi hissed at the doomed man. She dragged him along by the rope as several of the other vampires approached them. "Hesitation won't make you any less dead!"

The man began to walk, or rather shuffle, forward. He was sure to keep his steps slow, trying to enjoy his last few moments of life.

"Get a move on!" Vaylat roared at Manavi and the others. "Do make sure to bring a blood bucket!" He commanded one of the other vampires to turn back and retrieve the required item.

Manavi drug the man along faster in response to Vaylat's demands. The guard stumbled and nearly fell several times as they approached the designated spot.

"Stay still," Manavi told the guardsman. They now stood underneath the low-hanging branch among the rest of the group. "I need to tie your legs together before we continue," she said as she kneeled down in front of the man.

Manavi tightly coiled the rope around his ankles, rapidly pulling the rest of it back through.

"It will be so much worse for you should you fall." She stood back up to look the man in the face, a smile of delight on her attractive but dirty face.

"Lie down." Manavi harshly grabbed him by the shoulder and slammed him to the ground, the man hitting the dirt with a groan.

"Come on, string him up," said Vaylat as he held one clawed hand to his forehead.

One member of the group took the end of the rope and threw it over the branch. Two others caught the end and pulled on the rope with their substantial strength.

The man hung upside-down in seconds, his head five feet from the ground.

A fourth vampire placed the wide-rimmed blood bucket below the guardsman.

"Where is my blade-man?" Vaylat asked, his voice level as he turned to find Fischer standing beside him. "Cut his throat!" He instructed him.

"Yes, sir!" saluted Fischer, the knife reappeared in his hand.

Fischer skillfully sliced through the blood vessels on either side of the man's neck with the precision of a surgeon while the other vampires reached to hold the dying man in place. Dark red blood flowed from the wounds in torrents, over the bottom of the man's downturned chin, nearly all of it landing in the bucket. The vampire waited until his body went limp before he stepped away, blood continuing to drain into the vessel.

"Bring me a bottle in my tent, Manavi," said Vaylat as he clutched his forehead once more. His hunger headache had returned. "Make sure no one tries to eat this man's flesh, just as with the others. We are vampires, and we live on blood alone," he hissed as he stomped back toward his tent in a slump.

Manavi followed him, looking to retrieve the requested bottle. She returned to the hanging body a few seconds later, carrying the bottle, a cup, and funnel, all the tools she needed to transfer the blood from the bucket into the bottle.

"Waste, even if the guard was a filthy blood bag," grumbled Frater as he sat back down. He shoved the butt of his long rifle into the ground, holding it up as though it were a staff.

"'Bout tired of that stupid homo… Er, I mean hemato," said Fischer, shaking his head. He jumped over Anoura's log and returned to his seat beside his brother.

"If only he knew the real reason he's in charge." Frater's mocking grin was unmistakable even under his cowl.

"Can't wait to get out of here," Fischer muttered.

"What do you mean 'get out of here?'" Anoura returned to her spot on the log, curiosity in her voice.

"Can I tell her?" Frater turned to Fischer. "I don't think it will be a problem if we bring one more. Shame to lose one of Atropos's better lieutenants."

"What are you talking about?" Anoura grew slightly hostile.

"Can't imagine it being a problem," said Fischer. He picked at the ground with one of his knives, disinterested. "Go ahead and tell her."

"So it's like this," said Frater. He looked over at Anoura, his eyes concealed under his dark cowl. "This camp is full of some of the worst vampires in Atropos. These bloodsuckers are total morons. They do our organization no good. Vaylat is probably the worst, taken to only drinking blood as he has. I have no idea how he ever became an underboss. He probably goes through a human a day. Guys like him threaten to expose our organization with food demands like that."

"Why fill a search party with our worst personnel?" asked Anoura with an irritated look. "How does The Master expect to recapture The Surgeon's specimen using the worst of Atropos?"

"The Master has no intention of recapturing the specimen, at least not as far as this party is concerned," said Fischer as he sat up and returned his knife to his belt. "It's long gone by now, probably escaped somewhere off to the east."

"What's the point of any of this then?" Anoura managed not to yell.

"Since we're just sitting here, it's only a matter of time before the Legion attacks," Frater explained. "This party was formed for The Master to eliminate the dead weight."

"You can't be sure of that," Anoura insisted. "Wouldn't you be included in the worst of Atropos? Provided any of what you say is true."

"Oh, no, it's true as the day is long," said Fischer as he jammed his knife into the log and left it there. "Me and Frater are here on behalf of The Master. Wants us to make sure everything goes as planned. Wants us to make sure every pain in the neck Atropos vamp gets what's coming to 'em."

"Whole reason The Master turned us in the first place," said Frater. He laid his rifle across his lap, nearly hitting Fischer in the shin. "Heck of a fast way to get promoted."

"What about me?" Anora jumped to her feet as she half-shouted, half-whispered the words, careful should anyone overhear.

"Me and Frater already decided that you're coming with us." Fischer pulled the knife from the log and shoved it back into the loop in his bandolier belt. "No reason you should die here with the rest of 'em, here due to happenstance as you are."

"How do you expect to escape from here?" Anoura slumped back down in her seat. She grew frustrated, unsure why they had waited so long to tell her. "As stagnate as our movements have been, and the fact that we're a full company of vampires, I guess the Legion's preferred strategy would be to encircle us in some fashion. Probably send in half a battalion to make sure they account for all of us, maybe not quite that many if they bring their vampire-killing monster. It still lives, as I said."

"We got a man on the inside." Frater nodded and nearly dropped his rifle, his smug look concealed.

"Got a man on the inside?" Anoura frowned. "We've finally infiltrated the Legion?"

"That we have," said Fischer as he rose to his feet. "Guarantees us a path of escape when the Legion decides to attack. Soon as someone sounds the alarm, we're to run for those trees over that way." He turned around and pointed toward a space between two gigantic redwoods, near the southwestern corner of the camp. "Our man will be waiting for us over there. He'll let us slip right through the line and direct us to the helicopter they'll have waiting. After that, we'll fly off to join the real search party." He sat back down on the log.

"How do you know that this 'inside man' won't double-cross you?" asked Anoura, striking the log with her fist.

"The Master made him take a blood-oath," said Fischer. He took a dagger from his bandolier and threw it at the ground, the blade embedding itself in the dirt. "Had him swear fealty to Atropos. Gonna turn him as a reward." He pulled his dagger from the ground and took a handkerchief from his pocket to wipe off the dirt.

"We're the ones in charge of if he lives or dies," said Frater. He left his rifle sitting against the log and remained low to the ground as he made his way around the red lamp toward Anoura. "Rigged our man with explosives set to blow when I hit this button."

Frater pulled what looked like a plastic ring box from his pocket. He opened the lid to reveal a bright red button before quickly closing the box again.

"Going to remove the device from his person as soon as he directs us to the helicopter," said Fischer as Frater slunk back to his seat.

"I will need a guard to replace the one I had drained," proclaimed Vaylat.

He suddenly appeared behind Anoura, his aggression

vanished due to his drink of blood.

"We are beginning to run low on human personnel, so it will have to be a vampire. I've decided it should be you, Anoura." He placed a clawed hand on her shoulder.

"But, sir," she began to protest, carefully pushing his hand away.

"Do you have a problem, Anoura?" asked Vaylat.

"No, sir," she shook her head slowly.

"Very well," said Vaylat as he turned away. "I expect you to be standing at the front of my tent in the next few minutes."

He walked back toward his tent, his steps smooth and steady.

"Pff…" Frater scoffed under his breath, careful so that Vaylat couldn't hear him. "Got over his little hissy fit quick enough."

"Now you stop that, Frater," said Fischer as he pointed an accusatory finger at him, dead serious. "You know us vamps can only live on blood alone!" He dropped his hand to give his knee a hearty slap, the severity in his voice vanished away.

"The hunting parties have returned!" Someone shouted, several of the vampires rising to help with the human captives.

"Figured as much." Frater shook his head. "Another guard dead for nothing."

"Well, I suppose I will see you later," said Anoura. She gripped her AK-47 as she left, still unaccustomed to the feel. "I don't know when Vaylat will be letting me go."

"We'll try to stay over here until your shift is over." Frater looked up at her, the sincerity in his eyes concealed. "As soon as someone sounds the alarm for the Legion, we'll make a run for it. Just abandon your post and follow us."

"I will follow you if I so choose," said Anoura as she turned to leave their gathering. She was more than willing to abandon Vaylat's group, though she was unsure how far she could trust Frater and Fischer.

"You got the drive?" Frater asked Fischer, speaking at a whisper as they watched Anoura leave.

"Right here," said Fischer as he pulled an item from his combat vest pocket. "I imagine they'll be along any moment now."

He slung the object out into the grass, a glint of silver catching Frater's eye as it landed.

Anoura continued toward Vaylat's tent, walking no faster than she had to, in no hurry to perform the mindless task of guard duty.

The sun had slipped under the horizon, the last of its rays impossible to see through the extensively thick tree trunk bases. The red lanterns hanging overhead sparsely illuminated the vampire camp.

Anoura walked past the dead, still exsanguinating guard, Manavi having remained there to collect the blood. The underfed servant hastily corked the bottle and practically ran back towards Vaylat's tent. Anoura shook her head, still shocked by the level of servitude Vaylat demanded.

She stopped suddenly when she heard a rustling somewhere behind one of the massive redwoods.

Something ran through the undergrowth.

"We're under attack!" Anoura screamed.

A dark figure shot through the opening between the trunks of two giant trees near the other side of the camp, intent on Vaylat's tent.

Anoura turned to run, finding Frater and Fischer leaping from their seats.

They headed straight for the line of trees, leaving her little time to catch them. She ignored the mass panic in the wake of the Legion beast's attack, abandoning her fellows to suffer its slaughter as she rushed after her companions.

The fire of the Legion's automatic shotguns followed, their shots striking several nearby vampire soldiers, hastening Anoura's escape.

Frater and Fischer disappeared through the opening between the redwoods.

They never turned back, seemingly trying to leave her behind.

Anoura bounded past the red campfire lamp near where she had previously sat, blind to all but the dark portal between the great trees in front of her. The opening called to her like a homing beacon. The Legion's beast screamed like a leopard, its cries accompanied by the thunder of guns and high-pitched vampiric shrieks, the camp exploding into a whirl of chaos behind her. Anoura bolted through the opening between the trees, unconcerned with what lay ahead, her mind affixed only on escape.

Anoura ran headlong into Frater and fell backward onto the ground, the unnaturally tall man unaffected by her momentum.

"What's the idea?" Anoura demanded. She picked herself off the leaf-littered ground and readjusted the strap of her AK-47.

The gunfire, screams, and roars continued to sound behind her. The forest did little to muffle the sounds or to quench her anxiety. They needed to move before the Legion beast was finished with Vaylat's company.

"Huh, I could ask you the same thing," said Frater as he turned toward her and looked down. Anoura's head reached only to his chest.

He had removed his cowl, revealing his nearly translucent skin. His vampire blue eyes were visible in the low light, and his dark hair was mowed down in a buzz cut.

"Gotta get a move on before the Legion is onto us," said Fischer. He stood beside the traitor Legion soldier, both of their faces concealed, one with a helmet. "Just got to type in that code so you'll be free of those nano-charges The Master had injected into your head. Here we go." Fischer pulled a small device from one of his pouches.

The thing appeared to be a Rolodex crossed with a TV remote.

"7, 7, uh… 3, 4," Fischer typed in the code, the red buttons turning green before the device's lights faded away. "There you go." he slipped the device back into the pouch.

"Uh, that's better," said the soldier as he rolled his neck around, popping the vertebrae for emphasis. "Major stress reliever to have those things deactivated."

"Yeah, whatever blood bag." Frater rolled his eyes, nestling his beloved long rifle in his arms. "Just point us in the direction of the chopper, and we'll be on our way."

"It's a few miles over in that direction." The soldier turned around and pointed through the trees. "Shouldn't have any trouble finding it, well, as soon as you catch the scent of the other vamps."

"See you around, snack sack," said Fischer. He slapped a clawed hand on the soldier's shoulder, causing the man to flinch.

"The Master herself oughtta turn you any time now."

With that, the vampires fled through the woods in the direction the soldier indicated. They left the man standing there as though he had just finished a conversation with a group of ghosts.

Chapter IV

A Son Forever Lost

"Airports, taxi rides, crowds, lots of hurry up and wait," Lavali grumbled. The large man of Italian descent pulled his bulky body from the taxi and pushed himself out onto the crowded street. "You sure dis trip was worth it, boss? Real pain in the…"

"Would you kindly close your mouth for once, Lavali?" asked Mr. Dade. He looked the other man straight in the eye, his cruel, steely-cold blue eyes concealed under his sunglasses.

Dade raised his walking stick as though to strike his security agent, tired by his ceaseless complaining. He let his stick slide downward in his hand and then dealt Lavali a quick and much less than gentle tap to the shin.

Mr. Dade took a moment to look around, wary of any watching eyes, immediately growing content upon observation of the packed sidewalk. The streets crawled with people, just how he preferred, as the crowds allowed him to hide in plain sight.

"Ugh…" Lavali groaned. He knelt down to grasp his shin and nearly lost his own dark glasses. "Why ya got to go and do dat for?"

"Best to take Fumi's lead for now," said Mr. Dade as he ignored Lavali's complaints. "He hasn't said a word since we left the airport."

"Real easy to stay quiet when your tongue's been cut out," Lavali muttered as he rose to his feet.

"Uh…" Fumi let out a low bellow as he punched the open palm of his left hand with his right fist. The overly large, bald Asian man stood beside Mr. Dade and glared at Lavali through his own pair of shades.

"Regardless, keep your mouth shut, lest you reveal our business," said Mr. Dade as he turned his rotund back to them.

He gazed up the side of the towering hospital in front of him. The appearance of the tall brick structure was no different from any other healthcare facility.

"Come along," Dade instructed as he waddled toward the hospital entryway, leaning on his walking stick for support.

The heavy man was nearly as tall as he was round, his dark, thinning hair slicked back with gel, with his overall appearance like that of an overweight bullfrog. Despite his slow, labored pace, Dade's stride was merely an attempt to conceal his vampirism. He was much quicker than he appeared and felt he needed to walk slowly, as the sight of a rapidly moving obese man would be all too noticeable.

Lavali and Fumi followed Dade through the crowd, flanking him on either side. Both security agents were tall and heavily muscled, though a layer of blubber concealed most of it. All three wore expensive black suits. Their overall effect was like two smooth-moving sharks escorting a sinister walrus.

"Guess I can understand wanting to hide out under da morgue," Lavali remarked as the three of them approached the hospital's revolving door. "Does kind of make me feel like I'm visiting my sick granny."

Dade growled under his breath. He warned of impending homicide should Lavali utter The Master's title aloud.

"Oh, sorry, boss," Lavali caught himself. "Too many rules on dis trip."

The three men passed through the door. Dade bounded through quickly. His movements provided a brief glance at the speed he could attain.

The other two followed as they proceeded through the high-ceilinged, modestly-adorned atrium, walking over the grey, marble stone at a leisurely pace. They pushed through throngs of people as they approached the front desk's right side.

All three removed their sunglasses, their eyes safe from the sun's glaring rays.

"Is the Rat King holding court?" asked Dade. He put an arm

on the desk and checked to make sure no one was watching.

The hospital scrubbed receptionist's impossibly blue eyes grew large with recognition, and her body went rigid.

"Need to tunnel down to see him," Dade uttered the approved accompanying phrase to state his business.

"The King is in," the receptionist didn't hesitate. "I will escort you, sir. Follow me."

The vampiric woman stepped around the side of the long entry desk to wave them on behind her. She led them into the wide hallway that fed into the rest of the hospital and walked for several yards before suddenly banking left to continue toward the elevators. She pressed the button and took a cautious look over her shoulder as she checked to see if anyone had followed them.

"I…" Lavali started. Mr. Dade glared up at him with a deadly gaze, halting his attempt to break the silence.

"Here we are," said the receptionist as the elevator slid open and the four of them filed in. She hastily pressed the 'close' button multiple times, causing the doors to fly shut like guillotine blades.

"Ya gonna take us through da morgue?" Lavali asked, now safe from prying ears.

Dade shook his head at the man's insistence on conversation.

"That's the plan." There was an edge to the receptionist's voice. "To access The Master's tunnel via this hospital, we must first pass the morgue."

"Well, bite my head, why don't cha…" Lavali tensed, somewhat angered. "It's my first time down here," he explained, his words ignored as an awkward silence filled the elevator.

"Right this way," said the receptionist when the elevator door opened at last.

She led the others into an area strikingly different from the ground floor, the basement level seemingly constructed at least a half-century ago. Where the ground floor was marble, the basement flooring consisted of small, formerly white tile, grayed and cracked with age. Its walls were white, though considerably weathered, in desperate need of new paint.

"I will lead you to the door, and after that you're on your own," the receptionist told the three behind her.

She took them through a large doorway, the single word

'MORGUE' painted on the wall overhang above. They walked toward the front desk, the morgue's layout similar to what lay overhead, though the hallways were narrower and much less pristine.

Two male morticians staffed the front desk, both of whom looked up at the party as they passed in front of them. They nodded toward the receptionist, recognition in their ghastly, ice-cold eyes.

"Ya only got vamps down here?" Lavali tried not to speak too loudly, as he wished to avoid a reprimand.

"That is correct," the receptionist kept her voice level and nodded. She decided to put up with the ox-brained man for the moment. "We must keep The Master's secret from prying, blood bag eyes."

Lavali, Fumi, and even Mr. Dade gazed into the central mortuary as she led them around. They found several nude corpses hanging from a steel beam in the ceiling, all of the bodies stark white. Only small amounts of blood dripped from their lacerated throats now, this flowing down into blood buckets placed on the floor.

"It's delightful to see that our Master has set up such a successful front. It's an extraordinary feat given New York's population density," Mr. Dade mused.

The other three nodded vigorously, as they didn't want to appear disagreeable to their superior.

"Here we are." The receptionist waited until Mr. Dade's words faded away before she spoke.

She led them toward a steel door with a white sign that read DO NOT ENTER in bold, red letters.

"As I said a moment ago, you are on your own after this point. There are multiple exit paths connected to The Master's lair through which you may depart. After you, Mr. Dade," said the receptionist as she stepped to the side.

"Ah, yes, I nearly forgot," said Mr. Dade as he sauntered over to the thumbprint scanner. He placed the required digit down on the miniature, greenlit screen and waited as the locks disengaged.

"Allow me," said the receptionist as she went to open the door.

A dank, vaguely fungal stench washed over them, this born of a wet, subterranean realm. Ahead lay an almost shockingly dark passageway, the bare, dungeon-like walls illuminated by only a few bloody crimson electric torchlights.

"Shoulda guessed." Lavali looked down the tunnel and shook his head when he saw no end to it, able to cut through the darkness with his enhanced vampiric vision. "The Master sure likes deez long tunnels."

"That she does," said the receptionist. Her cruel blue eyes filled with hate as she kept the door propped against her back. "Would you mind proceeding so that I could get back to work?" She sneered.

"That is nothing against you, Mr. Dade." Her features instantly softened as she spoke to him. "You may take as long as you like."

"I understand your frustration." Mr. Dade nodded in agreement. "Lavali has a tendency to cause those around him to lose their composure. I find it best to keep him in line." He then jabbed the point of his walking stick into Lavali's giant foot.

"Ouch!" Lavali grimaced from the pain.

Fumi smiled when he saw his comrade's exclamation of agony, looking like an oversized, slightly constipated Pillsbury doughboy.

"Come along," said Dade as he picked up his walking stick and stepped into the tunnel.

"Well, looks like I'll get all my exercise for da week done in one day," said Lavali, undeterred by the punishment dealt him. "I knew I shoulda worn my gym shoes." His arms went slack at his sides as he followed Fumi, dragging his feet as he entered.

The receptionist flung the heavy door shut behind them, throwing the three of them into near-total darkness. She seemed intent on hitting Lavali in the back with it, causing the giant man to jump to attention. The door locks latched automatically, sealing Dade and his security detail inside.

"Not a pleasant woman," Lavali shook his head. He continued down the tunnel after the other two, his gorilla-like shadow barely visible upon the dark brick wall. "Think we oughta tell The Master, boss?"

"You are welcome to try, though I wouldn't recommend it," Mr. Dade answered in a rare display of sympathy. "Complaining about something so insignificant to The Master likely will not end well. Though our Mistress of Night is many things, she is not known for her sympathy."

"She?" Lavali frowned, confused.

"Uh…" Fumi groaned.

"Oh… oops, dear me," Mr. Dade's eyes narrowed, his voice full of sarcasm. "Forgive my slip of the tongue. It is a rule within Atropos never to mention The Master's gender aloud, lest we display bias," Dade mocked. "The utterance of her true name, for those who know it, is forbidden as well. Both practices derive directly from our leader's own insecurities. She believes that we would be less loyal to a woman."

"You sure you should talk about The Master like that, boss?" asked Lavali. He frowned again, unaccustomed to someone speaking so negatively about their leader.

"I will speak about The Master as I wish!" He attempted to hit Lavali in the shin as they walked, though the large man quickly stepped to the side to avoid it this time. "Lord knows I pay her more money than I ought, more than half my net profits anymore. Besides, as much as anyone sees The Master, the only way for her to police our vocabulary is for somebody to inform her of the infraction."

"Don't worry, boss. I'll never tell her." Lavali extended his lower lip and shook his head, his words sincere. "I'm no snitch."

Fumi groaned.

"It pleases me to hear that." Dade shrugged, his movement registering as positivity. "It's a rare thing for an Atropos vampire to have no desire to sell out his boss to The Master at the drop of a hat," he said as he led them farther down the tunnel. "Of course, those who snitch on me receive much worse than stitches," he muttered.

"Ow!" Lavali winched when Dade dealt him yet another quick, sharp blow to the shin. Lavali stopped, taking a moment to shake his injured leg as the other two continued onward.

Fumi let out something like a chuckle.

"What did I do that time, boss?" Lavali sprinted to catch up.

"Consider it a reminder to keep your mouth shut!" Mr. Dade suddenly turned around and pointed his stick up at the security agent. "One word out of you when we reach the Master's throne and both your employment and your life will be terminated! I simply cannot abide even the possibility of you revealing certain sensitive information!"

"I won't say anything, boss!" Lavali proclaimed, his pained expression evolved into understanding. "I swear it."

"Come along then." Mr. Dade turned around to continue down the passageway with Fumi in tow.

Lavali slowly followed.

Their massive forms moved beneath light after light, Dade's shadow resembling a giant weeble-wobble toy as it moved across the crimson-glowing wall. Their progression was monotonous, their way ubiquitous and unchanging.

They approached the end of the hallway some minutes later. A red tube light hung above another door, this one dented and disheveled, the bricks around it dirty and bloodstained.

"To the door, Fumi," Dade commanded. He pointed his walking stick at the rust-encrusted door, and the silent guardian slipped around him to fulfill his orders.

"How much farther we gotta go, boss?" asked Lavali, having recovered from Dade's scolding. His dead blue eyes went wide when he saw the length of the next tunnel.

"I believe there are three, possibly four doors, after this one." Mr. Dade frowned as he tried to remember.

"Nuts." Lavali shook his head and rolled his eyes, dissatisfied. "My dogs will be barking."

Fumi remained on the other side of the entryway, tired of holding the door for the other two.

"Let's move along," said Dade as he stepped past Fumi and through the entryway. Lavali reluctantly followed.

Lavali held the final door open some time later to admit Dade and Fumi, the large men rushing around him to arrive in a gasping huff, finally free from the oppressive smell's tyranny.

The last tunnel had run under a sewer pipe, imparting the expected putrid, fecal aromas along with a light glazing of the corresponding fluids. They planned to throw their shoes away the moment the opportunity presented itself.

Relieved of the smell, the oversized vampires found themselves in the foyer of what appeared to be an old-timey funeral home. The flowered, gaudy carpet forced his eyes downward immediately.

The red and orange petals clashed severely with the green plaid background. The walls appeared to be made of real wood, carved up with still more patterns. The smell of mothballs floated through the air, a relief from the scent that bathed the tunnel.

Fumi opened the overly adorned door. It was a delicate, wooden thing with a bright, stained-glass window that disagreed with the silent man's sensibilities.

"Can I help you?" asked the receptionist. She was a staggeringly short woman with impossibly bright, curly red hair. Her skin appeared so pale that it seemed to almost glow. Horn-rimmed glasses framed her vampiric blue eyes. She wore a metallic pink dress, complete with shoulder ruffles and elegant floral embroidery, the nametag pinned to her chest reading "Janoss."

Behind her stood a tall, thin, sickly-looking man dressed in a funeral director's suit. His skin was an unnatural shade of pale green. His nametag read "Thoop."

"Yes, I believe I scheduled an appointment," said Mr. Dade as he sauntered up to the front desk.

Both Fumi and Lavali dragged their feet behind him.

"Name?" the woman asked as she chewed the end of her pen, unable to recognize him.

"I am Primus Decimus Dade!" Dade exploded and struck the elaborately carved desk with his walking stick. "I have more than paid my dues to Atropos! I am second only to the Master herself! I could have both your heads! I need only utter the words!"

"Hey, you better watch it, mister!" the woman stood her ground and yelled right back. "I don't care who you think you are, but we won't put up with that kind of behavior here! Keep it up, and I will have Mr. Thoop escort you out!"

"You only need give me the order..." Thoop suddenly came alive, his voice airy yet confident. He popped his knuckles and glared down at the vampire boss and his security detail. Restrained murder raged in his bloodshot eyes.

All three of Thoop's potential adversaries could only look up at the threatening man. The feeling of fear was strange to them, but it coursed through their veins.

"My apologies," muttered Dade as he slowly moved his stick off the table. "I believe we have gotten off on the wrong foot. My name is Primus Decimus Dade, and I have an appointment with The Master."

"Can you tell me the nature of your appointment?" asked Janoss as she continued to nonchalantly chew the end of her pen.

"I would rather not." Dade sighed. "I do not wish to divulge certain sensitive information."

"Oh, yes, that Mr. Dade." Janoss flipped through the large appointment book that lay on the desk, a long, pink painted and highly manicured fingernail landing on his name. "Yes, I remember now, you are one of Atropos's primary financial backers. Sorry, I didn't recognize you. It's been a long time since The Master has held an audience with you. You have changed so much since the last time."

"Can you just point me toward our Master's lair, please?" Mr. Dade's eyes narrowed. The vampire lord was agitated by her insinuation.

"Yes, the elevator to The Master's lair is in that direction," said Janoss as she pointed off to her left. "Let me inform The Master of your arrival first, then you can move right along." She reached out and hit what looked like an intercom button.

"Yes?" asked a woman's predatory but patient voice, like that of a spider lurking within a web.

"Mr. Primus Dade is here for his appointment," Janoss told her, careful to speak clearly. "Are you still interested in holding an audience with him?"

"Oh, yes, Primus…" the woman mused. She paused to make a gulping sound as though she were drinking something.

Mr. Dade leaned on his walking stick as he tried to convey a countenance of rock-solid stoicism, though he shook as though he might explode in a rage-filled fury.

"Yes, send him down right away. I haven't seen him in ages," said the woman at last.

"As you wish, Master," said Janoss as she released the intercom button. "You are free to enter The Master's lair." She pointed off in the direction of the elevator once more. "I hope your encounter goes well."

"Thank you very much." Mr. Dade gave Janoss a slight bow, sure to mask his insincerity.

Lavali and Fumi followed Dade as he turned to walk around the desk. Both of the big men glared up at Thoop as they passed, taking a survey of the strength he conveyed despite his slender frame.

"All these regulations..." Dade grumbled under his breath. He strode over to the elevator door and reached for the button. "I don't know who she thinks she is. She forgets who pays most of the bills around here."

The elevator bell rang as Dade spoke, the doors sliding open to reveal an interior just as sickeningly flowered as the rest of the office. All three men stepped inside, cramped due to their exaggerated physical forms, shuffling around to fit.

"That makes things simple," said Lavali. He looked over Mr. Dade's head to find that the elevator control board consisted of only two buttons, up and down.

"Likely just a reflection on the intelligence of her staff," said Dade as he hit the down arrow.

The doors slid shut as the elevator began to descend.

"Must be a long ways down." Lavali looked at Fumi, who frowned.

"Yes, The Master's lair is many feet under the surface." Mr. Dade rolled his eyes at his bodyguard's stupidity. "Presumably, she likes to be as inconspicuous as possible."

The elevator jolted the three of them into each other as it came to an abrupt stop, a great mass of flab and elbows.

"Watch it!" Dade barked as he stumbled out.

"The Master sure has some strange digs," said Lavali as he stepped out behind him and gazed up at the vast underground cavern.

They entered a suffocating and dank, pitch-black underworld, viewable only with a flashlight or enhanced vampiric vision.

"Uh-huh," Fumi concurred.

The cave was expansive, filled with gigantic, slicked-down, stalagmite columns. Water dripped from the sharp, icicle-like stalactites that hung overhead. All was silent, except for the sound of the water and the far-off shrieks of bats. Ahead lay a narrow, gravel pathway, unnaturally carved through the cavern stone by humans or one of their derivatives.

"Yes, she has a flair for both the sinister and the dramatic." Dade shook his head, careful to whisper when he said the word 'she.' "Come along and do be careful. There are a few drop-offs on either side of our path." He sauntered forward, returned to using his walking stick for balance, his pace slowed. "I wouldn't want you to fall in," said Dade as he smiled in the dark. His grin was demonically warped, as he directed his words at Lavali.

"How much farther we gotta go, boss?" asked Lavali as he tried to draw attention away from himself. He let Fumi go on in front of him, directly behind Mr. Dade, as he wished to place someone between him and his vampire lord.

"Keep your voice down," Dade hissed at him in a whisper. "She generally resides somewhere beyond the ridge ahead. Remember what I told you about not speaking in front of her. Best you start now, as she has placed cameras at strategic points. There will be consequences if you fail to obey my instructions."

"Whatever you say, boss," Lavali spoke softly, though he still managed to throw an echo.

They made their way up the ridge, their hulking forms invisible in the darkness. Mr. Dade came to a stop atop the rise, and the three looked down into what seemed to be the cavern's innermost depths. Below sat a black obsidian furniture pair, one a simple stone table, the other a great ebony throne.

A slim figure reclined upon the obsidian seat, shrouded in a black cloak so none could discern its features.

The vampires squinted down at the figure to find that it drank from a glass filled with some viscous, bright red fluid.

"Ah, there she sits in all her glory," Dade grumbled, his words nearly inaudible. "Stop staring and come along," he ordered as he began his descent down into the cavern.

Fumi and Lavali reluctantly followed Dade. The latter left some distance between himself and his companions, suddenly in no hurry for a face-to-face meeting with The Master.

"Ah, Primus Decimus Dade," said the cloaked figure as they approached. She gingerly placed her half-filled glass upon the black stone table as she sat up on her throne. "To what do I owe this rare appearance? I haven't seen you in ages. You seem to have experienced substantial changes to your health." She cast an eye over at the three of them from under the hood of her cloak. She kept her face wrapped in a black shroud, her mouth left uncovered, so only her large, crimson lips were visible.

"I am here on behalf of my son Undecimus Dade, known as Icarus within our organization," said Mr. Dade as he stood before his master's throne. He ignored her backhanded comment.

Lavali and Fumi kept their distance behind him, glad to place another body between themselves and The Master.

"I never knew you had any children," said The Master. She caressed the top of her glass with long red fingernails, these stained with blood rather than painted.

"Yes, I had but one son," said Dade. He cradled his walking stick in his arms and shook his head in regret. "Unfortunately, Undecimus met his death some time ago, presumably while participating in a food procurement mission."

"Some time ago?" asked The Master. She placed her elbow upon her throne's armrest and rested the side of her head on her open palm. "Why are you telling me any of this? Are you now so powerless that you cannot handle such things on your own?"

Mr. Dade squinted back up at her, irritated by her insistence on keeping her face concealed, though he didn't show it. He suddenly felt a fifth presence lurking down in the cavern with them, his eyes pulled over past The Master's shoulder.

Out of the shadows arose another looming form. It surpassed Fumi and Lavali in both size and strength. It was in much better physical shape than either of the security agents.

The new figure approached The Master's throne from behind and remained off to the side. The giant creature kept itself concealed in much the same way she did. It had abandoned a cloak for close-fitting, black-plated body armor, its face hidden underneath its helmet's black visor. The head and neck appeared disproportionate to the rest of the body and suggested an abnormal visage.

"Who is this?" asked Dade. He grew anxious as a half-grin formed on his face.

Both Lavali and Fumi looked toward the monster, careful not to make direct eye contact as they sized him up.

"This is my new security detail, Bloodbath," said The Master as she took a brief glance over her shoulder, her voice flat.

The armored monster clutched the upper edge of the throne with his massive, pale white hand, its claws long, black, and staggeringly sharp.

Lavali shuddered when he imagined the wide and deep laceration wounds the thing's impressive weaponry could cause.

"I've never known you to keep security personnel," Dade spoke softly but with confidence, unafraid. "Have you become so distrustful of your own servants?"

"You never disappoint Primus," The Master smiled subtly as she mocked Mr. Dade. "Always one to talk, chastising me for keeping only one agent when you always travel with at least two."

"Beg pardon, master. I do live in a much more dangerous area of the country where it is much more difficult to hide." Dade struck the stone floor with the end of his walking stick, the sharp sound echoing throughout the cavern. "The District V Battalion is much more active than the others, always on the hunt. In addition to this, many of my underlings have tried to usurp me in the past. I cannot afford to be careless." He tensed but kept his tone level.

"I am well aware of the dangers you face in District V," said The Master. She sat up straight, waving Mr. Dade's problems away with her hand. "Bloodbath presented me with a gift, and I responded in kind, granting him his position. I have never had much need for protection, but I decided it was time to consider personal security before the need arose." The monster behind her grunted to emphasize her point. "Enough about my personal protection, though. Let us return to the issue at hand, the death of your son. Why have you yet to avenge him?"

"The situation is rather complicated, Master." Dade shook his head, a certain degree of regret in his voice. "I was not made aware of my son's untimely death until months afterward. I gained the information little more than a week ago, all of it second or even third hand."

"Why did you only recently learn of your son's death?" asked The Master as she came to attention. She gripped her throne's black stone armrest in her red-nailed hand, growing angry.

"I had grown estranged from Undecimus." Dade shrugged shamefully. "We had had a falling out, and I hadn't spoken to or heard from him in years. All of this aside, it seems the underboss in charge of Undecimus, Desmond was his name, declined not to inform me. Presumably, he is unwilling to take responsibility for what happened."

"Did you not have the underboss in question killed as soon as you determined he was the one responsible?" The Master propped her head upon her hand once more, bored by Dade's problems.

"That is precisely what I had intended to do, Master." Dade trembled with rage, the bright red of his face visible even in the darkness. "Unfortunately, this particular underboss seems to have been either killed or taken by the Legion after the failed counteroffensive at Wayward Packing. I found my son was dead only a few days after the Legion's attack."

"I see," The Master mused with a renewed interest. "Have you considered determining the whereabouts of those directly in charge of your son? I presume he was not one of our captains."

"I have looked for the individuals in question, but it seems they were transferred from my service, without my consent, some time ago," said Dade as he threatened to break the end of his walking stick. "They were given over to the service of The Surgeon at his behest. My apologies, Master, but it seems you were involved in that transfer."

"I had no way of knowing about their involvement with your son." The Master shrugged, unconcerned. "Had I known, I would have left your servants to you and not facilitated their transfer."

"Had they not been moved, I likely would have had my satisfaction." Droplets of sweat formed on Dade's forehead. "Regardless, I have given up on their apprehension for the present. After the Legion's defeat of The Surgeon's forces within his mountain laboratory, I presume they are dead."

"What would you have me do, Dade?" The Master cut to the chase, the scowl on her face concealed under her shroud. "Your underboss is likely dead, as are his former underlings. The only one left is the individual who actually killed your son. I presume it was not one of our own."

"Undecimus was killed by a human police officer, one who has yet to be identified," said Dade, his face clinched up even more. "From the little that has been gathered, it seems that that officer has been recruited into the Legion."

"Would you have me infiltrate the Legion for you, Dade?" The Master rose to her feet and instantly extinguished Dade's pressing rage.

The vampire lord took a step back, as did his security agents, all believing The Master had grown enraged. Their eyes shot toward her strapping armor-clad guard, though the monster remained immobile.

"Would you have me infiltrate the Legion?" The Master repeated the question with the same tone. "It is a feat none have fulfilled as of yet. The Legion's screening process is so extensive, its methods of dispatch so brutal, that it has been rendered impossible. So much so that no one dare attempt it. Is this what you want, Dade?"

"I come only to ask your assistance in finding if any of those involved in my son's demise still live." Dade reassumed his solid, confident stance. He remained guarded, somewhat confused by his master's actions. "I ask nothing more."

"I can do much more than that for you," said The Master.

She walked toward him, her step smooth and cat-like, though this only served to increase Dade's apprehension.

"The plan is already in motion as we speak. I have the perfect human candidate in my custody, a Legion soldier abducted during our defeat at Wayward, the gift that Bloodbath brought me to gain his position at my side."

"No disrespect Master, but do you sincerely believe that a captured Legion soldier is the best choice for a double agent?" asked Dade with a grimace. Lavali and Fumi exchanged looks of apprehension between themselves.

"In this instance, yes, I absolutely believe in the selected candidate," said The Master as she proceeded past Dade.

She gently laid a clawed hand on his shoulder as she floated around him, Lavali and Fumi stepping farther back as she approached.

"I don't care to reveal all the details, but I assure you everything is sliding into place," she said as she rounded Dade's other side, her delicate hand resting upon his opposite shoulder. "I have much confidence in my Legion soldier. Not only will his actions result in the death of your son's killer, they will lead to the downfall of the whole District V Battalion," she whispered in his ear, her voice soft and seductive.

"Is it advisable for you to place so much confidence in a plan involving a single human Legion soldier?" Dade was unfazed, though both of his bodyguards shuddered.

"Might we be forgetting who our master is?" The Master released Dade's shoulder and strode back toward her obsidian throne like a ghostly shadow. "It's either this or you can continue to seek your own justice, where the most you can possibly do is dispense punishment upon the heads of our own."

She turned to face the three and slowly descended back into her seat, reclaiming her position on the throne.

"I suppose I have little choice in the matter," said Dade. He cast aside any remaining anger he felt earlier and reluctantly accepted his fate. "My own methods have failed thus far."

Lavali shook his head, unaccustomed to seeing his overlord so thoroughly defeated

"You're a wise man, Dade. I knew you would see things the right way," said The Master. She gave him a broad smile, her sharp, white fangs contrasting with her ruby lips.

Chapter V

The Evolving Battlefield

Cyrus bolted for his target destination, the kresnik leaving the Legion soldiers behind. He rushed around the broad-based trees like a tracking hound, his nostrils filled with the smell of vampires' blood. Elysia remained back with the half battalion, as Commander Griffin wanted to test his new weapon to its full extent without assistance.

Cyrus rushed through the shadows; the sun nearly disappeared as the dusk settled in, his indiscernible phantom form concealed underneath the considerable foliage. His thirst to kill was unquenchable, though now contained by his nano-cranial implants, which kept a lid on his more bestial urges. He was a rational death machine in complete control of his own bladed arsenal, able to target his enemies, capable of strategy. He possessed the ability to hit the brakes and forgo the kill if he so chose.

The lust for blood always remained, though.

Cyrus kept a monster locked down in the confines of his mind, clawing into the walls. He charged through the woods as though pulled through the undergrowth by some hell-force. He craved solo combat, with the vampires soon to fall to the edge of his ever-changing blade.

Cyrus lunged through the opening between the bases of two redwood behemoths and bounded right into the vampire camp. He identified his destination immediately: an elaborate, black-cloth tent housing the lead vampire. Cyrus left the surrounding human guards to the Legion, instructed to eliminate as many vampires as possible, the easier kills left to his comrades.

The path to the tent was open, the kresnik's way lit by several strings of red lanterns, and virtually no guards were present nearby. Cyrus rushed his mark, his TAPSAW transformed into a sword.

"We're under attack!" Someone screamed, alerted to kresnik's presence.

Cyrus slashed open the tent's backside with his blade, the nano-metal edge crashing into several large computer monitors, the screens smashed on the ground. One of the vampires screamed when the kresnik leaped through the jagged opening, a woman in a bloody white dress.

Cyrus sprang at her, his sword instantly becoming an ax, the blade of which he buried in her forehead. He pulled his weapon from his victim and then went to decapitate another, sending the head flying out the front tent flap.

Blood flowing over the carpet, Cyrus grabbed the lead vampire from his seat with his good hand, taking hold of his frock overcoat. There was no doubt he had the right one, the man dressed in impractical, Victorian-era clothing just as described.

"Put me down, you stupid brute!" The man demanded as he struggled in Cyrus's grasp, unaccustomed to such violent handling. "Do you know who I am?"

Cyrus unleashed a leopard's roar as he threw the ridiculously dressed vampire through the flap at the front of the tent, his followers rushing after. The kresnik's TAPSAW became a sword once more as he sliced through the abdomens of three of the escaping vampire soldiers. The kresnik separated each into two halves, their blood spewing onto the ground as their entrails spread over the thick, expensive rug.

The sound of the Legion soldiers firing their X-12 automatic shotguns exploded across the evolving battleground as the half battalion encircled the vampire's sprawling camp. Several vampire soldiers held their ground, firing their weapons, though few of them seemed to know where to shoot. Most carelessly let their firearms fall to the ground as they fled, feeling little need to engage the enemy at all.

Cyrus charged out of the tent's front opening and into the erupting chaos. He found the frock-coated vampire captain scrambling onto his feet, the frightened man trying to take flight. Cyrus jerked the Atropos commander down onto the hard ground with his lash, his blade now transformed into a chain whip, the weapon wrapped around the man's ankles.

"Stay down, or I'll cut you in half the hard way," Cyrus leaned down to hiss in the vampire's ear.

The kresnik unraveled the links in his chain whip, releasing his prey for the moment. Cyrus spun around to knock several of the fleeing enemy down as they ran around him. Shifting his means of attack, he pulled back his whip, the long mass rippling and bubbling as it took the form of an ax.

Cyrus lunged for his downed victims, aiming for their prostrate necks as they tried to stand. The edge of the blade sliced through one and then another, the spent bodies falling into quickly forming pools of blood as the heads bounced across the ground. A third managed to rise from the ground before Cyrus was upon him; the kresnik's ax blade plunged into the vampire's back. The kresnik freed his weapon and then sliced through his victim's neck, beheading the vampire before his body could hit the ground.

"I told you to stay down!" Cyrus roared at the vampire leader when he caught the doomed man's movements in his peripheral vision.

He leaped around and lashed out at him with the chain whip, knocking him back onto the ground.

"Stay down or be rent to shreds!" the kresnik growled at him and then whirled back around to engage the enemy.

The Legion continued their fire as the line of soldiers entered the clearing, the red glow of the lanterns glistening against their black body armor. Despite all the gunfire, the Legion fragment rounds had no effect on Cyrus when they struck him. His advanced synthetic spider-silk armor protected him, his mouth vent up to shield his face. The rounds downed vampire after vampire and left him unharmed.

No longer concerned with express killing and needing only to delay the vampire's retreat, Cyrus let his TAPSAW become a mace and chain. The kresnik swung his weapon around rapidly, the bloody red light of the lanterns dancing over the black metal to create death's disco ball. Multiple bodies flew through the air and onto the ground, the victims desperately trying to rise to their feet, immediately gunned down by the Legion.

"Just keep it up a few moments more!" Cyrus heard Commander Griffin yell out from one of the Legion soldier's helmets. "They didn't stand a chance!"

Cyrus looked past the encircling Legion force as the bodies piled up to catch a glimpse of several of the escaping enemy.

A group of black-clad vampires ran for the southwestern corner of the camp, headed for an opening between the trees.

Cyrus bolted from the dwindling action of the Legion's fray, an impossibly fast, dark armored wildcat. He rushed through the circle of encroaching soldiers, leaving the rest of the defeated enemy to the Legion.

Cyrus roared as he raced for his prey. He lashed out at the first runner, cutting the vampire's legs out from under him and then decapitating him with his ax as he fell. The kresnik lunged for the next two, slicing straight through their necks with inhuman precision. He caught the fourth with a stab through the back, her chest cavity penetrated by his blade.

The woman screamed as she slipped from the blood-saturated, obsidian edge, falling onto the ground in a heap.

Cyrus followed up the blow with a clean chop through the vampire's neck, his sword an ax again. He turned and sped for the wide opening between the trees, unsure if any of the fleeing enemy remained alive, though the pungent scent of living vampire still filled his nostrils.

Cyrus darted through the darkened opening and into a heavily foliaged, blackened world. The light of the lanterns just reached the perimeter of the camp, but his enhanced black and white night vision allowed him to see where the Legion soldiers could not.

"What gives?" Sergeant Laveau shouted as he picked himself off the ground. Cyrus had run headlong into the soldier and knocked him down.

The kresnik smelled the air, suddenly going rigid. Something was very wrong.

"You smell…" Cyrus's eyes went wide when he took a whiff of Laveau. "You smell wrong!" He slapped Laveau's shotgun away with his prosthetic TAPSAW. The kresnik dug into the sergeant's body armor with his good hand and raised him up into the air. "You smell like a bloodsucker!"

Cyrus roared in Laveau's face. He was ready to level the sergeant to the ground, prepared to do to him what he had done to the vampires.

"Put him down!" Captain Dunkirk commanded. She appeared some distance behind Cyrus, holding up her shotgun with a death grasp.

Two other soldiers stood behind her, one with a tactical flashlight, revealing the soldier and the kresnik.

"Put him down, Cyrus!" Dunkirk commanded.

"The smell of vampire is on him!" Cyrus began to shake the sergeant.

"The smell of vampire is on everyone!" Laveau shouted. He ceased his struggle and held onto Cyrus's wrist with both hands. "It's on you the most! You're covered in their blood!"

"Put him down, Cyrus!" A young woman's voice rang out, causing Cyrus to turn around, though he retained a death grip on the sergeant. The woman was Elysia, her hood pulled down to reveal her face, pleading in her large brown eyes.

"You gonna put me down?" asked Laveau as he looked down at him through his helmet's visor, his voice flat.

Cyrus let out a low growl as he relented, planting the Surgeon's feet back on the ground. He skulked back toward the red-lit clearing, his anger slowly receding. His footsteps were heavy and forced as he left Laveau standing there, the kresnik making his way through throngs of Legion soldiers.

"We need your help to interrogate the vampire captain, Cyrus," said Commander Griffin. He appeared in front of him with an outstretched hand to stop him. His long white hair hung out of his helmet, made red under the lights. "We have him restrained and gagged. He's propped up against the base of that tree over there." The commander turned and pointed off to the side.

The vampire in question sat stationary against one of the massive redwoods, his frock coat removed. He resembled a wingless mosquito pinned to a block of wood.

"Pff…" Cyrus scoffed and then looked Griffin in the eye through his helmet. "Like I know anything about interrogations."

"You don't need to know anything," said the commander as he put an encouraging hand on his shoulder. "You only need to follow my instructions. We're going to put the fear of God back into that bloodsucker. Follow me." Griffin released Cyrus, stepping around him to walk toward the bound vampire, the monster attended by two Legion companies.

Cyrus remained off in the commander's peripheral as they approached.

The captured vampire tried to make eye contact with him through his helmet's visor, his deathly blue eyes seeming to glow through the lantern's red light.

"We only just got the gag in his mouth, sir," one of the Legion soldiers told the commander as he encroached upon the gathering. The man concealed his eyes under his transitions visor.

The soldier was Captain Lee, an officer whose name Cyrus had only just bothered to learn.

"Bloodsucker is a biter, nearly a miracle he didn't get hold of any of us. All of his screaming was about as bad." The captain shook his head.

"Sounds like a fun guy," Cyrus remarked.

The captain winced when he saw the kresnik's prominent canine fangs, Cyrus's mouth vent still open.

"I suppose it is safe to assume that he's unlikely to be very cooperative," Commander Griffin looked toward the captain as though he had asked a question.

"I would think so, sir," said Captain Lee.

"We'll just stick to the old 'bad cop, psychotic cop' routine," Griffin told Cyrus. He kept his voice down, lest the captured vampire should hear. "Need I assign your role?" he asked.

Cyrus tried not to smile at the remark.

The kresnik suddenly looked up to find Elysia somewhere off to the side of the large group of soldiers, her eyes friendly, her light brown hair bathed in the red light. Cyrus frowned when he saw Sergeant Laveau standing beside her, his helmet removed as he engaged her in conversation.

"Remove his bonds and gag!" Griffin shouted, returning Cyrus's attention to the captive vampire.

Many of the soldiers looked up at their commander in

confusion, unsure of the words that proceeded from his mouth.

"But, sir," Captain Dunkirk started. The tall woman had snuck up to them while they were speaking. "Do I really need to explain to you just how bad an idea that is?"

"Normally, it would be very bad," the commander admitted as he looked toward the vampire with critical scrutiny. "Times have changed though. We have the kresnik right here with us should anything go wrong. It is time for humanity to put the vampire back in its proper place."

"Do as you're told!" Captain Lee shouted at the soldiers nearest the vampire.

"I want you to take off your helmet and form your TAPSAW into the most brutal weapon imaginable," Griffin turned to Cyrus, his words stern. "We want to scare him as much as possible."

"Just another way to make an insinuation about my looks," Cyrus grinned with mirthful malice. "Personally, I think I look pretty good, in an unconventional way, of course."

"Follow me," said the commander.

Griffin proceeded toward the prisoner, his stride purposeful and confident.

Cyrus followed, his good hand on the back of his helmet as he prepared to remove it, thinking about what could be considered the most 'brutal weapon imaginable.' He pulled his helmet off his head, his large pointy ears slipping out the slits in the sides. He let it roll onto the ground and looked the bound vampire straight in the face, glaring at him through the red-tinted near darkness. Cyrus bore his ghastly sharp canines, a look of pure murder in his slit-pupil cat-eyes, the menacing orbs glowing some strange demon color under the red lights.

The vampire returned the intimidating stare, his glass-blue eyes partially covered by his messed black locks.

Cyrus formed his TAPSAW arm into a giant, crustacean-like pincer. He held it up for him to see, slowly opening and closing the apparatus in response.

"Hurry up with those bounds," Griffin spoke to his personnel in a level tone, the slightest hint of an edge to his voice.

The soldiers began to unwind the rope from the vampire's legs to let their captive rise to his feet, his quick, anxious movements suggesting thoughts of escape.

"Don't you try anything, bloodsucker!" Commander Griffin bellowed. He signaled the soldiers standing around the tree to raise their weapons toward the vampire, their red laser sights now dancing across the captive's forehead. "Remove the gag, but keep his hands tied," he nodded toward the soldier standing closest to the vampire.

"Get over there, Cyrus," Griffen directed the kresnik, though he retained his aim on the captive with his own X-12. "Got to put the squeeze on him early," he said with a clenched fist.

The vampire howled in rage when the soldier pulled the gag from his mouth.

Cyrus rushed straight for him, quickly changing direction and spinning back around to catch the vampire with his claw to hold him up by the back of the neck.

"Shut up, or your head goes 'pop,'" Cyrus made the sound with his lips as he whispered in the vampire's ear.

"There's no need for screaming, vampire." Griffin looked at their captive through his red laser sight, his finger on the trigger. "Only the information you give up could possibly save your miserable life."

"So you say," The vampire gave the commander a fanged smirk, revealing a face that demanded slapping.

"What is your name, vampire?" Griffin ignored his snide attitude.

"I'm surprised you haven't heard of me, commander, notorious as I am," the vampire's grin never faltered.

"He asked for your name, bloodsucker!" Cyrus tightened his grip around the prisoner's neck in an attempt to gag him.

"Very well," the vampire coughed as his eyes began to water, Cyrus loosening his hold. "I am Vaylat, The Un-surpassingly Powerful, Blood Prince of Darkness, The Bleakest Nightmare of Mankind, The Death Who Lurks in Shadow. Need I say more?"

"Lovely titles," Cyrus hissed. The smell of the vampire started to seep into his brain, his flesh beckoning to him like a juicy beef tenderloin.

His nano-implants seemed to have their limits.

"Nope, never heard of you," the commander shrugged.

The other surrounding soldiers began to talk among

themselves as they arrived at the same conclusion.

"My apologies," said Vaylat directly to the commander. He almost laughed as he ignored Cyrus's threatening manner. "I should have anticipated as much from a filthy blood bag."

"What is your purpose in these woods, vampire?" Griffin snapped. He was tired of Vaylat's arrogance, though he did want to catch him off guard.

"I am not a liberty to discuss such things." Vaylat refused to be intimidated. "The Master forbids it."

"Your life is at stake!" Griffin grew enraged. "We don't care what 'The Master's' orders are!"

"Order your mongrel beast to unhand me, and I'll gladly tell you whatever you want to know," Vaylat spoke as though he were at Sunday brunch.

Cyrus looked up at the commander, unsure what direction he would take.

"Release him, Cyrus." Griffin shook his head. "Move slowly though. We don't want him trying anything."

"Yes, sir." Cyrus hesitated.

He was unwilling to free Vaylat from his grasp, even temporarily. Every instinct he possessed, both human and bestial, screamed at him to hold on. He planted the vampire's feet firmly on the ground and loosened his grip as he backed away, retaining eye contact with the commander should something go wrong.

"Stand over there, Cyrus." Griffin pointed to a spot near Vaylat's eleven o'clock with his laser.

"Yes, sir!" Cyrus spoke so everyone could hear his response.

He turned and made his way to the designated spot, though he kept an eye on Vaylat. He held his crustacean claw at the ready, prepared to snap the vampire's neck as soon as the Commander gave the order.

"Your request has been honored, vampire." Commander Griffin's demeanor toward the captive softened. "Now, please tell me what your party's previous intentions were."

"I was told by The Master, directly and under the excruciating pain of death, never to reveal the mission objectives to the Legion."

"Once again, what your master says has no bearing here."

Griffin grimaced. "You will suffer the pain of death right here if you don't give me the requested intel."

"I suppose I could be convinced to give it to you, but only if you remove the bonds around my wrists." Vaylat held out his bound hands.

"I have already granted you one request, vampire," Griffin sighed in frustration. "Either talk or be blown away."

"I will not speak until all my bonds are removed!" Vaylat snarled, ferocity in his blue phantom's eyes. His prior composure had vanished. "I will not be bound like a beast by you human primitives!"

"I could care less about the painful death your Master has promised you for speaking," Cyrus hissed at the vampire as he repeatedly snapped his great claw open and closed. "I'm sure I can do so much worse." The vampire's threatening stance ignited his bloodlust, both the need to feed and eliminate the threat welling up inside.

"I will not speak unless all my bonds are removed." Vaylat returned to himself, acting as though his outburst never happened.

"You two! Remove the rest of his bonds!" Griffin commanded, indicating the soldiers toward the vampire with his gunsight.

The two men hesitated, then slowly lowered their weapons and ran toward the vampire, their comrades filling the gaps they left in the encircling line.

"Don't you dare try anything vampire!" Griffin continued to shout. "You touch any of my soldiers, and it's curtains!"

Vaylat remained motionless as the soldiers untied his wrists and then returned to their former positions. The commander's threats seemed to register at last.

"I will not be threatened by some blood bag made, mongrel dog!" Vaylat exploded into a rage and lunged at Cyrus, his fangs bared.

Cyrus roared as he caught Vaylat's mid-section in his claw. He buried his own fangs in the vampire's neck, crushing his vertebrae in his powerful jaws.

"Don't fire!" Griffin waved the surrounding soldier's weapons down. Several of them raised and then lowered their weapons, unsure of what to do.

Cyrus gripped ever harder with his giant claw and cut Vaylat in two. The vampire's severed lower half fell to the ground like half of a bloodied, intestine-filled piñata. The soldiers watched on in horror as they waited for the commander's next order.

"Wha…" Cyrus released Vaylat's neck from his jaws. He let the rest of the body fall to the ground in a heap as his giant claw formed back into an arm.

The kresnik turned and looked up at the encircling soldiers, his eyes glowing under the red light, Vaylat's dark crimson blood dripping from his mouth. He found Elysia standing in the same spot from earlier, Laveau still at her side.

She frowned and shook her head, making it impossible for him to tell if she was disgusted, disappointed, or both.

"Nice going, kresnik!" Sergeant Laveau slowly clapped his hands as he shouted over the crowd. "You have now destroyed all our potential sources of intel! So much for our superweapon!"

Cyrus glared at the sergeant through menacing cat's eyes, the all too familiar bloodlust boiling up inside yet again.

"Shut up, sergeant!" Griffin yelled at Laveau as he pushed his way back through the Legion soldiers. "That vampire had his mind made up. He wasn't going to tell us anything."

All eyes turned to the loaming spectacle as the soldiers anticipated a possible physical altercation.

"What is our next course of action, sir?" Captain Dunkirk called to the commander. She moved around the group of soldiers toward the other side of Laveau, revealed by her long red braid.

Griffin suddenly stopped. Dunkirk had taken him off guard, his anger toward Laveau suddenly dying away. "I suppose the best course of action now is to search Vaylat's tent."

"I doubt it will do any good, sir," Laveau spoke again, undeterred by Griffin's actions. "The kresnik already took care of the vampire's technological equipment. I doubt we'll be able to find much left in there."

"I could care less about your 'doubts,' Sergeant." Griffin turned to Laveau and gritted his teeth. "We will search every square inch of this campsite until we find the desired intel."

"I have already found something." Captain Dunkirk pushed

the others aside as she approached the commander. "I picked this up from over there." She handed Griffin a small silver flash drive and then pointed to a spot near the southwestern edge of the clearing.

"Excellent, Captain," said the commander. He took the flash drive and shoved it down into the pocket of his combat vest.

"What are your orders, sir?" Captain Lee asked as he appeared at Griffin's side.

"We will search the area with a fine-tooth comb." Griffin nodded and turned on his helmet's speaker.

"Dunkirk's company!" He commanded the soldiers, his voice resounding through his helmet. "You will search Vaylat's tent!" He pointed toward the designated area. "Lee's company will stand guard! The rest of you, search the area! I will have my intel, even if we   have   to   search   all   night!"

Chapter VI

The Death Company

"You ready to run this?" Corporal McCool almost had to jump to reach Asher's shoulder, the short man filled with overwhelming enthusiasm. The two stood among the rest of Captain Kilgore's company at the back of their transport truck, the soldiers growing agitated while they anticipated the start of their offensive.

Nine other companies stood nearby, swarmed near their own transports, the whole battalion all but mired in the swampy wetlands of southeastern Missouri. They had trekked over haphazard highway bridges and narrow gravel roads to reach their destination. The trucks and equipment were a strange sight in the area; a herd of black-plated war machines lost out in the low flood.

Their occupation of the site was the direct result of the additional information gained from the vampire Desmond, intel gathered through the threat of torture and Commander Greaves's series of threats. They were here to catch Atropos's money purse, Mr. Dade, at home. They sought to cripple the organization, to strike where it hurt most.

"I think we've got this." Asher nodded. He answered honestly, though he was unsure if he cared for the interaction. He approved of their new assault group leader, but he found his overblown optimism irritating. Their group had reformed a week ago, having trained with McCool only a handful of times.

Asher took a moment to survey their position, feeling almost disturbed by the disorganized Legion battalion.

A massive mansion lay above their assembly on the hill, its sharp, square design making it appear as though it could pierce the grey, clouded sky. The great stone structure resembled an old government building. It was not a home, but a fortress, an impenetrable barrier against the Legion's forces.

Though it appeared left without weaponized protection and lacked a physical barricade, Asher could see the movable stone slabs. Both of these stood embedded in the structure, laid out upon the hill, each concealing a heavy artillery piece.

"Come on, man! Get pumped!" pressed McCool, the corporal keeping his hand on Asher's shoulder. He attempted to make eye contact, his gaze stifled by his helmet's dark visor.

It was difficult to read any of the Legion soldiers, all of their eyes concealed. The unfriendly black of their uniforms suggested a level of hostility.

"We can't bring down the vamps with a bunch of wet blankets!" proclaimed McCool as he released Asher at last.

"Vamps won't be able to handle what we're packing!" Aaron returned McCool's bravado. He reached around to give the corporal a fist bump, as he saw Asher didn't care for the corporal's fervor.

Asher kept his eyes on the horizon, disappointed by the lack of sun this midmorning. He felt it could potentially hamper their operation, even if most of the fighting would likely occur indoors. The cursed, blackened storm clouds glared back at him, and he could see a thunderhead developing in the distance.

It threatened complications should their offensive not begin soon.

"Haha! That's what I like to hear!" declared McCool in response to Aaron. His hands returned to his X-12 automatic shotgun, the officer validated at last.

"You ready to take down the vamps?" McCool moved onto another group, met with similar looks from the other soldiers as he encountered multiple slack shrugs.

Someone swallowed hard, causing Asher to turn to the side. He found their group's medic, Milo Harkman, looking over at him from where he stood beside Aaron. Milo shook his head, his genuine dislike of their new leader apparent. The medic had a similar view of the corporal. He was always careful to give McCool a wide berth should his overdone attitude be contagious.

"Here she comes!" Greaves' forceful baritone voice

resounded through the speakers in their helmets. A decommissioned M1 Abrams tank rumbled into view as it rolled toward the chain-link barrier.

"To the side!" commanded Sergeant Ito. She stepped in front of her squad to order them back, the relatively short woman displaying a commanding presence despite her small stature. Ito was the last soldier assigned to Asher's unconventional five-man assault group, as Captain Kilgore felt someone higher ranking than a corporal was needed near the front.

The great machine lumbered through the ensemble of black-plated, sleepy soldiers on either side. Its mighty engines shook the ground as its immensely wide treads kicked up the loose gravel. The behemoth shambled onward, its metal-plated hide sandy brown like an arid, desert floor. Its grandeur was somewhat depleted by its lack of a heavy gun, the artillery deemed too weighty for their operation.

The vibrating machinery quieted as it approached the chain-link fence below, what looked like a brick storm shelter and the fortress on the hill set some distance beyond that.

"Give it the gas!" Greaves roared.

The tank's gas turbine engines revved up in response. The juggernaut rapidly gained speed as it thundered past the lines of watching soldiers, headed straight for the fence.

The tank tore through the chain-link, the flimsy, metal framework crushed under its rolling treads, leaving a mess of mangled, twisted debris. The machine slowed to a stop once more as it waited for the commander's next order, the Legion personnel following it with caution.

"Jamison's company!" Greaves called for his one hundred personnel-strong breaching company. "To your position!"

"My company!" Captain Jamison, the officer who stood across the road from Asher's squad, shouted and raised his fist to address his soldiers. "Move!" Jamison commanded. He sprinted toward the back of the tank, his black-clad Legion soldiers following behind him like a valor-fueled swarm of army ants.

"Kilgore's company!" Greaves continued down his list of Captains. "Support!"

"Move!" Kilgore gave the command with a raised fist and then rushed off toward the compound ahead.

Asher right behind him, Corporal McCool beside him, the two of them selected beforehand as the ones who would enter immediately behind Jamison's company. The rest of Kilgore's soldiers followed closely behind them.

"Take out the entry point!" Greaves called out to the Abrams tank.

The turbine engines roared back at him as the metal colossus grew enraged, its massive bulk lurching forward before it ran headlong at the concrete gatehouse. Metal slammed into stone with a mighty crash as the concrete bricks fell like a Janga tower, a dry cloud of dust filling the moist air. The Abrams stood over the wreckage, the shadow of its massive form cloaked in the smokescreen.

"Back it up!" Greaves roared.

The Abrams began to roll backward, its internal mechanisms capable of only so much speed. Jamison's company crossed over the wrecked fence, the soldier's forms barely visible through the dense dust cloud as they passed around the lumbering tank. They moved quickly, eager to put an end to the whole operation.

"Form up!" Captain Jamison's voice echoed through Asher's helmet, his company moving into position at the compound entrance.

Kilgore's company remained close behind as they followed them into the slowly dissipating filth cloud. The darkness created by both the dust and storm clouds obscured Asher's vision only slightly, as his visor's transitive lens helped him to see through it all. Kilgore raised an open palm in front of Asher. The private relayed the signal to those behind him, the company slowing down as they approached the entry point.

Jamison's company gathered in front of them, the soldiers up front arranging themselves against what remained of the concrete wall. They were careful to watch their footing as they proceeded over the debris-littered ground, hesitant on their entry.

The doorway stood in front of them, the surrounding dust illuminated in a foreboding red, a five-foot-wide gaping maw into the underworld. It was inadvisable to send a whole company down a long hall into a fortress, but the Legion was out of options. Crossing through the passageway was the only way to avoid the hill's guns and find their quarry.

Asher remained among the soldiers of his company, nearly fifty personnel on each side of the wrecked gatehouse. All of them clenched their double-drummed automatic shotgun, barrels pointed down as they waited for the signal for entry. From where Asher stood, it seemed the hallway was clear, though he knew even a slight shadow could remain indiscernible within the narrow space.

"Here we go," McCool whispered from somewhere behind Asher, his voice echoing throughout the cavernous space.

The first two soldiers from Jamison's company leaned against the wall nearest the doorway. They reached back for the shins of those behind them, the signal shared between both of their five-man assault groups. Without further fanfare, the two up front began to search around their corners.

They entered seconds later after they confirmed the hallway was clear.

The rest of Jamison's company slowly filed into the hallway, two personnel abreast, the level of caution they retained seeming unwarranted and ridiculous. The last soldiers moved through the entry point, disappearing into the dark, red lights.

Captain Jamison turned around and signaled back to Captain Kilgore's company with a wag of his index finger. He then went to join his soldiers, the short man's broad-backed silhouette vanishing with the others.

"Kind of dumb to leave the only entry point unguarded," Asher's mumbles echoed through the space. Milo, Aaron, and some of the others around him nodded in solemn agreement.

The unmistakable cries of a pack of feral vampires broke the relative silence. This reverberated through the hallway and out the door, the attackers enthralled by an unyielding bestial bloodlust.

Asher and his fellows clutched their weapons tightly and pointed their firearms at the entry point. Red laser sights danced over the darkened walls, periodically disappearing in the light emitted from the doorway. The desire to rush through the opening tore at Asher's composure like a wild, caged animal, the order for them to remain in place the only thing that held him there.

"They're coming out of the wall!" Jamison screamed like a dying animal. His company was already in the deathly cold grasp of the enemy, vampire tooth and claw rending armor and flesh.

"They're ripping us to shreds!"

Shotgun blasts followed and the Legion soldier's stout discipline devolved into panic. Their fragmentation rounds exploded all around as they tore into friend and foe alike. The company was effectively cannibalizing itself, their weapons more devastating against their own than any vampiric force.

"Fall back!" Greaves bellowed. He grew angered by the losses, enraged by what he registered as his own personal folly. "Send in the Sanguinarian Guard!" The commander roared.

His words rang through Asher's ears, the pain in his skull greater than his confusion. The private's muscles grew taut and he expected the enemy to emerge, the sound of gunfire beginning to steadily die down.

The soldiers in the hall fired continuously as they tried to both retreat and keep the ferals at bay.

"Roger!" Jamison responded. He had no other choice but to abandon his own troops, his company overrun.

Asher could see the captain's short, bulky shadow stretched over the red-lit wall as he raced for the door, his goal seemingly unattainable.

Jamison's dying screams were brief, the shadow of a clawed hand shooting out to grab him by the back of the neck. The talons wrapped around his throat and the sharp points penetrated his trachea, though the captain continued to struggle. The hand pulled the captain through the wall; his squatty form suddenly disappeared from beneath the lights.

"Where's the Guard?" Captain Kilgore yelled at Greaves through his helmet.

Asher jerked around to find his captain standing near the large pile of rubble left by the tank. Their company leader retained a stranglehold on his weapon, laser sight pointed toward the entryway, prepared for an incoming vampire onslaught.

"Your cavalry has arrived!"

A short, lean figure emerged from the still dissipating smoke at the company's back like a phantom, female from the sound of its voice and the cut of its body armor. Asher strained his neck to look at her, just able to see the name 'Murina' emblazed on the nametag on her chest.

"Better late than never," Kilgore told her, though he continued to look down his gun sights toward the doorway.

"So much for gratitude." Murina sauntered past the captain and through the large group of soldiers. She made straight for the entryway as she took up twin tomahawks from the holsters at her sides. She skillfully spun her weapons around in her hands, her firearm secured to her back.

A much taller, stocky male soldier followed her, clad in black like the rest of them, an oversized nightstick in his right hand. Asher squinted to read the name 'Balion' on the soldier's tag.

Behind the two was an onslaught of about one hundred more soldiers, their faces concealed under helmet visors. All carried bladed or blunt weapons, firearms strapped to their backs as an afterthought.

The whole of the Sanguinarian Guard gathered in front of the red-lit door as their leader turned around to speak to them, the shadow of her small form enlarged under the foreboding light.

"We will have blood for the Guard and blood for the Legion!" Murina shouted the Guard's battle cry, tomahawks raised above her head.

"Blood for the Guard! Blood for the Legion!" The Guard shouted back at her, blades and clubs in the air in a display of ferocity.

"Ahh!" Murina screamed. Her comrades dashed after her as she rushed through the doorway, the Guard moving with a striking lack of fear.

"What are you waiting for?" Kilgore barked at his surrounding company as the soldiers looked toward him for guidance. "Follow them through the entry point!"

"Move!" Sergeant Ito urged her group forward, never leaving her position behind the other four personnel in her group.

"But, sir!" shouted Lieutenant Tarango. He appeared beside Captain Kilgore to present his argument, the short, oversized man always the first to complain.

"Shut it, Lieutenant!" Kilgore waved him away with a dismissive hand, unwilling to deal with his protests. "Blackthorn! McCool! Pass through the entry point!"

"Yes, sir!" Asher rushed for the doorway just as the words

left his mouth, growing tired of their wait.

The private advanced with speed and efficiency, the rest of Kilgore's company copying his movements. He passed through the doorway to find himself inside a long, narrow hallway, the red light nearly blinding him even through his transitions visor.

The vampire screams burst forth in response, making Asher flinch. He waved his weapon around frantically as he searched the narrow pass for the enemy. Asher breathed deeply and regained his composure, his movements smooth and flowing as he rushed down the barren hallway after the Guard. Corporal McCool followed at his side, Aaron, Milo, and Ito behind them.

"Die, bloodsucker!" One of the Guard soldiers up front roared.

The red glint of a shining ax blade caught Asher's eye, the bloody edge quickly slashing through multiple vampire limbs and throats.

The Guard swept through the main body of enemy soldiers like a blackened, macabre tornado, the fighting concentrated just beyond Kilgore's entering company. The onslaught was a storm of blades and clubs, with vampire's blood splattered upon the naked walls in thick, gory sheets, bodies, severed limbs, and heads left in their wake. Vampire soldiers occasionally sprang from secret doorways hidden in the walls, the attackers caught and then laid low by the Guard.

The Sanguinarians left them hacked to pieces, the blood pooling together on the floor.

The Guard soldiers kept their firearms in reserve, and the passageway remained free of the sound of gunfire.

"Move it!" Captain Kilgore's voice rang in Asher's ear. He pushed the company forward, the soldiers distracted by the Guard's ferocious efficiency. "We can't leave everything to the Sanguinarians!"

"You heard him!" Sergeant Ito urged the four in front of her onward.

Asher smirked when he heard her high, delicate voice.

The private moved at double speed toward the force of Guard soldiers as he made for the long pile of dispatched bodies. Asher stepped over both dead comrades and foes, careful to watch his footing as he proceeded through the pools of blood.

He found no sign of the departed Captain Jamison, concluding that the officer's desecrated body lay somewhere within the walls.

One of the dying vampires screamed as Asher rushed onward, the thing springing from the hidden doorway to take Corporal McCool in its claws.

McCool shrieked as the monster drove its fangs into his throat, somehow able to penetrate his thick body armor.

Asher let his firearm fall to the side, the shotgun secured to him by its strap. His hand went for his beheading hatchet, the private yanking the blade out from the loop of his belt.

"Haven't had enough, bloodsucker?" asked one of The Guard soldiers as he materialized beside Asher.

A large gloved hand took the vampire by the throat, choking the frenzied monster and forcing it to release the corporal. The giant man turned and brutally flung the vampire into the waiting force of Guard soldiers. The miserable thing was beaten to the ground immediately, slashed to pieces by a storm of blades.

Eyes wide, Asher realized the soldier was Balion.

"Keep moving!" Kilgore shouted at Asher from somewhere in the back.

"Leave the corporal to me," Balion told the private.

The giant man slapped a bulky, technologically enhanced, pressurized bandage on McCool's bloody neck. He then lifted the soldier up and over his shoulder with little effort.

"Yes, sir," Asher replied to the Guard soldier. He remained dumbfounded and impressed, the soldiers behind him giving Balion similar looks of awe.

The soldiers followed the giant man as he turned to walk back down the tunnel. The noise of battle began to die down as the Guard moved to finish the remainder of the vampire forces.

Asher nearly had to climb over the bodies as Kilgore's company approached the end of the passageway; the dead Legion soldiers mingled among a multitude of slain vampires.

The other companies behind them would deal with the fallen Legion troops, going over the wounded and bitten. They would systematically behead them, lest they turn.

Asher pushed onward as he came to the end of the piles of bodies and pools of blood. The red light dissipated as he followed the Guard soldiers out of the narrow passageway.

Chapter VII

The Phantom Legion

"Hope that didn't bang you up too much, Blackthorn," said Captain Kilgore. He was about to laugh, unaffected by the fall. "Lift could use some work. Someone ought to tell maintenance."

Loud clicks sounded as the locks holding the car in place released.

Kilgore put the car back in gear, driving off the lift and onto the metal ramp, continuing downward until they reached the garage's concrete floor.

"Looks way bigger with all the lights on," said Asher.

He gazed off into the Legion base's vast parking garage, now recovered from his blow to the head. He reasoned the garage's total area had to be that of several football fields. The space was filled with vehicles of all varieties, cars, trucks, military transports, a few things that looked like tanks. The walls were like that of a cave, jagged and rocky, skirted by strings of white lights, which accented the floodlights that hung overhead.

"Got a pretty good setup down here."

Kilgore took a turn down one of the driving lanes, continuing past the vehicles parked on either side.

"I know you said there were up to a thousand soldiers stationed here, sir," said Asher as they passed vehicle after vehicle. "But there's a lot down here. Are you sure you need all this?"

"Oh yeah. In addition to all the personnel vehicles, we got a lot of special-purpose rigs. We can't be pulling up in the same jalopy every night. The vamps would be onto us. Got to have lots of different types of transport, and sometimes we got to show 'em the big guns." He nodded toward a group of tank-like vehicles.

They continued onward, weaving through the lanes past vehicles innumerable. Asher briefly caught a glimpse of a small clearing near the garage's center amid all the vehicles. He was certain that was where his interrogation had occurred.

"And here we are." Kilgore pulled into one of the few empty parking spaces, this one marked with a sign bearing his title. He took off his seatbelt and opened his door, pausing to rise from his seat as he spoke to Asher. "Suppose I might as well show you what we got down here." He paused to think. "We're proud of what we have. Some of them were actually kind of hard to get. You know what? What the heck, might as well give you the whole tour."

Kilgore climbed out of the car, as Asher did likewise, their doors slamming shut simultaneously. "This way." He pointed toward the group of mini tanks, taking off across the lot, causing Asher to break into a near run to keep up.

They covered ground quickly, going between the lanes and weaving between cars to reach the grouping of metal behemoths.

"Some of my favorite armored vehicles right here." Kilgore turned back around to address Asher. He rested an open palm on the metal hide of one of the mini tanks as he leaned against it, an M2 Browning machine gun looming overhead. "I'm sure you already know what these are."

"Yeah, those are Strykers." Asher was impressed by the machinery, though he didn't want Kilgore to see it. "Didn't see many of them during my service time. They used to be one of the Army's go-to's for quickly deployed heavily armored vehicles until they started to get old. How did you guys get ahold of so many?"

"We just got a few that were so heavily damaged that the Army didn't want to put out the time or money to have them fixed. We needed something similar to a tank, and this is what they gave us. Had our guys fix them up and repurpose them for our uses."

"What do you use them for?" A frown crossed Asher's face. "I mean, I can see the need for armored vehicles, but why these in particular?"

"We use the Strykers primarily to bust through and blow up structures to get at the vamps. It seems like they get more and more organized every day, and with that organization comes more vampire-controlled buildings and facilities, mostly for human slaughter and feeding. You can really give it to them by taking those out. Not sure if Greaves told you this or not, but the vamps have minions—humans that work for them thinking they'll turn them one day. The minions carry guns, and the Strykers are one of our defenses for that. Crazy as things are getting, a lot of the vamps have begun to carry guns as well. So there you have it. The Strykers are the Legion's mobile, all-purpose, mow-down weapon."

"Huh. Sorry, I asked that question, sir. Pretty obvious now that you said all that."

"Don't sweat it, Blackthorn." Kilgore's smile returned. "There are very few stupid questions here."

"You ever run over vampires with these?" Asher hoped he hadn't asked one of the few aforementioned questions.

"No, not yet." Kilgore shook his head. "Get out of the way too quick. Maybe if we ever come across a big gathering of them we will, but I hope that never happens."

"Do you have anything else to show me out here, sir?"

"Hmm… Guess not." Kilgore removed his hand from the Stryker to take a quick look around. "I'm going to take you on a short tour of the training facilities now." He turned back toward Asher. "Got to show you the range and the tactical training area, along with a few other things. I don't care to act as tour guide, but I suppose it's better than deskwork. We'll just go through the door down here."

The captain stepped away from the Strykers, motioning Asher to follow. They walked back in the direction from which they had come, passing through line after line of vehicles on their way to the large door at the other side.

"Here we are."

The door automatically slid upwards to let them pass through.

They entered a long, spacious, but minimalistic hallway, the structure built of nothing but bare, polished concrete. They continued down the hallway until they reached the elevator door at the end. Kilgore pressed the up arrow and turned to Asher.

"I'll be taking you up to the third floor to the bridge over the range and training facility," said Kilgore as the elevator door slid open and both of them stepped inside. "Sure hope you like gun training, Blackthorn." Kilgore reached out to press the button for the third floor. "You'll be doing a lot of it. Powerful as the X-12 is, you're going to need to be an expert with it if you don't want the vamps to have you for lunch."

"Just as I expected, sir."

Asher heard the faint sound of gunfire now. The noise steadily became louder with their ascent.

Ding!

The elevator announced their arrival, the noise from the range nearly drowning out the sound.

"Right this way."

Kilgore led Asher onto a metal mesh walkway hanging about 20 feet above the floor overlooking the range. On the other side of the bridge was the gallery itself, which consisted of multiple shooting lanes, each with a paper target toward one end and a soldier with a shotgun at the other. A glass wall separated the bridge from the range, placed there to muffle the noise of gunfire. Asher presumed it was shatterproof.

"As you can probably predict, we put a heavy emphasis on rate of fire, precision, and accuracy." Kilgore proceeded over the bridge, Asher following a half step behind.

"Isn't that pretty much everything there is to shooting, sir?"

"Exactly." The captain chuckled. "As I said, we need you to master your weapon. The vamps don't leave us much of a chance most of the time, so you'll need to make those first few shots count. I realize that, generally speaking, there really is no need to aim with a shotgun at close range, but that's only if the enemy is human. Whenever you're dealing with vamps you got to hit something every time without fail. If you don't, there is a very high probability that you and all the soldiers in your assault group will die. You need to eat, sleep, and breathe that shotgun until it becomes like an extension of your body. I expect between military and police training you should already be more than proficient with a firearm."

Asher remained quiet for a moment, not wanting to speak too quickly. He cast an eye back down on the soldiers below.

"What about long-range, sir?"

"Occasionally, we will have you do some long-range

shooting, though there isn't a lot of need for it. Most of the operations we do are in urban environments at close range, so distance isn't usually an issue. Typically, for long-range, we'll have you go to the outdoor gallery on the premises." Kilgore led Asher forward, eventually coming to the door at the end of the bridge.

"Ok, that should do it for the shooting range." The door in front of them slid upwards like the one to the garage. "The training facility is through here."

Kilgore led Asher into yet another expansive area. This one stood laid out in a manner similar to that of the shooting gallery. Instead of shooting lanes, however, a series of walled spaces divided the expanse. All of them lacked ceilings so that Asher could see down into them. Like the range, the bullet and soundproof glass separated them from the rest of the room.

"As you can see, and probably already concluded," Kilgore went on, "we practice a lot of room clearance drills down here. Those dang neck biters have a high preference for urban areas 'cause that's where the people are. This is where you learn to bring it to them where they live. When you're not practicing at the range, all the rest of your time will be spent here."

"Understood, sir." Asher was eager to move on so he could ask the captain one of his burning questions. "The commander said that you use a lot of explosives, and I'm assuming other special weapons. You know, like maybe a grenade launcher. Where do you practice using those?"

"There's a room back that way down the bridge where we practice with special weapons." Kilgore pointed to a door at the far end of the bridge. "Use a lot of grenade launchers, maybe an anti-material weapon every once in a while. Suppose you would expect us to use those outside too, but it would disturb the local populace. Since you're more or less a local yourself, you know people are pretty used to gunfire, but you start firing off a bunch of grenades, and they'll be onto us in no time."

Kilgore led Asher further down the bridge. Four-person groups of soldiers milled about under their feet as they ran their room clearance drills.

"I think we'll skip touring the classroom and office floor today." The captain stopped, turning toward Asher. "It's a range day, so we got the classrooms locked up. You'll be spending plenty of time down there anyway. You'll get to learn all we know about the vamps, their physiology, tactics, organization, etc. As for the offices, they are always busy, no matter the time of day. I can't think of a good reason to show you those. Lord knows I spend too much time there." He paused, considering his next thought.

"Guess that completes our tour of the training facilities," said Kilgore at last. "Going to take you down to the Command Center next. Depending on how active the enemy has been and the number of leads and intel we have, Command can either be packed full of personnel or deader than a graveyard. Right this way."

Kilgore turned around, leading Asher back in the direction they had come.

The elevator sounded, announcing their arrival on the second floor as the door slid open. Kilgore led Asher into another barren concrete hallway nearly identical to the first, continuing toward a grouping of several elongated windows.

"Well, here it is, the cerebral center of the place. We'll just hang back here and have a look through the window. No reason to go in there and disrupt all that activity."

Asher gazed through the window, greeted by what looked like a human beehive.

The expansive room was in a state of frenzied but controlled chaos. At least two hundred people occupied the vast space, with about half of them sitting at computers. The rest either stood around or ran between desks to deliver information to their coworkers. Despite the activity in the room, the hall remained silent, and Asher noticed the windows, these composed of soundproof glass. A giant computer screen hung on the far wall, which displayed an equally large map of the United States lit up by a scattering of red dots.

If Asher didn't know what he was looking at he would have assumed it was a control room at NASA.

"Hmm... Usually not this busy," Kilgore remarked. "Must be about to send out a whole company. Anyway, this is where we keep track of our drones and the vamps' known whereabouts, and both their and our activity throughout the country. The Command Center is the base's brain, where we receive the calls and roll out in response. In addition to that, we gather information and use it to plan our offensive ops, which we run from time to time."

"I'm starting to think there are more than 1000 soldiers living down here," Asher allowed the captain to finish.

"Obviously, Blackthorn. You can't keep this place running with just soldiers. We have to have additional personnel down here for maintenance and intel and everything else we need."

"Yeah, I guess I just wasn't thinking. Now that you mention it, Greaves did say you have your own scientists. Do they work down here too?"

"We do have our own laboratory facility on the base where a few of the Legion's scientists work. We have larger labs elsewhere. If the job's too big for our base's lab to handle, we'll send off to one of our larger, better-equipped labs."

"Are we going to tour the lab?"

"You can go visit the laboratory facilities on your time." Kilgore looked down at his watch. "Need to get down to the mess hall before they close up anyway. Trips to the lab tend to make it difficult to eat. All those dissected bodies." Kilgore shivered in exaggeration.

"I assume you have medical facilities as well?"

"That we do. That facility is comparatively minimal to everything else. Most of that's because the dang vamps tend to straight-up kill. Well, that, and our tendency to off anyone who's been bitten. Trust me, you never want to see that place." Kilgore's voice quieted to a whisper, the hallway growing silent. "You got any more questions, kid?" he asked, returning to normal volume. "I can answer a few more, but after that, we're off to the mess hall."

"Do you guys have a gym down here?"

"We do, but it's on the first floor back behind the barracks. Once again, something you can see later on your own time because we're running late." He paused. "That it, Blackthorn?"

"Yeah, that's all, sir."

"Good." A satisfactory smile appeared on Kilgore's face. "Our company should be down in the mess hall right now, about to finish up. Might be able to catch some of my company's officers before they leave. Right this way." He pointed back in the direction they had come.

* * *

Asher and Captain Kilgore made their way out of the meal line in the mess hall and began toward the tables. The place was reminiscent of any hospital cafeteria with white walls, white tile floors, and long, foldaway tables. Large industrial lights hung from the ceiling.

"You really lucked out, Private. Salisbury steak your first dinner at the base. All our food is gonna taste like crap after this."

Neither the serving staff nor the soldiers shared the captain's enthusiasm. A chorus of groans sounded every time he said the words 'Salisbury steak.'

Asher shared in their disgust, disappointed when he found the dish consisted of a fatty beef lump sitting in a pile of instant mashed potatoes, all of it drowned in a puddle of slimy brown gravy. He had had better food in the Army.

"The table assigned to our company is over there." Kilgore pointed toward a long table at the other side of the mess hall. "I'm going to have you sit over there by those two officers."

He motioned toward the only two people sitting at the table, a large Hispanic man and a young Asian woman.

"Usually privates and officers don't sit together, but we'll make an exception today."

Kilgore began towards the two other officers as Asher lumbered along behind him.

"Hello, Lieutenant and Sergeant," said Kilgore

Both the man and woman looked up from their trays.

"How are yuh?" asked the captain

"We're doing just fine, sir," said the man. He was in his mid-thirties and heavy-set, possessing a square jaw and virtually no neck. "How was your leave?"

"Can't complain, Lieutenant. Any break is a good break. Anyway, that's not why I'm over here. I thought I would introduce Private Blackthorn to some of my, our, company's officers while we got you tied up with lunch."

The man eyed Asher with interest, while the woman was more preoccupied with her dinner, ignoring him and the captain.

"Asher, this is Lieutenant Tarango."

The large man rose from his seat to shake Asher's hand. A broad smile swept across his face.

"Glad to have you in our platoon, Blackthorn." Tarango nearly crushed Asher's hand when he shook it. "We're always in need of new recruits."

"This is Sergeant Ito," said Kilgore.

The young woman remained seated as she leaned forward to offer Asher her hand. She was near his own age and possessed a complexion like that of porcelain.

"Hello, Private," said Sergeant Ito with an air of dismissal. Her grip was firm despite her size.

Asher found her attitude unsettling and was unable to determine if she was rude or just shy.

Finished with her introduction, Sergeant Ito turned her attention back to her meal.

"Here is where we part ways, Blackthorn," said Kilgore. "I'll be taking my dinner in the office. I imagine there are quite a few things I need to take care of now that I'm back from leave. I'll leave you here with Lieutenant Tarango and Sergeant Ito. See you all around." He cast a final look toward Tarango and Ito and then turned to walk away.

Asher placed his lunch tray on the table and sat down.

"So, how was your tour with the captain, Blackthorn?" asked Tarango as soon as Kilgore was out of earshot.

"Ah, it was an experience." Asher took a moment to think about it. "You've got quite a large operation down here." He cut off a piece of steak and took a bite. It was much better than it looked.

"Yeah, it's a big place, though I don't think it's as big as some of our other bases. I was wondering what you thought of the captain. He tends to leave an impression, as do most of the top brass."

"He's kind of a character..." Asher trailed off, unsure of what to say.

"Yeah, most people think he is kind of a nut at first. He's a great leader, despite his many... um... quirks, I guess you could call them. We're lucky to be serving under him, even taking all that into account."

"I guess I can kind of see that."

"You'll just have to see for yourself," Tarango chuckled, catching Asher's tone.

"Commander Greaves and our captain act a lot alike," Asher noted.

"You know," said Lieutenant Tarango, thinking. "You could say that about nearly all of the high-ranking officers. Well, I mean, you could say there are a lot of officers like Greaves. For my sake, I hope it isn't contagious, or I'm in real trouble. There's a lot of promotion within the Legion, so it's highly likely I will be a captain eventually."

"It's like the Legion just attracts a certain kind of person." Tarango took a bite of his steak and chewed it up before continuing. "I suppose since what we do is a grim business, only a certain kind of person can survive. I think you could divide us into two kinds of people—well, two kinds of people who make it: Those of us who are already adapted to the violence and mental stress and those who have to adapt after they are recruited. Greaves and Kilgore are the latter, though it seems in both their cases the cost of coping is the loss of sanity. At least that might explain why they act the way they do. It probably is better to come in here already somewhat adapted to this environment, though no one is completely ready for it at the start. Some are just more prepared than others. If you come in here with some experience with violence, death, and loss, it's less shocking later on. It really is survival of the fittest out there, both physically and mentally."

"You trying to be some kind of psychiatrist, sir?" Asher made an attempt at humor, only realizing he might be stepping out of line.

"No, not at all. I just have my theories." Tarango took no offense.

"So I've heard you have a military background, Blackthorn," Sergeant Ito cut in. "Is that correct?"

Asher was slow to answer, taking a moment to swallow.

"Well, is it?" she asked again.

"Yes, I have, but only for a year and a half," he replied at last.

"That's good," said Ito. "Most of the time, those with military experience make the best Legion soldiers. I bet survival will be easy for you." She smiled at last, though it looked less than friendly given what she had said.

"All this talk of death and loss has me kind of concerned." Asher was sure the Legion suffered considerable losses from time to time. He wouldn't have been interested in enlisting if he didn't think he was ready to deal with that, but he was starting to wonder just how bad it could get. "So what are we talking about, statistically speaking, loss-wise?" He made sure he didn't sound scared. "It sounds like over 50%."

"Would you try not to scare the recruits, Ito?" Tarango scolded ber before turning back to Asher. "It's way better than 50%," he said reassuringly. "Not sure exactly how high it is, but most people make it just fine. Granted, our stats are worse than the military's, but still not bad considering our enemy."

"I suppose I'll be leaving now." Ito abruptly rose from her seat. "It's been great to speak to you, Asher, but I really must go. I need to get back to the office as well. See both of you around." She gave Tarango a final look of acknowledgment before leaving to return her tray.

Tarango grew silent with Ito's exit, and the conversation ended.

It's just as well, thought Asher.

He was hungry anyway, this being the first meal he had since leaving his apartment. It was taking nearly all of his self-control not to stick his face in his lunch tray and wolf down his meal like some animal, all the while ignoring Lieutenant Tarango.

Several minutes later, Tarango said, "Since I'm the only officer from our company still down here, I'll be the one to show you to our barracks. If you'll hurry up and finish your dinner, we'll head down there."

"Just a moment, sir," said Asher, quickly scarfing down the rest of his meal, so unwilling to leave it that he didn't care if he looked like a pig.

"Well, if you're done," said the lieutenant, not expecting an answer from Asher. "I'll show you to your quarters in the barracks now. I'm not sure who your assigned bunkmate is, though you'll figure it out as soon as you get in there."

Asher finished, standing to follow Tarango as he walked away from the table. Both of them dropped off their trays before leaving the mess hall. Tarango led Asher down yet another barren hallway of polished concrete. This one was only slightly different from the others due to the large, ornate wooden doors resting open at the end of it.

At last, a recognizable landmark, Asher thought to himself.

"The barracks are just through those double doors down that way," Tarango turned toward Asher, pointing off down the hallway at another set of heavy wooden doors. "You should be in Room 17, which means you should take a left after the doors and then a right at some point. The officers' quarters are in a different direction, so I'm not entirely sure. We'll have training orders in for you soon. You can just hang out in your quarters for now. See you around, Blackthorn."

Tarango walked away, leaving Asher standing there.

Now alone, he continued past the doors and proceeded down the hallway, following Tarango's directions until he found himself standing in front of a simple white door with a large, black #17 painted upon it.

Asher paused before pushing his way through the door into his new home. He was surprised to find a generous-sized room, though he was disappointed to see it was constructed of the same barren concrete as the hallways and void of any decoration. Unlike the hall, the space contained several pieces of furniture, four desks, a few chairs, a flat-screen television hanging on the wall, and two sets of steel-framed bunk beds.

"Hello," said Asher. He found a small bespectacled young man sitting on one of the bottom bunks, his hair dark and spiky and his complexion pale. Asher thought it rather generous to call him a man, as he appeared younger than he was.

The spiky-haired man leaned over in his seat, staring at a spider scurrying across the floor.

"Are you my bunkmate?" asked Asher, feeling that it was a stupid question.

"Maybe," said the man, taking his attention off the spider, looking at Asher quizzically through his heavy lenses. "They said Davis would be replaced sometime soon. What's your name?"

"I'm Asher Blackthorn."

"Hello, Asher." The small man rose from the bed and extended his hand to shake. "My name's Milo. Milo Harkman."

"Nice to meet you, Milo." Asher shook the man's child-like

hand. "Suppose I might as well sit down." He pulled a chair out from under one of the desks and turned it toward Milo as he took a seat. Asher took another quick look at the beds, identifying the one above Milo's as his. It was unmade, and a pile of clean clothes and bedding sat stacked up at the end of it.

"So what happened to Davis, your last roommate?" Asher asked cautiously, trying to start a conversation with Milo. "He didn't…" he trailed off, his voice a whisper, a sick, nauseous feeling suddenly washing over him.

"He was killed." Milo looked up at him from his seat on the bed, his eyes locking onto Asher's with a kind of sheer bewilderment. "Why else would the Legion recruit a replacement?"

Chapter VIII

Slave to the Scalpel

Anoura and Desmond had seated themselves in white leather armchairs, a heavily polished, exquisitely carved wooden table separating them. Luther and Mara shared a white leather couch situated against the wall, adjacent to Anoura and Desmond.

"Who does this jet belong to, Desmond?" asked Anoura.

The noise and turbulence from the plane's takeoff died away.

The jet was unlike any Anoura had ever seen. Genuine gold composed the door handles and levers. The light fixtures were crystal, and all of the wooden surfaces were painstakingly hand-carved. Anoura hadn't looked, but she wouldn't be surprised if she found a diamond-encrusted toilet in the restroom. Regardless, whoever had purchased the plane had extravagant and gaudy tastes.

"I cannot say precisely." Desmond shrugged. "Well, that is, I cannot say who purchased it. Officially, it belongs to The Surgeon, though it's improbable that he would ever invest much money in interior design. Judging from appearances alone, it would seem the purchase was made by Mr. Dade, though I find such a scenario unlikely given the poor relationship between The Surgeon and Mr. Dade."

"More than likely, it's just a gift from Mr. Dade to The Master, who then loaned it to The Surgeon," said Luther, tired of Desmond's rambling theories. "I doubt Mr. Dade would be pleased if he were to find out The Surgeon was using his jet. The Master may have intended it to be a lesson to him about wasting money on unnecessary luxuries."

"Yes, I suppose that's the more likely explanation," said Desmond, hesitant to acknowledge the truth in Luther's words.

A low, soft moan suddenly proceeded from the back of the plane, breaking the silence. One of the children was due for another dose of sedation. They had placed each of them inside a large pet carrier, making them easier to manage throughout the flight.

"Stewardess, it seems as though the specimens are due for another dose of sedative," said Desmond as he pulled a set of needles from his suit pocket. "Would you be so kind as to take care of them for us, please?"

"Yes, sir," said the flight attendant as she took the needles from his outstretched hand. She walked past Anoura as she went to tend to the children.

"Exactly why does The Surgeon seek an audience with all of us, Desmond?" asked Anoura.

"As with many of our organization's affairs, information is only given out on a need-to-know basis." Desmond dismissed her question with a wave of his hand. "Even someone as high ranking as myself must be kept in the dark about some things. I really have no idea, though I do have some theories." He let out a low yawn, disinterested in the conversation with Anoura.

Desmond's eyes darted toward the flight attendant as an idea popped into his head. "Oh, how rude of me. I forgot to offer any of you a drink. I can't imagine you would be thirsty, Anoura, as you nearly drank your driver dry such a short time ago. Would you like a drink, Luther? Mara?"

Anoura doubted Desmond cared about anyone's thirst but his own, and he was likely just finding an excuse to access The Surgeon's exclusive stock. She was annoyed at his presumption that she was not thirsty. Luckily, he happened to be correct in this instance, which kept her from starting a fight that might have ended in a physical altercation.

"It has been a while since we've had something to drink." Mara nodded toward Luther.

"Yes, I believe we will have something, Desmond," Luther confirmed.

"I believe we could possibly have entrees as well, if anyone is interested," Desmond offered.

"The drink alone will be just fine," said Mara.

"Very well." Desmond turned toward the flight attendant, waiting for her to close the second child's carrier. "Excuse me, miss. We would like a bottle of your finest drink. Something young and robust, but not too metallic in flavor."

"I will have it right out, sir," said the flight attendant. She walked past them to disappear behind the curtain at the front of the plane.

She reappeared moments later, pushing a full serving cart up to the side of their table. She removed a bottle full of dark red, viscous fluid and three glass chalices, two of which she placed on top of the cart. The flight attendant then poured the red liquid into the single glass in her hand, filling it halfway up before handing it to Desmond. She went to fill the other two glasses, placing them on the table for Luther and Mara.

"May I see the bottle stewardess?" asked Desmond, stopping the flight attendant before she placed the bottle back on the cart.

"Of course, sir." The attendant handed the bottle over to him.

"Oh, this is quite nice," said Desmond as he scrutinized the label. "Taken from a young female fairly recently. I would presume she was a virgin, though I don't believe it affects the taste substantially. O positive is a little pedestrian to some, but it's one of my favorites."

"So, you are certain that this meeting with The Surgeon has

nothing to do with Icarus, Desmond?" Anoura grew tired of his pompous babble.

"I think it is safe to assume The Surgeon neither knows nor cares about Icarus's demise, my dear." Desmond smiled, finding the situation amusing. "Though I suppose, given his rivalry with Mr. Dade, The Surgeon might want to offer you a promotion for doing away with Icarus. Even if he cared about Mr. Dade's son, information doesn't travel that fast. Are you worried, Anoura?" Desmond smirked, pleased with himself. "Mr. Dade is a man of significant means, willing to employ unsavory tactics to achieve his end goals, especially when those goals involve retribution."

"Desmond, you know I would be lying if I told you I wasn't at least a little worried." Anoura hated to admit her fears. "We're all well aware of what Mr. Dade can do. He carries too much weight within our organization to be ignored."

She frowned, finding Desmond looking out the airplane window into a still dark but steadily brightening sky. He turned his head back toward her, acting surprised to find her sitting there.

"How many of these special missions have you carried out for The Surgeon, Anoura?" Desmond asked. "Yes, I know I'm the one responsible for ensuring assignments are properly executed, but I stopped keeping count a long time ago."

"There have been so many that I've lost count as well." Anoura paused to think. "I'm certain it's been more than a dozen."

"And all of these missions have been completed successfully?"

"Absolutely!" Anoura snapped, losing patience with Desmond's presumptive attitude. She glanced over at Luther and Mara, finding similar looks of irritation scrawled across their faces.

"Even you know all missions under my direction are handled with the utmost care and discretion!" Anoura continued to rage. "I accept nothing short of perfection from those under my command. This incident with Icarus means nothing. He was forced on us, Desmond. It was his fault for not following orders. I haven't made a single mistake since I've started running missions per The Surgeon's special requests. That's why he asked for me in the first place!"

"You have no reason to become upset, my dear." Desmond attempted to look oblivious to her rantings. "The only reason I ask about your success rate is that it now may be likely that The Surgeon would like to transfer you to his jurisdiction to work directly under him."

"And why would he do that?" Anoura caught her breath, her anger quenched. "I mean, I can see why he might want a highly competent procurement specialist, but why even mess with a transfer? I was hoping it might eventually lead to a promotion where I would take up your vacated position after you were promoted yourself."

"Yes, that is normally how it works, but we are quickly becoming a rather bloated organization, regardless of the low turning rate." Desmond swirled the blood around in his glass. "It just happens when many of your members have vastly extended lifespans. It would be logical for me to gain a position as one of the bosses over food supply and trafficking so that you could gain my position as underboss. Unfortunately, I do not see that happening anytime in the near future. All our boss positions are filled as they are. I know it's not ideal, and The Surgeon is, admittedly, quite strange and eccentric, but his research is so important I would assume any work done for him would be more satisfying than merely procuring food. The pay would be better as well, so it's nearly as good as a promotion, or at least I believe it would be."

"Yes, I suppose that is true, though I would be lying to you if I didn't say I prefer the promotion." Anoura made a pathetic attempt at a smile.

"One thing is for certain." Desmond took a sip of blood from his glass. "If Mr. Dade is angered over the loss of his son, and I think we can all agree he will be, you will be much safer under The Surgeon than you will be with anyone else.

"And why do you believe that, Desmond?" Luther cut in, gulping blood from his glass. "I don't know what special protection The Surgeon has, but he will need it should Mr. Dade decide to come after him. He's a very wealthy man, the foremost of our financial backers, and with all that money comes power. He might even be second only to The Master. If he wants someone disposed of, he will have them disposed of. It's only a matter of time. The best protection The Surgeon offers lies in putting a considerable amount of distance between Mr. Dade and us. Rest assured, though, he will eventually come for anyone he holds responsible for his son's death."

Luther went silent, giving Desmond a threatening look for dramatic effect.

Anoura smirked, amused by Desmond's frightened reaction to Luther. It was nice to see him put in his place. Despite her front, she retained a healthy fear of Mr. Dade and the things he could do to those who displeased him.

"The Surgeon is one of The Master's favorites, even above Mr. Dade for all his money," said Desmond, his panic quickly vanishing. "If he were to launch an attack against The Surgeon or attempt an assassination on him or his assistants, The Master would likely come to The Surgeon's defense or deal directly with Mr. Dade himself. When Mr. Dade is no longer seen as an asset, The Master will have him eliminated and his funds acquisitioned, regardless of circumstance."

"Yes, I suppose that's likely enough," said Anoura, continuing Luther's psychological assault. "But if The Surgeon was allocated such protection, then it obviously only applies to himself and those who work for him. Everything you have said only leads to the conclusion that Luther, Mara, and myself will be protected, not you. How do you know Mr. Dade won't just dispose of you for his satisfaction? You're the one responsible for deciding who goes on specific missions, after all. Who's to say he won't just go after you?"

"Just because you have been so successful carrying out The Surgeon's special requests doesn't mean he wants to add you to his number!" Desmond yelled. The fear had returned to his eyes.

Anoura had finally struck a nerve. She gazed down at the floor, a smile on her face. She knew she wasn't the only one dreading Mr. Dade's wrath.

"All of this is still highly hypothetical. Everything we have discussed thus far has yet to be proven true!"

Desmond abruptly stopped his rant, realizing he was about to fly completely off the handle. His attention shifted away from Anoura and back to the window as he took several deep breaths.

The sun hung on the horizon now, and the dark of night had slowly faded to a dismal grey.

Desmond might have several abhorrent qualities, but Anoura knew he was not an overly aggressive man. He was someone who liked to keep his emotions in check. She was certain he retained a low level of fear of her, preferring to keep her at a distance whenever possible. Given Desmond's less than impressive physique, she had no doubt who would win should things ever escalate.

"My dear, it would be very uncharacteristic of Mr. Dade to let anyone who has transgressed against him to escape punishment," said Desmond nearly a minute later. He gave Anoura a calm but cold look. "Even if he comes for me first, he will be led straight to you. You know I tend to have very loose lips when threatened. As the matter at hand involves the death of his only son, it is possible that Mr. Dade would willfully penetrate The Surgeon's defenses. After all, The Master's favor only goes so far."

Desmond fell silent again, this time staring intently at his glass, contemplating another sip.

Anoura glanced over at the couch against the wall, finding Luther leaned back against it, looking content and unworried. Mara's body language suggested she was of the opposite inclination, as she leaned forward and anxiously cradling her glass in both hands.

"Your transfer is only hypothetical at this point, Anoura," said Desmond, making direct eye contact. "There will be very little to stop Mr. Dade from laying hands on all of us without the protection of a more powerful benefactor."

"I guess we'll just have to see what happens." A look of defiance crossed Anoura's face as she attempted to hide her anxiety.

"I suppose we will." Desmond was unwilling to allow her the last word.

The red light rays of the rising sun suddenly appeared over the horizon. The four sitting within the jet's cabin closed their eyes, the searing light all but blinding them.

"I really would love to carry on our conversation," said

Desmond, his eyes remaining sealed. "Unfortunately, daylight is upon us. I anticipate we will have another long night ahead of us, and I know we all could benefit from some rest. Stewardess, would you please tend to the windows?"

"Yes, sir." The blinds made a quick swooshing sound as she pulled them closed. "That's all of them, sir," she said from the back of the cabin after she completed the task.

"Ah," said Desmond as all four passengers opened their eyes.

"Much better." Anoura glared at him, irritated by his tendency to speak for everyone.

"Stewardess." Desmond stopped the flight attendant on her way back toward the cockpit. "Would you please bring out some pillows and blankets?"

"As you wish, sir." The flight attendant continued past them to disappear behind the dividing curtain once again.

She returned moments later, carrying a large bundle of embroidered pillows and blankets, which looked highly expensive.

"Here you are, sir." The flight attendant distributed the requested items.

"Thank you very much, my dear." Desmond gave her a fanged smile.

Anoura rolled her eyes when Desmond wasn't looking, nearly yanking a pillow out of the flight attendant's hand. She'd long since grown tired of his insincere pleasantries. She retreated to one of the other couches against the wall of the jet and pulled her blanket over her head as she waited for the lights running down the aisle to go out.

"It looks as though we have all made ourselves comfortable, stewardess," said Desmond, moving to a couch somewhere away from Anoura. "We would appreciate it if you would be so kind as to turn off the lights."

"Of course, sir."

Anoura fell unconscious in less than a minute after the lights went out, thankful to escape Desmond's words and idiotic mannerisms. She had underestimated just how tired she was.

* * *

A tall, willowy man dressed in pure white clothing walked across a metal mesh bridge. He stopped, turning to place his hands on the railing, leaning in to survey the pit below. The man was ashen, even for a vampire, his skin and hair whiter than his lab coat. His eyes were a fierce, bright blue with a soft, serene quality about them, revealing a man content, regardless of what went on around him.

His many specimens looked up at him from the vast, red-lit pit below, secured in their cages, an audience for their overlord. They called out to him in various ways, some with screams and howls, others with shrieks and moans, their appeals for release always going unheeded. Theirs was a filthy, wretched gathering of both man and beast, all with a defeated, mournful look in their eyes. All would have their purpose, whether collected because of a genetic anomaly or lab born, each possessing a specific genetic feature.

"Sir," said one of his lab assistants, virtually materializing beside him. "Your guests are here, along with your requested specimens." The man was young with a look of naïveté in his brilliant blue eyes.

"And what guests would those be?" asked The Surgeon, irritated. "I don't recall asking to see anyone. I just wanted the requested specimens to be retrieved. I can't imagine why I would forget something like that."

"I believe the one you wanted to see was named Anoura," said the lab assistant, looking over the clipboard he carried. "She has proven herself to be quite the asset to her sector. She has commanded nearly all of your special request missions in that area for some time now. Anoura has been so successful that you have specifically requested that she and her associates be placed directly under your direction."

The Surgeon stared off into space for a moment, trying to remember.

"Oh, yes, that Anoura!" he proclaimed, recollection in his eyes. "We really should do away with this whole single name re-naming scenario. The other members of the old guard thought it was such a great idea in the beginning, but now it's just annoying. I haven't been able to remember anyone's name in such a long time!"

"If you're having such a high degree of difficulty with it, maybe you should take it up with The Master, sir."

"Hang The Master!" The Surgeon snapped, nearly grasping

for his assistant, feeling he needed to remember his place. "I haven't been granted an audience in ages. I'm one of the alleged 'favorites,' and I haven't seen The Master in years. Not that I have time to muddle with such mundane activities anyway. I have a research facility to run!"

"Understood, sir. Anoura and her associates should be down here shortly. I will leave you to them, sir." The lab assistant turned to leave, leisurely making his way over the bridge.

The Surgeon turned back around, admiring the sheer size and layout of the holding area where he stored his vast specimen collection. He was pleased with the lighting scheme most of all, as he had helped to design it. Red light, being of the lowest wavelength, was the least damaging to vampiric eyes and was the lighting he preferred most. It allowed the staff to work as efficiently as possible and for the specimens to see everything they did to them. The whole place was perfect in both form and functionality.

The Surgeon checked his watch, looking up when he heard the sound of multiple footsteps approaching, one set quicker than the rest. Expecting a woman, he scowled when a splotchy-skinned man greeted him.

"Hello, sir," said the man, extending his hand to shake. "It is an absolute pleasure to meet you. I suppose you already know you are a legend within our organization, and it is an honor to be meeting you in person at last. You have a lovely facility down here, which I'm sure you operate with a considerable amount of efficiency."

"Yes, I am quite proud of this facility. I helped to design much of it." The Surgeon had no intention of shaking the man's hand. Instead, he stared him down with a cold, venomous look until he withdrew his hand.

The man recoiled, confused.

"It offers me the seclusion I desire, in addition to providing a large amount of space to store my specimens and the ability to carry out my research at any time, day or night." The Surgeon frowned, regarding the man before him with a lack of recognition. "I welcome your compliments. Who are you?"

"I'm Desmond, sir," said the man with a smile. "I'm responsible for managing one of the slaughterhouses in the Midwest sector. I'm the one who has been doling out your special request assignments for Anoura and her subordinates."

"Good for you!" said The Surgeon with over-the-top sarcasm. "I still have no idea who you are."

"You surely have some idea about who I..."

"Where is this Anoura I have heard so much about?" The Surgeon cut him off.

"Hello, sir. I'm Anoura." A shorthaired, leather-clad woman stepped around Desmond. She approached The Surgeon and extended her hand to him.

"Ah, finally, the   person I was expecting to   meet." The Surgeon took her hand in his and leaned down to kiss it.

Anoura flinched when his soggy lips touched the base of her fingers, recoiling away the moment she had the chance, unaccustomed to the strange contact. If any of her subordinates, or even Desmond, dared place their lips on her in such a way, they would come away with a broken nose.

"Now, where are my requested specimens?" asked The Surgeon, shooting Desmond a deadly glare.

"Here are the requested specimens, sir." Desmond cringed.

Luther and Mara shambled around him with the pet carriers, setting them down on the bridge.

"Let's see what we have here." The Surgeon walked toward the two carriers and squatted down to look inside. "Yes, two young, heterozygous Sickle-cell disease gene carriers. I will have to do a check of their medical data to make sure. Their blood will be perfect as a negative control in some of my experiments, among other things."

The Surgeon rose back onto his feet, turning his back to them, searching the holding area for something.

"One of my assistants has to be around here somewhere. That's one of the few things The Master is good for: making sure you have plenty of personnel. Unfortunately, quantity comes at the cost of quality. It never fails that every time you need them, you can never find them. It looks like it could be a while before I have someone up to retrieve my specimens." The Surgeon turned back around to look directly at Luther and Mara. "We'll just set them here for the time being."

"May I ask what your interest is in these particular

specimens?" Desmond interjected. "All your research is quite fascinating, and I'm sure you have something extraordinary planned for them."

"Would you kindly remove your lips from my posterior?"

"Beg pardon?" asked Desmond.

"Oh, you heard me." The Surgeon's voice went flat. "No one likes a butt-kisser. All your pleasantries are just exhausting."

Anoura fought to hide the broad grin she now displayed by staring at the ground, but it was just too much for her. She let out an audible snort as she suppressed her laughter. She glanced up at Luther and Mara, finding similar expressions on their faces.

"I... I..." Desmond stuttered. "My apologies, sir."

"Besides," The Surgeon snarled at him. "I already said they would serve as negative controls."

The Surgeon gave Anoura, Luther, and Mara an awkward smile, turning off his rage.

"However, I suppose since a few of you are about to become part of my staff shortly, there's no harm going into more detail. I plan on carrying out a full analysis of the specimens' DNA to confirm what I gathered from their stolen records. After all of that is completed, we'll keep them in holding until we are ready to use their blood and clone their DNA. We won't have much use for them after that. I guess we'll pump them full of hormones to grow them up quickly and feed them to the staff. We're a little backed up, so it may be a while before we get to them."

"Hey!" The Surgeon reacted as though he experienced a mood swing. "Over here, you useless bloodsucker!"

"What can I do for you, sir?" asked the lab assistant, standing behind the group gathered on the bridge.

"Oh, isn't it obvious?" The Surgeon's voice was sarcastic as he slid a gloved hand down his face. "I need you to find someone to help you take these carriers containing human specimens to the holding cages."

"Have you fed them yet?" asked the assistant.

"No, we have not," said Desmond. "They have been sedated for several hours."

He turned to Anoura, who nodded for confirmation.

"They have not been fed in that time," she said.

"Yes, I expect you wouldn't have fed them as of yet." The Surgeon looked thoughtfully at his cornered assistant. "Very well. Have these specimens redressed, disinfected, and then fed. I expect they should come out of sedation very soon, and once conscious, they will likely begin to whine for food. The whining is always so irritating."

"As you wish, sir," said the assistant. "I will be back with assistance shortly, and we will fulfill your request." He turned to leave, hastily making his way back across the bridge in the direction he had approached.

"Sir," said Anoura, doing her best to sound humble. "It looks like you have plenty of assistants here to help. Why have us brought all the way out here when our skills would be better utilized in the food procurement sector? We are better out in the field. Why go through with our transfer?" Anoura intended to sound as though she didn't want the protection he could offer. She didn't want to appear weak.

"I've had you transferred over to this sector because I need someone with your skills and abilities. As you have already observed, though I have a considerably large amount of help, most of them are rather incompetent. Honestly, if they weren't vampires, I would use them as food. That's all some of them are good for. I have put in for new procurement specialists several times, but all The Master ever sends me is more lab assistants, nearly all of them worthless. Seems to believe quantity is more important than quality. Since good help is so hard to come by up here, I had you transferred over to serve as my personal assistants."

"I doubt we will be much help in the lab, sir."

"Ha!" The Surgeon scoffed, causing Anoura and all her accomplices to jump back a little, fearful of what he might do next. "I highly doubt you would be any less adequate than any of my current personnel. They never fully learn their way around. Besides, you won't be working in the lab at all. I still need some better lab assistants, but given my tumultuous relationship with The Master, I anticipate that won't happen for some time."

"Anyway," The Surgeon paused before continuing, "due to the poor help I keep receiving, I have given up on requesting good assistants and decided to focus on procurement instead. You will keep essentially the same position. The only difference is you will no longer be involved in general food procurement operations. You will be fulfilling my requests only." He looked directly at Desmond as he finished, singling him out with a sinister glare.

"Yes, that does make sense, sir," said Anoura.

"I'm glad you understand," said The Surgeon, looking genuinely pleased and then suddenly disappointed. "You're not going to turn into an insufferable suck-up like him, are you?" He pointed at Desmond.

"I would never dream of it, sir, nor would my other associates," said Anoura, her rare grin returning.

A strange noise suddenly sounded from within the far wall, starting as a low moan and quickly increasing in volume. It was unlike any other recognizable sound, the mechanical groans of a machine mixed with a bestial howl reverberating throughout the stronghold. The noise came from a living creature, one that steadily became more and more enraged.

Though she couldn't fully discern it, Anoura was sure she heard the words "I will find you" slowly repeated several times. She looked toward Desmond and then at Luther and Mara, seeing concern and fear written on their faces.

"What is that?" Anoura yelled over the noise.

"It is absolutely nothing to worry about," said The Surgeon, unaffected by the noise and irritated by Anoura's words.

"That's ridiculous," Anoura retorted, unwilling to accept The Surgeon's aversion to the question. "Nothing that sounds like that can just be overlooked. So what is it really?"

The noise subsided, steadily returning to a low, mechanical moan before finally going silent.

"It is nothing to concern yourself with!" The Surgeon's voice echoed throughout the cavern, no longer masked by the noise. "There is one thing I need to make completely clear," he snarled. "One condition of your service to me is that you will not be permitted to ask any questions regarding that noise. You may ask me about anything else, but never that noise. In addition to this, you are not to interfere with any of the experiments performed within this facility. So long as you abide by those two rules and do everything else that I ask of you, we should get along just fine. Is that clear?"

"Perfectly," said Anoura, her usual severity returned.

"How about you?" The Surgeon turned to Luther and Mara.

"Understood, sir," they replied nearly in unison. Luther saluted.

"What are you still doing here?" The Surgeon turned to Desmond, staring him down. "I only requested that Anoura and her immediate subordinates be transferred to my facility. I have no need for you."

"I… I was just leaving, sir," said Desmond. He immediately turned away from the group and made his way back down the bridge toward the exit.

The metallic howls of the creature behind the wall sounded through the stronghold once again, causing Desmond to sprint for the   door.

Chapter IX

Cure at Cost

Cyrus, awoken by the sheering pain in his head, found himself hanging upright, still shackled to the examination table. He opened his eyes slowly, anticipating another assault on his retinas by the room's blinding lights, certain it would worsen his headache.

A dull, red glow flooded his vision instead, barely illuminating the darkness. The low light gave the room an unnatural, eerie quality.

Sweat poured down Cyrus's face as his headache intensified. A vein in his forehead pulsated from his pain. He instinctively surveyed the room. His blurry eyesight made it difficult for him to make out the machines and furniture placed around the examination table. Cyrus gazed into the elongated mirror in front of him. He squinted as he discerned the dark figure glaring back at him.

"Dr. Shen!" His rage exploded forth when he realized the dark shape was his reflection. "What have you done to me?"

The procedure had stripped away all of what had made him human. Black scales replaced his hair and skin. His ears had grown pointy, like that of a cat, and his jaws were much more robust, suggesting an ability to crush bone. A powerful, hulking build replaced his frail body, and his formidable musculature rippled underneath his scales. The nails on both his hands and feet were weapons, blackened, sharp like knives. Even his eyes had changed drastically. An electric yellow had replaced the original deep blue of his irises, and his pupils were now slits, like that of a venomous snake.

Cyrus snarled at the mirror, revealing a complete set of

fangs, all of them needle-sharp. "What have you done to me!" He howled once more, now realizing his voice was deep and gravelly, as though he suffered a severe case of demonic laryngitis. The pain in his head reached its apex, bringing with it overwhelming madness and rage.

"You'll all pay for this!"

He flailed and thrashed around in his bonds in a frenzy, the metal restraints bending and growing loose under the incredible force he exerted. Out of his insanity came a surge of primal hunger, the savory scent of nearby human flesh and blood drifting into his nostrils, fueling his blood lust.

"I will find you and make you pay!"

Cyrus flexed his right arm, tearing the loosened restraint from the bed, the metal clattering upon the hard tile floor.

"I'll rip you to pieces!" He continued the tirade, now assured he was more than capable of freeing himself.

Cyrus ripped the left arm restraint from the bed with his free hand, brutally throwing it at the mirror in front of him, shattering it. He then turned his attention to his ankle restraints, kicking out with both feet, slamming the shackles against the wall.

"Better run! Better run, or you'll regret it!"

Cyrus grasped the final bond around his middle with both clawed hands, pushing down upon it with his immense bulk, contracting his abdominal muscles. He pulled the restraint from its bolts with one last heave, dropping from the bed onto the floor. His claws made clicking noises upon the cold tile.

Cyrus roared as he tore the tubes from his chest. Black blood spewed from the wounds, splattering all over the broken mirror in front of him.

The alarms outside his room blared, alerting CyberGen personnel to his impending escape.

Cyrus grabbed the monitor nearest him and slammed it against the wall. Machine parts and broken plastic exploded everywhere. He flew through the room like a storm, shattering tables and chairs, smashing through monitor screens.

The floor quickly filled with wreckage and debris.

Cyrus bellowed, lifting the upright examination table into the air, pile driving it back down into the ground. "This is it, Shen!" he thundered. He turned his focus to the heavy door at his right as he prepared to charge into it. "You're all dead!" He launched himself at the door, slamming into it with his shoulder, ripping it from its hinges, and sending it crashing through the drywall of the adjacent hallway.

The alarm blared above Cyrus's head, and the red lights swirled over the darkened walls and ceiling.

"Security to basement floor two, there has been a breach from Room 7734!" A voice shrieked over the intercom. "Security to basement floor two, there has been a breach from Room 7734!"

Cyrus stood to the side of the doorway, his chest heaving up and down as he tried to control his anger. He felt a need to save it until the guards arrived. He stepped to the side, squatting down beside the opening, waiting to catch the incoming guards by surprise.

"Move, move, move!" Someone yelled from the other end of the hallway.

Numerous booted feet struck the floor as the guards raced toward Cyrus's room and stopped at the doorway.

Cyrus sprang from his position and grabbed the end of the first guard's gun just as he rounded the entryway. He tore the weapon away and let it fall to the floor. He then grabbed the man by the edges of his body armor and tossed him through the door to crash into the wall.

His bones broke with the impact.

Cyrus leaped after him, landing on top of the screaming man, tearing out his throat with his impossibly sharp claws. The blood splattered everywhere.

"Kill it!" shrieked one of the guards.

A torrent of bullets spewed forth, but nearly all of the shots were off target and either buried themselves in the wall or ricocheted down the hallway.

Cyrus screamed. The few bullets that struck him felt like hornet stings, enraging him even more. He leaped at the guard immediately in front of him, jabbed him in the stomach with his claws, and tore out his intestines.

The man screamed and fell to the floor.

Cyrus flew at the rest of the guards, unleashing a frenzy of unrelenting, blood-drunk violence. He ripped through flesh and sinew and tore off limbs and heads, biting through throats and spines as fresh, warm blood flooded the hallway.

The guards continued to fire upon him, intent on bringing him down, even as their comrade's butchered corpses fell to the floor, one after the other. The gunfire eventually ceased altogether.

Cyrus palmed the side of the last guard's head, crushing the man's skull against the wall.

The blare of the alarm stopped, and the hallway grew silent.

"Cyrus! Stop this! We only wanted to help you!"

Cyrus released the dead man's head from his grasp, letting him collapse onto the floor as he turned to see Viddur approaching him. The red alarm lights danced over a face full of shock and horror.

"Is this what you call help? I'm a monster!" Cyrus bellowed. He yanked the gun away from the dead man nearest him to rush at Viddur, charging at him, barrel first.

Viddur screamed when Cyrus stomped down on his foot, nailing him to the ground with his claws. Cyrus rammed the gun barrel up under Viddur's ribs, impaling him upon the blunt-ended weapon.

"You didn't have to do this, Cyrus," Viddur whispered, blood pouring from his wound as Cyrus pulled the weapon from his chest. The light faded from his eyes as he fell to the floor.

Cyrus looked up from his gruesome work to find a single figure at the end of the hallway.

"This experiment was a mistake. I see that now." Dr. Shen's voice echoed out through the silence, full of regret. He pulled a pistol from his waistband and pointed it at Cyrus.

Seeing the gun, Cyrus let out a feral roar and charged down the hallway toward him.

"It's over, Shen!" screamed Cyrus, rushing for the doctor.

Dr. Shen stood his ground and fired upon Cyrus as he sprinted toward him. Shot after shot rang out through the hallway, all missing their mark.

The doctor moaned and put the gun up against his temple.

Cyrus sank his claws into the doctor's arm just as he pulled the trigger, tearing the limb from his body.

The wasted bullet ricocheted down the hallway.

A torrent of blood flowed from the doctor's wound onto the floor, and his shrill screams penetrated the air. Cyrus dropped the severed limb and dove for Shen's neck. The doctor's spine broke under his powerful jaws.

Shen stopped screaming as his body went slack and lifeless.

"Cyrus, why are you doing this?" Elysia shrieked. She suddenly appeared from around the corner, causing Cyrus to look up from the slaughtered doctor.

"I don't know!" he cried, letting Shen's body fall to the ground. "The rage in my head is driving me insane!"

Cyrus launched himself at Elysia, his jaws open wide and claws extended, unable to comprehend why he was so intent on butchering her.

* * *

Cyrus jerked awake, opening and then immediately closing his eyes, the blinding lights hanging above him not helping the pain in his head. He lay drenched in sweat, flat on the padded examination table, unsure how he had managed to dream up such strange and terrifying images. The nightmare was even more vivid than any he had had involving Talon's death. He hoped Shen's treatment hadn't done any lasting psychological damage.

Cyrus tried moving his arms, finding himself still tethered to the table, frowning with curiosity when he strained against the metal restraints. He wasn't sure if he had imagined it or not, but it felt as though his arms had exerted more force than usual. He pushed against the restraints once more. The tightness of his shackles rendered him incapable of discerning if the sensation of force was indeed due to an increase in strength.

"How are you, Mr. Blackthorn?" Dr. Shen's voice echoed throughout the room, catching Cyrus off guard. The doctor was eager but also worried. Cyrus was so preoccupied with his restraints that he hadn't noticed him come in.

"Been better," Cyrus groaned, finding his back sore.

"Viddur, would you raise the examination table, please?" The doctor turned toward his lab assistant and found him standing against the wall. "I would like to converse with Mr. Blackthorn, and I believe things would be less awkward for him if he were upright."

Viddur moved off to the side to access the table. A motor

buzzed as it ascended.

Cyrus slowly opened his eyes once more, re-accustoming himself to the intense lights. As the blurry white dissipated, he looked over his surroundings. He quickly realized he was in the same room as earlier, doubtful he had ever moved. Two figures whom he assumed were Shen and Elysia stood in front of him, but the light obscured their faces.

Metal struck metal as the table reached its apex, leaving Cyrus restrained upright to look down on the rest of them.

Viddur's blurred form moved away from him and back toward the far corner to stand against the wall.

"Thank you very much, Viddur," said the doctor.

"Why am I still in the same room?" Cyrus asked with a yawn. "Did the treatment not work out?" He might have panicked if he hadn't felt so lethargic.

"Oh, no, Mr. Blackthorn." Dr. Shen shook his head, his awkward, uneasy grin coming into view. "The treatment went splendidly, even better than expected. You responded to the nanobots perfectly. They successfully rebuilt your damaged skeletomuscular system and corrected the deletion in your DNA. You have been returned to this room as we felt a more intimate environment would be best for the initial evaluation."

Cyrus looked past the doctor and into the mirror in front of him as his vision returned. He was relieved when he saw his reflection.

He remained draped in the same hospital gown as before, and his skin remained pale and smooth as always. His eyes were still blue, and he possessed no vicious claws or deadly jaws. If anything, he looked better than before. His sickness and frailty had disappeared overnight, replaced by a healthier, more robust form. Cyrus flexed the muscles in his arms, finding them significantly larger. The doctors had granted him the strength denied him at the very last.

"How... How long was I out?" asked Cyrus, snapping back into reality, exasperated by his muddled thinking.

Elysia stood just off to Shen's left, wide-eyed. She appeared to be the only one concerned for his welfare. Viddur took the opposite attitude and leaned against the wall, nonchalant, looking as though he slept.

"Well, let's see, today is Thursday." Shen's face contorted in thought. "That means we put you out a couple of Wednesdays ago. So it has been just a little over two weeks."

"What? Two weeks?" Cyrus came out of the mental haze entirely.

"The procedure took much longer than anticipated." Dr. Shen shrugged, unconcerned. "It's a complicated process, Mr. Blackthorn, one that must be carried out properly to ensure its success. What is losing fourteen days to sleep compared to regaining the rest of your life? Are you absolutely sure you feel well, Mr. Blackthorn?"

Dr. Shen pulled out the clipboard he held behind his back and took a pen from his lab coat pocket. "What symptoms are you experiencing?"

"My head hurts pretty bad." A frown remained plastered on Cyrus's face. "And I'm sore from being strapped to this table."

"Very good." Shen sounded oddly delighted. "Both can be easily remedied." He hastily scribbled something down on his clipboard. "Do you believe you feel well enough to be released from your restraints so we may see if you have successfully regained the ability to ambulate?" He gazed up at Cyrus. "I'm confident you will be capable of walking once again."

"Sounds great, doctor," said Cyrus. The smile that appeared on his face felt strange to him. He had waited for this day for most of his life. But, excited though he was, something felt off.

"Will I be able to go home after I prove to you that I can walk again?" he asked, his smile suddenly disappearing. "I realize I have become very unaccustomed to walking, and you may want to hold me over for physical therapy or something. Maybe you just want to hold me for observation. I don't know. I didn't really expect to be released immediately. I just thought if I showed you everything you needed to see that you would let me leave soon."

Elysia stared up at Cyrus once more, looking as though she desperately wanted to speak. Unfortunately, Shen had likely ordered her not to say a word.

The doctor gazed up at Cyrus as well. His awkward smile suggested dishonesty.

"We had indeed planned on keeping you here for a few more

days for observational purposes, Mr. Blackthorn," Dr. Shen barely blinked as he spoke. "Before you are released, we must assess if the treatment was successful. The first item we are to evaluate is your ability to walk. You will need to attempt to demonstrate other abilities in order to facilitate your release, but we will address things one item at a time. You will be released upon full completion of our assessment and not before." The doctor let his words sink in. "Now, are you ready to attempt ambulation, Mr. Blackthorn?"

"Yes, I am," Cyrus's grin returned. He was unable to believe this moment was finally happening. "Let's do this."

"Viddur and Elysia, would you release Mr. Blackthorn from his restraints, please?" Shen stepped back. The doctor stood in front of the mirror to observe.

Both Viddur and Elysia moved from their positions and approached Cyrus's bed.

The lab assistants unfastened the restraints around Cyrus's arms and ankles, both turning to give Shen looks of hesitation before they undid the final restraint around his middle. They awaited further direction.

"Well, what are you waiting for?" asked the doctor, nearly as a reprimand. "Let him catch himself, but make sure he doesn't fall on his face. He should be ready to stand and walk on his own. Any problem Mr. Blackthorn experiences will be related to forgetting how to ambulate properly."

"As you wish, doctor," said Elysia. Both Viddur and she grasped a side of the final restraint.

"Here we go," said Viddur, preparing to pull the restraint open. "1, 2, 3…"

Elysia and Viddur pulled the restraint open.

Cyrus slid down from the bed. He felt muscles he had forgotten he possessed tighten as the soles of his feet made contact with the cold floor. He instinctively reached out with his right hand and attempted to catch himself as the upper portion of his body leaned toward the floor. The muscles in his back simultaneously stiffened to prevent his full descent to the floor.

"Don't let him fall," said Elysia. Both she and Viddur barely had time to react to Cyrus's sudden release from the restraint. They stood off to either side with arms outstretched, ready to catch him should he suddenly veer off and stumble toward them.

Cyrus held his arms out to either side, retaining his balance as he cautiously placed one foot in front of the other, teetering slightly off to one side as he moved. Though uneasy, he took several slow, careful steps until he was walking. The feeling was beyond euphoric, and Cyrus couldn't help but beam as he moved around the room. He couldn't recall a time he had ever felt this happy. He could cry out with joy.

"How does it feel being able to walk, Cyrus?" Elysia smiled gleefully at him.

"It's better than a dream!" he exclaimed, attempting more steps and nearly tripping over his own feet due to excitement.

Though Cyrus was overjoyed to be back on his feet at last, an odd thought suddenly entered his mind, which caused him to stumble yet again. It was strange to walk even with the nanobotic reconstruction.

"Uh, doctor, how is it that I'm walking without any therapy or anything?" Cyrus asked, concerned. "Surely, it's never been this easy to get back to walking just like that."

"That's very simple," explained Dr. Shen. "In addition to the nanobots that repaired your DNA and rebuilt your muscle tissue, the infusion cocktail contained nanobots designed to stimulate your brain and neural cells. These nanobots deliver a small electric shock to the cells of your cerebellum and the motor neurons connected to your muscle tissue, helping to unlock your muscle memory. This, along with the muscle tissue rebuild, has allowed you to quickly regain the ability to walk without extensive therapeutic intervention."

"Get over here, doctor!" Cyrus felt a sense of overwhelming gratitude surge over him. "I've never been a hugger, but I think I can make an exception just this once."

Cyrus awkwardly stumbled toward the doctor, taking him in a hardy embrace, repressing the impulse to tear up. Dr. Shen wasn't much of a hugger either and remained silent and limp.

Cyrus continued to hold the doctor in his cumbersome clasp until he gazed up into the mirror.

He flinched when he saw his reflection. There was something very wrong with his eyes. They had changed from the dull blue of a moment ago, and his irises now glowed copper yellow.

"Doctor, I think there is something wrong," said Cyrus, releasing Dr. Shen as a sickening feeling hit the pit of his stomach.

He pushed past the doctor as he made for the mirror and leaned in for a better look.

"What's wrong with my eyes?" he shrieked.

"Just relax." Dr. Shen turned to face him in the mirror. "It's nothing to worry about, Mr. Blackthorn. It's just one of the side effects of the treatment. It's purely cosmetic and is no reason to become upset."

"That's one heck of a side-effect!" Cyrus flew into a rant. "Would it have killed you to at least tell me this might happen? How much information have you been keeping from me?"

"Elysia. Viddur." Shen ignored Cyrus. "Would you please leave the room so Mr. Blackthorn and I can speak privately?"

"Whatever you say, doctor," said Viddur, turning to leave.

"Are you sure that's a good idea?" asked Elysia, immobile where she stood.

"I'm sure I will be quite alright here with Mr. Blackthorn," Shen assured her. "Thank you for your concern, Elysia."

The lab assistant's eyes darted toward Cyrus and locked onto him for a brief moment before she regained focus, reluctantly following Viddur. The heavy door slammed shut behind them.

"Mr. Blackthorn, I told you everything you needed to know at the time." Shen turned his attention back to Cyrus. "I told you that we would cure you of your disability, and we have. As you can see, you are no longer disabled. Isn't that good enough for you, even if the gift was bestowed under a few minor false pretenses?"

"Hey, what's this?" Cyrus felt a bristling at his neck. There was an object hidden underneath his hospital gown, something he hadn't noticed due to all the excitement. He stood erect, grasping for his neck, his fingernails striking something metallic and hard.

Cyrus pulled down the top of his gown to find a black metal collar.

"Why is there a collar around my neck?" he asked, turning around to face Shen.

"It's a shock collar," Dr. Shen's voice was blunt. "It has been placed around your neck in case you suddenly step out of line. It's a precaution, placed there to protect all of us, including you."

"Why does anyone need protection from me?" Cyrus shouted. "I was more than harmless a couple of weeks ago, and now that I'm cured, hurting anyone is the farthest thing from my mind. I suppose I'm more dangerous than I was, but trust me, I have no reason to attack you."

"I'm happy to hear that." The doctor attempted a friendly smile. "I never doubted you. The collar is merely a precaution. Given your display of gratitude, I'm sure it will be removed very soon." Dr. Shen stepped away from Cyrus, continuing toward the upright examination table before turning around to face him.

"I believe you may want to sit down for what I'm about to tell you, Mr. Blackthorn." He pulled a rolling chair out from under the table nearby and gently pushed it toward Cyrus. "I must confess to something I'm sure you will not approve of."

"What is that, doctor?" Cyrus folded his arms across his chest, letting the chair hit the side of his leg. "You know, I would say it better not be something you should have told me before I consented to the treatment, but I think we passed that point a while ago. If you really are going to start telling the whole truth, I do want to be sitting down, you know, just in case I pass out from the shock."

He took a seat in the rolling chair and nearly fell out of it when he plopped down. He could use some practice in the fine art of sitting.

"You likely won't believe most of the things I tell you as of right now," Dr. Shen continued, hands folded behind his back.

"In time, I am certain you will find everything I say from this point onward is indeed true." The doctor found a rolling stool and moved it closer to Cyrus before sitting down to face him. "The first of the few things I neglected to mention is that not only have we corrected your disability, we have also improved your abilities to a point far beyond that of the average man. For example, your physical strength will soon exceed that of even the most powerful weight-lifter."

"OK," said Cyrus, still feeling a little overwhelmed. "How much stronger are we talking?"

"Possibly six times stronger than the average human male

once the nanobots fully complete their work." Shen shrugged. "Maybe even stronger. We won't be sure until it is tested."

"Wow, that much…" said Cyrus, suddenly hoping what the doctor said was true, excited by the prospect.

"Only after the nanobots have completed the repairs and improvements to your body will we know for sure."

Shen's words caused a light to appear in Cyrus's eyes.

"You will reach that level of development soon. In addition to the increase in strength, you will also be much faster, much more agile, and will have more stamina than the average human."

Come on, doctor," Cyrus scoffed. "Nice try, but you'll have to do better than that if you want to pull one over on me. Suppose I might as well start wearing tights and a cape. What else you got?" Even as he rebuked him, Cyrus wanted to believe everything Dr. Shen said was true. He supposed that maybe he should give him the benefit of the doubt. After all, he was a goner a mere two weeks ago, and now he could walk.

"I assure you, Mr. Blackthorn, everything I have just told you is true, providing the procedure went as anticipated." Shen blinked multiple times, his eyes void of any sense of humor.

Cyrus looked past him, distracted by his reflection in the shiny, black screen of the shutoff monitor just off to the doctor's left. A cold tingle crept over his spine, a terrible thought entering his head when he looked into his yellow eyes.

"You're not going to let me leave, are you?" Cyrus suddenly felt downcast, his voice growing soft. "Even if you don't have something sinister planned, you can't let me leave."

"Mr. Blackthorn…" Dr. Shen started again

"Why did you even bother telling me I would be able to leave?" Cyrus cut him off. "It seems like you just lie for the heck of it. Your talents have been wasted on science. The way you lie, you probably could have been a good lawyer, or maybe even a politician."

"We plan on releasing you in due time." Dr. Shen stopped him, ignoring the slight against him. "As previously stated, there are conditions for your release. Tests that need to be performed. Data which must be gathered. Your physical appearance and regained abilities will have no bearing on your release. After all of our conditions are met, you will be allowed to leave. It's a minimal price to pay, Mr. Blackthorn, to perform several simple tests in exchange for a healthy body."

"Well, when you put it that way, it does kind of sound like I owe you." Cyrus's mood lightened. "Nothing comes free, after all. Though, I would like to point out that I was right about there being a catch."

The doctor stared off into space, refusing to grant Cyrus any acknowledgment.

"You know, doctor, keeping me around for tests isn't all that big of a deal." Cyrus attempted to press Shen again. "Why didn't you just tell me everything you had planned to do before you started the procedure? I'm sure I would have agreed to it. Unless... No, surely not..."

He paused, tripping himself up, lost in thought.

"What exactly do these tests involve?" Cyrus asked, his eyes narrowing.

"The tests to be performed should not present a problem." The doctor gave him a look of deep sincerity. "They will require only a little effort on your part. I realize, given the degree of distrust you are displaying, you would like more information than what has been given, but unfortunately, I am not at liberty to tell you any more regarding the tests. You will just have to believe me."

"Well, if I have no other choice..." Cyrus decided to believe the doctor. A deep frown formed on his face as his suspicions returned to prior levels.

"What else aren't you telling me? How far down does this iceberg go?"

"You are very perceptive." Dr. Shen raised an eyebrow. "In the interest of full disclosure, there are other reasons as to why you must be kept here, in addition to what I have just mentioned."

"OK, let's hear them." Cyrus crossed his arms. "You are mak ing quite an effort to drag your feet."

"Just be patient. I will tell you everything you wish to know. Some of it must be said with a certain degree of finesse, which is difficult to fulfill in haste. I apologize if I'm overly subtle, but there is no other way to go about it."

Cyrus readjusted his position in his chair, making himself

comfortable, feeling Shen was a long-winded talker.

"Given your background in molecular biology," the doctor continued, "I am sure you are very aware that there exists a considerable amount of human metabolic disorders. For example, there are diseases in which the affected either cannot or have great difficulty breaking down certain organic molecules."

"You mean something like... umm... something like phenylketo..." Cyrus was becoming frustrated, having difficulty remembering the name. "Something like PKU, where phenylalanine can't be metabolized?"

"Precisely. There are certain metabolic disorders like phenylketonuria where individuals cannot break down certain substances. Among these metabolic disorders, there are also a few where the patient cannot metabolize a number of organic substances."

"I'm not surprised that there are." Cyrus shrugged, unsure how what the doctor said had anything to do with him. "I suppose someone could potentially have more than one of those disorders and survive, though it would be difficult. I'm certain if someone couldn't metabolize most of the nutrients required for survival, they likely wouldn't last very long. That's if they even made it out of the womb."

"That's an accurate enough statement." Dr. Shen could never let him be entirely right. "Unfortunately, it is not entirely true. An individual can survive and be incapable of metabolizing many substances, difficult though it may be. In fact, in recent years, another one, or I suppose you could say another two, of these metabolic disorders was discovered. In fact, a disease in which the affected are incapable of metabolizing a great many substances exists. Sufferers can only subsist on a very limited, very specific diet."

"What is it called?" Cyrus's patience ran low, and he doubted the information Shen gave.

"We will arrive at the name in a moment." Shen raised a hand as though trying to stop him. "Anyway, the disorder of which I speak is quite different from any other metabolic disorder otherwise discovered by man. It is most peculiar, as the affected are so limited by what they can metabolize that all of their nutrition must come from one particular source. They cannot break down any plant material whatsoever or anything significantly distant from themselves phylogenetically. This leaves them only one source from which to draw sustenance. Human flesh and blood. They are essentially obligate cannibals."

"OK, what?" asked Cyrus, suppressing a laugh.

He looked at the doctor and saw a face of stone-cold severity.

"You surely don't mean, or it sounds a lot like…" he trailed off.   "Sorry, it's just   that what you described sounds a lot like zombie-ism or something."

The doctor remained silent as Cyrus awaited his answer, the eerie, noiseless moment lasting an eternity.

"The   term   'clinical zombie-ism' could be applied to   one form of   the   disease," the   doctor   answered at last,   relieving Cyrus's anxiety. "In the case of the other related disorder, I believe vampirism is more accurate. One of the only major differences between the two diseases is what happens to the mental faculties. With the vampiric form, these remain   mostly   intact, while   those afflicted with zombie-ism seem to lose most of them. Those with vampirism also display a slight preference for blood as opposed to flesh, whereas those   with   zombie-ism   don't   usually have a preference at all."

As much as he didn't want to believe the doctor's words, Cyrus's skepticism had dwindled away. Shen made some ridiculous claims, but he used language that made what he was saying almost credible. Nevertheless, he needed more information if he wished to discern the truth.

"Well, I suppose when you put all of it in technical terms like that, it's feasible that both clinical, physiological vampirism and zombie-ism could exist."

Cyrus leaned forward in his chair, looking Shen in the eye.

"I would assume it is easier to deal with than the vampirism from folklore. I mean, there's not a modern society that is OK with the consumption of human flesh and blood. But, I think there is a possibility that people would understand having to resort to it when you have no other choice, so long as you do it the right way. You know, only eat people who are already dead. We couldn't just allow them to die. I'm sure it's easy enough to find a cadaver to feed them.

Their metabolic needs shouldn't be any higher than that of the average person, so I wouldn't think it would take all that many bodies."

"There is a little more to the disorder than that, Mr. Blackthorn. In addition to causing obligate cannibalism, those affected with either form of the disease also have increased nutrition needs, similar to that of a large predator, like a lion or another of the order *Panthera*. This means their caloric needs are up to five times that of the average individual."

The doctor removed his glasses and clean them on his lab coat.

"Unlike the other metabolic disorders, clinical vampirism imparts certain physical advantages to the affected." Dr. Shen put his glasses back on. "Individuals display increased strength, speed, and stamina, in addition to increased sensory perception. Though I suggested it does not affect the mental faculties, some people can display certain behaviors associated with psychopathic individuals. There are indeed instances where mental functioning is reduced somewhat, though not to the extent of what we see in zombie-ism. More accurately, it is believed that the disease tends to reduce one to a more primal way of thinking, where the frontal lobe of the brain sees a great reduction in function, causing one's cognitive abilities to become more animalistic. All of that is theoretical, of course. We have yet to formally analyze the psyches of anyone with vampirism. It could be that feeding on the flesh and blood of other humans itself is enough to lead to the development of severe psychosis."

"What's the initial cause of either disorder?" Cyrus grew more convinced by the second, though he would have never admitted it. "I would think it would be inherited genetically, like nearly all of the other metabolic disorders."

"The disease's method of conveyance may be its most interesting attribute." Dr. Shen gave him a sly smile. "You see, the disease develops via viral infection. There are two different but very similar viruses, one for each of the two types of this disorder. Both are transmitted through bites and only affect humans. As I'm sure you know, infection through a bite isn't the most efficient means for transmission compared to transference through the air. This is a good thing, of course, as infection with either virus nearly always leads to the development of the disorder. It's just that potent. If someone with a significantly compromised immune system were to be infected, they could potentially die due to some complications, though this has been observed in very few cases. However, so long as the individual survives the initial attack, they have a good chance of survival."

"What do you mean 'attacked'?" Cyrus interrupted, unable to contain himself. "You surely don't mean that those infected with the virus are actually assaulting other people, do you? It's starting to sound even more like you're talking about mythological vampirism. Whatever credibility you gained, you're starting to lose it."

"I wish I hadn't let it slip as I was attempting to arrive at that point later," Shen admitted. "Anyway, yes, that is indeed true. Those who have developed either disorder do routinely attack uninfected individuals for sustenance. Those with zombie-ism, having lost so much of their brain functioning, are incapable of controlling their more basal urges. They will attack nearly any living thing, both humans and animals. Those with vampirism possess more self-control, but yet, still attack others. As I have stated earlier, this form of the disorder tends to cause what might be termed 'severely sadistic behavior.'" The doctor leaned forward in his seat, addressing Cyrus in a near whisper. "I understand why you would doubt what I'm telling you. I sincerely wish what I just said was not true, but, unfortunately, that is just not the case."

"All that sounds interesting." Cyrus frowned, arms still crossed. "Metabolic disorders like that always are. The only thing is, what does any of this have to do with me?"

"It has everything to do with you," the doctor continued to whisper, quickly returning to normal volume. "I'll tell you exactly what it means to you if you will just entertain my subtlety for a while longer."

"I'm having a difficult time believing any of this."

"Is there anything I can say to convince you?"

"I can't imagine that there is. You've made some pretty ridiculous claims."

"Well, if there is nothing I can say to convince you..."

Shen rose from his seat, making toward the door with a kind of defeated walk. He had taken some offense to Cyrus's doubts. The doctor turned the door handle and looked back at him.

"Come with me, Mr. Blackthorn. I have something to show you," said Shen, just before disappearing into the hallway.

Cyrus shook his head, rising from his seat and reluctantly following him, stumbling at first but managing to keep his balance.

Chapter X

The Plague

"Here we are," said Dr. Shen, straining to open the heavy sliding door.

Cyrus stood behind him, along with Elysia and Viddur, anticipating the end of their surprisingly long trek.

Originating from Cyrus's room, the doctor led them through a labyrinth of hallways. The place was a maze of nothing but bone-white walls, tile floors, and the occasional chrome-plated elevator. Strenuous though the walk had been, Cyrus found the soreness in his feet exhilarating, a sensation he had all but forgotten.

"After you, Mr. Blackthorn," said Dr. Shen.

The open doorway revealed a dubious-looking stairway, only the topmost portion exposed by the light of the adjoining hallway. Darkness blanketed all the rest.

"I would prefer not to enter first if that's OK." Cyrus stared down the dark hallway.

Suspicion spiked in his head. The feeling was similar to what he had experienced when he first met Dr. Shen. He still had every reason not to trust him, even when he considered what the doctor had done for him. Shen already neglected to tell him about all of the cure's side-effects, after all.

"Very well," said Dr. Shen, understanding his hesitation. "Viddur, you go first."

"Sure thing, doctor," said Viddur. He walked past them and down the darkened stairs, a light switching on moments later.

"Elysia," said Shen as he motioned toward the door. "Mr. Blackthorn and I will follow you."

Elysia wordlessly proceeded through the doorway and down the stairs, leaving Cyrus in the hallway with the doctor.

"You first," said Cyrus, failing to hide the suspicion in his voice. "Forgive me. It's just sometimes I have difficulty fully trusting medical professionals. It's what you get out of a lifetime of disease. All the poking and prodding and the false hope they sometimes give you..." He let his abduction go without mention, as he found it the most apparent reason for his mistrust.

"Of course." Shen remained beside the door. "All of your precaution is unnecessary, I assure you. You have been a very successful subject thus far. On behalf of all CyberGen, I'll say this: We wouldn't wish any harm to befall you."

"I'd rather not take any chances." Cyrus gave him a cynical smile. "Surely you can understand that."

"Very well." Dr. Shen's frustration showed as his shoes hit the floor louder than usual.

Cyrus followed behind him, silent as he made his way through the doorway and down the stairs.

The air instantly became suffocating. The stairs descended into a sparsely lit, poorly aerated passageway, the whole atmosphere dank and dusty, in great contrast with the rest of the facility. Where the other halls were clean and sterile, this passageway was left filthy; the walls fouled with dirt. The closed-in walls and cobwebs made Cyrus feel as though he had stepped into a tomb. He hoped it didn't turn out being his.

"Viddur, would you please close the door?" asked Dr. Shen, nervously looking back to see if Cyrus had entered the doorway.

"Sure thing." Viddur punched the red glowing button on the wall beside him.

"CyberGen ever think to clean this place up?" Cyrus suppressed the impulse to sneeze as his eyes begin to water. "It's dusty as heck down here."

The door closed behind them, and the locking system immediately snapped back into place. The noise sent chills down Cyrus's spine. His body went stiff, ready for the impending attack.

Dr. Shen looked up at him from the bottom of the stairs,

bored by his antics.

"It's simply not an option," said the doctor. "A cleaning crew cannot be allowed into this area. There's just too much of a chance someone will discover what we're keeping down here. Most of our staff don't know about many of the things we do here, and I'm sure they will not be at all pleased by what they might find. The only way to tidy up the place would be for someone fully aware of our activities to volunteer."

"For the last time." Viddur turned back around to glower at Dr. Shen. "I'm not cleaning up down here! You can stop with all the hints!"

"Why have Viddur clean down here?" asked Elysia, a hint of mirth in her voice. "Everything will still be dirty even after he's done."

Viddur glared at her. Cyrus grinned, trying to keep from laughing.

"Let's keep any bickering to a minimum," Dr. Shen cut Viddur off, denying him any kind of retort. "Mr. Blackthorn has made things difficult enough with his distrustful attitude, so let's not fight amongst ourselves."

"Yes, sir," said Viddur, both he and Elysia proceeding down the passage.

Dr. Shen and Cyrus stepped off the stairs to follow them. The group walked on for another hundred yards, the hall dirty throughout with large dust stains occupying the majority of the once white, brick walls. Cyrus continually suppressed the urge to sneeze.

"Here we are," said Viddur, stopping beside an unremarkable wooden door in the middle of the passageway.

"Give us a second, Viddur." Dr. Shen stopped him, paying his words little heed. "There's no reason to rush in. We don't want to startle Mr. Blackthorn if we can help it." The doctor moved past those gathered, directing Viddur away from the door while wrapping his hand around the handle. "Mr. Blackthorn." Shen failed to conceal the anxiety in his eyes. "Try not to be too alarmed by what is behind this door. We do not need you to become overly excited as it will be hazardous to the health of everyone here, yourself included."

"Understood." Cyrus tried not to sound anxious, but a cold sweat suddenly appeared on his palms.

"Very well." Shen braced himself against the door. "Here we go."

The doctor pushed through the door with a considerable amount of force. He continued through the entryway and into the next room, propping it open before making a move for the lights. A powerful smell floated out of the room, so horrendous Cyrus felt it could nearly raise the dead.

The shrieks and cries of what sounded like a highly disturbed man echoed throughout the passageway, this a reaction to the doctor's sudden entrance into the room.

"Come in!" Shen yelled back at them. "Don't worry! He won't do anything to you! We have him in a cell!"

"Here we go again," said Viddur, oblivious to all the noise as he shuffled through the doorway, strangely bored by what was going on. Elysia followed him, possessed by the same lackadaisical attitude, leaving Cyrus alone in the passageway.

"Come in, Mr. Blackthorn!" Dr. Shen yelled out once again. "Everything is perfectly safe! He cannot harm you!"

Cyrus moaned, finally following them through the door, his eyes watering from the strength of the smell.

The screams greeted him as he entered.

"What the heck, doctor?" Cyrus jumped to the side as an extraordinarily disheveled and bewildered man in tattered clothing reached for him through the bars of his cell.

In addition to his crazed behavior, there was something very wrong with his appearance. His eyes were an unnatural, sickly yellow, bulging from his head; his skin ashen, yet tinted green, like a corpse that had begun to decompose.

"You're keeping one of them down here?" Cyrus continued to react. "What's the matter with you?"

The man in the cell suddenly stopped shrieking, raising his head to take a quick whiff of the stale, musty air. His eyes widened as he glared at Cyrus, full of what looked like recognition.

The man screamed one final time before retreating to the opposite side of his cell, tripping over his own feet as he went, landing in the corner face down. He remained there, shaking and occasionally looking back at Cyrus, reacting with a terrified whimper each time.

As his heart rate slackened, Cyrus saw the room extended back past the lit area. The decor was bare and dirty, reminiscent of a medieval dungeon, though few would give much thought to how things looked. The stench in the room overpowered all else. The mixture of the man's filth and excrement could knock a person down.

Repulsed though he was, Cyrus took a sniff of the air, finding another scent buried underneath the others: the smell of spoiled meat, savory yet pungent with the odor of growing microbes. He licked his lips, finding the smell strangely appetizing.

"This man has zombie-ism, Mr. Blackthorn."

Shen stood off to the side of the cell, not at all perturbed by the crazed man.

"As I said earlier, this condition is caused by a variant of the same virus responsible for vampirism. As for holding an infected individual, it's a difficult situation to avoid. Moreover, it's impossible to perform any research without any live specimen to study."

"You're a scientist, for crying out loud!" Cyrus shouted, riled up anew, disregarding what Dr. Shen told him earlier. Seeing was much different from merely hearing.

Cyrus gazed toward the opposite wall, finding Elysia and Viddur standing off near the empty cells. He shot them both a pleading look, looking to garner support for his argument and finding none.

"You don't actually believe this man is a zombie, just like from the movies? You told me they were just sick people." Cyrus was over his initial scare and took a closer look at the deranged man. Though he looked like a sickening wreck, Cyrus felt there could be other explanations for his appearance.

"I hope I didn't waste my time explaining the disorder only to have you spontaneously forget everything I told you, Mr. Blackthorn." Shen's voice was flat. "The zombie virus is not unlike rabies, except instead of merely causing inflammation of the brain, it degrades and even reorganizes brain cells, eventually reducing the infected to an animalistic state." He indicated toward the man in the cell.

"I haven't forgotten what you told me." Cyrus matched

Shen's tone. "It's just this… It's all still a little hard to believe, even after seeing somebody like this." He looked over at the man in the cell, finding him sitting in the corner, watching him with unhealthy yellow eyes.

"Do you know why he's acting like that?" Cyrus frowned back at Dr. Shen. The answer he wanted suddenly entered his mind. "He acts like he's afraid."

"It certainly appears that way, Mr. Blackthorn."

"Do you know why?"

"I can't say for sure," Shen paused to think. "It may have something to do with the way you smell."

"What do you mean 'the way I smell'?" Cyrus was confused, unsure if he was being intentionally insulted. "I know I haven't bathed since the procedure, but…" he started toward the doctor.

"It has everything to do with the virus's method of action, Mr. Blackthorn." Shen failed to read Cyrus's reaction. "As the infection progresses and damages the brain, it begins to affect the senses, some more than others. The vision is reduced, the hearing is typically unchanged, and olfaction actually increases. In addition to this, the infected individual has a greatly reduced ability to perceive certain stimuli like temperature and pain. Anyway, with the increase in their olfaction capacity comes the additional ability to smell other individuals like themselves. It makes them capable of recognizing other infected individuals, so they don't attack each other. Given how his behavior changed the moment you entered, it seems he has the ability to recognize other genetically modified organisms such as yourself. As you also smell unfamiliar to him, it is only natural he react with fear."

"Hmm… That's very interesting." Cyrus felt the doctor had somehow missed something.

He moved over to the opposite wall where Elysia stood, finding she displayed a similar look of confusion.

"Do you really feed him human flesh?" his tone went cold.

"That we do," replied the doctor, speaking as though he could be talking about the weather.

"And there is nothing else you can give him?"

"We've tried to give them other things in the past, but it always caused vomiting." Shen shook his head as he looked over the man in the cell. "Multiple tests have been performed, and it seems that they're just not capable of metabolizing anything else. They are obligate cannibals in every sense. Human flesh is quite easy for us to obtain. We just take it from cadavers. There is no need to become too excited, Mr. Blackthorn."

"So there have been others?" Cyrus was genuinely curious, though confident he wouldn't care for most of Shen's answers. He would try to remain calm.

"Yes, there have indeed."

"What happened to them?"

"We euthanized them. We didn't have a choice. The condition is not reversible."

"You couldn't treat them with nanobots?" Cyrus asked, frustrated by the loss of life. He knew there was nothing to do for it, but he felt it all the same.

"We have tried, but without success, as you can see. We have seen some results, but they are always limited. We have been able to restore a very slight amount of brain function, though nowhere near enough to bring them back to where they were. The human brain is just too complicated and elegant an organ to recreate with nanobots. There are just too many neural connections to replicate."

"Do you think the condition causes them any pain?" Cyrus continued, a certain idea popping into his head.

"They experience little pain, well that is, other than what they unintentionally inflict upon themselves."

"And the infection is deadly one hundred percent of the time?"

" One hundred percent of the time."

"How long does it usually take for the infection to kill them?"

"Days, months, maybe years," said Shen, considering each. "It varies considerably. Believe me, his mind is too far gone to comprehend his condition." He found the angle Cyrus was trying to play.

The man in the corner let out a howl like a wounded animal and darted back toward them, sticking both arms between the steel bars to grasp for Shen with his dirty, clawed fingers. Whatever fear he felt earlier wholly disappeared for the moment.

"Huh, must be hungry." Dr. Shen turned to find Viddur standing at his immediate right, both unperturbed by the zombie man's sudden outburst. "Viddur, would you feed him, please?"

"Yes, sir," said Viddur. He walked past the doctor into the darkness at the other side of the room, entirely disappearing from view.

Cyrus glanced over to where Elysia was standing, finding she had moved to a corner of the room farthest from Shen, likely to avoid the chore of feeding the specimen.

Viddur re-emerged moments later, carrying a heavy bucket.

Cyrus did not attempt to see what it contained, as he didn't want to know what filled it.

Viddur shoved the zombie meal through a slot at the bottom of the man's cell with a booted foot. The man immediately lunged for his meal, shoving his head into the bucket as he began to devour its contents.

"*Omm... Omm... Omm...*" The man gnawed and smacked his lips as he ate. He took part of an intestine in both hands and tearing into it like a gluttonous child, wolfing it down like an uncooked hot dog. Dark red blood and an unidentifiable black fluid dripped from the man's chin as he bit off a piece and immediately swallowed it.

Elysia moaned and faced the wall, disgusted by the way the man ate. "It's always so gross. I can't watch."

"What plans do you have for this specific specimen?" asked Cyrus, eager for any reason to look away from the man, feeling he might vomit.

Shen and Viddur looked bored by the zombie's method of feeding.

"If all of your attempts to cure zombie-ism have failed, wouldn't it be better to euthanize him instead of leaving him down here like this?"

"As I said before, we are currently still performing research," said Shen, a weary grin on his face. "We still seek both to create a vaccine to prevent the condition and to find a cure for those who have already developed the disease. This requires us to care for and monitor live specimens for a period of time. As of the moment, we are far from accomplishing our goals, but we will keep trying until we have it right. This man has lived longer than any other specimen after receiving our current version of the vaccine. We are still holding him for observation."

"Do you work to create the vaccine as well?" asked Cyrus.

"No, that's Dr. Gupta's department." The doctor suddenly became excited for no apparent reason. "If you like, we can show you to her lab."

* * *

"Here we are," said Dr. Shen, pushing down on the door handle as it refused to budge. Undeterred, he knocked on the door, impatiently tapping his foot as he waited for someone to open it.

The doctor had taken their group less than one hundred feet away from the zombie holding cells, leading them to the end of the crypt-like hallway to stand beside a white, very sterile-looking door. Its appearance greatly contrasted with the surrounding filth.

Dr. Shen knocked on the door several more times; his persistence rewarded moments later as the door handle began to turn.

"Oh, hello, Daniel," said Dr. Gupta, speaking with a barely detectable Indian accent. She held the door partially open, peering up through the crack at Dr. Shen. "What can I do for you?" She kept her voice calm and cheerful, sounding as though she genuinely wanted to help.

"Well, I have a unique and unexpected problem," said Shen.

"And what is that?"

"I have a naysayer with me who is somewhat disinclined to believe anything I tell him," Shen explained. "His skepticism is admirable, possibly surpassing any scientist I've ever worked with. He needs additional concrete evidence before he comes to a final conclusion."

"Well, excuse me." Cyrus frowned and shook his head, somewhat exasperated. "A lot of what you said before we came down here sounds like nonsense now that I think about it, even with all the things you've shown me. I don't see anything wrong with being thorough, especially in this case. Well, that and I wanted to see the lab." He grinned, uneasy.

"Well, if you want to take a closer look at one of the infected, then you are in luck." Gupta nodded toward him.

She unlatched the door, opening it wide so the four of them could pass through.

"We are performing autopsies right now."

Dr. Gupta was middle-aged and very small, a head shorter than Dr. Shen. She wore a lab coat and long, purple, nitrile gloves. Her face shield and mask further concealed her tan skin and face.

"Oh." Gupta jumped a little when she looked at Cyrus, startled by his cat-like eyes.

"Don't we probably need to put on some kind of protection before we enter a room full of zombie contagions?" asked Cyrus. He stared at Dr. Gupta's face shield and mask, determined not to be offended by her reaction.

He suddenly felt a strange tingling sensation around his gum line, immediately writing it off as nothing, odd though it was.

"Not that I can think of," said Dr. Gupta, quickly recovered from her surprise. "I'm sure Dr. Shen has already told you that the virus is not spread through the air, so there's no need to wear a mask. I'm just wearing the shield to protect my eyes from splatter and the mask to deal with the smell. I doubt you will be in here long enough to necessitate wearing either. You might want to put on gloves if you intend to touch anything. Right this way, please."

Dr. Gupta turned from where she held their group near the door and led them further into the room. The white light was nearly as blinding as it was in Cyrus's room.

As his eyes adjusted to the light, Cyrus saw that the room was essentially a morgue, clean and sterilized, filled with body vaults and medical examination tables. On nearly every table rested an ashen-skinned zombie cadaver, each in a different state of dissection, most of which was heavily focused on the head. Most had their brains removed from their skull cavities, and several more brains rested on medical examination trays. Many other specimens remained whole as the members of Gupta's laboratory staff stood scattered about the room, intensely involved with dissecting the corpses.

The scientists remained focused on their work, ignoring the group that entered. The overall effect reminded Cyrus of an automotive chop shop, full of partially deconstructed bodies instead of cars.

"OK, I think we will need the masks, Dr. Gupta," said Elysia. She cupped her hands over her nose and mouth, finding the smell in the room extremely off-putting.

Viddur and Dr. Shen did likewise.

Cyrus admitted the stench had a certain penetrative quality, st abbing at the eyes, wafting up the nose in such a way it poked at the brain. But, just as with the man in the cell, he found the scent oddly appealing.

"Oh, come on, is it that bad?" asked Dr. Gupta, a good-natured smirk on her face.

"I would say it is," said Viddur, gasping for breath.

"Very well, the box with the masks is over there." Gupta pointed toward the box hanging on the wall near the door.

"Thanks, doctor," said Shen just before bolting for the box, beaten to it by Elysia and Viddur.

Nasal protection secured to their faces, the trio returned to where Cyrus and Dr. Gupta stood to wait.

"This way." Dr. Gupta led them toward a table near the far corner of the large room.

"What's with all the bodies?" asked Cyrus as they walked. "I thought there would be only a few infected individuals, but this is a little excessive. It makes it look like we're right in the middle of a zombie crisis."

"That is because we are wrapping up the most recent trial of the latest version of our zombie-ism vaccine," Dr. Gupta shook her head as she stopped to speak, staring down at the floor with regret. "I will admit it was very effective, just not it in the way we would like. It relieved nearly all of our specimens of their suffering, killing all but a single man in only days. It is back to the drawing board once again."

"That is unfortunate." Dr. Shen gave Gupta a forgiving look. "I'm sure you will have a working vaccine for us very soon."

"I can only hope." Gupta gave him a beleaguered smile. "Come on, the specimen I want to show you is over here." She waved their group onward, taking them to an examination table near the back of the room, a partially covered, shaven male corpse resting upon it. "Here we are." Gupta stood beside the table where the man's head rested as the others in the group gathered around. "Just give me a second to open up his skull and pull the brain out of the cranial vault."

She picked up a vibrating saw sitting on the instrument table, positioning the blade near the man's head. She turned it on, forcefully but delicately cutting into the skull, the saw blade screeching even louder when it made contact with bone.

"Almost there." Gupta completed her sutures, turning off the saw and placing it back on the instrument table. She stuck her gloved fingers into the incisions she made, pulling the bloody bone fragment from the rest of the skull and placing it on an examination tray.

"There we have it," she said, going back in for the brain.

Gupta carefully pulled it from the cranial vault, holding it up in the air for all to see. Like all brains, it resembled a head of flabby, pinkish-grey cauliflower, appearing to be normal, yet off somehow. They all leaned in for a closer look, too desensitized by watching the man in the cell eat to find a single brain unsettling.

"I'm not sure if you can tell without a healthy brain for comparison, but there is something very wrong with this one." Gupta rotated the brain around in her hands. "For starters, it is significantly smaller than average due to the cell death of much of the ganglia in the cerebrum. The virus typically hits the frontal lobe the hardest, shrinking it down so that the brain takes on a more rounded shape. Due to this size reduction, an individual with zombie-ism is incapable of most forms of self-control. The virus also tends to cause some extreme changes to the limbic system. The amygdala, the portion of the brain responsible for anger and fear, is larger than what is seen in an uninfected human, explaining why the afflicted become so aggressive. We'll have to cut it open to see that, though even then certain things will still be difficult to see."

Dr. Gupta placed the brain on the examination tray, quickly slicing it in half with her scalpel. She held the right half against the tray so they could see the cross-section.

"As you can see, the damage is much more apparent when we take a look at the inside."

Gupta pointed at various parts of the brain with a purple-gloved finger.

"The most visible damage is to the cerebrum, making it significantly smaller than what is considered normal. As I said, though the frontal lobe has seen the most shrinkage, all the other lobes show significant shrinkage as well. Sections of the cerebrum are hollowed out, a feature not unlike what is found in some very severe psychological illnesses, though it is typically much worse in zombie-ism. There is little of the cortex left for higher-level thinking, though portions like those devoted to certain senses seem to be more or less OK. Strangely enough, in most cases, the subjects actually grow another olfactory bulb, giving them a sense of smell powerful enough to rival that of a canine."

Gupta took her hands away from the brain and removed her gloves, tossing them into a nearby trash can.

"Oh yeah?" asked Cyrus, excited by what Gupta had said, nearly forgetting they were looking at a brain afflicted with zombie-ism. "That last part sounds kind of awesome."

"Mr. Blackthorn," said Shen, causing Cyrus to look up. "Nothing is an advantage when the overall result is the degradation of the mind."

"The virus is very capable of targeting specific areas within the brain," said Gupta, intending to stop a potential lecture by Dr. Shen. "It's as though the virus itself is displaying some level of intelligence. It's kind of miraculous that anyone suffering from this much damage to their brain is walking around at all for any length of time. Granted, this individual was in the final stages of the disease, but it's still quite extraordinary that he didn't perish much sooner. It's almost as if the virus itself helps to prolong the lives of those it infects."

"So, are you convinced yet?" Elysia asked, giving Cyrus a gleeful smile.

"I guess I will have to be at this point," Cyrus shrugged. "Having it explained from several different angles helps a lot. Hard to refute all the evidence presented here. Given the situation, I don't think anyone would go through all this trouble just to fool me."

"I'm glad I could help you, Cyrus," said Dr. Gupta, beaming.

"OK, so you've shown me the stupid zombies," Cyrus turned to address Dr. Shen. "I can't think of any other disease that would cause someone to look the way they do and display the behavior they display. It really only puts one of my questions to bed, though, since I still don't see how any of this has anything to do with me."

The strange pain under his teeth intensified to a nearly unbearable point as he spoke, making him unsure if he could stand it for much longer.

"You still haven't told him why he is here?" asked Dr. Gupta, rolling her eyes at Shen and shaking her head in disappointment. "I would think that's something you should have told him before you released him from the restraints."

"Yes, I suppose it is time to tell you the other reason why you are here, Mr. Blackthorn," said Dr. Shen. "I commend your patience. I didn't expect you to last this long without asking that question again."

"Ahh! Oh, my gosh!" Cyrus howled, the tooth pain erupting into a torrent of agony so severe he thought it would put him out of his mind. He slowly fell to his knees, bearing down on the floor tile, pressing his palms against the ground.

"Oh, yes," said Dr. Shen as he looked down at his watch. "Right on time, I nearly forgot."

Many of the lab workers turned from their tables, startled by Cyrus's sudden outburst.

"It's OK!" exclaimed Viddur, turning toward the workers. "My friend likes to overreact! It's just a way to get attention!"

The staff members immediately turned back to their work, whatever concern they may have felt extinguished.

"Why does it hurt so much?" Cyrus screamed

"Tooth pain can be excruciating, Mr. Blackthorn," said Dr. Shen, remaining irritatingly calm.

"Why is this happening?" Cyrus looked up to find Elysia staring down at him, only slightly concerned.

Everyone remained in place, acting as though ordered not to approach him.

"I'll spare you the details for the moment," said Shen. "Your old canines are simply being replaced by longer, sharper ones."

Cyrus screamed again.

Something hard flew out of his mouth, hitting the white tile floor. Cyrus's hand immediately flew to his mouth, feeling for his top right canine. He pricked his finger on the new tooth, or rather, fang, and nearly drew blood.

"Last one," said Dr. Shen.

Cyrus screamed as the second tooth flew out of his mouth.

"Exaggerate much?" asked Viddur sarcastically.

"Oh my gosh." Cyrus slowly rose to his feet, his pain dissipating at last. "Yet another thing I wish you would have told me before you let it happen."

He gave Dr. Shen an accusatory look.

"Kind of getting tired of this, doctor. Are you going to tell me everything now, or should I just assume that I'm slowly transforming into a cat or something?"

Cyrus bent down to pick up his old, discarded teeth off the floor, shoving them into his pants pocket.

"Yes, Mr. Blackthorn, I suppose you are right," said Shen. "It's high time I tell you everything that has been done to you and what we have planned. I'll start by warning you that you can expect your new bottom canines to erupt within the next few hours."

"That's just great," said Cyrus snidely. "What else you got? Surely you did more than change my dental plan without my permission."

He walked closer to where Shen now stood, casually leaning on the examination table nearest him.

"Very well," said Shen. "Take a seat, and I'll tell you."

Cyrus took a rolling stool out from under the examination table and sat down to face Dr. Shen. The rest of their group gathered around them.

"Since you prefer a policy of blatant honesty, I will arrive right at the point," Shen continued, looking directly at Cyrus. "Both the zombie and vampire populations are exploding. Even though the two diseases cannot spread as quickly as what may be described in myth, they still need some sort of control to ensure their numbers remain manageable. The best-case scenario would be to find an apex predator, or the equivalent, and unleash it upon its natural foe. It would serve as the control, creating a situation like that on the African savannah. I realize we're speaking about something only moderately similar, but most of the same principles still apply. We need an unnaturally created predator in order to control the unnaturally created prey. That's where you start to become part of this, Mr. Blackthorn. You will become the first such predator."

"What do you mean?" Cyrus was unsure how to feel. "You cured my disease, but…"

"The process is not yet completed." Dr. Shen raised a hand to stop him. "However, the procedure has been successful thus far, giving us no reason to assume the total transformation will not be successful as well. I personally look forward to our future partnership after the change is complete. We'll all be working together for a common goal. You needed a cure, and we provided it. Now you will be our cure. It is only fair."

The way Dr. Shen spoke put Cyrus on edge. It was all just too unbelievable, and it made him feel paranoid.

"Who's in charge of all of this?" Cyrus asked abruptly.

"I won't get into technicalities, Mr. Blackthorn," said Shen. "The whole project is supported by the United States government. They provide the funding and support our efforts in many other ways, all in secrecy, of course. This need for secrecy is why we can't let you leave, at least not anytime in the near future. The government would like to keep the fact that you are still alive a secret, as any information to the contrary could potentially lead to mass panic. After all, if the public learns of your existence, they will soon learn of the existence of zombie-ism and vampirism."

"Your stay here will be a comfortable one." Shen skipped to what he felt was the conversation's natural conclusion. "As you know, we are a multi-billion dollar organization, and we're more than capable of providing you with everything you need. You will not be permitted to venture outside under any capacity, however."

"I see," said Cyrus, thinking what he was about to say might start an argument. "What if I don't want to do this?"

"Excuse my phrasing, but you don't have a choice in the matter, Mr. Blackthorn. We've given you a gift: the one thing you have always wanted but could never obtain. Since we have now given you this thing, this 'cure,' it's now your turn to return the favor. Besides that, you are intended to be the first of your kind, and if everything proceeds as planned, the most effective defense against a plague that could get out of hand at any point. Humanity will need you."

"Forget all-access and the various amenities or whatever." Cyrus felt he might become enraged at Shen's call to duty. "This is indentured servitude, or borderline slavery even. Surely none of this is legal."

"Normally, it wouldn't be," Shen admitted. "However, in this case, we don't have the convenience of adhering to the law or deciding what is ethical or not. Either way, the decision has already been   made.   You   will   remain   here."

Chapter XI

Sadistic Savagery

"Hey man, how's it going?" Asher asked as he sat down across from Milo at their company's table.

He'd had an entire morning of firearms practice, all but sprinting away from the range when the clock struck twelve, eager for a break at last. Asher had progressed through the cafeteria line in no time since the place was nearly void of any personnel.

"Can't complain." Milo shrugged and gazed at Asher through his extremely thick glasses, his blue eyes magnified by the lenses. "Food is good, or at least it's improved from the slop they used to give us. Hard to beat scrambled eggs and bacon."

"Hmm…" Asher frowned down at his tray, trying to pick up the eggs with his fork as they slid off. "So what's with the breakfast food?"

"Oh, I don't know." Milo looked back up from his tray. "We always have breakfast for lunch at the base. It's because we have to follow the vampires' schedule. Most of the time, they want us up before dusk and down right after dawn, though it depends on what rotation you're on. It will make more sense when we're off the daytime rotation. Whichever way, the officers like to have breakfast when they wake up, which is usually late afternoon."

"So the reason the place is so empty right now is that nearly everyone else is asleep?" Asher looked up from his meal, his voice echoing throughout the nearly empty cafeteria.

A few of the soldiers sitting at a nearby table turned to frown at him, displeased with the volume of his voice.

"That would be correct," said Milo, taking a bite of egg. "The base doesn't come alive until like five or so, when the majority of our soldiers are up."

"I take it that our whole company is on a daytime rotation?"

Asher brought a bit of egg into his mouth, frowning when he found that it lacked flavor.

"Our platoon is, but not the rest of the company." Milo paused to think. "They should have us back on nighttime rotation pretty soon after they bring the platoon numbers back up."

"What do you mean 'bring the numbers back up'?" Asher felt a sharp tingle going down his spine and a chill growing in the air.

"We haven't experienced any major losses for quite a while now, or so I've been told. The Legion's been kind of nickeled and dimed lately, personnel-wise, and they're taking a while to bring in some recruits and reorganize the platoons a little bit. It's not anything to be excited about. Just kind of business as usual around here." Milo grew silent, unwilling to say anything more, remembering something painful.

They both focused solely on their plates for a while. The sound of their silverware upon the plastic trays served as the only noise coming from their section of the table.

"So how did you find out vampires were real?" asked Asher, unable to stand the silence any longer. He knew it was better than trying to persuade Milo to tell him about his deceased bunkmate.

"I would rather not talk about it." Milo looked up to speak to Asher directly before immediately turning his attention back to his meal.

"Come on, man, you gotta tell me something." Asher smiled, trying not to sound as though he were pleading. "You haven't wanted to talk about anything. Well, at least not since I started bunking with you. The whole thing about me shooting that vampire in the face with a 9mm is already common knowledge around here. The least you could do is swap stories with me."

Milo sighed, frustrated. "I suppose when you put it that way, I might as well." Even as he said it, he sounded doubtful that he would tell Asher his story.

"OK," said Asher, hoping to lead him into it. "How did it happen?"

"Hey, don't rush me." Milo put up his left hand, stopping the line of questioning. "It's not the easiest story to tell, and I don't care to relive it. I'll tell you. Just give me a minute."

Asher went silent and waited for Milo to go on with his story.

Just when he had nearly given up, Milo looked up from his meal and began. "So I used to be an EMT."

"Tough job. Terrible hours for terrible pay."

"Do you want me to tell the story or not?"

"Oh, sorry, I thought we were having a conversation." Asher's face went red. "Go ahead."

"Anyway, so I used to be an EMT in St. Louis, probably about a year or so ago," Milo continued. He looked blankly at the wall, his thousand-yard stare giving off a dramatic effect. "Me and my partner, Darrell, we used to work mostly downtown. Darrell was supposed to be kind of like my mentor, you know, showing me the ropes. We got this call. Stabbing victim. Not at all out of the ordinary for the particular location. I'm sure the locals wished it wasn't like that, but that's the reality. Anyway, so we head out to rendezvous with the cops and go pick him up. We didn't know there were ferals out."

"Sorry, but what exactly is a 'feral'?" Asher frowned, feeling it was important to the story. "Don't mean to interrupt, I just don't know what you're talking about."

"A feral is a rogue vampire."

Milo stabbed at a hash brown.

"Most of the vampires we kill are part of the organization, but not ferals. They're too animalistic to be involved with them. Can't be trusted to carry out any task without getting sidetracked. Not good for their bottom line. Anyway, most ferals still hunt in groups, but every once in a while you get a loner that's too wild to be part of any hunting party. That's what found us that night."

Milo paused once again, remembering something traumatic. He was affected by some kind of inner pain. He sat there motionless for several seconds.

"Milo," said Asher, trying to pull him out of his trance.

"Yes, what?" Milo asked, suddenly snapping out of the spell.

"So, as you were saying…"

"Oh, sorry." Milo gave him an embarrassed grin. "Well, anyway, on this call, we were already near the location, so we got there way before the cops did. There was no sign of the perp, so we thought we were safe. Well, as safe as we could be in this particular part of town. Me and Darrell, we had a hard time finding the victim. The guy wasn't where they said he was. Not sure if he walked away or what, but we tracked him by following the trail of blood. We found him a couple of blocks away, but there was somebody already there, crouched down, leaning over his body. I thought it was just some ordinary gangbanger at first, but when it looked up at us with those ghostly blue eyes, we knew we weren't dealing with anything human. I had no idea what I was looking at. Just knew I was terrified."

Milo stopped, trying to remember, his magnified eyes wide with intensity.

"He… He came at me first," Milo started again, his voice labored. "Guess I wasn't what he was looking for because he just threw me against a wall and broke a few of my ribs and my arm. Yeah, I know it sounds terrible, but it was nothing compared to what it did to Darrell. He went right for his throat, like they do, and fed. Nearly ripped his head clean off when he tore into him." His voice shook when he spoke, causing him to choke up on his words.

"All I could do was lie there and watch that monster feed, too broken to do anything but scream. Once he got done with Darrell, he got up and started coming back for me. He started walking toward me slowly, just toying with me. He was nearly on me right when I heard a bunch running footsteps. It was an assault group from the Legion. One of the Legion's drones of already had the vampire spotted and called them in. Before I knew it, they blew the filthy vamp's head clean off. His brains and skull fragments splattered all over the place…" Milo finished, trailing off.

"Whoa, that's sure some heavy stuff," said Asher. Sweat had begun to condense on his palms, and the remnants of his meal lay forgotten on his tray.

"Yes, it was." A weary smile crossed Milo's face. "It will haunt me to my grave. I used to have nightmares about it all the time. They only stopped after I began to go on ops for the Legion.

Then I got a whole new set of them."

"I'll say." Asher was certain he would have his own nightmares very soon, finding it strange that he had escaped them thus far.

"After the attack, I was stuffed into my own ambulance and taken to the hospital to treat my injuries," Milo explained. "About a month later, when I was nearly healed back up, Lieutenant Tarango and some other guys from the Legion picked me up and recruited me. It didn't take long for them to convince me to join up. Felt like I owed Darrell at least that much. Hardly left the base since, except to go out on a call." Milo went silent again, the regret in his voice dying away as he stared down at his now-empty tray.

Asher sighed, deciding to end his line of questioning. He was sure he wouldn't be able to convince Milo to say anymore. He turned back to his food. The awkward silence continued for several minutes as he finished his meal.

"Hey, Ash!" A familiar voice suddenly called out.

Asher looked up and was surprised to see Aaron Pritchett walking along the side of the table toward him.

"Oh, hey, Aaron!" Asher exclaimed, surprised. "What's up? I can't tell you how surprised I am to see you."

"Yeah, they told me you would be down here, so I can't say I'm surprised to see you," said Aaron, sitting down across from him. "Just finished up the tour with Lieutenant Tarango and came down here for a late breakfast or lunch or whatever this is."

Aaron briefly glanced to the side at Milo, unsure what to make of his less than cheery body language.

"This is my bunkmate, Milo." Asher tried to make the situation less awkward. "Milo, this is Aaron Pritchett. We used to work together for the St. Louis Police Department."

"Hello, Aaron. It'll be great to have you." Milo suddenly became pleasant and alert. He was genuinely pleased to meet Aaron and offered to shake his hand.

"Yeah, nice to meet you." Aaron accepted his hand to shake.

Milo returned to his usual gloomy, dismal state as Aaron released him. He could only manage the illusion of happiness for moments at a time.

"How did they rope you into all of this?" asked Asher, receiving a blank stare from Aaron. "I didn't think you would be one to respond to people who recruit by kidnapping you first," He suddenly stopped. "Wait, they did kidnap you didn't they?"

"It's kind of interesting that you would ask me that, Ash." Aaron frowned, his demeanor changing from carefree to severe.

Asher stared at him blankly for a moment before he realized what was affecting his mood.

"Why didn't you tell me you had been kidnapped by vampire hunters when you came to see me in the hospital?" Aaron's voice suggested he might snap. "If you would have said something then, you could have saved me a lot of trouble. At least then I would have been prepared for it when they came to grab me."

"Aaron, all I can say is that I'm sorry." Asher gave him the most sincere look he could manage. "I had no idea that they were so extreme in their recruitment. I thought maybe mine was just a special case because I got lucky and killed that vamp."

"Well, you were wrong." Aaron was still steaming. "Sounds like nearly every recruitment kind of happens like that, or at least that's what it looks like."

"How exactly did they grab you?" Asher tried to break the tension.

"They jumped me on the way back home from the hospital last night. Got me just after I got out of the car, before I had a chance to walk through the doors to my apartment building. There was this big, white utility van that pulled up right behind me. I barely had time to close my car door before four guys in body armor jumped out and grabbed me. Shoved a black bag over my head and threw me in the van. Next thing I know, I'm down in the garage tied up, talking to Commander Greaves."

"What all did they do to convince you?" Asher was curious as to how Aaron had submitted to recruitment faster than he had.

"Well, at the start, I didn't want to believe vampires were real in any way at all." Aaron had a kind of cynical squint in his eyes. "I've never really cared for any of that supernatural stuff, and I like to think it took a lot of convincing. Greaves asked me a bunch of questions about what I saw, and I just told him about everything it might have been other than a vampire."

"Yeah, I was about the same way." Asher nodded in solemn agreement. "There's just so many other things it could be attributed to with all our technology these days."

"Greaves kind of changed his tone after he started trying to reason with me."

Aaron took a bite of eggs, grimacing as if he might spit them out.

"He started asking me a bunch of questions about how that vampire moved, asked me if I had any other explanation as to how a human could throw me against a wall and crack my skull. When I couldn't come up with a good enough answer, he brought out a sack with the vampire's head in it. Nasty as heck. Just cut it off and left it in there to rot. As gross as that was, I still wasn't convinced. I told them there was probably something you could do to make a pig's head look like that."

"Yeah, that's pretty much what I told them." Asher smiled, seeing Aaron was in a better mood.

"After that, they tried the whole guilt angle." Aaron chewed a bit of bacon. "Talked about how I needed to think about Hernandez and Nelson. They told me it was my duty to avenge their deaths or whatever. Said they would have wanted me to help rid the world of this vampire menace. That didn't work. It just made me mad that they would put words in dead guys' mouths, especially ones I cared about."

"If they did all that, then how did they convince you to join?" Asher crossed his arms under his chest. "Doesn't seem like there would have been anything else for them to do."

"When I still wasn't buying it, Greaves pulled out a voice recorder of you calling them and saying you wanted to join the Legion." Aaron shrugged. "They told me all about how you killed that thing. About how it was nearly impossible with a 9mm unless you hit 'em in the eyes. I always thought you were no dummy, somebody who could kind of see through people to tell what was real and what wasn't. I never thought of you as someone who would do anything stupid, and I was sure if you were willing to do it, then I might as well too. I was kind of finding being a cop to be a little stale anyway, so I thought, well, what the heck."

"Thanks for that endorsement, Aaron, I guess." Asher

was almost sarcastic, though he was admittedly happy about the prospect of working with someone he knew from before.

"Yeah, we have kind of gotten a little aggressive in our recruitment," Milo chimed in, suddenly becoming part of the conversation, awoken from his daydream. "It didn't use to involve kidnapping, but I guess we're just that desperate now. They didn't use to have anyone above a lieutenant do it either. Must think Greaves is more effective than anyone else, I suppose."

"Yeah, I think they might want to reconsider." Aaron finished his hash brown. "Greaves is a little too aggressive. About kept me from enlisting for sure."

"Well, looks like I'm finished," said Milo, absent-mindedly scraping his fork across his tray, making a grating sound. "I've kind of been lounging around our room all day, and I think it might be time to head out to the range. See you guys later." With that, Milo rose from his seat to return his tray.

"Well, guess I'm off to the range too," said Asher, looking down to find his tray empty, barely remembering he had eaten at all. "Sounds like all they have privates do is arms training until they hook us up with some kind of vampire education course or whatever. They really want us to have some crazy good accuracy." He swung his legs over the other side of his seat, rising to his feet.

"I'll be joining you as soon as I'm done here," said Aaron, taking another bite. "Can't wait to try out one of those X-12's that Greaves likes to harp on so much. I hope the kickback is like he says it is, though. I don't want to get beat up by one of those things."

"Kickback is not bad. I was surprised." Asher turned to leave. "Well, alrighty, I'm off. See you down there, man."

* * *

"Cease fire! Cease fire! Captain on deck!" Asher heard a shrill voice cry out into his headset.

The range was typically mind-numbingly loud from near-ceaseless gunfire. It went silent in an instant as the soldiers put down their weapons and removed their ear protection.

Asher flipped on his weapon's safety and placed his headset down on the shooting booth table, turning to see Captain Kilgore walking along the glass wall behind the shooting lanes. Another young soldier followed closely behind. Asher and Aaron saluted the captain when he approached. Kilgore returned the gesture when he stopped in front of them.

"I have the new assault group assignments, so listen up!" The captain proclaimed, taking a moment to look for Milo and frowning when he found him several lanes down. "Harkman, get over here so you can hear it!" he commanded, stomping his foot impatiently.

"OK," Kilgore continued, looking down at the clipboard as Milo hurried to stand beside Aaron. "I have you guys, that's Harkman, Blackthorn, and Pritchett down for the same assault group."

"But, sir," asked Asher, confused by the announcement. "Aren't there supposed to be four people in an assault group? I mean, I can't imagine you would send us into anything with less than four."

"I was getting to that Blackthorn." Kilgore gave him a sullen look. "There are four men in an assault group in the Legion, bringing me to the point I was trying to make."

The captain turned to the young man standing beside him. The soldier's features were difficult to discern through his helmet.

"This is Corporal Draven Driscoll, and he will be your group leader. We had him transferred over from another company. He needs a group. You need a group leader. It's perfect. We're going to have another bunk moved into Blackthorn and Harkman's quarters. That way we can keep you all together. It's imperative to make sure you're together. It helps to foster cooperation. Or teamwork. Or something..." He looked up at Asher, then at Aaron and Milo, frowning when he saw none of them shared his enthusiasm. "Aren't you going to shake hands?"

He stepped aside so Corporal Driscoll could introduce himself to the group.

"It might help if you would remove your helmet, Corporal."

"Yes, sir," said Driscoll, pulling the helmet from his head, revealing a doughy, pasty-skinned visage. Both his hair and eyes were a dull brown.

"Hey, Corporal." Asher went in to shake Driscoll's hand. "I'm Asher Blackthorn, and this is Aaron Pritchett and

Milo Harkman, our medic." He gritted his teeth on the last syllable, unprepared for Driscoll's deliberate, bone-breaking handshake. It was as though the corporal intended to crush his hand.

Driscoll finally let go of him, moving on to greet Aaron and Milo.

"Well, I suppose since you're now part of this assault group, corporal," said the captain, having failed to see Asher grimace when Driscoll took his hand. "I'll leave you to it then."

"Yes, sir!" Draven saluted Kilgore and then stepped away from the group to retrieve his weapon.

"Just try not to give each other a hard time," said Kilgore, as soon as the corporal was out of earshot. "Not sure Driscoll is going to be the easiest man to follow, but you're just going to have to make it work."

"Yes, sir!" Asher saluted. Aaron and Milo did likewise.

"Well, that's all I got for this group." Kilgore turned to leave. "Got to be moving along. Several other assault groups to assign. They'll give you the all-clear as soon as I finish. I got your assault group assignment right here!" He walked away from them, continuing along the glass wall, barking out orders.

"Dang it! Evans, take off your headset so you can hear me!" the captain yelled as he moved down the line.

Corporal Driscoll reappeared just as Kilgore walked away, taking the empty booth at Asher's left. He had a protective headset in hand, his shotgun slung across his back.

"Sir," said Aaron. He stepped around Asher to where Driscoll stood, determined to improve the corporal's first impression of his new assault group. "Congratulations on your promotion, sir. You must have had to work hard to get it."

"Thank you, Private." Driscoll displayed a genuine smile this time. "I can't say I had to work very hard to advance to corporal. Not sure exactly what I did to get it. I just woke up one day, and they gave me another stripe. Some of my former group leaders liked to say I could clear a room better than anyone. I like to think maybe that had something to do with it."

Probably just looking for any excuse to get rid of you, Asher thought to himself. He leaned against the wall separating his shooting booth from Driscoll's, knowing he should attempt to find an entrance into the conversation.

"Promotion is still a pretty big deal, sir, no matter how you get it," said Aaron. "Just out of curiosity, though, does the Legion ever use any tactics that don't involve room clearance? Don't you ever do anything that doesn't call for boots on the ground?"

"Wow, you guys are new." Driscoll's smirk reappeared. "Aren't they teaching anything in those classes anymore? They were pretty in-depth when I took them, but maybe the instructors have gotten kind of lax."

"Blackthorn and Pritchett are very new, sir," said Milo from where he stood beside Asher, a bespectacled elf next to a giant. "Blackthorn arrived last night, and Pritchett only just this morning."

"OK, I'll just give you some information in advance, Pritchett," said Driscoll. "Yes, we do employ other tactics where we can. Sometimes, if we believe the vamps haven't taken anyone or if we've just found a coven, or nest, of them, we'll just send out a drone and level the place. The Legion doesn't do that itself, of course. We usually have Homeland Security fly one out and take down the target under false pretenses or whatever. That's how we would like it to go down every time if we had the choice. Unfortunately, that method just isn't practical most of the time. Vamps prefer heavily populated areas, places that are kind of hard to bomb, creating delicate situations. The Legion routinely lays down explosive charges on their own to destroy vampire crime scenes, but never as the primary means to deal with vampiric perps. Since the vamps like to attack civilians and usually never gather in numbers large enough to warrant the use of explosives in a fight, our only choice is to use projectile weapons. That's why we rely on room clearance so much."

"I can understand the need to avoid explosives, sir," said Aaron, finding Asher and Milo with similar confused looks on their faces. "What I mean is, do you ever use any projectiles or other non-explosives more powerful than a shotgun? Maybe even something futuristic, like, I don't know, robots with guns too heavy for a man to carry?"

"Ha! Robots!" Driscoll nearly laughed. "The government gives us plenty of funding, but never enough for anything like that. Besides, as far as I know, there aren't any robots quick enough to bring down a vamp."

"So is anyone even trying to develop any new anti-vampire tech at all, sir?" asked Asher, his interest stimulated. He decided he would try to save Aaron from any further underhanded rebuke. "It seems like it would be a major concern by now, you know, since the vampires are such a big problem."

"As far as I know, there still hasn't been much of that going on at the moment," said Driscoll, pausing to think about it. "I'm not an authority on anything like that. Someone could be working on something, I suppose. A lot of the top brass like to make it sound like they have become a major problem, but I don't think their numbers are that high just yet." Driscoll grew quiet, looking past the three gathered around him.

"Here comes the captain," said Aaron, indicating to the others to turn around. All four of them saluted Kilgore as he passed.

"Better get back to your booths," said Driscoll, never afraid to state the obvious. "They'll give an all-clear here in a moment."

"Yes, sir," said Asher. Aaron and Milo joined in, none of the m enthusiastic.

Asher moved from where he stood against the dividing wall and stepped into his booth while the others passed behind him to do likewise. He shoved his headset back on his head with his shotgun at his side as he waited for the all-clear.

"All clear!" shrieked the voice into his headset seconds later. "You are free to resume usual range activities!"

Asher assumed his shooting stance on reflex, a deadeye aim on his paper target's head as he pulled the trigger.

Chapter XII

Up from the Depths

"Lights out at 10:30," said Driscoll, letting the door to Room 17 close behind him.

His entrance caused Asher to look up from where he sat watching TV with Aaron.

"Don't worry. It will only be 10:30 until they put us back on the usual rotation."

Asher produced an audible groan, failing to keep it in.

"What's that, Blackthorn?" asked Driscoll. He remained near the door, his eyes blinking rapidly as though he couldn't believe what he heard.

"Nothing, sir." Asher didn't want to risk a scene and made sure Driscoll didn't see his irritated expression. The corporal wielded his power like a club.

"Come on," Driscoll coaxed. "I know you said something, Blackthorn. I'm not deaf. Let's hear it."

"Trust me, sir," Asher reaffirmed. "It's just a complaint, and you don't need to hear it."

"Try me."

Asher rose from his seat and turned to face the corporal.

Driscoll's eyes narrowed when he looked up at Asher, irritated by his superior height. The light from the TV danced over his face, illuminating his pudgy features in the dark.

"Sir, it's just that I normally crash around like 12:30 or so. It's going to be hard to sleep if I have to go to bed that early. We haven't been required to wake up early yet, so there's no reason to go to bed at 10:30."

"That was then, and this is now," Driscoll's voice was dismissive. "When you're under my command, you will be up at 5 AM for the morning run."

"But, sir," Aaron craned his neck to speak to Driscoll from his seat. "The captain already makes us go for a morning run at 8:30."

"You'll be going on two runs then." Driscoll grew frustrated. "You'll need to be in real good shape if you're going to last long hunting vamps. Trust me, I would know." He looked at Asher as though he stared down a potential attacker. "Aren't you kind of tired, Blackthorn? We had a long day at the range, and then we had to set up that second bunk for Aaron and me. Sure made me tired." His gaze grew less severe as he spoke.

"No, sir," said Asher, barely able to keep from rolling his eyes.

The corporal hadn't lifted a finger to help assemble the second bunk earlier. He had stood by as the others worked, sure to point out their mistakes.

"I must admit that I do not feel tired, or at least any more tired than usual."

"Very well." Driscoll realized he couldn't convince Asher. "Regardless, lights out at 10:30. I hope you don't plan on defying my orders, Blackthorn. I wouldn't want to write you up on my first night as your group leader."

. "I have absolutely no intention of defying your orders, sir," said Asher, flabbergasted by the corporal's insinuation.

"I'm happy to hear that, Private." Driscoll smiled. "We will all get along just fine so long as you do what I tell you."

Asher grew tense over the remark and felt a sudden urge to strike his superior, though he knew he would never dare act on it.

Driscoll turned around and started for the door.

"Where are you going, sir?" Asher crossed his arms over his chest. "That is if you'll allow me to ask."

"I have some business to attend to." Driscoll stood with the door open, failing to produce the volatile response Asher expected. "I should be back at ten at the latest to see if you're all following my orders. I like to lead by example, so you can expect me to be in bed by 10:30 as well. I'll see you later." He remained by the door, motionless, expecting Asher to say something.

"See you later, sir," said Asher at last.

"That's it." Driscoll's smile was sincere this time. "Keep it up, guys, and we'll be a fully functioning assault group in no time." He passed through the doorway, letting the door gently close behind him.

Asher remained where he stood, listening to the corporal's footsteps become more and more distant.

"Ah, that guy." Asher turned to speak to Aaron, confident Driscoll was out of range. "He is insufferable! I hope he's not in charge of us for long. It's going to be tempting to just hand him over to the bloodsuckers."

"Don't say that!" said Milo from out of nowhere, sitting up to speak to them from where he lay on the bottom bunk.

Asher and Aaron turned to look at him, taken aback by his sudden outburst.

Milo set down the book he held and looked over at them, his already large eyes magnified by his glasses.

"OK, yeah," Milo's voice returned to its normal volume. "I know Driscoll is a jerk, but we really should show some respect. I mean, he surely did something to attain a higher rank than us, and I think that in itself deserves at least some respect. We'll just have to give him the benefit of the doubt before we call final judgment. We'll have to learn to get along if we hope to survive. You got to be at your best at all times when you're going after the vamps. It's like they can sense our weaknesses and exploit them. I don't know how many more of my comrades I can see slaughtered."

Milo gazed down at the floor and shook his head.

"Yeah, I suppose you're right," said Asher, ashamed of being so willing to complain moments earlier. "I'll do what he says and try my best to be respectful, but just for the benefit of you guys and everyone else who ends up working with us. I'll just have to get used to it."

"That's more like it." Milo gazed back up at Asher, a kind of glee in his eyes. "I can't say it's the best attitude to have, but it's better than the one you had a second ago. At least it's a start anyway. How about you, Aaron? You OK with Driscoll as group leader?"

"I guess I'll have to be." Aaron shrugged, turning to look at

Milo through the darkness of the room. "I can't do anything about who gets promoted and who ends up assigned to a certain group. As far as I'm concerned, having a superior who you don't really like is just an incentive to do better in the hopes that you can be promoted yourself. Other than that, I'll do whatever it takes to get us all back home in one piece."

With that, their conversation ended, and the tension in the room died away. The lull from the TV was the only noise.

Asher was satisfied. He only wanted to relax and enjoy his time without Driscoll, certain such opportunities would be rare in the future. Asher slunk back over to his seat to continue watching TV with Aaron.

Thud!

Milo closed his book and rose from his bed, heading for the door.

"Where you going, Milo?" asked Aaron. Both he and Asher craned their necks to look at him.

"Nowhere, really." He held the doorknob in his hand. "Kind of feeling riled up. I think I'll go run the track to blow it all off. Might go down to the range and practice since it's open for free shooting."

"Have fun," said Asher, waving goodbye. "Remember Driscoll's curfew. You don't need a wad like him chewing you out."

"Oh, I'll be back way before that." Milo opened the door. "See you guys later."

"Hey, Aaron, I think I'm going to turn in early tonight," said Asher nearly an hour later, preparing to rise from his seat.

"What?" asked Aaron, sounding addled. "Coming right off your standoff with Driscoll? He's not even back yet himself."

"I'm just tired from the sudden change of pace," Asher admitted. "I wasn't going to let Driscoll have the satisfaction of knowing that. Anyway, I went from cop to vampire-hunter-in-training in less than twenty-four hours. It's already starting to wear on me."

He rose from his chair and walked toward the bathroom to change clothing and brush his teeth. He emerged moments later to make his way to the bunk opposite the door.

"I suppose you need me to turn down the TV and stay quiet,"

said Asher as he stepped past Aaron. "You can do whatever you want. Sound doesn't usually get to me. I can sleep through most anything."

"OK, I'll try to be quiet anyway." Aaron pointed the remote a t the TV and turned down the volume.

"Yeah, if you don't mind," said Asher as he climbed onto the top bunk. He took the blanket from the foot of the bed and rolled himself up in it, facing the wall so he wouldn't be bothered. "See you in the morning, man. Bright and freakin' early."

"That's why Driscoll insists on the earlier bedtime. Night, Ash."

Asher yawned, closing his eyes. The light from the TV's LED screen danced upon the bedroom wall. The rise and fall of the voices caused him to drift off into a state of unconsciousness.

* * *

Asher awoke with a start, feeling as though he slept for only a few minutes. He heard a strange sound echoing up from the depths of the underground barracks. He brushed the trappings of sleep away by rubbing his eyes with his fist, listening for the sound.

He wasn't disappointed.

The noise, the unmistakable howls of a pack of canines, and big ones at that, reverberated through the base once more.

Goosebumps popped up all along Asher's back, and his heart rate rose. Terrifying, blood-filled thoughts about the noise-makers raced through his mind. Whatever it was, the sound came from inside the barracks. Asher knew it contradicted every survival instinct he possessed, but he felt an urge to investigate.

"Hey, Aaron, you hear that?" Asher turned over to ask Aaron, who was asleep on the bottom bunk across from him. The howling came to a stop before the words left his tongue.

"Uh… Man, hear what?" Aaron gave him a less-than-friendly answer. "I don't hear anything. You're probably having a nightmare or something. Just go back to sleep. It's like 2:30."

The howling resumed, louder this time, but still requiring a certain amount of concentration to hear it.

"You surely heard it that time," said Asher.

"OK, yeah, I kind of heard it that time." Aaron was up on one arm to speak to him through the dark of the room. "I have no idea

160

what it could be, and I honestly couldn't care less right now. Whatever it is, I don't think it would be anything that can hurt us. Isn't this place supposed to be secure or something?"

"Yeah, I guess you're right." Asher reluctantly rolled himself back up in his blanket to face the wall once again.

The howling started again, just as he closed his eyes.

"OK, that's it," he said, pulling off his blanket to slide from his bunk, his bare feet landing directly on the cold tile floor, nearly causing him to lose his balance. "I've got to find out what's making that noise."

"You just going to go out there in a t-shirt and boxers?" Aaron groaned. "Better hope it's just a dog or something, or all you'll be doing is giving it a nighttime snack."

"That's ridiculous." Asher tried to remember where he put his shoes as his feet felt as though they might freeze to the floor. "Of course I'm not going out there like this. I've got to get my shoes on first."

"Oh, that'll help." Aaron's voice was sarcastic to the core. "Though, I guess if you get desperate, you can throw a shoe and distract whatever it is while you make a run for it."

"My thoughts exactly."

Asher bumbled around the bottom of the bunk, surprised to find Milo still asleep. He discovered his lost shoes only when he nearly tripped over them. He slipped them on, eager to separate his skin from the ice-like tile floor. Asher remained near the bed, crouched down in the darkness as he waited for his eyes to adjust, wanting them to be at their best before he left the room.

Content with his vision, he slowly made his way toward the door, arms outstretched in an attempt to keep from running into something. As he neared the wall, he reached for the doorknob, grasping at the air before his fingers came in contact with the dull, cool metal. He pulled the door open, looking back to see Aaron still lying motionless in the bottom bunk.

"You comin' Aaron?"

Aaron hastily threw his blanket off and sat up in bed to look over at Asher. "Guess I have to, now that you've got me all woke up. Not like I'm going to get much sleep anyway since you won't shut up. Just give me a second, OK?" Aaron stared at his feet for a few moments, rubbing both eyes with his fists, unable to shake the tiredness away.

Just when Asher was sure he was about to have second thoughts, Aaron slowly rose from his bed.

"Dang, this floor is cold," he said, immediately making for the dresser at the other side of the room. "Let me go put on some socks or something."

Asher could have laughed seeing him move, his fellow private looking like a chicken walking a tightrope, making sure his feet made as little contact with the floor as possible.

Finally fed up with the cold, Aaron all but sprinted for the dresser, barely stopping before he slid into it. He yanked open the top drawer and groped for his socks.

"Come on, man, just hurry up." Asher impatiently waited for Aaron to pull on his socks. "The howling could stop at any moment, and then we won't be able to tell where it's coming from." He briefly considered leaving him, concerned that the howling might stop altogether if they didn't leave the room soon.

The howling sounded once more, increased in volume this time, remedying Asher's concern. Milo groaned from the bottom bunk at the opposite wall, acting as though he might wake this time.

"Hurry up, Aaron," Asher hissed, trying to hold his voice down to the softest level possible. "You're going to mess around and wake up Driscoll. He's just waiting for a chance to bawl us out."

"You keep talking this much, and somebody will absolutely hear us," Aaron hissed back, finally finished putting on his socks.

Asher held the door for him as he waited to venture out into the hallway. Asher proceeded through the entryway, the hallway just as void of illumination as the room. Aaron followed, both of them using the now continuous howling that came from underneath the base to guide them down the lightless hallway. They kept as low to the floor as possible, their arms spread wide to avoid running into walls. It was the only way they could move both quickly and quietly through a near pitch-black environment.

They neared the heavy wooden doors that separated the

sleeping quarters from the rest of the base within seconds. Asher held out his palms as he felt for the dense wood. Finding the door, he searched for the handle. The cold metal nearly caused him to pull away as he wrapped his hand around it.

He opened the door, his movements cautious and methodical. Light from the adjacent hallway poured through the ever-widening opening, revealing that the base did indeed stay busy both night and day. Aaron caught hold of the door just as Asher proceeded through the entryway, closing it quietly behind him.

They rushed onward, the two young men in t-shirts and boxer shorts racing down the well-lit hallway, one stomping through in untied shoes and the other sliding around in socked feet. They scrambled past the cafeteria, stopping for only a moment to peer through the open doors. Instant relief washed over them when they found nobody within.

Ding!

The elevator rang as they approached, stopping them in their tracks as the doors slid open. As though on cue, the far-away, underground howling suddenly came to a stop. Before they had time to turn and run in the other direction, the doors slid open and Lieutenant Tarango stepped out.

"What are you doing out of bed?" asked Lieutenant Tarango, his face folded in a deep frown. "Privates aren't allowed access to this area at this time without permission. Sometimes it's allowed in case of emergency, which this isn't." He didn't look upset, though the edge in his voice suggested otherwise.

"Tell you what," the lieutenant continued, a strange, slightly crazed-looking smile forming on his face. "I don't consider being up after hours to be a real big deal so long as you return to your quarters now. I'll just let you off with this warning."

He stopped, and the howling resumed, even louder than before.

"Can't you hear that, sir?" asked Asher, feeling courageous. "We just wanted to figure out what it was, since it's kind of keeping us up."

Aaron looked over at Asher and then at Tarango, expecting the lieutenant to lose his cool.

"Of course I can hear it, Blackthorn." Tarango's frown

returned, revealing his irritation with Asher's question.

"Would you care to tell us what it is, sir?" asked Aaron, directing the lieutenant's attention away from Asher.

"I'm not at liberty to give you that information until the appointed time," said Tarango. "I recommend just getting used to it for the time being."

"It sounds like you have a pack of werewolves chained up in the basement," said Asher, the hairs on the back of his neck stiffening as he spoke. It wasn't the most unlikely of assumptions. "You can at least give us something, you know, so we can sleep at night. I swear we won't tell anyone."

"Absolutely not!" Tarango roared, his rage exploding and his carefree demeanor gone. Angry though he was, the lieutenant only stood looking up at the ceiling, silently counting to ten before continuing. "What's classified is classified, and you have to respect that." His voice went flat as it returned to a regular volume. "There is nothing down there that will harm you, and that ought to be good enough. Now go back to bed before I have to write you up for insubordination. I can't tell you how much I hate filling out that paperwork, but I'll do it if I have to."

Tarango covered his face with his left hand, pointing toward the heavy wooden doors with his right.

"Yes, sir," said Aaron and Asher in unison. They rose to their feet, turning around to start the sullen walk back to their quarters.

"Hey, guys!" Tarango called back to them in his typical pleasant tone, causing them to turn back around. "Hey, no hard feelings." He gave them a genuine grin. "Just don't do it again, and there won't be any problems."

"Yes, sir."

"OK, off to your quarters then."

"Yes, sir," they both said for the last time. They followed the lieutenant's orders, all the while making a mental note to step lightly when they had to be near him.

Chapter XIII

The Kresnik

"Where exactly are we, doctor?" Cyrus yelled into his headset over the mechanical sweeping sound of spinning helicopter blades.

"Once again, Mr. Blackthorn, we are taking you to a training facility," said Dr. Shen, giving the same answer for at least the third time. "It is to be the site of your first field test."

"Yeah, I have that part figured out." Cyrus grew frustrated by the doctor's refusal to crack. "Maybe I should rephrase. Where are we headed in terms of geographic location?" he asked, beginning to grow tired of Shen's side-step response to his questions.

Cyrus had made several subtle attempts to coax their destination out of the doctor over the five-hour helicopter ride and now considered forcing the answers out of him. Only the shock collar around his neck stopped him.

Cyrus suddenly felt eyes upon him and looked across the aisle. Elysia greeted him with a smile.

"Mr. Blackthorn, I am not at liberty to give you that information," Shen explained. "I would think that merely viewing the scenery would reveal enough about our location."

"Whatever."

Cyrus decided to leave Shen alone for the moment and look out the window. He closed his eyes the instant he peered out, the waning light of the setting sun searing into his overly sensitive retinas.

Undeterred, Cyrus opened them once more, ignoring the light's painful intensity as he managed to make out a multitude of green blobs, which he assumed were cacti. He could make out little else. The relatively barren landscape added strength to the sunlight, as all the sand and rocks reflected an intense light.

Cyrus averted his gaze from the window when the savage, scorching pain became unbearable. Dr. Shen had told him he would experience increased sensitivity to light as his transformation neared completion. It was yet another gradual adjustment that Cyrus loathed.

Regardless of the light, he found his first helicopter ride rather enjoyable. The steady, constant spinning of the blades and the gentle motion of the machine moving through the air felt relaxing.

"How about letting protocol slide just this once?" asked Cyrus, resuming his harassment of Dr. Shen. "I'll never be able to figure out where we are just by looking, at least not with my eyes the way they are right now. I only want to know out of curiosity. I swear I won't tell anyone where I was after this 'field test' is over. How could I let any information get out? I'm not allowed to leave any of the facilities you bring me to, and I'm pretty much at your mercy thanks to this shock collar you psychos make me wear. I'm not likely to escape and say anything, at least not any time soon."

"You might as well tell him," said Viddur, glaring at Shen. "It won't matter, and it will finally put an end to all his irritating questions."

The doctor sighed and frowned at Cyrus. "I suppose the odds of such information leaking out are quite minimal. We have no plans to release you from our custody anytime soon, denying you any chance to do so. I suppose there is a small chance you might try to escape, but I don't think you possess the motivation. Even if you did make such an attempt, I highly doubt you would be successful."

"Thanks for your support, doctor." Cyrus showed his fangs and wrapped his now-clawed fingers around his security collar. "Such an escape attempt would be futile." Even though he owed him his life, he grew impatient with the doctor.

Elysia looked over at Cyrus with stern disapproval.

"Very well." The doctor ignored Cyrus's threatening display. "We are currently flying over the Sonoran desert, somewhere outside of Phoenix. Everything else will be revealed once we land, leaving no need to continue this game of questions."

Cyrus let out a yawn, stared down at his feet, and decided to give up on the doctor. Ever since undergoing the procedure, he'd had considerable difficulty sleeping. He knew it was because of his transformation and likely had something to do with his gradual conversion from a diurnal creature into a nocturnal anti-vampire. Cyrus reasoned he probably ought to ask Dr. Shen about it in the future when he was more receptive.

"We're approaching the drop point now, doctor," announced the helicopter pilot, some thirty minutes later.

"Take a look out the window, Cyrus." Elysia smiled at him from across the aisle. "The sun has nearly set. It shouldn't hurt your eyes any longer."

"Let's have a look then." Cyrus tried the window again, his muscles tensed in anticipation of the burning pain, desperate for his first look at their destination.

He was pleasantly surprised. He could see through the low light. His ability to see in the dark had increased tremendously, giving him the capacity to make out the sandy, rugged terrain of the desert below. The landscape held Cyrus's attention for only a moment before the quickly approaching lights distracted him.

"Wow, that is quite the setup." Cyrus scanned over what appeared to be a small town several miles in area, entirely enclosed by an extensive chain-link fence.

"We would like to think so," said Dr. Shen, a proud look on his face as he surveyed the area.

Along the length of the fence stood several guard towers, all of them simple, steel-framed constructions. The whole of their forms lay masked in the dying light. Two additional towers stood among them near the middle of the town, impossible to miss due to their height and the immense amount of light they projected.

The helicopter made its way toward the tower farthest from them, crossing over the various structures. As they flew ever closer to the far tower, the other, smaller and more sparsely lit buildings came into view. Some scattered structures were recognizable as gas stations, stores, houses, and one school building.

"Those towers kind of mess with your eyes," said Viddur.

The two structures grew nearer, revealing themselves to be considerably narrow. The backdrop of the night's sky and their many lights gave them the illusion of girth. The travelers approached the first one, and the bright blue letter H on the landing pad growing ever larger as the helicopter descended.

Four armed guards approached them just as the landing skids touched the ground. The security officers gathered near Cyrus's side of the helicopter. Cyrus spotted a dozen or more guards as he took a more discerning look at the various points along the tower roof, fully automatic weapons in hand.

"Please remove your headset and step outside, Mr. Blackthorn," Dr. Shen instructed once the helicopter blades ceased their rotation.

The screams of what sounded like a group of crazed animals echoed throughout the town below, causing Cyrus to remain seated. He had no desire to be down there in the dark with whatever made those sounds.

"Mr. Blackthorn, I would advise doing what you have been instructed." Shen acted as though he hadn't heard the noise.

"Just do what he says, Cyrus," said Elysia. A pleading concern glistened in her brown eyes.

"Whatever you say, doctor," said Cyrus as he slid the door open. He took off his headset and handed it to Shen.

The guards moved in closer as he climbed out, their guns trained upon him. All four red laser pointers steadied on his forehead.

Beads of sweat formed on the back of Cyrus's neck. He supposed their guns might only contain rubber bullets, but he didn't want to take a chance to find out.

"I'll try to make this brief, Mr. Blackthorn," said Shen, remaining in the helicopter.

"Exactly what kind of 'field test' is this?" Cyrus spoke to Shen through the helicopter's open door, careful not to appear threatening in the presence of the tower guards.

"We call it a 'survivability' test. It is a test to see if you can survive a dire situation without the benefit of being properly supplied with food, water, equipment, and proper shelter. Essentially, we want to assess your ability to survive in the 'wild' among the creatures you have been designed to hunt."

"What kind of place is this?" asked Cyrus. He knew the

doctor would fail to give him full answers but decided to test his luck anyway. "I mean, are we dealing with a town that's experiencing an outbreak of zombie-ism that the government has covered up or…"

"It is a life-sized model of a town designed to simulate a zombie-ism outbreak among the local populace." Shen's voice was devoid of emotion. "It's a mock-up of a hypothetical disaster situation, complete with actual infected individuals captured from various areas of the country. Don't worry, Mr. Blackthorn. You have been made immune to their bites."

Cyrus found the doctor's answer dubious at best. Shen's aversion to his gaze was disconcerting. He briefly considered asking some follow-up questions but quickly decided against it, believing he was fortunate to receive what little information Shen cared to give out.

"So it's pretty much a zombie Jurassic Park down there."

The dumb smile on Shen's face seemed out of character. "Yes, I suppose that is an accurate enough statement. However, the infected haven't escaped to run amok. The test will be considered a success if you both survive for the allotted time and meet us back at the exit pad at the appointed time." Shen shifted gears. "In this case, the time will be one month from now at sundown."

"What do you expect me to do for food?" The proposed timeframe left Cyrus dumbfounded, and he was unsure how much he should protest.

"Whatever you can," answered Shen. "This site is meant to be a replica of any small Arizona town right down to the houses, stores, and gas stations. Though I doubt you'll be able to find much in any of those places. Most of the food will likely have spoiled due to the high temperatures. In order to obtain nutrition, you will have to do things you are uncomfortable with. Eat things you normally wouldn't think to eat. Don't expect to go without eating either. Due to the strict diet that we've kept you on, along with your now rapid metabolism, going without nourishment would be most unwise."

"How do you expect me to survive when there isn't any food?" Cyrus shouted, showing his teeth and wishing he could take hold of Shen.

The guards pressed in closer, recognizing the glint in his

eyes.

"So you're just going to leave me out here in the middle of nowhere with no food or equipment or anything?" Cyrus asked with a hushed tone, his rage still simmering.

"That would be the idea." Shen nodded. "It wouldn't be a proper survivability field test if you were appropriately equipped or provided food. You need to scavenge what you can in order to survive. As I said, 'survivability' probably isn't the best word to use. Our board of directors simply thought calling it a 'scavenge or die' test was a little disconcerting."

"Maybe this will help," said Viddur, speaking over the doctor. He pulled something out of his tracksuit pocket and slung it out of the helicopter.

The object slid across the ground and hit Cyrus in the foot. It was an odd-shaped knife, its blade curving away from the handle near its base.

"What the heck kind of knife is this?" Cyrus squatted down to pick it up, holding it in front of him to scrutinize the blade.

The guards moved in even closer when they saw him pick up the weapon, muscles taut as they held their firearms.

"It's an inverted bread knife." Viddur gave Cyrus a maniacal grin. "I stole it from one of the kitchens the other day."

Elysia groaned, putting her palm to her forehead, disappointed but not surprised by her brother's thievery.

"Thanks," said Cyrus as he rose to his feet. "It's not much of a weapon, though. Do you really expect me to kill zombies with it?"

"Since it's all you have, I'm sure you'll make it work." Viddur found humor in Cyrus's situation. "It should be as useful as any other kind of knife. I did bother to sharpen it for you."

"Yes, I suppose it is much better than nothing," said Cyrus, shoving the knife into his waistband.

"One word of advice, though," Viddur continued. "The only real way to be absolutely certain that you have killed one of the infected is to separate the head from the body. I came up with the moniker 'remove its head and make it dead.'"

"Brilliant." Cyrus frowned.

"Mr. Blackthorn," said Shen. His voice was severe, as though he were chastising a small child. "The CyberGen board of directors has ordered me not to allow you into the facility with a weapon." Shen's serious edge suddenly disappeared, replaced by a broad grin. "I have decided to allow this small infraction. The board likely won't be happy with me should they find out, but I suppose if having a small weapon like that knife helps you to survive the test, then so be it. Your survival means they keep their asset, and they can't argue with that. You likely won't need it anyway. Your new abilities have developed to the point that you will no longer need a weapon."

The infected screamed up from below, interrupting the relative calm.

"And that brings me to my next point." Shen referred to the screams. "Keep in mind, the immediate disposal of the infected is secondary to the rest of your concerns at this point. I would advise you to find shelter before the sun comes up. Due to your increased metabolism, I assume you will be alright over the cold nights, but I don't believe it would be a good idea to overexpose yourself to the light and heat of the sun. There is an obvious need for caution. Both you and the infected are mostly nocturnal, and you will likely be at odds over the course of your test. You will compete with the infected for nearly every resource except food, which has been provided for them."

"I have no intention of killing anyone down there if I can help it," Cyrus stopped the doctor from going off on a tangent as he anticipated the next argument. "I know I asked for a weapon, but I have no intention of using it on anyone unless I absolutely have to." Even as he uttered the words, Cyrus doubted he could last a month without killing once, at least.

"That is a noble ambition." Shen scoffed at the notion. "Unfortunately, the avoidance of killing would be most unwise in this scenario. Your best chance of survival is to kill as often as possible. Ideally, they will come to fear you. If they recognize you as the apex predator that you are destined to be, they will avoid you, and you'll have fewer dangerous encounters with them."

"You can say whatever you want, doctor." Cyrus's tone remained calm but defiant. "Besides, I'm not saying I would never kill one of the 'infected.' If I'm placed in a situation where it's them or me, you can bet I'll do whatever I can to make sure it's them and not me. I will kill to survive. What I mean is that I won't seek them out to kill them. You call it whatever you want, but I feel that constitutes murder, whether they're infected or not."

"Unfortunately, the lines of morality will likely blur given the situation. Make no mistake, Mr. Blackthorn, I am not trying to persuade you that murder is an acceptable practice, but in this instance, whatever killing you do is an act of mercy. Think of the infected as already dead. Their minds are gone and, with no effective vaccine, there is little chance they will ever be restored to their original state. They are mockeries of their former selves now, destined to wander the land searching for subsistence from the most morally reprehensible source imaginable. To refrain from killing them would be to deny them a dignified end, leaving them to a fate worse than death."

"Yeah, I suppose when you put it like that, it's really the right thing to do." Cyrus scratched the back of his head.

"I highly doubt you will even be able to stop yourself from killing them. You were designed to be a predator specializing in only two types of prey: the zombie and the vampire. On the positive side, all the killing you do will be instinctual, and it's unlikely you will remember any of it. Regardless, in order for us to have an accurate picture of your enhanced abilities, the test demands that you make several kills. If you don't kill, it will throw off the test, and we won't have any footage to assess. The procedure will have to be repeated. I know none of us want that to happen, especially you."

"How exactly do you plan on recording any of this, doctor?"

"The collar around your neck has been fitted with several, nearly undetectable, cameras that will monitor everything you do."

"And just how long have these cameras around my neck been functioning? Surely not from the beginning." Cyrus gave Shen a look of uncertainty.

"The cameras will be functional as soon as we leave the landing pad."

Shen caused a smug smile to appear on Cyrus's face. No matter what he said, there was never any guarantee he told the truth.

"All it requires is that I press a button," said the doctor.

"So, is this all the information you can give me, or do you have more?"

"Oh, yes, I nearly forgot." Shen pushed his glasses back up his nose. "As we approached the landing pad, I'm sure you saw several guard towers around the fence. They're easy to spot as lit up as they are. Anyway, it is advisable that you avoid them. You will be fired upon should you dare approach the fence or guard towers. Such an action will be seen as an attempt at escape."

"None of you seem to trust me much," said Cyrus.

At the mention of trust, the guards around him leaned in closer, their posture becoming even more wary and rigid. Cyrus knew it was irrational for CyberGen to blow him away without just cause, but keeping the guards so close to him was too much.

"Mr. Blackthorn, if it were my decision, your collar would be removed, and the guards would be instructed to avoid you. The fact of the matter is that you are a potentially dangerous genetically modified organism, and several important individuals within CyberGen would rather not take the risk. We're not exactly sure how we ought to treat a being such as yourself. As a general rule, the more tasks and tests that you successfully complete for us, the more we will trust you."

"Will the guards be firing on the infected as well?" asked Cyrus.

"Of course. We cannot risk any of the infected being released into the populace. That's one of the reasons why this facility is in such a remote location."

"Sir!" One of the guards from the tower's perimeter shouted at Shen, dashing to the helicopter. "We need you to wrap it up! We are running behind schedule."

"I'll not keep you much longer." Shen remained calm, despite the guard's haste. "I just have to make sure Mr. Blackthorn knows exactly what he needs to do to complete the test."

"Do you see the tower over there, diagonal to our position?" Shen pointed to the far end of the facility at the tower dominating the nightscape.

"It's impossible to miss," said Cyrus.

"That will be the retrieval point, Mr. Blackthorn. When we return to retrieve you in a month's time, we will pick you up at that tower. Until the retrieval time, you must remain within the perimeter of the fence and survive on whatever resources you can find. As I have said, failure to stay within the perimeter could result in your permanent termination. There are a number of infected individuals within this facility with whom you will compete for survival. You are permitted to do with them what you wish. Failure to adhere to the test regulations will result in the collection of unusable data, and the test will be repeated. Failure to survive is indicative of a failed test, though we will still learn something from the collected data. Obviously, we cannot repeat the test if that happens. To achieve a positive result, it is required that you survive to be retrieved within the time allotted. Do you understand these instructions as they have been given?"

"Yes, I do."

"Sir, the sun has nearly set," said the guard to Shen, intent on rushing them. "We need to get the kresnik off the tower now."

He nodded at Cyrus when he said the word 'kresnik.'

Cyrus frowned, unsure as to what exactly the guard had called him. The word itself was benign enough. Regardless, he didn't feel as though it was an insult. Instead, there was power in the word. He liked it.

Cyrus turned toward the guard and smiled, displaying his prominent fangs. The man winced.

"Now then," said Shen, as Cyrus turned to face him through the helicopter's open door. "I have told you all I can. These men will escort you to this tower's exit point, that ladder over there, and monitor you as you climb down."

The armed guards moved in on Cyrus as the doctor spoke, guns still fixed on his forehead.

"Why do I need to exit the tower from a ladder?" Cyrus asked, hesitant to move. "It's like ten or more stories from up here to the ground, isn't there some kind of elevator?"

"There is indeed an elevator," said Shen. "Only certain personnel are permitted to use it. It is to be used sparingly, lest the infected somehow learn to enter it and access the tower. They're not coordinated enough to climb a ladder."

"Whatever you say."

Cyrus turned toward the ladder to find the

guards standing even closer. They were now so near him that they could prod him with the barrels of their guns.

"Let's get on with it." Cyrus grew anxious.

"Right this way." The guard in front of him stepped to the side so he could proceed through.

"Be careful, Cyrus!" shouted Elysia as he walked away. She had finally escaped the silent spell that enthralled her every time Shen spoke at length.

"I'll try, but no promises!"

"Please remain calm, sir!" A guard shouted at Cyrus, as though he might pull the trigger of his weapon if he didn't have a coronary first.

All four guards followed closely behind Cyrus as he made his way toward the ladder. The caution they displayed elevated to near ridiculousness. One of them passed in front of Cyrus, hastily unlocking and then pushing open the heavy gate which separated the cage-encompassed ladder from the rest of the tower roof.

"Proceed," said the guard, motioning Cyrus through the gate with his gun.

The guard slammed the gate shut behind him without warning, causing Cyrus to stiffen from surprise. He turned around to see the man produce a large set of keys, hurriedly selecting one and shoving it into the keyhole.

"Now this gate is shut," said the guard. He looked up at Cyrus, the lock snapping into place as he turned the key. "You will not be allowed to re-enter. You will be allowed to exit the tower, but only after the test's one-month time period has elapsed."

"Whatever you say." Cyrus sneered at the man, irritated by his unnecessary hostility.

"Get a move on!" The guard aggressively aimed his gun at him. "I won't hesitate to shoot! I don't care how much you're worth!"

"Chill out," Cyrus frowned at the man with exasperation. "I'm going."

He proceeded toward the ladder, turning back around to begin his descent, disappearing beneath the tower wall. Modest though the height was, a kind of mild vertigo instantly struck him. The distance to the ground felt nearly infinite. Cyrus closed his eyes as he faced the wall, hoping maybe that would help cool his nerves as he made his way down.

"One foot in front of the other," he said as he steadied himself on the ladder. It had been a long time since Cyrus had climbed down anything, and he was less than eager to re-learn the process at such a height.

As he descended the rungs, he was pleasantly surprised by how quickly he took to climbing. The physical movements came much easier than he anticipated. Cyrus's apprehension rested in his psyche alone. As he continued ever downward, the urge to look below became increasingly intense. He felt as though the climb down lasted for an eternity.

Unable to wait any longer, Cyrus stopped, slowly opening his eyes to let out an audible sigh of relief. He was now far enough down the ladder that a fall likely wouldn't result in serious injury. Several of the town's denizens screamed up from below, causing Cyrus to freeze and briefly consider an ascent back up the ladder. He would rather take his chances with the guards and their guns.

"I doubt I'll ever get used to that," Cyrus muttered, looking over his shoulder both ways while seeing no sign of nearby attackers. Hearing no more additional noise, he continued his descent, quickly reaching the bottom rung and jumping from the ladder.

Landing firmly on his feet, Cyrus ran for the nearest alleyway across from the tower. An assailant might lurk somewhere along the narrow passage, but it had to be safer than continuing down the street in the open. Behind his cover, he put his back against one of the walls and slowly peered around the corner.

The sun had wholly vanished below the horizon now. The tower at the other end of the facility pulled at Cyrus's eyes. Its brilliant lighting and immense height dominated his view of the blackened sky. It wasn't all that far away from the starting point and conveyed a sense of security and comfort within its walls. Despite what feelings the tower radiated, seeing it still put Cyrus on edge. Its proximity alluded to spending a month confined in a small area with a limited number of hiding places.

Survival would be difficult; the horde of bloodthirsty infected providing only one potential cause of death along with heat exposure, thirst, and starvation. Cyrus needed to find shelter and nourishment as quickly as possible.

He shifted his gaze away from the tower, and his eyes landed on the busted gas station light further down the street on his left, one of the bulbs inside flicking on and off at random intervals.

"Here's hoping there's not a nest of them in there," Cyrus muttered.

He sprang from his hiding place, rapidly zigzagging his way down the street, bounding between alleyways as he made for the gas station. He tried to stay low to the ground as he moved, trying to remain inconspicuous. His vision, though advanced above average, was like unto that of most nocturnal animals. Cyrus could not detect color in low light, everything appearing in black and white, the images crisp and clear. The gas station sign signaled to him like a beacon, calling him forth.

Cyrus crept past the sign and gas pumps to approach the front of the station. He cautiously peered at the building, a chill filling the air as he looked in, half expecting something to jump out at him.

"No good," he said. He found the windows shattered and the inside darkened, everything scattered and broken.

Whatever food there was within likely had either spoiled or been trampled underfoot long ago. Even discounting the food, the station would make an inadequate shelter sitting out in the open as it was. The building appeared void of occupants, and the lack of noise suggested safety. It remained eerie regardless, as if there was something skulking about in the shadows nearby.

Cyrus considered entering the building through one of the broken windows but took the thought back almost immediately. He knew he would only waste time if he stopped to sift through the debris.

Disappointed but not surprised, Cyrus stealthily slunk back across the street to look for something more promising. He needed to find shelter soon. It was a matter of time before he came upon one of the infected, or worse, a group of them.

Cyrus continued down the street using his sneak-between-houses method for a considerable length of time. He found the rest of the buildings even less promising than the gas station. All of them were in shambles, grievously dilapidated and burnt or simply boarded up.

"There we go," he muttered when he found another potential food stash location, this time a grocery store.

The building was well-lit from the outside, just as the gas station had been.

Desperate, Cyrus moved in for a closer look, forgetting his cautious movements to sprint down the open street. He was upon the building in seconds, covering even more ground when he saw the structure remained intact through transparent windows. He found the interior lit up as brightly as the exterior.

Cyrus rushed into the abandoned grocery store, the automatic doors sliding open. He immediately regretted stepping foot inside.

The place smelled like an unholy union of rancid, spoiled food and an excess of human excrement. The stench could melt his eyeballs. The store's undamaged lighting system had deceived him. The overturned shelves lay extensively ransacked with whole packages of food thrown to the ground and smashed. The culprits had no interest in their contents.

Cyrus immediately realized his chances of finding something edible were slim, but he decided to forage anyway. It was still more promising than the gas station, despite the smell and wasted food. Knowing he was foolish to run down the street moments ago, Cyrus returned to his cautious stance, going low to the ground as he began his search.

He took only a few steps before a flash of red caught his eye, his color vision returned under the store lights. Turning towards what he saw in his peripheral, Cyrus spotted the bright red plastic wheels of an overturned dessert snack cart, this fallen near the end of a nearby aisle.

"Looks promising." He hoped to find non-perishable, plastic-wrapped snack cakes just around the corner. "Stupid things got no respect for a Twinkie," Cyrus said aloud for all to hear, frustrated.

Something had already been at the snack cakes, smashing the sweet desserts to mush without even attempting to eat them. Cyrus bent down and picked up one of the cakes, holding it in his hands like a dead puppy.

He let the crushed dessert fall to the ground when he heard

the sound of heavy, frantically running footsteps of an unknown creature striking the floor and scrambling around the aisles.

Cyrus jumped, turning from where he stood to see the creature staring at him from the opposite end of the aisle as it sized him up. It was one of the infected, man-shaped with yellow-green postulated skin, its filthy clothing in tatters, rotting off its body. All similarities ended there. Its features were much more bestial and simian than the zombies Cyrus had seen at CyberGen. The beast was incapable of maintaining normal human posture, down on all fours, walking on the knuckles of its oversized hands, its arms long and lanky yet impressively muscled. Its face was the most unlike a man's. Its mouth was remarkably large, its nostrils like that of a gorilla, and its eyes red like a demon.

The thing pushed down on its knuckles and roared, revealing rows of sharp, shark-like teeth. The beast rushed at Cyrus, barely giving him a chance to reach for his knife as it barreled into him, sending him flying toward the wall at his back. The creature lunged for him, diving for his soft, gasping throat.

Cyrus was ready this time and pushed up at his attacker with all four limbs just as it went for him. He shoved the creature off to the side with all his strength and threw it into the shelves nearby.

Cyrus leaped to his feet, slowly turning his head to the side to find a second creature waiting for him at the end of the aisle. Anticipating its attack, he pulled the knife from his waistband and brandished it as the creature charged at him.

It roared, jumping for him, its snake-like jaw opened wide.

Like a flash of light, Cyrus stepped to the side and out of the creature's path, jamming the knife between its eyes, all in a motion so quick it surprised him. The second creature fell to the ground, the knife buried in its face, just as the first emerged from the overturned shelf.

It bellowed at Cyrus just as before, rushing for him as it sought another chance to tear into his throat.

Taking advantage of his newfound speed, Cyrus slid to the side before the beast could make contact and turned around as it made for him. He drove his elbow into the base of its neck and slammed its body to the ground. He dove at the creature as it fell, firmly pinning it down from behind.

The creature howled, violently jerking and writhing as he fought desperately to hold it there.

Cyrus screamed as a strange urge struck him. Pure instinct overtook his mind.

Before he could stop himself, he bit into the creature's neck, tearing into it with his now formidable jaws. The dark black blood poured onto the floor like thickened wine. He continued to hold the creature's throat firmly in his mouth, driving his fangs farther into it. He shook the thing's head around for good measure.

The monster slowly went limp as its wretched life ebbed away.

Cyrus retched, realizing what he had done. He released the creature's neck from his jaws, its viscous blood falling from his mouth in great globs. Repulsed, he sat down beside the body, the urgency of his situation melting away. The action had been so instinctual, so immediate and tenacious. It was as though he had become a machine that had no choice but to perform the order given it.

Reality seeped back in, and Cyrus impulsively touched a hand to his mouth. He had ingested much of the creature's blood, his palm soaked by the black fluid.

He groaned, trying to stay calm as he looked around to find himself sitting in an enormous puddle of the creature's blood. He frantically scooted across the floor away from the body, wanting to cry out hysterically but refraining from it, fearful he might alert other nearby creatures. The stress made him feel sick.

Cyrus gagged on the creature's rancid, black blood, coughing heavily, spewing it all over the floor in a torrent. He continued to vomit violently for a few moments more, the oil-like blood finally giving rise to just saliva.

Thoroughly disgusted, Cyrus slowly rose to his feet and walked toward the first downed creature, feeling a need to review his work. Though he staked the knife deep into its skull, he remembered what Viddur told him earlier. He needed to separate its head from the spinal column to ensure it was dead.

Cyrus pulled the knife from the creature's skull and began sawing through its thick neck. The blade barely cut through the skin, and while he appreciated Viddur's gift to him, it was much better suited for slicing bread.

The horde of bloodthirsty creatures cried from somewhere outside the store as Cyrus reached the downed creature's spine with his knife.

"Must be time to go." Cyrus dropped his knife and sprinted toward the nearest window at the front of the store. "Oh... that's not good," he muttered as he looked through the window.

He found a mass gathering of creatures bounding toward the store from nearly all sides. Many of them were gorilla-like, similar to the two he had killed, while the rest of them were smaller, more like chimpanzees or orangutans. Their wild, shrill screams reached a deafening volume now, their numbers far too great for Cyrus to do anything but flee. He ran back toward the other end of the store, searching for the double doors leading to the storage area and hoping they might provide passage to the outside.

Frustrated, Cyrus looked through the small windows of the swinging doors and found them blocked by several heavy overturned shelves. He dashed back to the front in a breakneck sprint, skidding to a stop on the claws of his feet as he took a last look out the window. The creatures pressed in close, eager to turn the store into a tomb of Cyrus's own choosing.

"Here we go..." Cyrus hesitated only for a moment before leaping headlong through the window.

Glass flew everywhere as he tucked and rolled into it, bowling over several members of the attacking mob.

Cyrus jumped to his feet. He spread his arms wide as he tore through the assembly, slashing faces and throats as he went. The force of the massive horde was on him, and his only hope for survival to hack and slash his way through lest the demented creatures catch hold of him. The human part of his consciousness disappeared again as he fought like a caged animal, barely tearing his way through the overwhelming infected gathering.

Just when it appeared that the crowd would engulf him, he pushed into them with every ounce of strength he possessed, bulldozing through the throng of monsters. Free from the grasp of the crazed mob, he ran for the nearest building and leaped onto the roof.

The beasts called after him, giving chase.

Cyrus ignored them as he bounded from roof to roof, never thinking to look back.

The sound of feet and knuckles struck both shingles and ground.

Given their physical forms, Cyrus wasn't surprised that they could climb onto roofs as well. He just hoped that the addition of added obstacles would give him a chance to outdistance them.

Cyrus moved across the moonlit skyline at a pell-mell sprint, the fence perimeter becoming visible in the distance. A thought entered his head. If he could lure his pursuers to one of the towers around the fence and within range of the guard's guns, he would all but guarantee his escape, so long as he could keep from being hit himself.

As he considered the insane idea, he noticed the noise of his pursuers had ceased. Their howls had quieted, and their footsteps had stilled. He knew he couldn't run forever.

Cyrus slowed to a stop and turned to look back for the mob. He nearly dropped to his knees, relieved when he saw the monsters had vanished from his sight. Having outdistanced his pursuers, he decided against remaining on the roof. Cyrus dropped from it onto the ground as he abandoned all thought of luring the creatures within range of tower fire.

Hidden in the darkness under the shadow of the replicated town's buildings, Cyrus re-assumed his stealthy movements. He systematically and silently zigzagged through the alleyways, carefully peering around every corner as he went. He could almost believe the infected, or whatever they were, had vanished from the facility altogether as quiet as the place had become. With his heart rate slowly slackening, Cyrus was exhausted from the stress of the chase and decided to sit down against the wall of the nearest house to catch his breath.

"If they ever were human, they certainly aren't now," he mumbled in the dark. Regardless of his adversary's species, he needed to find shelter and at least some morsel of safe food before the morning. "It's going to be a long month."

Cyrus rose to his feet and slinked off into the surrounding darkness, the blue-white crescent moon hanging above amidst the magnificent lights of the towers.

Chapter XIV

Jaws of Justice

Asher and Aaron took the lead, a silent Milo following behind them as they strolled through the base's barren hallways. The three of them made their way toward the classrooms.

"What do you think Tarango's going to talk about this time, Ash?" asked Aaron, a mischievous grin on his face.

Asher frowned at Aaron. "Geez... I sure hope it's not room clearing tactics this time." Asher shook his head. He had grown bored with the routine in the past few weeks, tired of all the arms training, workouts, and incredibly redundant tactical classes. "I didn't get enough of that in the Army."

"Haha," Aaron chuckled. "Yeah, never get enough of it."

"Yeah, Milo, what..." Asher felt Milo's hand on his shoulder. They all stopped outside their classroom, having almost missed their destination.

Asher looked up to see Commander Greaves sitting on the instructor's desk, gazing back at them through his sunglasses, waving them through the open door.

"Hello, sir," said Aaron, strolling into the classroom in front of Asher. "This is Lieutenant Tarango's class. What are you doing here?"

"Just take a seat, Private," Greaves commanded, his voice casual. "There will be no class today. I have to show yuh something. Taking you on a field trip down to the basement."

"Yes, sir," said Aaron as he took a seat near the center of the room.

Asher took the desk beside him, scanning the plain room and

finding it empty except for the four of them.

"Whatever you planned for us, sir, I'm sure it will be much more interesting than what Tarango has been giving us lately," said Milo. He stepped around Asher and Aaron to take a seat near the front of the room.

"It really would be nice if the rest of you had Harkman's attitude," Greaves noted. "Sure beats all the sass from you and Blackthorn."

"Whatever you say, sir," said Aaron. Greaves's ridicule had no effect on him.

Asher grinned but said nothing, not wanting to push the commander out of his good humor, degrading comments aside.

"So exactly what's in the basement, sir?" Aaron asked, genuinely curious, though his scheming smile had returned.

"Oh, not a whole lot." Greaves shrugged. "Just a new weapon we plan on trying out here real soon."

"Got something cool for us to look at down there, sir?" Aaron pried. "Mind telling us what it is?"

"You can ask all you want, but that's all you'll get out of me until we get down to the basement."

With that, Aaron ceased his questioning while the rest of their platoon slowly filtered into the room. Asher might have spoken to some of the privates now entering, but as their training was very involved and four-man-centric, he saw little of anyone except the company officers and the other members of his assault group. He had always thought of himself as a friendly person, and the lack of social interaction was strange to him.

Asher looked up to see Sergeant Ito smile at him from where she stood at the front of the room with some other officers. He had missed her entrance.

"Hey, guys. Guess I'll be joining you today."

Asher turned to find Driscoll taking the seat beside him.

We can never shake this guy, he thought to himself.

"Oh, hey, Corporal, sir." Asher rolled his eyes but kept his head down so Driscoll couldn't see.

"Greaves has something special to show us," said Driscoll enthusiastically. "A new weapon, he said. That's exciting. We haven't gotten any of those for a while."

"OK, looks like most of you are here now," said Greaves, rescuing Asher from Driscoll. "For those of you just arriving, I have taken the lieutenant's class this afternoon. I have something to show you down in the basement."

A flurry of hands shot into the air just before Greaves finished his last word.

"OK, just cool it a while," said the commander, waving the hands down. "Does anyone have a question that isn't about what I'm taking you to see?"

Lieutenant Tarango suddenly burst into the room in a huff.

"Well, hello, Lieutenant, nice of you to show up," taunted Greaves. "Just because I'm in charge of your class this afternoon doesn't give you an excuse to be late."

"Sorry, sir," said Tarango, his speech labored. "Just running a little late." He remained at the back of the room.

"Let's get going then," said Greaves. He rose from his perch atop the desk and ambled toward the door. Once out in the hall, Greaves stood to the side of the doorway, waiting as the room's occupants slowly filtered back into the hallway.

"Just walk down to the end of the hall over there," he said. "I'll take you around the corner and show you where the door is. The precise location of the basement is supposed to be classified, and I assume most of you have no idea where it is. Come on! Look alive, guys!" Greaves shouted. "You ought to be excited about what I'm going to show you! It's going to make all of our lives easier!"

"And here is the door to the basement," said Greaves sometime later when the group stopped in front of a heavily reinforced door.

Asher felt like they had walked forever, rounding corner after corner like rats in a maze. All of the base's hallways looked virtually identical, and he wondered if the commander knew where he was leading them.

"Just give me a moment to find the key..." Greaves took the ring from his belt and sorted through the keys before finally settling on a single one. "Here we go," he said, shoving the desired key into the lock, twisting it around before taking it out again.

The commander grunted as he turned the handle. He pushed the door open with a considerable amount of effort. Greaves turned around to hold it in place as he addressed the platoon.

"I need everyone to remain quiet while we're down there," he spoke nearly at a whisper. "They're not supposed to be dangerous to us, but as far as I know, they haven't been around large groups much. I just don't want to spook 'em."

Greaves glared at the platoon expectantly, motioning them to pass through the doorway. He frowned when all of the soldiers remained stationary, none wanting to go first. "Well, don't everybody run through the door all at once," he said, slapping his palm over his bald head and sliding it down his neck.

Everyone in the platoon tried to look as inconspicuous as possible.

"Let's not get excited. I don't want a stampede."

A loud howl from the basement disrupted the tranquility. It was the same howl Asher had heard every night for the past three weeks.

"I never thought I would see the day that I had to make a bunch of professional vampire hunters go down a dark stairway on their own base." Greaves pretended the noise hadn't happened.

"Sir, the fact that we are vampire hunters makes us leerier of dark passageways," said Tarango from the other end of their procession. "Personally, I've forgotten the last time I went down a dark stairway and didn't find something that wanted to kill me at the bottom."

"Oh, there you are, Lieutenant Tarango." A devious grin formed on Greaves's face. "Why don't you go down there first to make up for your tardiness?" He looked at the lieutenant expectantly.

Tarango didn't share his level of enthusiasm.

"Come on, you already have the advantage of knowing what's down there," Greaves reassured him. "Show the troops that their ol' lieutenant ain't scared of nothin'."

"Whatever you say, sir," sighed Tarango before reluctantly pushing his way through the huddled platoon. "Didn't care for them the last time I was down there," he mumbled, passing by Asher. The lieutenant proceeded through the doorway into the darkness, grumbling as he went.

"Hey, grab those lights while you're in there, Lieutenant!"

Greaves yelled back at him.

The light on the other side of the doorway flipped on, revealing nothing but the same bare, concrete walls within.

"Just try to remain quiet," Greaves reminded his troops, waving them onward through the door. "They're not designed to be aggressive towards humans, but let's not take any chances."

"Sir, are you going to tell us what these things are?" asked Asher, tired of the commander's coaxing. "You keep telling us how they don't attack humans, yet you insist on being cautious."

"Shut up, Blackthorn!" Greaves's good mood evaporated instantly. "It's bad enough that Tarango's being a wimp! I don't need you asking stupid questions and scaring people!"

Asher's cheeks flushed red, both from anger and embarrassment from Greaves' singling him out. He had only said what everyone else was thinking.

"OK, then, everyone down into the basement, and that's an order." Greaves waved everyone through the door.

The hair on Asher's neck stood on end as he and the rest of the group passed through the opening. The heavy metal door slammed shut behind them.

Greaves engaged the lock, sealing them into what felt like a tomb. "Just got to get the other light over here real quick."

The commander passed by Tarango, the lieutenant standing against an unadorned wall.

"Try not to be alarmed when you see them," Greaves continued, fumbling around as he found the switch. "They're quite a sight, especially when you see them caged down here. OK, Here we go."

Greaves disappeared around the corner, Milo right behind him and the rest following after. The concrete floor gave way to a metal mesh walkway overlooking the lower part of the basement. Greaves led them into what looked like a squared-off, empty cavern overlooking a ravine. Strings of lights hung from the uneven, rugged walls and illuminated the place.

"Holy!" Milo nearly yelled as he looked over the railing.

"Harkman!" shouted the commander, forgetting what he had said earlier. "I would expect it from Blackthorn or Pritchett, but not you!"

Asher gazed downward from where he stood on the walkway to find the source of Milo's surprise.

He saw two dozen or so massive dogs at the bottom of the basement's fifty-foot ravine, all of a breed he did not recognize. Each was taller than a Great Dane and possessed twice the muscle. Their dark, shaggy hair, piercing eyes, and colossal jaws gave them the look of lupine monsters. Each animal resided within a barred, concrete-floored cell, which Asher presumed was there to protect onlookers. It was easy to see why Milo was afraid of them. Luckily, most slept in beds in the corner of their cells, with a few standing up when they saw the platoon.

"Sorry, sir," said Milo as he leaned over the railing.

The rest of the platoon filed in behind Milo, the soldiers gathering around him to look down into the ravine. Lieutenant Tarango remained at the opposite side of the bridge, never bothering to look at the dogs. He tried to put as much distance between himself and Greaves as possible.

"Don't sweat it, Private," said the commander, turning around to speak to him from where he stood farther down the bridge beside the stairs. "These animals are supposed to look terrifying. That's one reason why we keep them down here in the first place."

"Exactly what are they, sir?" asked Aaron as both he and Asher took their places beside Milo.

"What do you mean 'what are they'?" Greaves frowned. "What kind of question is that?"

"Obviously, they're dogs, sir," Aaron recanted. "What breed are they exactly? I've never seen a dog like that in my life. I mean, my parents have a St. Bernard back home, and these things look like they could have him for breakfast."

"They are hellhounds, or at least that's what I'm gonna call them." Greaves' tone of voice revealed he was just giving Aaron a hard time. "They were created by a private company, one that usually designs pharmaceuticals, but they dipped their toe into bioengineering at the government's encouragement. We contracted them to make us a vampire huntin' dog. The eggheads over there said most of the hounds' genetic makeup comes from some kind of extinct wolf mixed with the DNA of certain modern dog breeds, along with a little bear and hyena thrown in there for good measure."

"Would the animal you're talking about be the dire wolf, sir?" Milo asked, bursting with excitement.

"Dire wolf..." said Greaves, trying to remember. "Yeah, that would be the one. How do you know anything about animals, Private?"

"Before I joined the Legion, I studied biology in college, sir."

"So we plan on using these in combat, sir?" asked Asher, nearly interrupting Milo. "Not just for finding vampires, but for running them down and killing them as well?"

"Absolutely," Kilgore confirmed, the captain seemingly materializing beside Greaves. "We've had a lot of difficulty with escaping assailants in the past. These guys were created to put an end to all that."

"Sir, what exactly makes them any different than a normal dog?" asked Driscoll skeptically. He was some distance behind Asher and nearly had to yell. "Well, I mean other than their size and their relation to those other animals."

"I was getting to that, Corporal," Greaves continued for Kilgore. "These hellhounds are physically superior to any naturally bred canine. They are made to be bigger, faster, stronger, and more ruthless. They're great trackers, and once they catch a vamp's scent, they will hunt it down and kill it all by 'em selves."

"Sounds pretty impressive, sir." Driscoll remained unconvinced, however, and was eager to trip up the commander. "Aren't there some disadvantages to working with these dogs? Seeing as they were artificially created, I would think there would be a few."

"Hmm..." Greaves cupped his hand around his chin, "No, not really anything that I can think of, other than they eat a whole lot. Kind of work up an appetite when you're running down vamps all day. You know," Greaves started up again before Driscoll could stop him, "I didn't intend to just stand up here answering questions all day. Come on, let's get on down there for a closer look."

The commander started down the stairs with a spring in his step, his heavy boots striking the metal mesh. Asher left his place at the railing, following Milo and Aaron. The other soldiers behind him did likewise.

"And you're sure these things will never turn on us, sir?"

Driscoll asked Greaves while pushing past some of the others to catch up to him.

"I'm certain these hounds would never harm any of us," said Greaves as he stepped onto another flight of stairs. "Poor temperament towards man is not something we want. We made sure these hounds were designed with an undyin' loyalty to the Legion's soldiers and other humans as well. They only get mean when vamps are around. There's one disadvantage for you, Corporal: You never want to get between them and the vamps. Get all bloodthirsty and crazy when they're around. That would probably be the only situation when they might harm you, unintentionally of course."

"Have these hellhounds been successfully field-tested, sir?" asked Ito, nearly shouting as she cut through Greaves' tangent. She had just taken the first set of stairs.

"If you mean 'have we exposed them to vampire blood and tissue to see if they could identify it,' the answer is yes," Greaves told Ito, though he knew he couldn't give her the answer she wanted. "If you also mean did we gauge their reactions during this exposure, then yes, they have been field-tested."

"You know that's not what I meant, Commander Greaves." Ito rolled her eyes. "Have they been put in a real-world situation where they have been successfully used to destroy assailants?"

"No, they have not, Sergeant." Greaves shook his head. "We plan on taking them out on an ops here real soon, and if they can handle that, we'll know they're worth keeping around. I'm certain it will all work out, though."

"And who exactly will be working with these animals?" Ito continued. Nearly a whole stairway separated her from Greaves, the commander having stepped onto the ground below. "I highly doubt any of us are qualified."

"Witchburn has created a special force to work with the hounds!" Greaves shouted back up at Ito. "Would have had their handlers meet us down here, but they're off to lunch or something! I was only going to show them to you anyway!"

The majority of the platoon had now joined Greaves at the bottom of the stairs. The soldiers remained close to the commander. Seeing they did indeed have visitors, most of the hounds rose from their beds, regarding them with interest though they held themselves in reserve.

Asher frowned, finding their behavior strange.

None of the hellhounds jumped at their cell bars as many dogs might and instead sat staring at the soldiers through their fierce yellow eyes. Asher remained instinctively cautious due to their terrifying appearance and sheer size. They were just too big, too hairy, and possessed bone-crushing jaws.

"That's enough questioning for the moment." Greaves stood just to the side of the cells, his back turned to the hounds. "No reason to act afraid and make them all nervous. I figured you would want to pet one of 'em, Harkman."

"Oh, no." Milo shook his head, remaining off to the side with the rest of the group. "I always found the dire wolf fascinating, but I never really wanted to meet one of them or their modern-day equivalent." He nodded toward the hounds.

"Whatever you say, Private. Does anyone want to try and pet one?" Greaves asked the group. "They aren't designed to attack humans, I swear. Any volunteers?"

His request met with silence. No one raised a hand or came forward. The soldiers stared down at the ground or to the side, avoiding the commander's gaze. Asher thought of volunteering but decided against it, typically never one to go against the crowd.

"Oh, come on." Frustration grew in Greaves's voice. "At least one of you has to be a dog lover." The commander continued to wait for someone to make a move, but his words received only blank stares.

"How about you, Sergeant Ito?" Greaves spotted the sergeant as she stepped down the last flight of stairs. "I know you like dogs, or at least you keep a lot of pictures of them around anyway."

"No, sir, it's fine," said Ito, frozen in place, her attempt to remain unseen failed. "I don't need to pet anything."

"Come on, get over here." Greaves waved her forward. "I got to have somebody touch one of 'em. Got to show the troops that they're harmless. They can't be scared of something they're going to have to work with in close proximity."

"I don't need to pet one, sir." Ito gazed upward at Tarango, the lieutenant still at the top of the stairs. "I'm sure the lieutenant would be up for it, sir. It would really show the rest of us not to be afraid of these things if the leader of our platoon was to do it."

"Way to shove me under the bus, Sergeant!" Tarango called down to her. "Sorry, sir, but I'm going to have to take a hard pass on this one. I'm allergic to dogs. I break out in hives. I swear."

"Dang it, Sergeant!" the commander shouted, not finding any humor in the situation. "I didn't want to do this, but I guess I have to now. Get over here and pet one of these things, or I'll get you for insubordination."

"Yes, sir," said Ito. The sergeant pushed through the crowd. "There's no reason to get so bent out of shape. Which one would you like me to pet?"

"Hmm… Let's see here…" Greaves walked down the line in front of the holding cages, taking a good look at each of the hounds. "This one right here." He pointed to the only hound not sitting at attention at the front of its cage.

The beast lay in its bed at the far corner pretending to be asleep. Sensing the commander was talking about him, the hound sat up to take a look at them. He was one of the largest of the hellhounds, a considerably terrifying specimen with his coat solid black, his eyes bright green, a scar over the right one.

"Over here!" Greaves called the hound as he approached the cell. "Come 'er, the sergeant wants to pat yuh!"

The hound rose from his bed and trotted over to him.

"Name's Garm," said Greaves, reading the hound's tag before squatting down to take a look underneath. "Looks like a male. Obeys commands better than most of you already."

Greaves rose to his feet and turned around to find the sergeant standing out in front of the rest of the group. Ito was unwilling to come any closer until commanded to do so.

"Excellent choice, sir," she said, sarcasm filling her typically good-natured voice. "I would like to commend you for choosing the biggest, scariest one."

"Oh, come on." Greaves smiled, the mirth in his eyes concealed by his sunglasses. "Do you want to mess around and hurt his feelings?"

"I suppose not." Ito shook her head. "It wouldn't be a good idea to be on bad terms with him." Ito approached the hound's cell and closed her eyes, cautiously moving her hand between the cell bars.

Asher's heart raced from the suspense, and the platoon became silent with anticipation.

The hound remained unmoved from where he stood, somewhat confused by Ito's actions.

"Don't do that." Greaves grabbed Ito by the shoulder, causing her to withdraw her hand. "You don't want to act scared. You'll just make him nervous enough to bite."

"Sorry, sir," said Ito, her voice shaking slightly. "I'm just not used to dealing with something that looks like him."

"You kill vampires for a living, Sergeant. You can't be scared of some dog. Just pet him already. I don't think he'll bite. He seems to like you. Can't imagine why you're stumblin' around with your eyes closed like that."

"Well, when you say it like that..." Ito trailed off. She placed her hand back between the cell bars. "Here we go," she said as she reached out to touch Garm.

The hound stood up and bowed his head to her. He allowed Ito to stroke him a few times before vigorously licking her hand with his black tongue.

Ito pulled back a saliva-drenched glove.

"Was that so bad, Sergeant?" asked Greaves, a broad smile across his face.

"I would prefer he didn't slobber all over me, sir," Ito admitted. "Other than that, no, it wasn't so bad."

"OK, looks like the sergeant is the only one brave enough to pet these things." Greaves turned back around to address the rest of the group. "Anyone else want to try to pet one?"

Not a single hand went up, just as before. Their encounters with vampires made them leery of large teeth. Asher saw no point in petting one of the beasts, reasoning he would likely see enough of them later.

"Come on, not even after all that?" Greaves shook his head, exaggerating his disappointment. "Well, suit yourselves then. These guys were put here to make our jobs easier, and you're gonna have to get used to fightin' alongside 'em. Guess we'll have to work on that later, though not too much later. We will begin using them as support real soon."

"Is that all you wanted to show us, Commander Greaves?" asked Tarango from atop the stairs.

"Yes, Lieutenant," said Greaves, his patience with the man wearing thin. "That is all I need to show you. Back up the stairs, everyone! I'll meet you at the entry point to let you all out!" he commanded the soldiers."

"Bunch of wussies," Greaves muttered as he followed the platoon back up the stairs.

.

Chapter XV

An Unfortunate Assignment

"OK, guys, that last run was pretty good, but we still need to pick up the pace!" Driscoll yelled back at Asher and Aaron from the next room.

They were in the residence mock-up area of the range, practicing their room clearing tactics.

"Just a few more runs, and we should have it!"

"Uh…" Asher sighed, disappointed. He hoped their last run would be it for the day.

Though the facility was air-conditioned, Asher was sweating like a workhorse in the desert sun. It was always a hot, miserable time when you ran around in full body armor. The dust from the gravel worsened things further, as it made the air dry and difficult to breathe.

Asher stood up straight from his crouched position and gazed over at Aaron, who looked as though he were on the brink of his own meltdown. Asher grinned at him, glad to know he wasn't the only one having a difficult time with repeated drills.

Aaron returned Asher's smile with a look of hostility.

Milo and Driscoll burst into the room and interrupted whatever dispute they might have had. Milo was exhausted, his skin a deep shade of red, the sweat dripping from his face where his goggles contacted his skin. Driscoll didn't look much better, though he would never admit to drill fatigue, even if he were sweating blood.

"I think if we can get the next few runs down without a mess up, we'll be done for the day!" Driscoll shouted over the unrelenting gunfire from the other cinder block houses. Despite his attitude, the corporal had proven himself a capable, reliable group leader. Asher might even hazard to say he was a great one, though never to his face. The man was insufferable and arrogant enough as it was.

"OK, move back to the door." Driscoll waved a gloved finger around in the air, indicating a restart. He hastily moved through the open door of the mock-up as the rest of his assault group trailed behind him. "Come on guys, stack up and get this drill over with!" he yelled, turning to see his three comrades saunter out the door.

Driscoll turned back around to hunch down beside the open doorway. Asher positioned himself in front with Aaron, and Milo filed in behind them. Asher remained stationary, waiting for Aaron to squeeze the back of his arm, the signal for entry.

"Cease fire! Officer on deck!" called the voice over the intercom, stopping Driscoll from signaling to the rest of them. "Officer on deck!"

The soldiers straightened their postures, turning to see Captain Kilgore walking toward them through the bulletproof glass surrounding their section. He twisted the door handle and entered the room.

"Who's ready for their first op?" Kilgore's voice was inappropriately casual. Everyone looked at him dumbfounded, even Driscoll.

"Come on, Captain," said Asher, already feeling as though he might collapse. "There's absolutely no way we are ready to go on ops yet. Me and Pritchett have only been here a few weeks, and the company isn't even fully restored. We'll get destroyed out there!"

"Calm down, Blackthorn." Kilgore was unaffected by Asher's words. "There's no reason to get your drawers in a wad. This one's supposed to be easy. Even have those new hellhounds to help us out."

"As much as I hate to admit it, I agree with Blackthorn, sir." Driscoll moved in between Asher and the captain. "We're just not ready for ops yet."

"Greaves hand-picked this mission specifically for our company," Kilgore explained. "If you haven't noticed, our rebuilding efforts have been extensive. We're nearly back to full strength now. I can't let you guys sit around getting fat and lazy for too long."

Kilgore paused, letting his words resonate.

"You know I don't like being like this, Driscoll." His voice grew severe. "Orders are orders. It doesn't matter what you think. If the commander says we're going out on ops, then we're going out on ops."

"Understood, sir," said Driscoll, backing down.

"That's more like it," Kilgore's tone relaxed once more. "Now go pack it up and meet me in the briefing room at 1500. It's going to take a while to tell the rest of the platoon."

"I don't mean to criticize, sir." Driscoll caught Kilgore as he started to move around them. "But wouldn't it have been easier to tell us over the intercom?"

"Under normal circumstances, it would," admitted Kilgore. "I anticipated some resistance from most of you, so I figured it would be best just to go around and tell you in person. Anyway, briefing room, 1500, no more questions."

Kilgore made for the door, his heavy boots sending gravel flying.

* * *

"We going to watch some kind of movie, sir?" Aaron asked when Captain Kilgore strolled into the room. He sat beside Asher and Milo near the edge of the crowd.

The whole company had piled in the briefing room, the soldiers sitting or standing in front of a large screen.

"Haha. You should try stand up, Pritchett." Kilgore rolled his eyes. The captain walked past Aaron and through the group of soldiers, taking his position behind the desk up front. Kilgore grabbed the remote off the desk and pointed it at the screen.

Multiple photographs of confirmed vampires glared down at the soldiers. All of the individuals were young and attractive, their eyes ghostly blue, their skin almost translucent. Most had jet-black hair, and a few blondes were thrown in for variety.

"Here are our target assailants," Kilgore declared. "Just the everyday, run-of-the-mill vamps. Nothing we can't handle. They differ from our typical targets in that they appear to operate solely on their own, independent of the organization. Best we can tell, this coven started with one domestic vampire, likely formerly of the organization, who decided to go out and form his own coven for whatever crazed reason vamps have for doing anything. Probably thinks he's vampire Jesus or something."

Kilgore smiled, expecting someone to find the humor in his statement. The room remained silent.

"None of that matters to us, though," Kilgore continued, walking back around the desk to stand directly in front of the crowd. "As far as we're concerned, they're just a bunch of kooky bloodsuckers living out in the middle of nowhere with no idea how dangerous and abominable they are. They primarily feed on unfortunate travelers who come too close to their residence or whatever homeless people they pick up when they go into town. They might have even tried to sustain themselves by feeding on the blood and meat of livestock before going back to humans when it just wouldn't satisfy. Regardless, it doesn't matter how they think of themselves. They're a rabid menace to humanity. A plague that must be eliminated!"

"Where is our target located, sir?" Tarango inquired, cutting into the start of a miscued pep talk.

"Oh, let's see," said the captain, pulling up what Asher felt was an all too familiar map. "Somewhere around the suburbs of Springfield, Missouri. The specific area where they roost is relatively isolated. It's too far out there for them to survive on random visitors."

Asher was shocked to discover that vampires were so close to his hometown, keeping the surprise to himself.

"Here is our target locale." Kilgore flipped to the next page.

A house appeared on the screen. Its architecture was modern contemporary, the structure possessing an excessive amount of windows.

"What's the deal with this house?" Asher asked abruptly. "What kind of vampire would want to live in a place with so many freakin' windows?"

"Yes, they have a thing for tinted windows." Kilgore ignored the fact that Asher had spoken out of turn. "Their fascination worked in our favor. Made it real easy for us to map the interior with drones. They're some kind of new-age bloodsucker. Like I said, it should be a real easy takedown. Their eccentricities, along with their preference to remain in one place, make them sitting ducks, so much so that I almost feel sorry for them. Almost."

"What about the floor plans, sir?" asked Ito. She raised her hand from where she sat at one of the desks near the front of the room. "You might want to show us those before you go off into space. You know how you tend to go on tangents."

Kilgore scoffed at her. "I appreciate your concern, Sergeant. I was getting to that." He hit the screen remote, pulling up 3D blueprints of the house. "So thanks to our targets' strange love of windows, we have a pretty good idea of the layout of the top three stories." He used the red laser pointer at the end of the remote to indicate the individual floors. "We also know they probably have an extensive basement."

"How do you know that, sir?" asked Tarango. He frowned with skepticism, his arms folded across his chest as he leaned against the wall at the back. "You didn't say anything about it earlier when I talked to you."

"Well, we don't know about the basement for sure, but we kind of just expect it," Kilgore explained, shrugging. "There aren't any other structures surrounding the house, and they have to be taking their kills somewhere. Several people are missing from the area, yet we haven't found any bodies. They have to be keeping them somewhere and I, we, hypothesize the only logical place for them to keep them is underneath the house."

"Yes, it does make a fair amount of sense, sir." Tarango squinted, scrutinizing the screen further.

"We estimate that there are about nine or ten assailants and probably at least one juvenile. Those are always tons of fun. I don't know why the dang vamps like biting the kids so much, though I guess in this case, it might have been born that way, which is even worse. Poor kid has probably never seen the sun. Either way, it just makes an otherwise easy job difficult. You think these guys are ready to deal with a juvenile, Lieutenant Tarango?"

Kilgore gazed up at the lieutenant before shooting a glance in Asher and Aaron's direction.

"I'm sure they can handle it, sir." There was confidence in Tarango's voice.

"Wait, what?" asked Aaron, looking around, the full

magnitude of the conversation finally hitting him. "What's all this about shooting some kid?"

"It's what I just said, Private." Darkness hung about Kilgore. "We have reason to believe there is a bloodsucking juvenile in this house, and we're going to have to take it out just like the rest of them."

"Is there no other way, sir?" Aaron was surprised no one shared his apprehension.

"Nope." Kilgore shook his head. "Kid has to be eliminated just like the rest of them. I realize this is your first outing, and you haven't seen one yet, but believe me, child vamps are absolutely the worst kind."

"How so, sir?" asked Asher, the whole room turning to look at him as if he were denser than a concrete slab. "OK, I mean, obviously it's going to be way harder to go through with killing a kid than an adult, even if they are a bloodsucker. It's just that the way you are talking suggests that there's more to it than that."

"No, as far as we can tell, the kids don't have any special abilities that the adults don't," Kilgore explained. "They're weaker, as you would expect, regardless if they've been bit or were just born that way. Not sure if you've gotten to that in your classes yet, but yes, vampires can reproduce sexually. So, you guys think you can handle it?" Kilgore looked over to see Ito staring at him expectantly. "Excuse me," he grinned apologetically. "Do you think you all can handle it? Better not leave it to Pritchett anyway. Beginning to have some serious doubts about the rest of you as well."

"There will be more experienced personnel in there with them, sir," said Driscoll. He put his hands behind his head and gave Kilgore a smug smile. "I'm sure I'll be able to handle it if the other, newer, recruits can't."

"Sir, given the nature of this particular target, isn't it more likely they would take whatever children they have with them into the woods when they flee?" Tarango asked, hoping to stop Kilgore from going off course to lecture Driscoll.

"What makes you so sure they will flee?" asked Ito, turning toward Tarango before the captain could answer. "This is their home. Why wouldn't they try to protect it?"

"Yes, I am also quite interested as to why you believe they

will flee," Kilgore interjected, allowing Ito's interruption.

"I just don't think they are fighters, sir," Tarango looked anxiously around the room for support and found none. "They're not with the organization, and they're not regular ferals. That generally means they use deception to lure their prey in rather than attacking them directly. They should be out of practice and out of shape compared to what we usually deal with. They're also just out there playing house, trying to act like a 'vegetarian' vampire family unit. They'll want to protect the child, rather than just leaving them out there to deal with us. They will take whatever young ones they have and flee into the woods."

"I hope that ends up being the case." Kilgore stepped back, whatever hostility he displayed vanishing. "It's what we would like them to do as it would allow us to use the hellhounds to run them down. They don't discriminate between children and adults. I thought we had successfully instilled a shoot first, ask questions later approach on killing vamps into our newer recruits, but, as I said, now I have my doubts. Luckily, there's still several of us veterans around to do what needs to be done, should the newer stock be unable."

Kilgore searched the room for veteran officers, frowning when all he could find were Ito and Tarango.

"Anyway, back to the floorplans." The captain broke the awkward silence he had created, pointing his laser at the screen. "There are three floors, four if you count the basement... 1, 2, 3, 4." He pointed to each one. "We will arrive around 1900 and park off over here at this adjacent property, approaching the house through the woods. We'll make our approach at sunset and catch them when they are at their weakest, right when they wake. Shouldn't be any vamps on the first two floors when we hit it. Presumably, they will all be in their coffins."

Kilgore grinned and looked around the room to see if anyone caught what he said. Instead, several glares met his words, specifically those of Ito and Tarango.

"Just testing you. Don't care for jokes, I guess? Anyway, don't presume there won't be any bloodsuckers on the first couple of floors, as they should be in bed. It shouldn't be hard to clear the place, you know, compared to some other places we've cleared. Not many hallways and we have the floor plans thanks to our drones' spy cams. There are quite a few problem areas, though. Have a lot of these half walls that we'll have to look around, which is always a pain. Another problem area will be up here on the third floor in this hallway that all the bedrooms feed into."

Kilgore pointed toward the top of the map.

"Kind of a chokepoint there. Just have to make sure we get up there quick to clear it and hope the vamps aren't in a fighting mood. If they're going to swarm us, it will be there. That's why we'll be flooding the place. Put so many men in there so quick the vamps won't know what to do."

Kilgore paused as he scanned the room, receiving nods of understanding from his soldiers.

"This chokepoint could still get pretty brutal, and I think it would be best if we picked someone at random, right here and now, to approach it first. Yes, I realize that it's kind of dumb to do that, seeing as we could just order someone up there when it comes time to clear that spot, but I think it will help to choose somebody before that. We routinely encounter obstacles like this, and we have a randomizer computer program to deal with this kind of situation. All you do is hit a button, and it spits out a name. Wait, just a second. Hit this button right here. Oops, no here..."

The captain fumbled around with the remote, an eerie silence filling the room as he did so. Asher wished he would move more quickly, his palms growing sweaty as a strange, foreboding aura filled the room.

"OK, here we go," said Kilgore at last, finding the correct button.

A slot machine-like graphic suddenly appeared on the screen, and the reel began spinning. Everyone held their breath as it steadily slowed.

ASHER BLACKTHORN suddenly scrolled across the screen in big, black letters.

"Come on, Captain!" Asher protested, nearly falling from his seat before rising to stand. The nauseating pain made him feel as though he might vomit. "Surely you don't want to put one of us new guys out there like that on his first op. Wouldn't it be much better to use a veteran?"

"Are you questioning the validity of my methods, Private?" Kilgore roared. His red hair seemed to catch fire, effectively extinguishing Asher's own anger.

"Well, no," he squeaked, sitting back down. Though Asher was a head taller than the captain, he still found him intimidating.

"I can see why you might think sending in new personnel might be a bad idea." Kilgore stroked his chin. His angry mood gave way to an apologetic smile.

Asher gave him a scared look, hoping he might change his mind.

The captain walked toward Asher, bending down slightly to talk to him. "I'm still going with the machine's pick," Kilgore spoke to him directly. "We do a pretty dangerous job, and we just hemorrhage personnel sometimes. You're going to be put in some pretty tough spots, and you might as well get them over with now and hope things go better later. This is a soft target, and I think if you stick to your guns and don't hesitate when it comes time to clear that spot, you ought to come out just fine."

Kilgore stepped away and went back toward the desk to continue addressing the company.

Asher regretted his outburst immediately. He was frustrated by his inability to repress his feelings and that his fear had manifested itself as rage.

"Sir, I would like to volunteer to be positioned behind Blackthorn on the stairs," Ito spoke abruptly. She rose from her seat, and the captain turned back around to face her. "I'm sure it will be much easier to clear the corner if Blackthorn has back up from an officer."

"Very well, Sergeant Ito." Kilgore nodded, understanding her reasoning. "It's about time someone took some initiative." He paused as his eyes fell on Pritchett. "Of course, with the sergeant volunteering to follow right after Blackthorn, it means we'll rearrange things a little. Private Pritchett will be moved back, essentially taking up the sergeant's former position."

"That's just fine with me, sir," said Aaron, suppressing a sigh of relief.

"Sorry for having to leave you, man." He tapped Asher's shoulder with his fist.

"It's no big deal." Asher stared off into space, the fear building within him as he considered his assignment. He had barely heard Aaron or the captain.

"Now, for the rest of you new people, remember our M.O.," said Kilgore.

All of the soldiers' backs straightened as though they were at attention.

"Kill everything that moves and make sure none of the assailants are left with their heads still attached. Got to know they are dead. Don't worry too much about escapees. We got the dogs for that. They'll catch them for us and probably already have them taken care of before we even have to pull a trigger. It seems like I haven't said a whole lot, but that's all I have for now. You got any questions?" He took a moment to scan for raised hands.

"Oh, so it's like that." The captain looked almost bewildered, seeing the air free of hands. "Nothing at all? You're making me feel a little concerned."

"I think you did a great job explaining everything, sir," Ito answered, trying to sound reassuring. "Very thorough."

"OK. Do the rest of you feel that way, or is the sergeant just being a suck-up?" The captain looked around the room once again as Ito rolled her eyes.

He received several unenthusiastic but approving nods.

"Good, guess we're off then. We can discuss more of the particulars on the way down there. Finally get to use those new fancy helmets. Got speakers, microphones, and digital image interface. Follow me out to the garage, and we'll load up in the transports now."

Asher rose from his seat and turned to leave with the rest of the company. He was a pulsing bundle of anxiety and intensifying dread as he made for the door.

"We going to load the whole company up in a bunch of armored trucks, sir?" asked Aaron as they filtered out of the room.

"Oh, that's right," the captain mumbled to himself. "Glad you brought that up, Private. I nearly forgot. Yes, since we will be traveling in a more or less populated area, we had to come up with an alternative method of transport. Needed something more inconspicuous than usual."

"And what kind of transport did you come up with, sir?" asked Ito.

"School bus," said the captain, a smile slowly materializing on his face.

Chapter XVI

The Dying Light

Asher gazed thoughtfully out the bus window, catching glimpses of the brilliant pink-purple sunset through the trees. The branches were bare, yet prepared to burst full with buds as the last of winter's bite had nearly fallen away. The school bus careened down the narrow, winding highway and over the rolling hills as though the driver had some kind of strange death wish. They were only about twenty minutes away from their arrival at the drop-off point.

Asher's anxiety increased with each passing minute.

There hadn't been much talking over the course of the trip. The captain had issued the order for quiet early on, instructing his soldiers to keep their helmet speakers on so he could continue his lecture en route to the destination. The silence presented Asher with the rare opportunity for a nap, but sleep was impossible due to all the stress placed upon him. All his arms training aside, he was still nervous about his assignment, unsure what would happen when he came face to face with another cold-eyed, fanged monster.

"You OK, Blackthorn?" asked a female voice to Asher's left. He looked up to see Sergeant Ito staring at him, her big brown eyes full of concern. He hadn't noticed her sitting there earlier. "The first op is always the hardest," Ito said with a smile. "But you do have to keep your head in the game if you want to come out all right."

"I'm fine." Asher frowned, somewhat offended by the sergeant's inference of weakness.

Ito stared at him blankly, unconvinced.

"You OK, Pritchett?" The sergeant turned her attention to Aaron, who sat directly across from her in the aisle seat next to

Asher.

"I'm more than fine." Aaron tried to sound confident though his tone suggested otherwise. "We've been practicing taking these bloodsuckers out for a while now, and it's nice to finally put that training to use."

"Pfft…" Ito dismissed his words, waving them away with her hand. "Neither of you sound as confident as you should. Are you absolutely sure you're alright, Blackthorn?" She looked back over at Asher. "You sound worse off than Pritchett."

Asher sighed, reluctant to answer. "It's just been a while since I've seen one," he said, sensing the sergeant likely wouldn't leave him alone until he gave her what she wanted. "They're freakin' terrifying, and if you haven't heard, the one I shot nearly got me! It's those freakin' blue ghost eyes. Makes them look like a living nightmare!"

"The vampire you killed sounds a lot like a feral, given its matter of attack," explained Ito. "They're always the worst. Much more terrifying than any of the others. These ones shouldn't be anywhere as scary. They're 'wanna be vegetarians' like the lieutenant said."

"Yeah, suppose you're right about that," Asher admitted. "It doesn't mean they won't put up a fight. Why wouldn't they? We're here to eradicate what they consider to be their family. Surely they'll do something. Heck, even if they do run, that doesn't mean something won't go wrong." He cringed, imagining the possibilities.

"You know you can't think like that, Blackthorn." Ito shook her head, displeased. "You have to have confidence. If you go in there thinking something is going to go wrong, then it definitely will. You've been training non-stop for nearly three weeks now. Your skills should be developed. Realistically, you don't even have to be at the completion stage to handle this target. Don't sweat it too much."

"Suppose you're right." Asher gazed down at his boots, letting himself sound hopeless.

"I feel like you don't understand the gravity of what I'm saying, Private!" Ito's supportive demeanor became harsh, giving way to full command mode. "You can't have doubts like that. You'll endanger the whole company. You'll be a risk to all of us. As your squad leader, I order you not to worry!" She yelled, causing all of the bus's occupants to turn and look over at them.

Asher's face turned a deep shade of red due to both embarrassment and the bluntness of the sergeant's words.

Aaron, who had been trying to stay out of their conversation, looked as though he might bolt for the back of the bus.

"Yes, sir... um... I mean, ma'am." Asher saluted just to be sure.

The sergeant smiled at him, amusement in her eyes.

"We're nearing the drop-off point now!" Lieutenant Tarango called from the front of the bus, ending Asher's encounter with Ito. "Make sure you have all your gear and put your helmets back on so I can talk to you over the speaker!"

"That's my signal to get back to the front of the bus." Ito rose from her seat. "See you later."

The bus took a wide-arched turn some minutes later, leaving the highway for the loose gravel of a rural driveway. A second bus transporting about a dozen handlers and their hounds followed them. Two more buses continued past the drive, going down the highway to the drop-off point on the other side of the target property. One of these contained the company's second platoon, while the other carried another hellhound squad. They were to rendezvous at the target house after both platoons made their initial sweep of the surrounding area.

"Wow, we are in the sticks," Aaron mumbled, Asher barely catching it.

Ahead lay a simplistic farmhouse flanked by ill-kept fences and empty, forgotten barns. The whole scene was serene and pleasant, contrasting with the horrifying and gruesome events that would soon occur down the hill. Their target location lay just past the farm's wooded field to their right.

Asher shook his head, smiling. He had no idea what kind of fantastic lies Greaves told the owners to warrant their arrival here.

The bus pulled in front of a battered, old barn, rust holes riddling its blue, tin sides, the second bus parking right behind them. Their mission was already dangerous from the start. The noise from the buses' engines served as an instantaneous proclamation of their arrival. They were to approach the house on foot, quickly establishing a perimeter so they might prevent any early flight attempts by the assailants.

None of that might even matter, Asher thought to himself. They were already making quite an assumption when they anticipated that their quarry would be asleep at this precise time of day.

"OK, everybody off the bus!" called Lieutenant Tarango. "Go to your initial position by that fence and try not to be seen!"

Obeying his command, the 50 or so platoon personnel rose from their seats. They strapped on shotguns, checked ammunition packs, and adjusted body armor in preparation for the approach.

"Ready to rock and roll, Ash?" asked Aaron through his helmet, his eyes visible through his now transparent face shield. He leaned down to pick up his pack.

"Ready to rock." Asher signaled back with the metal horns hand sign before shoving his helmet onto his head. He waited for Pritchett to strap on his pack before bending down to reach for his own gear, taking it from where it sat beside the seat.

The platoon filtered off the bus as Asher threw on his pack and then slung the strap of his X-12 around his back.

"Come on, people, let's get moving!" yelled Tarango through the helmet speaker, much less easy-going on operations than he was at the base. "We're not going to take down any vamps if we never get off the freakin' bus!"

"Hey, see you when this whole thing is over, man," said Aaron, placing a hand on Asher's shoulder. "Stay positive." He went to assume Ito's position farther up in the line-up, still close to the action but in a slightly safer spot.

"Yeah, so long as everything goes well," said Asher with a hint of sarcasm, an attempt to hide his anxiety. He immediately wished he hadn't said those words.

"Hey, don't say stuff like that," said Milo as he turned from where he stood in the aisle. "You'll jinx the whole thing!"

Asher joined the others in the lane. As the soldiers edged their way toward the front of the bus, he felt his attention shift to the rapidly waning sunset and the darkness approaching within the next hour. To him, dusk always seemed the best time to be leaving the woods, but yet here he was rushing into it.

"You ready to clear those stairs, Blackthorn?" Tarango asked as Asher met him at the front of the bus. The lieutenant was attempting to rattle him, his voice coming from both the soldiers' helmet speakers and his mouth. "Sorry about that. Forgot to turn off the microphone," he apologized, realizing the whole platoon could hear him.

"I'm ready as I'll ever be, sir!" Asher proclaimed, unwilling to let the lieutenant shake him up.

"That's good to hear, Private," said Tarango, receiving the enthusiastic answer he wanted.

Asher climbed down the stairs and out the door, his boots hitting the gravel drive. He was thankful to stretch his legs after so much time on the bus. His height always made him feel cramped, no matter how or where he sat.

"Go, go, go!" Asher heard one of the dog handler's command, causing him to move to the side of the open door. He turned to watch the hounds and their handlers exit the bus behind them.

The hounds bounded out of the back door, their handlers after them. The soldiers nearly fell on their faces due to the door's distance from the ground as they struggled to keep up with their designated canine wards. It was strange to see the hounds on leashes. Their large size made them capable of easily dragging their handlers through the woods if they wanted. It almost seemed more appropriate for the soldiers to ride them like horses.

"I'll be right behind you, Blackthorn, as soon as we get all personnel off the bus," said Ito. She stood beside the bus's front tire while a few more soldiers passed around her.

"Thanks for keeping the captain from feeding me to the wolves, Sergeant," Asher told her. "I appreciate it."

"I'm sure you would do the same for me." Her helmet concealed her smile.

Asher looked past her as she turned to leave, finding standing Aaron near the fence giving him a thumb's up, a gesture he immediately returned.

"Hey, Blackthorn," said Driscoll. He approached Asher from behind as he made his way across the drive and onto the grass, lightly punching him on the shoulder. "Guess I'll be the one behind you down the hall after the sergeant moves to the side."

"Yeah, that's exactly what it sounded like, sir." Asher tried not to sound too sarcastic, annoyed by the physical interaction with Driscoll. "Don't goof up and shoot me."

"Ha!" Driscoll was genuinely amused. "With my aim, that is a possibility!"

Asher rolled his eyes behind his helmet's visor, regretting what he said.

The two started walking once more, closing the ground between the road and the fence, finding Milo waiting for them there. They returned his salute without a word. The time for talk was over now.

Asher took his position behind the fence with Driscoll and Milo on either side. Ito approached him from behind. Asher turned his attention toward the quickly darkening woods.

The brush and trees were thickly packed, and an abundance of dead leaves lay on the ground, making it impossible to pass through without making considerable noise.

Asher took his shotgun in hand and looked down the sights as he took on a shooting stance. He waited for Tarango's orders to proceed, Driscoll, Milo, Ito, and the rest of his fellows doing the same. A cold sweat formed on his palms as he waited for the order, and a frightful dread filled the air. Asher gazed through the dense wood, periodically believing he saw movement under the shadows.

"Proceed," said Tarango, half-yelling, half-whispering into their helmets' speakers. "Try not to take too long passing under that fence."

Their platoon would hear only Tarango's voice until they surrounded the house. They could speak only if they encountered an escaping assailant.

Asher grabbed the fence's bottom wire with a gloved hand, pulling it up. He felt it more appropriate to apply a wire-cutter to the fence, but they wished to leave no evidence of the company ever being there. He waited for Ito to take the wire from him and then passed under it.

"Form the line!" Tarango ordered, seeing the platoon had passed the fence. He took up his position somewhere in the middle of the line.

The rest of the soldiers quickly fell in beside him, remaining approximately ten feet away from each other, ready to make the sweep. The line of black-clad soldiers stood in place, their chests heaving up and down rapidly.

"Make the sweep!" Lieutenant Tarango commanded at last.

The line moved in unison, quickly but stealthily pushing their way through the woods, careful to watch their footing. Asher's concentration was mainly on the terrain in front of him, though he occasionally glanced to either side. He maintained a visual on both Ito and Driscoll, careful to keep a similar pace. The captain had been sure to point out how important it was to keep each other in sight.

Asher crushed the leaves under his boots, the sound continuously repeated by both him and his comrades, the noise impossible to prevent. He frowned, finding it strange that the soldiers made the most noise. Not a single howl or cry came from the hounds still on the other side of the fence. Regardless, Asher was sure they would make their presence known once they closed in on the house. As soon as they smelled their first whiff of living vampiric flesh, a frenzied hellhound attack was certain.

The soldiers under Tarango's command continued through the woods, the walk taking an eternity. Dried, discarded foliage crackled underneath their boots with each step. The line of soldiers approached the fence, the second platoon behind them now preparing to make a second sweep of the area as a precaution against escaping assailants.

Asher had forgotten just how loud dry leaves could be, and each step seemed to reverberate through the woods, threatening to reveal their position. He frequently encountered obstacles in his way, stepping over branches and the occasional bush. He knew there were more straightforward means to access the house. They had forsaken these for the woods and its cover, the need for concealment outweighing all else.

Asher made another quick check of his three and nine before returning to what was straight in front of him. He could see the house through the densely packed trees now; its overly angular architecture and window-walls impossible to miss, all of it out of place there.

Asher grunted as he felt his foot suddenly catch on a tree

root, causing him to stumble. The sound of crushed leaves echoed throughout the woods. He might as well have set off a car alarm.

"Blackthorn!" Tarango hissed through his helmet. He instinctually singled out Asher, as he was the tallest of the recruits.

Ito, Driscoll, and all of the other platoon personnel briefly glanced over at him, trying not to notice his error. Kilgore had ordered them to keep moving at this point, the captain telling the soldiers to ignore such a misstep.

Asher kept a firm grip on his weapon and quickly regained his footing. He continued through the brush, careful to watch his feet more closely. He kept his eyes on his peripherals and what lay ahead of him as he proceeded forward. The soldiers soon passed the tree line and stepped onto browned grass, leaving their cover. Several, mostly evergreen, trees were here, though not as compacted as what now lay at their backs.

"Hold!" called Lieutenant Tarango.

Their line stopped some fifty feet from the house. Asher took several more steps to regain his position. His stumble over the root had left him behind the others.

Back in line, he gazed upon the house once more, his hands firmly on his weapon. An extremely modern and open structure, it normally would look non-threatening, even comical, if it wasn't for the aura of foreboding stemming from the inhabitants who resided within. Captain Kilgore was confident it was a soft target, as much as a house filled with vampires could be.

Asher remained unconvinced. The sky darkened ever so quickly, and all those windows would give any enemy waiting inside an excellent view of their position. The platoon stood near the tree line waiting for further orders.

"First sweep of the west side complete!" Tarango announced through their helmets.

Asher wasn't sure if he would ever become accustomed to hearing the lieutenant's voice inside his head.

"First sweep of the east side complete!" a male voice unfamiliar to Asher came over the speaker. It was the second platoon's lieutenant. He thought the captain had said his name was Roth.

"Proceed on to the house!" commanded Kilgore, his

disembodied voice sounding strange in their helmets. He had positioned himself somewhere behind the target point, watching their movements through a pair of binoculars. A circling drone provided him a complete visual.

On Kilgore's word, Asher and his comrades continued toward the front of the house. The line quickly became a V before it broke into two horizontal lines. The soldiers' dark helmets and armor made them look like a flock of giant ravens, intent on their next feast of carrion.

Ahead, Asher saw the personnel who had approached from the east side. They remained distant from them, arranging themselves in a loose circle around the house. They would guard it while Asher and his comrades cleared the interior. Whatever assailants made it through the outside platoon's line of fire would be met by the merciless hellhounds. The beasts and their handlers had formed an even wider circle around the house.

Asher gazed up at the structure once more, finding it more and more intimidating by the moment. Its abnormally square angles and straight lines cut a sharp edge across the darkening sky. He shuddered, imagining the bloody, wretched horrors they would find inside.

"Hounds are now in position on the west side!" said another voice, female this time. Asher had no idea what the woman's name or rank was. She was in charge of half of the force of hounds and their handlers.

"Hounds in position on the east side, sir!" sounded another unfamiliar voice.

"Confirmation by all units!" Captain Kilgore roared into their headsets. "Proceed into the house, Tarango! Stack up and bring down those vamps!" An icy chill filled the air as he spoke, and the dreadful anticipation of the raid weighed down on Asher.

"Yes, sir!" replied the lieutenant. His personnel moved into position, stacking up against the side of the house. "Enter!" commanded Tarango.

The first man approached the door and found it unlocked, saving them the hassle of a breach. The man immediately behind him pulled a flash-bang from his comrade's pack, launching it through the open door. The front man charged through the open door just as the light dissipated, a loud *BANG!* from the non-lethal explosive punctuating his entry. His helmet and visor protected him from the device's effects. If there were any vampires on the first floor, they were now wide-awake and left momentarily blind and deaf. All of it happened in milliseconds, giving Asher little time to comprehend the series of events.

The rest of the soldiers rushed in, one after the other, a relentless force of speed and aggression, intent on total elimination. Though he couldn't see them from where he stood, Asher heard the sound of multiple booted feet striking wood and concrete as the house flooded with soldiers.

"Going in, sir!" Tarango called out to the captain, following after the last assault group assigned to the first floor. He neared the house behind the last man.

Tarango needed confirmation from each of the assault groups before they went on to the next floor. A better strategy might have been to flood all the floors at once, as was the usual practice, but this time the circumstances were different. The goal here was to flush their quarry from the house so the hounds could perform most of the heavy-hitting.

Asher could hear the sound of the lieutenant's boots on wood as he ran back toward the door.

"First floor cleared!" yelled Tarango. He was visible through the only slightly tinted window, motioning the soldiers to continue to the second floor.

No shots fired, no vamps.

The personnel assigned to the second floor rushed through the doorway, a swift, efficient black line of destruction headed straight up the first flight of stairs.

Asher quickly moved into position to the side of the house behind the last man assigned to the second floor. Ito, Driscoll, and then Milo filed along behind him. Asher's grip tightened around his weapon as he braced himself for the second all clear. The sounds of yet more booted feet echoed out of the house, still only footsteps and no shots. Asher began to sweat from his forehead, his dread nearly at its apex as he took up his position by the open door.

"Second floor clear!" Tarango bellowed.

Two floors cleared and nothing. No shots and no fleeing

vamps. It all but guaranteed Asher an encounter with a whole coven of bloodsuckers. He remained motionless in his shooting stance, paralyzed by the intensity of the task before him.

"Time to get to the top of those stairs, Blackthorn!" Tarango shouted, anticipating his hesitation.

Asher took a deep breath and entered the house. Sergeant Ito and the others followed close behind him. He made his way around the open door, continuing in a straight line toward the west side of the house, his gait swift yet steady. Asher stopped at the corner leading to the first flight of stairs and took yet another deep breath, readying himself for the onslaught. He shuffled his feet as he made his way around, careful to search every angle before he proceeded further.

Corner cleared, they continued up the stairs, moving sideways, careful to place the soles of their boots on the studs to prevent any unnecessary noise. The personnel kept the muzzles of their guns pointed toward the ceiling, keeping a close watch on all angles in between.

Just as Asher turned the second corner, he heard the sound of footsteps swiftly approaching. The muscles in his arms drew tight as a pale, dark-haired man lunged for him.

BOOM!

Asher instinctively pulled the trigger of his weapon, dealing the man a blast straight to the gut. He fired from the middle of the torso up to the head, his shots reinforced by those of Sergeant Ito, their repeated fire deafening. Their fragmentation rounds tore through the vampire's body, shredding the walls, the blood spraying them dark crimson. Pieces of the bullets even made it past the stairs, shattering some windows on the third floor.

The first vampire had only begun to slump and fall when another assailant followed him around the corner. Their shots tore into him, quickly grinding his body to a bloody pulp. He fell onto the stairs, half his face gone, blood, brains, and bone fragments splattered over both the ceiling and what remained of the windows.

Asher breathed deeply. What he was told about the speed and near unnatural durability of their foe barely prepared him for the reality. The vampires withstood blast after blast, taking up to ten or more rounds right to their unarmored bodies before finally going to the ground, falling in front of them only a couple yards away. Only the power of his shots and the enemy's irrationality saved him from death. The vamps were fools to attack them on the stairs. Few things survived a close-range cascade of shotgun blasts, no matter their athletic prowess.

"Proceed!" Ito yelled for him to continue up the stairs.

Asher obeyed her, taking considerable care while stepping over the bodies. Sweat now poured from his forehead as the stress of the situation continued to rise. He stopped when he reached the end of the stairs, catching his breath.

Asher continued to search around the corner of the stairs when he heard a third assailant charge down the hallway from the nearest room. The vampire moved so fast that Asher saw little more than a flash of his blonde hair. He was slightly more intelligent than the other two, knowing it was better to wait for his prey to come to him.

Asher and Ito sprayed him down, round after round piercing his body, shredding his intestines into a filthy pulp.

Smart though he might be, the vamp had made a mistake coming around the corner at all. His patience did him little good as he underestimated his speed and neglected to account for the destructive power of a fully automatic shotgun. His body tumbled backward and collapsed on the stairs, blown to pieces, the same as his more reckless comrades.

Shaken by the onslaught of assailants, Asher refused to lose his nerve. He was already dead the second it was gone, possibly even bringing a few of his comrades down with him. He completed his search of the final corner and entered the third-floor hallway.

Asher took a few steps down the wood floor before a fourth vampire came out of the room directly in front of him, a redheaded female this time. He felt the inner workings of his shotgun catch as he pulled the trigger, stifling the intended barrage of bullets.

"Jam!" Asher screamed at the top of his lungs. He dropped to his knees to allow Driscoll a clear shot, his desperate cries answered by the deafening blasts from both Ito and the corporal's X-12s.

Still undeterred, two more assailants rushed from the room at the end of the hall after the first, the vampires realizing it was better to attack in unison.

With the introduction of the new threat, Ito slumped down on the floor to give Milo a clean shot, obeying the unwritten rule that there must be at least one gun on every assailant at all times. It was the only way to guarantee all personnel survived.

All patience with his weapon lost, Asher abandoned the half-spent double-drum on the floor. He snapped a fresh one into his shotgun as the redheaded vampire finally fell, her blood slowly soaking into the wood floor.

"Got it!" Asher shouted, taking aim at the two remaining assailants. He remained squatting down beside the wall, careful to stay below Driscoll.

With three shotguns on him, the third dark-haired male stood no chance. Asher had no time to regain his sites before the vampire's pulverized body fell to the floor, the wood slickened with blood.

The last assailant, a young, blonde female, sped past the male's body, a defiant, rage-fueled bloodlust in her ghostly eyes. Asher dealt her several rounds to the gut, his comrades ceasing to fire as they watched her stumble backward and land against the wall near the far room.

Asher let out an audible sigh as he rose to his feet. There were still at least two more assailants unaccounted for, and he still hadn't entered the room he was to help clear. He took a brief, ill-advised glance at the blonde female on his way to the room, finding her body relatively whole compared to how a human assailant would have looked. All she sustained was an, albeit devastating, wound to the gut.

Asher continued further down the hallway, halting at the door of the first room, once again searching all angles of the entryway before proceeding. He burst through the open door and moved to the right. Sergeant Ito followed and went left. He could hear the sound of booted feet behind him as Driscoll, Milo, and then the rest of the personnel assigned to the third floor moved onto the other rooms.

Asher stopped in front of the bed before taking a wide step around to inspect it, jumping even though he found nothing. He leaned down to look under the bed, sweat pouring from his forehead as he did so, nearly expecting a clawed hand to lash at his face.

Asher raised a hand and gave Ito a thumb's up, indicating he had found nothing.

"Clear!" Ito yelled back to Tarango through the open door.

Asher moved back to his point of domination. He and Ito stood, holding their positions, as several more all clears echoed through their helmets. They were all ordered to wait in their assigned rooms until Tarango gave the confirmation.

Asher heard the sound of gun blasts coming from the far room, followed by the sound of more gunfire from outside. He was certain the remaining vampires had leaped from an open window, escaping their first line around the house. He heard the howls of the hounds in the distance, excited by the scent of their intended prey, finally losing their composure and becoming feral beasts. They were the living nightmare of all fool bloodsuckers.

Asher heard the screams of the vampires as well. One of the cries was higher and shriller than the others, suggesting a smaller individual. The vampires' screams suddenly became higher in pitch, transforming into the tortured shrieks of dying hellspawn. It would have been better if they had stayed in the house. Death by shotgun blast was preferable to bloodthirsty hellhounds tearing them apart.

"All clear!" yelled Tarango, having finished his check of the third floor.

Asher and Ito abandoned the room as soon as they heard the order, exiting to find the lieutenant waiting for them at the end of the hall. Driscoll, Milo, and a half dozen other personnel joined them.

"Hatchets! Let's take care of those heads!" bellowed Tarango, rushing back toward the stairs. "I see six assailants! I want to see six headless vamps!"

He apparently hasn't spent any time looking over the corpses, Asher thought to himself.

Several personnel, Asher included, took their light but extremely sharp hatchets from their belts.

"Will six body parts do, sir?" Ito yelled back at Tarango. "Let's see..." she turned to look down the stairs and counted until she reached the end of the hallway. "I can get you three heads, two arms, and a foot!"

"Don't be a smart aleck, Sergeant Ito!" Tarango shouted back at her through his helmet. "I just need proof that we found six assailants and eliminated six assailants!"

"You go take care of the blonde over there, Blackthorn!"

Driscoll shouted at Asher, pointing his hatchet toward the female at the other side of the hall. He rushed past the blonde's corpse on his way to whatever vamps still had their heads. Milo followed close behind him.

As Asher approached the felled vampire, he thought he saw her begin to stir as though from sleep. The movement was so slight he thought his eyes deceived him, stressed as he was. He was no more than ten feet away when the vampire suddenly looked up at him, making him jump backward.

"Mercy?" she pleaded, pure insanity reflected in her crystal blue eyes.

"Sorry, no mercy for vamps," said Asher coldly. He advanced, his hatchet raised to strike.

He felt a strange sensation wash over him as he looked into her eyes, something alluring yet psychotic, promising pleasure but intent on pain. Regardless, Asher just couldn't look away. She promised to give him everything he ever wanted with her gaze, though he could feel it would come at great cost. He didn't care anymore. He was willing to pay the price. The only thing he could see now was the beautiful woman before him and her enchanting cool, blue eyes.

"You don't show mercy to your victims," said Asher, barely uttering the words before surrendering to her cruel seduction completely. "You're pretty torn up anyway. You won't last much longer. Death is your mercy."

"We only kill because of what we are!" The vampire gave him a venomous glare, her alluring gaze suddenly disappearing. "It's what we have to do to survive!" Asher's words had struck a chord, agitating her to such an extent that she could no longer keep up her spell.

"No, you murder to survive." Asher returned to his senses. "You give in to your primal urges and murder, never seeking any other way. I kill to protect the innocent from you."

"You won't kill me," she whispered, beginning her seduction anew.

Asher stood there motionless, trapped in her hypnotic spell once more.

The vampire slowly rose from the pool of blood in which she

sat, her tattered entrails hanging loosely from her wound as she walked toward him. Asher lost sight of everything but her eyes. She was nearly upon him now, reaching for his throat.

Just as she grasped for him, a hatchet suddenly flew across the room, striking the vampire in the forehead.

She hissed as she fell to the ground in a heap.

Asher turned back around to see Milo looking back at him, panicked astonishment reflected in his large, pixie-like eyes.

"Don't hesitate, Blackthorn!" Milo yelled at him. "The most dangerous vamp is one that isn't quite dead yet!"

Asher stood there, slowly recovering from his confusion.

"Well, don't just stand there, Blackthorn," said Sergeant Ito. She walked toward him behind Milo. "Tarango needs whatever heads he can get."

"I'll take care of it, Sergeant," said Milo, rushing around Asher. "Need to get my hatchet back anyway," he muttered.

Asher remained rooted in place as the last effects of the vampire's spell wore off, watching Milo as he took care of her head.

Milo took a firm hold on her hair as he wrenched his hatchet free from the center of her forehead, pulling her neck forward so that it lay prostrate before him. He plunged his hatchet into her neck and, after two quick chops, separated her skull from the vertebrae, blood pouring from the headless neck like water from a faucet. Holding her severed head, he pulled a cloth sack from his belt and slipped the grisly trophy inside. Milo twisted the top of the bag closed, tying it around his belt to rest beside the other head he had taken.

"What the heck did she just do to me?" Asher asked, turning to find Ito still standing behind him. "She used her eyes to put me under some kind of spell."

"Yeah, I suppose you new guys probably haven't addressed it in class yet." Ito shrugged. "Some vampires, actually quite a few really, have hypnotic abilities. Nothing supernatural or anything. They can just use their eyes to hypnotize and disorient you for short periods. It works best on the opposite sex, so you'll have to watch the females."

"Let's pack it up, people!" Tarango yelled over Ito. "The captain wants our platoon gathered back on the first floor!"

Chapter XVII

Spoils of Victory

"How did the hellhounds do out there, sir?" Tarango asked Kilgore as the captain stepped through the house's open doorway.

Night had fallen, and Tarango's platoon had remained in the house as they waited for Kilgore's order to pack it all back in and head home.

"Not bad, though not as good as I would have hoped," said Kilgore as he went to stand at the side of the stairs. "One of them, Garm, is a beast. He got loose from his handler when those vamps were making their way out of the house. Tore one apart by himself and started on another before the rest of the hounds caught up. Those dogs are savages, which is what we want, though they're a little hard to handle sometimes."

"How many did they end up catching, sir?" Tarango casually leaned against a column embedded in the wall. "We got six in here."

"They took care of the last two, or at least what we hope was the last two." Kilgore stared into space, thinking. "I guess there's the possibility that we miscounted, and one of them got away. As quick and brutal as those hounds are, I highly doubt they would miss one."

"Have any trouble rounding the hounds up, sir?" Tarango asked, his curiosity aroused.

"No, not at all." Kilgore shook his head. "After they took care of the vamps, they became their big, slobbery selves again, just covered in blood."

"What about the kid?" Tarango looked at the floor regretfully. "Did they tear her apart too?"

"Left the child alone completely," said Kilgore, still slightly dumbfounded by the fact. "Wasn't a vampire at all, just some abducted child, or at least that's what it looks like. She might be the offspring of one of these vamps before they were bit, I don't know. It looks like they kept her around as some kind of pet."

"I will never understand some of these bloodsuckers!" Tarango shook his head. "I take it you haven't got an ID on her?"

"We haven't been able to identify her yet. That's why we have no idea if she was abducted or belonged to one of them. She's around five or so and not much for talking. No idea if she's just being quiet or if she actually can't. Not giving us much at all either way."

"What are we going to do about the little girl's memories of past events?"

"Not really much of a problem at the moment, you know, since she doesn't say anything. She'll have no problem remembering something like this, though no one will ever believe her. On the other side of it, maybe some of the things she saw were just so traumatic that she'll drop them from her mind. Who knows? One thing is certain, though, somebody's going to have to cough up a fortune in counseling for her." He paused for a moment, expecting at least a chuckle from Tarango.

All he received was silence.

"And the basement still hasn't been cleared, Lieutenant?" Kilgore moved onto the situation at hand.

"The basement has stayed untouched as you ordered, sir." Tarango looked concerned. "I posted guards by the door, just in case more assailants are unaccounted for. Just as a personal concern though, sir, exactly why are we leaving the basement unclear? It kind of goes against common sense, sir. Dangerous to leave it like that."

A foreboding called out to them as they spoke, echoing to them from the heavy metal door at the corner of the living room.

"Did you try to blind any occupants with a flash-bang or soften them up with a grenade?" Kilgore ignored Tarango's objections.

"No, sir. You never really clarified earlier. You said you didn't want it cleared, so we left it untouched."

"Has the door been breached yet?"

"No need, sir. It's unlocked."

"Kind of reckless for them to leave it like that." Kilgore chuckled, shaking his head. "No evidence of any kills around or even in the house, and there they go leaving what is likely their larder unlocked. I tell you, these vamps, they must be blood drunk off their butts 24/7."

"It's a heavy door, sir. Too heavy for a single man to open. I doubt they felt it needed a lock."

"Evans! Salvo!" Captain Kilgore turned to the mass of personnel loitering on the other side of the room. "Put your guns down and go open that door!" he commanded, pointing toward it.

A short, squatty blond man and a wiry, Hispanic woman rushed from the crowd to the assigned point, each grabbing one of two handles.

"Wait a second." Kilgore held up an open palm to stop them. "We might have miscounted the number of assailants. Let's get someone to cover you." He gazed upon the gathered crowd once more, choosing carefully. "Harkman! Rogers! Get over there and cover that door!"

"But, sir, Evans and Salvo will not be clear of our shots!" Milo objected, dragging his feet.

The chilling presence in the room continued to intensify.

"Hazards of the job, Private!" The captain smiled, acting oblivious.

Milo looked at him as though he were insane.

"If there's a vamp hiding down there, we don't want to risk it getting loose," Kilgore told them. "Evans and Salvo are already dead if one of them breaks out right now! Best to shoot first and ask questions later when we know there are vamps around!"

"Stand off to the other side of the door!" ordered Kilgore. "It will be your best bet if you don't want your guns pointed right at them!"

Milo and Rogers took up shooting stances as they stood to the side of the door, prepared to follow the captain's orders no matter how apathetic he acted.

Evans and Salvo struggled with the door, unable to make it budge.

"Come on, you're going to have to do better than that to get that door open!" bellowed Kilgore, frustrated.

"Going to need more than two of us if you want it open," said Salvo, letting go of the handle.

"Let's see..." the captain looked toward the crowd once more, his eyes quickly settling on Asher. "Blackthorn, go over there and help them with that door. It's heavier than I thought."

Asher tightened his gun strap and made his way over to the door. He put both hands on the higher of the two handles, above Salvo's.

"All at once, guys," said Asher as they pulled in unison.

Though the door was heavy, Asher's added strength tipped the balance, and the apparatus slid open.

"Oh, my gosh..." Asher gasped, the door open only a crack. "What the heck is that smell?" Even as he asked, he knew what the odor was.

It was the stench of rotting human flesh, so strong and severe that it made him light-headed.

"Ahh! Captain, the smell is bad enough to make my eyes bleed!" Salvo complained, looking as though she might bolt from the door.

Several of the remaining personnel waved their hands around in an attempt to dissipate the foul odor. Several more put their hands over their noses.

"They're freakin' vamps, people!" the captain yelled back at them. "Their food caches always smell like festering dung heaps. Heck, if you think that's bad, you should check their bathrooms. That always makes for a good time."

Asher and his comrades had the door open now, a task nearly halted because of the smell. He alone leaned against the door to keep it open. The opening, dark and foreboding, made him anxious.

"Turn on your flashlight attachments, people!" demanded Kilgore. "No telling what's down there!"

"You go ahead and hang back, Blackthorn," he spoke directly to Asher. "I already fed you to the wolves once tonight."

"Evans! Salvo! Harkman! You come down into the basement right behind me and help clear the place! You over there!" The captain turned back to the group of soldiers who still stood in the living room, bored with idly standing there. "Follow us down there and back us up!"

Multiple soldiers moved toward the doorway. Kilgore quickly had all the personnel he needed, thirty or so of them all around him.

"Don't you think that's a little over-cautious, sir?" asked Tarango, still leaning against the column off to the side of the captain. "Even if we miscounted, it's unlikely there's more than a couple down there."

"Don't give me that, Lieutenant! Hard to have too many men when you take out the vamps. Like I always say, ain't no kill like overkill! Here we go!" Kilgore alerted the gathered personnel.

The captain took a flash-bang from the pack of the soldier in front of him and lobbed it through the doorway. A parade of quick steps moved down the stairs ringing out as the line of personnel disappeared into the darkness.

Hearing no shots fired, Asher moved away from the door, forgetting he was the only thing keeping it open. As he turned to catch it, he found it was stuck there in a resting position, too heavy to close.

"We're all clear down here!" Kilgore called back from the bottom of the basement, his booted feet striking the wooden stairs as he made his way back up. "Tarango! Get the rest of your platoon down here to see this! It is absolutely disgusting! Ought to be a good learning experience for them. Have the message relayed outside to Lieutenant Roth as well. Might as well show everyone the sights!"

Kilgore made his way back up the remainder of the stairs and peered around the doorway, turning to where Asher stood stationed at the door.

"Blackthorn!" he proclaimed. The captain spoke to Asher as he stepped back through the doorway. "You need to see what's down there!"

"Come on down!" Kilgore yelled at the remaining soldiers still standing near the staircase, waving them toward him. "You stay up here, Tarango, and make sure Roth's platoon gets in here." The captain sprinted back toward the door, fifteen or so soldiers following him.

Asher proceeded into the basement, finding it no longer dark. Someone had found the light. He gasped as he crossed the threshold, the smell more awful than he had imagined. Below lay an indescribable horror show, the scene unfit for the eyes of man. Though it was necessary to light the way, the illumination revealed every morbid detail. Asher remained at the top of the stairs, hesitant to proceed down, frozen in place by what he saw. The smell continued to burn into his eyes and nasal passages as though it put a stranglehold around his brain.

Shaking his head, he regained his senses and descended into the basement. He needn't traverse the stairs to see the innumerable corpses and body parts littering the place, all in various stages of decay. Partially skinned corpses hung from meat hooks with blood buckets situated underneath. Many of the other corpses, some of them quite small, were no more than piles of bones, the flesh stripped away. Bloody, severed limbs and heads sat on jagged, wooden tables, some partially eaten.

Asher only managed to view the sight for a few moments at a time. He looked away periodically and retched slightly, barely holding onto his last meal. The inhuman barbarism repulsive and beyond enraging, made him feel as though bullets were too merciful for the wretches responsible for the carnage below.

We should have crushed them with a steamroller, he thought to himself. *Starting from the toes up so they would feel every ounce of pain.*

Ill as he felt, Asher fared better than most. Several of his comrades actively vomited. Some managed to find a bucket, while most spewed the contents of their stomachs onto the bloodied floor.

Asher neared the bottom of the stairs, finding Aaron and Sergeant Ito standing nearby.

"Don't they believe in refrigeration?" asked Aaron, turning to Asher. "It smells like the bowels of Hell down here!"

"How's it going?" asked Asher, stepping onto the floor, ignoring Aaron's complaint.

"Not bad. Well, except for the smell," Aaron enthusiastically shook his head. "No action on the second floor, which is good, I guess. I missed out on giving it to the vamps, but whatever. Better than what you guys saw on the third floor. The sergeant told me there were six up there."

Asher's gaze shifted to Ito, who smiled at him and then

shrugged.

"Must have been intense. It sounded like a war was going on up there," Aaron finished.

"Yeah, it was bad up there." Asher nodded. "Things got close. Not sure if I was going to make it."

"Oh, my gosh! Why would they do this!"

The second platoon entered at the top of the stairs, their cries of disgust and repulsion drowning Asher out. A few of the soldiers made their way down, but most remained where they stood, crowding the doorway, just as hesitant to descend the stairs as Asher was earlier.

"Come on, guys!" shouted Lieutenant Tarango, appearing behind the sluggish platoon. "Captain Kilgore intends for this to be a learning experience for all of us, and it will last much longer if you never get down there!" The remainder of the company slowly filtered down.

"Try to hold onto your lunches, people!" Kilgore commanded, hearing Tarango give his title. "You might as well get used to the gore. It gets even worse than this sometimes." Kilgore stood off in the middle of the grotesque, barbaric scene waiting. Asher had missed his entrance, still preoccupied with all of the bodies.

"Who does this?" Salvo shrieked, suddenly losing all composure. "Freakin' bunch of psychos!" She stood in front of Asher and his friends now. "Why can't they just stick to blood?"

"It's always the clean-cut and good-looking vampires that have the nastiest basements," Ito noted. "Hope this teaches you a lesson about hesitation, Blackthorn."

She placed her hand on his shoulder. "No matter how harmless some of them might make themselves seem, they always have some sort of horror show going on behind the scenes."

"Lesson learned, Sergeant," said Asher.

He was proud of himself for not vomiting earlier, though he knew he couldn't keep his stomach contents down for much longer.

When the reflex finally took him, he sprinted for the nearest bucket, finding it already filled with blood, which made him retch even more. Stomach empty, Asher returned to where his friends stood. He wiped the edges of his mouth with his sleeve, acting as though nothing had happened.

"Why would they leave all these bodies right out here to rot like this?" Salvo asked, gagging as though she might vomit again. She remained standing in front of Aaron and Ito.

Asher passed around them to retake his spot against the wall.

"I think some of them prefer their meat like this," said Milo, materializing from nowhere to answer Salvo's question. "A lot of wild carnivores will leave their meat out to rot for the same reason. It's a means of tenderization. The bacteria break down the meat so that it is easier to tear off and chew."

"This is just nasty!" Salvo's face turned green. "Surely they could have done something other than let it get like this."

"Yeah, you would think." Milo nodded in agreement. "Vamps just have some peculiar tastes."

"Quiet!" Captain Kilgore yelled. He raised his fist into the air, causing all talking to cease immediately. "Good," he said, his arm back at his side. "Now that most of the company is down here, we'll get started. It looks like the majority of you have had a hard time keeping your dinner down. I don't blame you for it, this being the first operation for most of you. I wish I could say it gets easier, but it doesn't. It's just the nature of our enemy. They're dangerous, disgusting, and cruel. They have to be stopped." Kilgore searched over the company, his hidden rage beginning to seep out. Most of the soldiers were disinterested in what he said, distracted by the gore and their stomach sicknesses.

"This is why we do what we do!" roared Kilgore, violently kicking a blood-filled bucket with his boot. It struck the adjacent wall with a loud crash, its contents splattering all over, catching some nearby soldiers.

"We have yet to find a vamp, no matter how civil and domesticated it might act, who wasn't a bloodthirsty killer. It would be nice if they would just stick to the killing. There's no telling what these wretches did to these people, freakin' some of them children, before they killed them! This is why they must all be exterminated!" Kilgore looked over the faces of the gathered company, expecting to see his dark enthusiasm reflected there. He frowned, finding a bunch of tired, blood-splattered, and grossed-out personnel.

"Well, looks like that's all she wrote," said Kilgore, reading the room, seeing it really was time to pack it up for the night. "Nice job on your first op for all our new people. This was about as open and shut as an operation can be, so don't expect things to come out this clean. Uncommon not to have any losses."

Kilgore paused to look over the corpses. His eyes widened as though he had only just realized he was standing in the middle of Satan's morgue.

"Suppose we can leave the vampire food cache now. Forensics is on its way to catalog all this. Hopefully, they can work through this and identify most of the deceased before we destroy the house. That's all I have for you, so everybody out! Tarango! Roth! Take your platoons back to the buses!"

The company withdrew up the stairs as soon as he uttered the word 'out.' None desired to remain in the grotesque slaughter-dungeon.

Asher had never seen so many people exit a basement that quickly.

Chapter XVIII

An Unlikely Epidemic

The creature moaned, sounding more like a cow than the mutated zombie-ape monster it was. The desert heat died away with the twilight, though it was unbelievably hot and miserable out in the open. All rational beings had escaped to the shade.

Cyrus instinctively kept to the shadows. He stayed low to the ground as he maneuvered the town's streets, slipping between houses and buildings in a haphazard attempt to remain unseen by his quarry. Not only did the shadows provide cover and protection from the heat, it kept the glaring light of the sun's rays from hitting his retinas. The fiery sphere descended in the sky now, its vivid, vibrant colors visible between the run-down houses of the facility.

Cyrus's hypersensitivity to light had improved substantially throughout his stay in the facility, though his ability to see the color red had disappeared entirely. His vision was like that of a feline now. He could only see colors within the green, yellow, and blue portion of the light spectrum during the day. All color vision gave way to black and white at night.

The creature moaned again, causing Cyrus to stop in his tracks. He took a whiff of its vile odor, a stench that became more putrid and pungent as he drew near. His heart rate increased as he closed in on his prey, allowing him to anticipate the coming change to his psyche.

Cyrus felt the urge start to claw at him.

The savage animal would soon escape the cage of his human mind. Cyrus knew he wouldn't be able to resist it much longer, no matter how much he tried to hold it back.

The creature continued its moaning, still unaware of the kresnik's presence.

Cyrus had yet to determine what made them act like this. Zombies abhorred the sunlight even more than he did. Cyrus had no idea what possessed them to venture out on their own like this, out into the open, the sun's rays shining right in their eyes and the heat radiating over them. Their brains, bogged down from the extended effects of their affliction, rendered them incapable of even the most instinctive thoughts. This level of sickness was becoming a common occurrence amongst the infected.

Regardless, the ultimate causation of their maladaptive behavior mattered little to Cyrus. It saved him from having to hunt during the darkest hours of the night, when the tables turned and the infected hordes stalked him. Moreover, he had a genetically enhanced affinity for these failing, irrational creatures. Cyrus could hear and smell them from miles away, even before he could see them. They were the perfect prey, made even more so by their obnoxious moans and foul stench.

Cyrus squatted beside the corner of the house, concealing himself as he prepared to make his next move. He looked to his right, through the chain-link fence and out onto the Arizona desert, the terrain spotted with cacti and patches of wildflowers dispersed among the rocks and sand. Cyrus couldn't describe how much he wanted to leave the facility, though he tried not to dwell on the thought. If he were to escape, it would be into a world of desolation and unbearable heat, with even less access to food and water.

Remaining in place, Cyrus shifted his gaze from what lay beside him to what flew above, casting an eye toward the top of the nearest white-painted guard tower. The acuity of his vision had improved to a superhuman level, allowing him to obtain a visual. All four tower guards hung hundreds of feet above him, the armed personnel walking the perimeter of the tower platform along the railings. Cyrus knew they wouldn't hesitate to fire upon him should they see him, but he wasn't terribly concerned.

Though the guards refused to believe it, their shots had little to no effect on him, failing to penetrate his nearly impervious hide. The rounds from their assault rifles simply were not of a high enough caliber to cause any real, lasting damage. Cyrus had felt the bite of their bullets numerous times over his stay at the facility, and though each shot certainly hurt, they presented him with only a mild inconvenience. His experiences aside, Cyrus refused to willfully step in front of the towers. There was always the chance that one of them might get lucky.

The creature moaned for the last time, announcing its position and shifting Cyrus's focus back to it once again.

The kresnik rested his back against the wall of one of the houses now, preparing to take the corner. Cyrus's hunger, which had nagged at him from the start of the hunt, exploded into an all-consuming wildfire. He tensed, making a vain attempt to keep his rage contained. Fearful of what he would soon become, he was unable to hold back any longer.

Cyrus closed his eyes as the bloodlust seared into his mind, occupying his every thought. His humanity vanished, replaced by an animalistic psyche. Only slightly aware of all his actions, he would have no way to quell his urges. Cyrus was only along for the ride. He shook as though to burst, and then his reality snapped.

Cyrus roared, speeding around the corner like death's javelin, bounding over rocks and debris toward the zombie near the side of the fence. His prey didn't even have time to turn its head before he was upon it.

Cyrus ran down his target with devastating speed and tenacious ferocity. He struck the creature in the back of the head with razor-sharp claws and leveled it to the ground. The kresnik pounced upon the back of his doomed victim, clamping down on its windpipe with a wide, savage bite as he tore into the flesh.

The zombie continued to struggle despite the ferocity of the attack, a futile attempt to preserve its worthless life. The creature could only resist its inescapable fate for so long and finally succumbed to asphyxiation and blood loss.

* * *

Cyrus felt his rage subside as he transcended back into himself. His humanity returned, and the feral hunger burned away.

He nearly screamed when he looked down and saw his clawed hands, stained black with the blood of a creature that so closely resembled a human. He gazed over the corpse, finding the head nearly severed from its body, the abdomen shredded asunder with the internal organs partially ripped out.

Cyrus retched and choked, suppressing his disgust, knowing there were always potential adversaries lurking nearby. He felt something oddly chewy in his mouth and slowly reached up to remove it. Cyrus held the slimy morsel out in front of him, squinting to see what it was. He winced as he tossed it away, realizing it was a piece of intestine.

Cyrus crawled away from his kill and toward the side of the wrecked house, fearing he might vomit. He desperately wanted to avoid throwing up pieces of zombie. Cyrus remained on all fours by the house, continuing to gag, black blood occasionally spewing from his mouth.

Satisfied he could keep the rest of his hellish meal down, Cyrus sat up. He looked over his kill once again, finding various parts of the zombie's corpse tossed all about. The infected always appeared much less intimidating once torn asunder. Cyrus hated turning to them for sustenance. He had searched everywhere for other sources of nourishment, checked every crevice of the enclosed facility for some morsel, some scrap of unspoiled food.

Cyrus had turned to rancid zombie flesh much sooner than he wanted to, his hunger great, yet still nowhere near the starvation level when his killer instincts first kicked in. It was as though his body was unwilling to let him return to a state of weakness and took action to prevent it. All of it was ghastly and barbaric, but Cyrus had no other choice. He hadn't even had the option to let himself starve.

Cyrus heard the howls of several of the infected, surprised by how close they were. He was so preoccupied with his kill that he hadn't noticed how late it was. The sun was barely visible above the horizon now, and the sky took on a dark blue hue, signaling the coming darkness. The hordes of infected would eventually find him if he didn't move soon.

The kresnik rose to his feet and walked over to the zombie carcass. Cyrus took the body up in his arms and slung it over his shoulder, crouching down as he snuck down the alleyway. Though he was perfectly adapted for hunting at night, the massive zombie hordes gave him no other choice but to seek shelter. Cyrus moved cautiously through the streets of the facility, careful to stay quiet as he went.

The horde called out from the approaching darkness, sounding as though it had increased in size and proximity.

Cyrus needed to reach his hovel soon, lest his primal urges emerge once again when he neared the horde. Ever since his first encounter with the infected, he avoided mass groupings of zombies. He had no idea what would happen should he run into them this evening. Though drawn to single sickly individuals, bloodlust enraptured Cyrus whenever he was close to any of them. He was always careful to go out only during the dawn and dusk hours, encountering only handfuls of zombies at once. His encirclement by a horde would undoubtedly result in a bloodbath, one in which he would kill many but ultimately be overwhelmed.

The cries of the horde became weaker and more distant as the creatures prepared to attack one of the towers.

Cyrus continued through the streets and alleys of the town on cat's feet, his kill's body hanging limply over his shoulder. He occasionally scanned the tops of the houses, gazing westward toward the giant tower. The spotlights illuminated the continually darkening night. He had built his shelter only a few hundred yards away.

The distant fire of guns confirmed Cyrus's guess. The horde would attack en masse, each individual making a run for the tower, always cut down before they reached it.

Cyrus stopped and shook his head. He had lived with the infected for almost a month now, and they never grew any smarter. The horde would attack the guard tower until nearly all lay dead, the zombies entirely oblivious to their fallen comrades through the onslaught. The kresnik smiled a dark smirk, his face concealed in the shadows. He was always happy to hear the wails of dying zombies.

The mindless assault continued as Cyrus turned down yet another alleyway. The kresnik knew the hordes could only be distracted for so long. He often wondered how any zombies remained, between those he killed and those gunned down by the guards.

Despite the promise of easy pickings, the multitude of bodies never appealed to Cyrus. They never called out to him the same way the living zombies did, never awakened the bloodlust sleeping within. It was just as well. The act would significantly increase his exposure to the tower's blazing guns. The prospect of sifting through bullet-riddled zombie bodies was even more horrifying to Cyrus. He didn't have much time to pick through them either way. All of those killed near the fences were always mysteriously removed before the dawn.

Cyrus heard another of the infected moan, this one surprisingly close. The cry was low and nearly inaudible, all but drowned out by gunfire, but his enhanced hearing abilities allowed him to pick it up. Cyrus broke into a run, almost dropping his kill as he did so. The sound was more terrifying to him than any other, threatening to unleash his uncontrollable, primal fury while simultaneously calling more zombies to him. Once near a large group of the infected, he would slaughter all around him, cutting down his opposition while the full force of the horde enveloped him, leading to his nightmare scenario.

Another moan came from only a few blocks over.

Cyrus was now in an all-out sprint, rushing down alleyways and bounding around corners, quickly changing directions multiple times to confuse his potential pursuers. He would have no other choice but to do the unthinkable if he didn't reach shelter soon. Zombie flesh wasn't an appealing meal, but he had put a substantial amount of time and effort into hunting it.

Feeling desperate, Cyrus skidded to a stop, taking in a whiff of air. His cat eyes widened with familiarity. He could smell his hideout now. Horrid as it was, the smell was what kept the hordes away.

Cyrus heard multiple moans, and he feared the infected would likely find him at any moment. His bloodlust began to tingle.

Cyrus tossed his kill to the ground. He grabbed one of the corpse's ankles in his talons and stretched the leg backward as he stomped down on the back of the pelvis with a clawed foot. The kresnik pulled and twisted the limb out of the socket with a crack, tearing the flesh as he wrenched from the rest of the body, black blood spewing forth. The leg wasn't a lot, but it would keep his hunger at bay for the time being. He slung the prize over his shoulder and leaped for the rooftop. He bounded from roof to roof, the claws of his feet scraping the shingles as he went, granting him traction and adding to his speed.

The moon all but dominated the sky now. The pale, glowing

crescent silhouetted Cyrus's quick-moving form against the darkened veil of night. The howls of the main horde grew louder yet remained distant. They concentrated on the tower, and none were alerted to the kresnik's movements.

Cyrus continued his run, but his haste gave rise to caution as he kept an eye to the streets below. There was a chance he had misinterpreted the positioning of some of the nearby infected, and the possibility of being ambushed by his urges remained a danger.

Something familiar caught Cyrus's eye. He could see his hovel hideout now. The rotting zombie corpse propped up on the roof illuminated in the moonlight acted as a scarecrow of deep depravity.

Cyrus made a b-line for his shelter, forgetting his sense of caution entirely. He knew if he closed the distance quickly enough, he would have protection from all zombie-kind, shrouded in the unholy stench of rancid decay. The kresnik hurtled over the houses, practically floating through the air, a cat-like creature flying through the early night's sky. The infected had no hope of catching him before he was within the perimeter of his shelter's zombie-repelling fumes. The stench was strong, and despite its repugnance, it was like the warm embrace of a loving parent.

Cyrus descended from the last rooftop and rushed for the door of one of the dumpier looking houses, dragging his prized leg behind him. He knocked over his display of piled zombie skulls as he pushed through the heavy door, the eyeless sockets staring up at him in indignant disdain. His hovel was nearly pitch black inside, cut off from any electricity like all the other houses in the facility.

Cyrus threw the severed leg across the room, where it landed on the chopping table as he entered the door. He slammed it shut behind him, turning back around to bolt the locks. His repellant could only do so much, never accounting for the possibility that the infected might throw him a curveball and suddenly change their behavior.

Satisfied that the locks were secure, Cyrus walked into the middle of what he had always assumed was the living room toward a large hole in the floor. It served as his cooking pit, the source of most of the horrible smell. Situated above the fire pit was a massive hole in the roof that served as a makeshift chimney. The irregular shape and burnt edges were a testament to Cyrus's inability to find any tools to carve them out. Instead, he had used matches to burn a hole through both the floor and ceiling, partially setting his shelter ablaze.

Cyrus reached down into the middle of the fire pit and removed what was once a marshmallow skewer, taking it off the two burnt, twisted Y-shaped hangers on which it sat. He returned to the kitchen and picked up the severed leg, jamming his skewer into the limb's severed end and pushing it through flesh and muscle until it exited through the foot. Cyrus put down the skewered leg and ambled over to another corner of the living room. He took a few boards from his modest collection of firewood, which consisted of paneling taken from some of the surrounding houses.

Cyrus dumped the wood into the fire. He searched the pit's perimeter for his lighter and hairspray can, finding them in the seat of his salvaged lawn chair. Cyrus crouched down beside the pit. He held the lighter in front of the aerosol can and squeezed their buttons simultaneously, setting the wood ablaze.

Content with his handiwork, Cyrus retrieved the skewered leg from the table and placed it down by the ends of the improvised spit, setting it securely between the bent Y hangers. He remained beside the fire, occasionally turning the skewer with his claws to ensure the meat cooked evenly. He reflected on his new barbarous ways as the leg roasted on the spit, thinking he should feel worse for what he did.

I suppose it's not much different from killing and dressing a deer, even if these things were human at one point, he thought to himself.

Cyrus's cat ears suddenly pricked up, causing him to rise from his crouched position. He left the blazing fire and went to the window at the corner of the living room. He was sure Dr. Shen's helicopter had returned at last. Cyrus had fully intended to keep a tally of the days spent at the facility after he arrived, but he had lost count early on due to his frequent primal outbursts. Regardless, he knew retrieval day was soon. Standing at the window, he separated the blinds with two clawed fingers and peered through.

Cyrus was disappointed by what he saw. He caught sight of the zigzag, fluorescent orange stripes of a lift helicopter, this particular craft sight a common sight within the facility. Lift helicopters flew over nearly every other day.

"Infected," Cyrus whispered, seeing the massive crate hanging from the helicopter. It was only his best guess, as he never confirmed precisely what the helicopters carried in the massive crates. It was the best explanation as to why the zombie's numbers never dwindled, even though the guards' assault weapons resulted in massive carnage on a nightly basis.

Bored by the view, Cyrus left the window for the fire pit and returned to his zombie leg. He crouched, continuing to rotate the skewer until the limb lost its green tint. A brown shade indicated a light roast, which singed off the hair. Cyrus found that the cooking time had only a small effect on taste. A burned leg was almost as horrible as a rare one.

He picked up the hot poker by his side and jammed it into the leg at the back of the knee, careful not to drop it as he brought it back to the table to cool. Cyrus had always heard that for best results, the meat needed to rest. It seemed no matter what he did to the meat, no matter how he cooked or seasoned it, it never tasted right.

Cyrus waited for a few more minutes before taking the leg in both hands and tearing into it with his razor-like teeth. He gagged frequently as he chewed. It was putrid, bitter, and a little on the stringy side, but he was hungry, and it was all he had. Sadly, it would not be enough to satisfy him for long. His metabolism had increased substantially, just as Dr. Shen had predicted. The more ravenous he became, the more prone he was to submitting to his primal urges. He would need to make a kill and return with the majority of the body soon.

Cyrus stripped the leg to the bone within minutes while still standing right at the table, unable to take a seat until he finished. His meager meal ingested, he carried the bare bones to the door and quickly unlatched all the locks, propping it open against the wall as he tossed his scraps through the doorway. He slammed the door shut and immediately fastened the locks. It was all part of his end-of-meal ritual. The flesh left on the bones quickly rotted under the Arizona sun, adding to the infected-repelling stench.

Finished disposing of his meal from hell, Cyrus made his

way to the restroom to retrieve a towel to wipe his face. After finding one on the side of the sink, his attention moved to the open medicine cabinet door hanging above it.

The mirror on the other side was hidden from view.

Cyrus hadn't looked at his face much since the change, and though he knew there was a high likelihood he wouldn't like what he saw, he was curious to see how he looked. He clasped the side of the door in his claws, closing it slowly at first and then slamming it shut against the cabinet.

Cyrus could only take a brief look at himself before throwing the door back open, shocked by his bloodstained vestige. He nearly broke the mirror when he hit it against the wall. He appeared only slightly human. His facial features had changed so much that he resembled a hairless cat, his skin translucently white, his ears large and pointed, his eyes still yellow. Cyrus moved a clawed hand over his head, stroking his nearly bald scalp, pleasantly surprised when he discovered fine white hairs growing there.

"Looks are still a game killer," he muttered. He skulked off to the kitchen for water, bloodstained towel in hand.

Water was one of the few things found in abundance within the facility. It was air-dropped every three days, always arriving in bulk, bottled, and wrapped in large palates. The infected usually got to it before he did, pilfering through and tearing into the bottles, lapping the spilled water from the ground. They never ruined all of it, though, which allowed Cyrus to create a considerable stockpile amassed within the unpowered refrigerator.

Once in the kitchen, Cyrus yanked open the refrigerator door and took out one of the bottles. He poured water onto the towel and wiped his face, removing all the blood. He knew he couldn't do anything about ugly, but he could at least stay clean.

Cyrus returned to the living room and stretched out in his salvaged lawn chair as he gazed up at the ceiling. He was unsure what he ought to do next, as he was so certain Dr. Shen would pick him up this evening. He supposed it was feasible that when Shen used the word 'month,' he meant thirty-one days. There also existed the possibility the doctor had lied yet again.

Cyrus couldn't bring himself to give credence to the thought. It just didn't make sense for CyberGen to put in all that time, effort, and money only to leave him here. Regardless, he knew the time spent in the mock-up facility was irrelevant. It would be a long time before he saw his loved ones again if the opportunity ever presented itself.

Cyrus thought about his mother and younger brother Asher often. He wondered what they were doing now, wanting to be near them once more. He knew they thought he was dead, passed away in a manner typical to those with his disease. They would grieve and then come to some acceptance of his death, never learning what truly happened to him. They would never recognize him in his new, ever-changing state. His former life was over now. He knew he would accept it in time.

Cyrus frowned, slowly rising to his feet once more, believing he heard the whooshing, sweeping blades of yet another helicopter.

Confident he was wasting his time, he leisurely walked over to the window and peered through the blinds, ready to find another lift helicopter. Scanning the horizon, his cat eyes widened with surprise.

A smaller, darker aircraft flew toward the facility, difficult even for him to make out.

Convinced without confirmation, Cyrus bolted from the window and made for his burnt-out chimney, leaping through the hole to land on the roof, making for the departure tower. He had no idea how long the doctor would wait.

* * *

Cyrus bounded over the roof of the last house and dashed for the base of the exit tower, relieved when he found the doors separating the ladder from the rest of the facility wide open. The helicopter had landed moments earlier, now concealed from him at the top of the tower.

Cyrus dashed for the ladder, not bothering to check for zombies at any point on his run. He focused solely on the base of the tower. The night had reached the apex of darkness, and the only light came from the crescent moon and the towers. The passage of time intensified his resolve. He rushed through the doors to the ladder and ascended toward the top of the tower. The moonlight barely caught Cyrus in its rays. The kresnik nearly ran up the side of the wall on all fours. His physical prowess enabled him to clear the distance in no time.

Quickly ascending the tower, Cyrus slowed down as he prepared to clear the ledge at the top. He knew the guards would be displeased should he suddenly bolt onto the roof.

The muzzles of two assault rifles greeted him just as his head appeared over the ledge, warranting his concerns. Each weapon rested in the hands of nervous and uneasy tower guards.

Neither man looked pleased to see him.

"Hey, what's with all the hostility?" Cyrus asked, looking up at them, red laser pointers dancing across his forehead. "I'm just here to go back home," he said as he crawled over the ledge to stand in front of the guards.

Both armed men wore black body armor. Both remained silent, likely surprised that the creature below was capable of speech. They stepped back to give Cyrus room.

"The last thing I want to do is harm anyone," Cyrus continued, giving the guards a broad, toothy grin. He decided to channel his own misgivings back at them.

Both guards moved farther back when they saw his prominent fangs.

"Sorry. Just following orders." The guard retained his deadly aim. "Can't be too careful."

Each man stepped to the side so Cyrus could approach the helicopter. The aircraft sat motionless on the pad. He felt the guns follow him as he passed.

"Hello, Mr. Blackthorn. I trust you are ready to go back home?" Dr. Shen turned and identified himself. He walked toward Cyrus, his glasses gleaming in the moonlight. He stared at the kresnik, taking in his new appearance.

"Heck yes," said Cyrus, leisurely walking toward the doctor. "It's been no fun at all. No one to talk to for a month. Nothing but those things down there. It was a real drag." Though he was excited to leave the facility, he wanted to seize the moment and make Shen talk. "Before you take me back, I have a few questions I need answered." Cyrus lowered his voice, letting out a low growl. He couldn't keep up his casual ruse much longer.

"Do your questions need to be answered here? This is neither the time nor the place, Mr. Blackthorn. If you'll come back with me,

I'll answer whatever questions you might have."

Sensing Cyrus's hostility, the doctor pulled a strange-looking device from his lab coat pocket. It was a remote control. The doctor placed his thumb over the big red button in the middle, prepared to press it.

By the way he held it, Cyrus knew it was the remote to his shock collar.

"Can you tell me what those things down there are exactly?" Cyrus ignored Shen's wordless threat. "They move and act like zombies, I'll give you that, but they sure don't look like they were ever human." His anger grew. It had been brewing since he stepped foot in the town mock-up. Cyrus would make the doctor admit to his lies. He couldn't tolerate Shen holding his cure over his head and using it as a tool to force him around any longer.

"They are human infected. The disease only occurs in humans. I told you that. The infected we have quarantined here are in the advanced stages of the disease. That's why they look like they do."

"Wrong answer!" Cyrus howled, suddenly flipping into full predator mode. He broke into a run and charged at the doctor.

The guards kept their weapons trained on him, ready to fire once given the word.

"Don't shoot him!" commanded the doctor. "We don't want to injure him! He's far too valuable to us!" Shen pressed down on the red button.

Cyrus screamed as the overwhelming pain of the collar's electrical charges coursed through his body, stopping him just before he could reach the doctor. He continued to howl, fighting through the pain. He somehow managed to stumble the last few feet, grasping for Shen's throat.

"You might as well throw that away, doctor!" Cyrus roared. He grabbed Shen by the shirt collar and hoisted him up into the air. "The shocks aren't working!"

Shen dropped the red-buttoned remote, and it skidded across the roof.

Cyrus spun the doctor around, holding him up in front of the guards, the way an angler might hold up a big catch. "Hold your fire, or I give the doctor the world's worst tracheotomy!"

The kresnik put his free hand to the doctor's throat, the tips of his claws pressed against Shen's windpipe.

The guards looked at Shen in desperation, their eyes asking what they should do next.

"Lay down your arms and do what he says!" Shen ordered. "You'll barely be able to scratch him anyway. Your weapons aren't of a high enough caliber. Even if you could kill him, he is now more valuable to CyberGen than I am."

"Put the guns on the ground and slide them away!" Cyrus commanded. "The doctor and I just need to talk. So long as he answers my questions, no one gets hurt!"

The guards hesitantly placed their weapons on the ground and pushed them across the rooftop.

Satisfied, Cyrus turned his attention back to Shen. "Tell me the truth!" he roared in the doctor's face.

"It's the truth, Mr. Blackthorn," the doctor replied calmly, though his body trembled. "It doesn't matter if you believe it or not."

"Doctor, were those things human infected, or weren't they?" Cyrus softened his voice slightly.

"They are human infected, just like I said." Shen resisted, though Cyrus knew the doctor could only hold in his fear for so long.

"Dang it, doctor!" Cyrus's hungry glare became a frown. "There's no way those things are purely the result of a viral infection! You made them in the lab, didn't you? Tell me the truth! You know I'm perfectly capable of killing you right here!" He scratched the side of the doctor's neck with one of his claws, drawing blood, a droplet running down his throat. "Tell me what I need to know!" He raised Shen farther up into the air. "I don't want to have to make good on my threats!"

'It seems one of the side-effects of your transformation is heightened moodiness and aggression," the doctor remarked, disregarding the deadly claws so near his throat. He was determined not to give Cyrus any satisfaction that his threats were leaving an impact. "I'm sorry, Mr. Blackthorn." Shen shook his head regretfully. "I'm not at liberty to give you that information!"

"How stubborn can you be?" Cyrus snarled.

He placed his free hand against the doctor's stomach, right under his ribs.

"What did you do to make them? Tell me what I need to know, or I'll kill you in a much slower and much more painful way! Worse than having your throat torn out!"

"Alright, I'll tell you!" the doctor screamed hysterically. He finally snapped, failing to keep his fear in check. "The infected down there are not human! You might even say they aren't infected at all."

"If they're not human, then just what are they?" Cyrus returned to a civil tone. Finally hearing what he wanted, he lowered the doctor to the ground, retaining his grip on Shen's collar.

"They are laboratory-grown specimens, never bitten or infected." Shen lowered his voice, still sufficiently terrified. "Their genome consists mostly of chimpanzee or gorilla DNA with the viral genes already integrated in. The genes of several other primates were also spliced in to give each type of zombie the desired look."

"Why would you ever want to do that?" Cyrus tightened his grip on the doctor's collar.

"We needed stronger zombie specimens." Shen's tone changed in kind. "We wanted to give you a challenge! We wouldn't have been able to properly subject you to selective pressures if we pitted you against a bunch of infected human weaklings. We've also had difficulty finding very many humans infected with the virus. What can I say? It just doesn't spread very quickly."

"Why couldn't you tell me they aren't human?" Cyrus was flabbergasted now. "Wouldn't it have made things easier? I've spent the last month believing I was committing cannibalism!"

He removed his claws from the doctor's throat, content with the answers given him.

Realizing the doctor was no longer under immediate threat, the guards went for their guns and pointed them at Cyrus's head.

"It is a relief to hear that, though." Cyrus gave Shen an awkward half-smile. He knew he appeared to have an extreme mood swing, but his rage was simply an act to make the doctor talk. "Makes me feel much less like a monster, even if I am beginning to look like one." He wanted to believe his own words.

"Believe me, if it were up to me, you would be briefed on every detail." Shen grasped his throat with his hand, making sure it was still intact. "I don't know why CyberGen's board of directors likes to retain such a high level of secrecy."

"Where are Elysia and Viddur?" Cyrus ignored the doctor's excuse and looked toward the helicopter for the siblings.

"They couldn't be here this evening as they have other duties to be carried out," said Shen.

Cyrus might have asked what these other duties were but decided against it. "Are we going back to the CyberGen facility where I underwent the treatment?" he asked instead.

"Of course." Shen raised an outstretched arm. "Where else do you think I would be taking you?"

"Well, after everything I've been through here, I thought I might ask." Cyrus remained where he stood. "I don't need any more surprises. What do you have planned for me now that I have completed your survivability test?"

"Oh, we have many things planned for you, Mr. Blackthorn." Shen finished straightening his collar. "Our work is just beginning. That's why we're taking you back to the facility in which you were initially treated. Once there, you will be put through an intensive training regimen."

"That's just great." Cyrus gave Shen a sarcastic frown as he started toward the helicopter, a clear lack of enthusiasm in every step.

Chapter XIX

The Trappings of Terror

"Hey, man, wake up," said a male voice.

A hand shook Cyrus by the shoulder. He nearly jumped from his bed, his fatigue and weariness the only thing stopping him.

"What?" Cyrus slapped the hand away and reluctantly opened his eyes. He found Viddur standing over his hospital bed, his face barely visible through the haze of bright lights.

Cyrus vigorously shook his head, the weariness still holding him down as he tried to determine precisely where he was. He groaned and sat up in bed, his eyes slowly adjusting to the light. The room was solid white, typical of nearly any room at CyberGen, and contained only a few pieces of furniture. It was almost identical to his room from before. The only difference was a startling lack of machines and monitors.

"How did you guys get in here?" asked Cyrus, rubbing his eyes. He felt groggy, as though he awakened from a deep, drug-induced sleep. He had no memory of arriving back at the facility.

Dr. Shen likely hit me with another sedative.

Cyrus decided to let his frustration with the doctor go for the moment. He looked down and felt a lack of air flowing through the holes in his clothes. His tattered grey tracksuit was removed and replaced with a new one.

Cyrus gazed toward the door, finally able to see through all the white, realizing Elysia was in the room as well. She grinned at him, holding up a bent paperclip.

"It was pretty easy to figure out which room you were in," Viddur explained. "Door was locked when we got here, though.

Elysia picked it." Viddur turned to Elysia, then back to Cyrus, a wicked grin on his face. "She can be as bad as me sometimes."

"Viddur, you're a terrible influence." Elysia tucked the paperclip back in her pocket and remained near the door.

"Don't you think Dr. Shen's going to be at least a little upset that you're in here with a potentially dangerous monster?" Cyrus asked. He only now remembered his ordeal in the quarantine facility and the physical changes that had accompanied it.

"Probably, but he'll get over it," said Viddur, his words reenforced by his carefree attitude. "He did say you only go nuts when you're around zombies and vampires, so I thought we would probably be safe. Besides, you're no monster. You're just a big, white pussy cat." He leaned toward Cyrus, reaching for his ear.

Cyrus raised a hand to stop him, catching him by the wrist.

"Come over here, Elysia." Viddur wrenched his hand from Cyrus's grasp. "You like cats. Don't you want to pet the big ugly kitty?"

Elysia blushed but remained where she was, hesitant to approach.

"What are you doing standing over there like that?" Viddur was suddenly aware of his sister's reluctance.

"Sorry, Cyrus, but as much as I wanted to see if you were OK, I would prefer we had Dr. Shen's final word before I get too close," said Elysia.

Cyrus might have taken offense if not for the stagnating effects of the sedative.

"I know you wouldn't willingly try to hurt us, but I would rather be on the safe side." Elysia gave him a half-smile, genuine concern plastered on her face. "I'm sure you wouldn't want it on your conscience if you unwittingly harmed one of us."

A series of knocks at the door silenced anything else she had to say.

"Hello, it's Dr. Shen," said the muffled voice through the door, keys jingling as the doctor rummaged through his lab coat. "That's strange. The door is unlocked," Shen grumbled as he twisted the door handle.

Elysia stepped out of the way, moving toward the wall away from the door, still weary of Cyrus. Viddur remained near the bed, undeterred by Dr. Shen's arrival.

"Hello." Dr. Shen stepped into the room, his eyes narrowing when he saw Viddur. "I see you have decided to disregard direct orders, as usual, and reintroduced yourselves to Mr. Blackthorn before I had a chance to re-evaluate him." Dr. Shen shook his head as he pulled out a stool and sat down beside Cyrus's bed.

"We just wanted to see him." Elysia stepped forward. "You did leave him at the quarantine facility, out in the middle of nowhere for a month, without any human interaction. So what if we just wanted to see how he was doing?"

"I appreciate your concern Elysia, but it was just a formality," Dr. Shen explained, unsurprised to find her in the room as well. "As you know, we have engineered Cyrus to be dangerous only towards organisms infected with the vampirism virus and its derivatives, but this does not mean we should forego all precautions. Would you be so kind as to leave the room now?" Shen gave Elysia no chance for a retort, his lab assistant glaring at him with agitation.

"I would like to begin Mr. Blackthorn's examination. You can wait in the hall. The examination will not take long."

"Whatever you say, doc," said Viddur. Both he and Elysia made for the door.

"Goodbye, Cyrus," said Elysia as she left the room.

"See you later, man." Viddur followed her, closing the door behind him.

"Do I need to undress for the examination?" Cyrus rose from the bed, ready to remove his pants.

"Oh, no, that will not be necessary, Mr. Blackthorn." Dr. Shen raised an open palm to stop him. "You survived a month trapped in a 'quarantine' facility and made it out alive. You have to be in at least decent physical condition to have made it through those trials. I only said I was here to perform a physical evaluation to keep Elysia and Viddur out of the room."

"Whatever you say." Cyrus sat back down. "What would you like to talk about?"

"First, I would like to ask if you had any questions regarding absolutely anything you have experienced here at CyberGen?"

"Yeah, what gives with all these sedatives?" The memory of his previous bout with Dr. Shen returned. He reached for his own throat and found the shock collar around his neck.

"It was for safety and also convenience, I suppose. You had just threatened to kill me, so it should come as no surprise that we had to sedate you."

"Yes, I suppose. You realize I had no intention of harming you. You're just so thick-headed and closed-lipped sometimes that the threat of violence seemed to be the only way to make you talk."

"I would have told you everything you needed to know at some point in time." Shen placed a hand on the end of Cyrus's bed. "You only needed to remain patient for a little longer."

"Understood," said Cyrus, trying to avoid a scolding. "Can you tell me what exactly your intentions are for me? I know we have talked about it before, but there's something you aren't telling me."

"Mr. Blackthorn, you were created to combat the growing vampire threat."

"Yes, you have told me more than once, doctor. I just don't quite understand why you want me to kill them. I mean, they're not like the zombies, if what you said earlier is true. If they retain most of their mental faculties, they're not much different from any other human. They're just sick people that we have no medication for yet. I understand how they can be dangerous, but why have me kill them? Can't we, I don't know, just lock them up until there is a cure?"

"You are somewhat correct." Shen stepped in front of Cyrus as though he were about to give a long academic lecture. "These people are indeed ill and as such should be allowed treatment. That I will not argue. However, there exists a large portion of those with vampirism that seek to take advantage of the side-effects imparted to them by the disorder."

Cyrus felt his rage cool upon hearing the doctor's words. He hated the doctor's habit of not telling him everything upfront.

"I've told you this before, Mr. Blackthorn, and now you have observed it in our lab-grown zombies at the facility. The disorder comes with a considerable increase in physical strength, speed, and stamina."

"That sure isn't the case with zombies, at least not after a while." Cyrus gazed up at Shen. "Many of the infected routinely became ill, or that is, more ill than they were. I don't think it would have taken much effort for a healthy adult to take them out when they got like that. Those were the ones I liked to feed on. They were the easiest ones to bring down."

"Yes, I've heard as much from the guard's reports." The doctor nodded in agreement. "It makes absolute sense that you would prefer to feed in the way you did. It's only the most rational method."

"Exactly," Cyrus concurred. "But, did you design your zombies to act in a specific manner?" He asked while suspicion flooded his head. "Or, I suppose more to the point, did you design them to expire after a certain period of time?"

"I suppose I should have addressed it earlier." Shen pulled his stool toward the wall adorned with the one-way window. He sat there, staring down at his shoes before looking back up at him. "The reason those particular infected acted the way they did was that they were approaching the end of their lifespan. As I have said before, it is rare for one inflicted with zombie-ism to survive for more than a few months before they succumb to its effects. It's even worse when those individuals are conceived with the viral DNA already integrated into their genome, as is the case with our artificial zombies. Our clones were designed to mature at an accelerated rate so that the disorder couldn't kill them before they were mature enough to be placed in our quarantine facility. There is no scenario where something like that is going to have a very long lifespan. It's another one of the reasons zombie-ism is not a real threat to humanity. That, and the fact that it is considerably difficult to spread disease via bite, along with several other issues."

"Makes sense," Cyrus spoke nearly under his breath. He found what the doctor had to say about zombie-ism interesting even though he had heard most of it before. It awakened the long-sleeping genetic engineer within him.

"Severe mental degradation is not something that usually occurs with vampirism," Shen moved on. "Their human intelligence along with the strength and durability that their disorder grants them tends to give rise to those with vampirism developing a belief system wherein they think themselves superior to all. They feel they are the next step in human evolution. This idea can then lead to a desire to enslave or even eliminate those they see as being beneath them. It doesn't help that humanity is essentially their food source, which reinforces such beliefs."

Cyrus frowned. He felt as though the doctor neglected to mention something. "So what are you saying, doctor?" he asked. "I can understand how they would be an obvious threat, but... I mean, they should be killable. You said yourself, bites don't spread pathogens around as efficiently as even the air does. Unless... no..." He was finally catching on. "Are they organizing?" he asked, worried that his intelligence was slightly diminished by stating it.

"Precisely. Their numbers are on the rise, and they are indeed organizing. There is one organization, in particular, that is steadily becoming very powerful, according to reports from our military connections. They must be stopped before their numbers rise to the point where they are capable of bringing humanity to its knees, twisting it to their needs. It is for this reason you were created."

"Is there no other way to stop them?"

"Various anti-vampire weapons have been developed, but none have been very successful."

"Why not?"

"Oh, for several different reasons. When the government first learned of the existence of this particular vampire organization, Atropos, conventional weapons were used. Assault rifles and weapons like that. They typically didn't work very well, given the impenetrability of a vampire's dermis. Those dedicated to facing the vampire threat now carry more powerful weapons, such as automatic shotguns and grenades. They use those and their own ingenuity, but they need more if they wish to eliminate the threat."

"Exactly who is responsible for facing the vampire threat?" Cyrus interrupted, unwilling to hold the question down too long.

"So far, it has been a paramilitary branch of the US military known as G96 or Legion 96. They are responsible for the field testing of all of the anti-vampire weapons, both with and without our collaboration. They have seen moderate success keeping the vampires in check, more or less, though they haven't been able to significantly reduce their numbers."

And exactly how did they obtain any realistic numbers? Cyrus thought to himself, deciding to let it go.

"Is there a specific reason as to why you want a purely

biological weapon?" he asked instead. "Wouldn't a robot be a better hand-to-hand combatant for a vampire?"

"We've tried to come up with a robotic solution for some time now, but the field just isn't there yet."

Dr. Shen rose from his seat again and stood between Cyrus and the one-way mirror.

"Granted, we have some technologically advanced prototypes at CyberGen, but they are complex and cannot be produced in quantities large enough to deal with the vampire menace. There will likely come a day when robots will be the primary method of eliminating rogue vampires, but that day is not here yet."

Probably the day they let me go home, Cyrus thought.

"That leaves the biological weapons," said Shen. "We have tried to create other viruses that specifically target vampires, but we've had no success at all. This brings us back to the visceral. We have artificially created a breed of dog in one of our other facilities, one that sniffs out vampires and then eliminates them. Legion 96 calls them hellhounds. As of right now, I have little information regarding the status of that project."

Shen took a breath as he prepared for a shift in their conversation.

"Even from the beginning, we knew we needed something more intelligent, a creature with reasoning abilities like our own, one we could communicate with verbally. You are only our latest attempt at a prototype. If you show promise, or that is, if you survive your early operations, there are plans to create more of your kind. More kresnik, as we have decided to call you. I'm sure you heard the word at the quarantine facility."

"I suppose that means I won't be going home?" Cyrus nearly added the word 'ever' to the end of his question. He refrained, not wanting Shen to read into it further. The doctor hadn't given him much confidence. Cyrus believed the only way he would be going home would be in a body bag. He decided to leave the subject for a better time.

"No, you will not be going home anytime soon, Mr. Blackthorn." The doctor shook his head. "We did have an agreement. We would cure you of your genetic ailment so long as you agreed to assist us in our venture. Furthermore, as much as I detest the phrasing, you are the combined property of both CyberGen and the US military via the nanobots that now reside within you. If you were to be released now, you would be essentially stealing that property. I couldn't let you leave if I wanted to."

Shen made a failed attempt at eye contact.

"Have you forgotten what we have done for you, Mr. Blackthorn? You have been saved from inevitable death and saved from a lifetime of weakness and pain. Does that warrant at least some loyalty?"

"Doctor, I will never forget what you have done for me." Cyrus tried to rise to his feet but let himself fall back onto the bed, suddenly weak at the knees. "There are few things I wouldn't do for you, but you ask a lot. Almost too much, really. I'm not sure I realized what the trade-off entailed. A life of sickness and death for, basically, a life of indentured servitude." He gazed toward the one-way mirror in front of him, paying little attention to his reflection and staring into space.

"Do you really believe we can release you back into the world after what you have become?" asked Shen.

"I suppose not." Cyrus's gaze fell on his reflected image in the mirror. He looked into his yellow eyes. His attention then shifted down to his hand. Cyrus extended his fingers, scrutinizing his sharp, blackened claws. He retained only a few human features.

Cyrus was sure the doctor was right. He couldn't return to human society like this, no matter how much he wanted to. He had made Dr. Shen a promise. His predicament was no worse than it had been, though the circumstances had changed. He would play the doctor's game for the time being.

"Do you have any other questions?" Shen interrupted his thoughts.

"I have no idea what else to ask. It's a lot to take in, though I suppose I need to ask if there is anything else you need to tell me." Cyrus gave the doctor a critical look, doubtful that he would provide any additional information.

"There is one thing, Mr. Blackthorn."

"What's that?" Cyrus raised an eyebrow, or tried to, both of his missing.

"As I'm sure you are aware, your genetic 'alteration' has caused you to undergo several aesthetic changes."

"If you're going to call me ugly, you can just go out and say it."

"I wouldn't say that, Mr. Blackthorn." Dr. Shen almost smiled. "All of the changes to your appearance serve a purpose. Anyway, I was trying to say that you now look so unique that you can no longer go out in public without raising concern. In order to keep your new appearance from drawing unnecessary attention, a special uniform has been made for you."

Dr. Shen walked toward the wall in front of him and pressed a black button near the elongated one-way window. A section of the adjacent wall pushed into the surrounding surface and moved to the side to open where it became a sliding door.

The wall moved to reveal a glass-enclosed display containing a black, form-fitting set of body armor suspended within the uniquely shaped holes of a white, leather-covered foam block. The armor was complete with a helmet, fingerless gloves, and toeless shoes to accommodate Cyrus's claws. The skin of the armor had a dull gleam to it, as though it were made of polished cast iron.

"Aww..." Cyrus unexpectedly voiced his excitement.

He had never thought much of the clothes he wore yet was enamored with the ensemble. Cyrus ambled toward the body armor, and a light appeared in his cat's eyes. As he approached, he saw that the armor was not exactly black, but rather a dark grey, composed of a multitude of snake-like scales.

"Oh, that is sick." Cyrus touched the glass to catch his balance, failing to mask the awe in his voice. "Is that Dragon Skin?"

"I had planned to detail you on your new wardrobe. It will be discussed."

"OK, let's hear it." Cyrus barely heard him as he continued to stare at the armor.

"Capstone Armors created this set. I was told it is one of the best ballistic armors available. I'm not sure exactly what they called it... Black something... Black ada... Adamant? Something like that."

Dr. Shen put a thumb on his chin, staring off into space as he tried to remember.

"Anyway," the doctor continued, giving up. "I was told it's composed of a material stronger than Dragon Skin. As you can see, it was made with functionality in mind, though some liberties were taken to give it a certain intimidating quality. The helmet, gloves, and toeless shoes were altered here at CyberGen, as any collaboration with another corporation ran the risk of potentially revealing classified information. They needed to be specially designed to accommodate your needs."

"How did you convince them that CyberGen needed a set of ballistic armor like this? Sounds suspicious to me."

"Oh, no, that was not an issue. Our Robotics Department is currently developing several different types of battle drones for the military. We just told them we needed multiple sets of ballistic armor to test them on. We had to order a surplus so as not to raise suspicion, though, in all likelihood, you will need spares."

"I see."

"As I was saying," Shen suddenly remembered something. "This armor is made primarily of Black Adamant, which offers more protection than even Dragon Skin. The material itself is made of the strongest substances on earth, consisting of the teeth of the limpet mollusk laminated in fabric made of specially designed, synthetic spider silk. The whole set is made up of it, including the helmet, gloves, and toeless shoes. Though it is a ballistic armor, it provides ample protection from attacks by most bladed weapons."

"Do you think it will protect me from the vampires' claws?" Cyrus felt Dr. Shen had missed something. "That is provided they have them?"

"They do indeed have claws. And, no, the armor was not tested against any vampires. We had intended for your genetic alterations to cause the growth of a thicker, more durable dermis, which should provide additional protection should the armor be breached. So long as you are careful and don't put your trust entirely in the armor, you should come out alright."

"Wait a second," said Cyrus, his admiration for the armor replaced by concern. He was angry with himself for forgetting the meaning of the word 'ballistic.' "What's this about being shot? I thought we were dealing with vampires?"

"Did you forget what I said?" The doctor tried not to sound

critical. "You will be working closely with Legion 96 and will often be in close proximity to those with powerful projectile weapons. There is only one of you, and you will experience several situations where that added firepower will be essential to keep the enemy at bay. The armor will serve mostly to protect you from friendly fire, though you will likely have at least a few encounters with armed vampires. Some of them are sensible enough to carry weapons."

"Yeah, I guess I can see that happening."

"Now, on to the CyberGen alterations," the doctor continued. "I suppose it is obvious that we removed the tips of the gloves and shoes to allow you the use of your claws." Dr. Shen stepped forward, pressing a second button near the display, causing the glass to slide upward into the wall. He took the helmet from the display and held it out for Cyrus to see.

"The helmet is state of the art. The visor is photochromic in accordance with your light sensitivity and vision needs. You have computer interface via the visor, allowing you internet access and the ability to discern the location of yourself and others. All of that is voice-initiated, of course. It is equipped with the latest in communication technology, allowing you to speak with your handlers remotely."

The doctor pressed a button underneath one side of the helmet, causing small windows on either side of the helmet to open. "So that your hearing is not restricted, we installed ear slits. We're not sure as to how well your hearing compares to the decibel detecting devices in the helmet, so we've given you the option to switch to manual, so to speak."

Dr. Shen cradled the helmet in the crook of his arm.

"Exactly when will I be able to interface with any of this equipment?" asked Cyrus, his enthusiasm quenched at the mention of 'handlers.' "If you haven't noticed, I tend to go nuts on the hunt."

"You will have plenty of time to interface with the equipment." Shen blinked rapidly. "You will not be surrounded by zombies and vampires all the time. You will use the equipment in between encounters. The computer interface system is designed to shut down when your heart rate reaches a certain number of beats per minute."

"Any other disadvantages?"

"The helmet does not offer anything in the way of mouth protection when the vent is open." Shen hit another button, causing the mouth portion to fold open, the material seeming to melt away to accommodate Cyrus's jaws. The doctor moved a hand through the resulting hole. "Your fangs are one of your most formidable weapons, and we would like you to be able to use them. I would advise not letting yourself be shot or stabbed in the face."

"Always great advice."

Dr. Shen stepped toward him, handing him the helmet.

"OK, there's another thing," Cyrus wished the doctor would say what he needed to the first time. "You said you only want to conceal me from people without the clearance to know I exist. Do you expect me to run around in a full suit of armor all day?"

"Of course not. I only ask that you wear the helmet when you step outside your living quarters."

"Oh, is that all?"

"Yes. We absolutely cannot risk you exposing yourself."

"I suppose I can understand that." Cyrus sighed before slipping on the helmet. It fit his head perfectly and didn't even catch on his ears on the way down. "One heck of a helmet," he said. He found the visor tinted like a pair of sunglasses that compensated for the brightness of the room. "Too bad I have no idea how to turn it on."

"Just say 'activate.' It only recognizes your voice, so there's no danger of someone else turning it on. If you wish to turn it off, say 'disengage.'"

"OK, activate," Cyrus commanded the helmet.

The visor lit up, glowing a ghostly translucent blue, the word 'ACTIVATED' glaring back at him. The display lasted only a moment, and the visor returned to its previous tint.

"You can now interact with the computer interface. Ask it to display your location."

"Show me my current location." Cyrus was reluctant, but he was relieved when the visor display showed him positioned somewhere outside St. Louis. He had returned to the same facility as promised. The helmet glowed and displayed a map of the Midwest.

"I feel like I could be Ironman." Cyrus gave the doctor a fanged grin. "What else should I ask it to do?"

"I'm afraid we have a hectic schedule, Mr. Blackthorn," Shen killed Cyrus's mood. "There will be more time to experiment with the software later."

"Understood. Disengage," Cyrus ordered the helmet to turn off the software.

"That concludes your 'examination,' Mr. Blackthorn." Shen pressed the button to the side of the body armor display and closed the open portion of the wall.

"Come with me. I have something else to show you." He walked past Cyrus toward the door.

"It's not another zombie, is it? You don't want to see what happens when I get near them," said Cyrus as Shen opened the door.

Chapter XX

A Worthy Opponent

"Here we are, the Robotics Department." Dr. Shen stopped in front of what looked like the entrance to a high school gymnasium, the door possessing narrow, tinted windows.

"Dr. Ingram should be in." Shen gave the door several quick knocks and turned back toward Cyrus, Viddur, and Elysia. They waited as they listened for approaching footsteps.

"Yes?" asked a woman's voice, the door held ajar by the faceless speaker.

"Hello, Dr. Ingram." Dr. Shen spoke through the crack in the door. "You have a robot to show us?"

"That would be correct." Dr. Ingram pushed through the doors and stepped into the hallway. She was an African-American woman in her mid-thirties, her hair grown into an afro. She wore a welding apron in contrast to the usual lab coat.

"OK, I guess I might as well say it." Dr. Ingram crossed her arms as the door shut behind her. "I'm not pleased about today's set-up. The whole floor has been shut down for the remainder of the afternoon. No lab techs or assistants have been on the floor since noon. It's cost us half a day's worth of progress. I don't know why the higher-ups insist on such a high degree of secrecy surrounding your project."

"Yes, it is quite bothersome at times." Dr. Shen attempted to sound empathetic. "Though, I do understand the need for such precautions. The project is highly classified."

Dr. Ingram glanced at Cyrus. "Speaking of which, Daniel, don't you think the helmet is a little unnecessary?"

"Sorry, we didn't want to risk exposing him to anyone on the way over," Dr. Shen explained. "His appearance can be somewhat startling if you're not prepared for it."

"Oh, give me a break!" said Dr. Ingram, exasperated. "He can't be all that frightening. Besides, there's no one on this floor but us right now."

"Would you like me to take it off now?" Cyrus grinned, revealing his elongated canines. Both clawed hands clenched the back of his helmet as he began to remove it.

"Oh no, that's OK." Dr. Ingram stepped forward and held out her hand to stop him. "You can keep it on."

"You sure?" Cyrus kept his hands in place. "I'm quite the looker anymore."

"Yes, I'm sure you are." Dr. Ingram put her hand down and stepped back. "I just don't want to hurt Dan's feelings. We can't have you outshining him in the looks department."

Viddur and Elysia turned toward Dr. Ingram, surprised to hear anyone talk about Dr. Shen in such a manner. Cyrus thought he might start laughing.

"Dr. Ingram, could you please show us the robot?" asked an irritated Dr. Shen. "We're not here for a comedy routine."

"Relax, Dan, I'm getting to it." Dr. Ingram gave him an apologetic smile. "Nothing wrong with some fun at work. It's how the rest of us keep from turning into you."

Dr. Shen looked at her expectantly.

"Come on in, and I'll show it to you." Ingram opened the door, holding it in place with her foot as she motioned for them to enter. The group passed through over the threshold and stepped into a wonderland of plasma computer screens and magnificent metal forms.

The vast room was less of a laboratory and more of a technological workshop. Wall-to-wall weaponized robots and drones of all varieties, some fully assembled, others in various stages of build or repair filled the area. All looked futuristic. Many were equipped with guns, though several were outfitted with bladed weapons. Near the middle of the room sat dome-covered vats, each containing a pool of metallic, gleaming goo. It was like Willy Wonka's chocolate factory, except, instead of candy, it was full of highly advanced computers and deadly war machines.

"Pretty impressive, huh?" Dr. Ingram held her arms outstretched at both sides, palms up as she turned around in front of them, presenting the expansive workshop to them.

"You bet it is." Cyrus made a futile attempt to disguise his awe.

"Feel free to look around, but don't touch anything," Dr. Ingram instructed. "Some of the bots and other devices are dangerous, obviously. We don't want anyone losing a limb or worse."

She turned to Viddur and glared.

"What?" asked Viddur, flabbergasted. "Like I'm any more prone to breaking things than anyone else."

"Yeah, tell that to someone who doesn't know you." Elysia rolled her eyes.

"There is a reason why I specifically asked for you to be banned from this room until now." Dr. Ingram's voice grew intense. "I don't want a repeat of last time."

"Is this still about that stupid battle drone?" asked Viddur.

"Well, what else do you think it would be?" asked Elysia, shooting an irritated look in his direction.

"How was I supposed to know it was armed?"

"You shouldn't have been anywhere near it!" Dr. Ingram was hysterical. "It shot up the whole lab, destroyed half our prototypes, and nearly killed several of the staff! You single-handedly set the Robotics Department back ten years!"

Cyrus walked around the massive workshop, ignoring the episode between Viddur and Dr. Ingram, taking stock of all the devices and robots. He approached the middle of the room, making his way toward the glass-domed vats of goo.

"What's this?" he asked, reaching out with a clawed hand to touch the glass.

"Don't touch that!" Dr. Ingram shouted back at him, still in the middle of her fight with Viddur. Cyrus jerked his hand away, surprised by Dr. Ingram's reaction.

"Sorry, I had assumed 'do not touch' didn't apply to glass displays," he said.

Ingram practically sprinted toward him. Elysia, Viddur, and

Dr. Shen followed her.

"'Do not touch' applies to everything!" Ingram scolded.

"What gives doc?" Viddur asked, saving Cyrus from Dr. Ingram's wrath. "What's the deal with the goo?"

"Hey, don't call it 'goo,'" Dr. Ingram pointed a finger at Viddur, drawing close to address him further. "The only reason I don't slap you now is that I know what you say is due to ignorance."

"What exactly is it, doctor?" asked Cyrus.

"It is a type of programmable matter," Dr. Ingram answered, turning away from Viddur.

"What's programmable matter? Sorry, I have a background in biology, and I really don't know anything about robotics."

"Well, as the name implies..." Dr. Ingram trailed off, her mind suddenly on another matter. "Excuse me. I don't think I ever got your name. I can't just go around calling you 'kresnik' forever."

"My apologies, Dr. Ingram." Shen moved to stand beside Cyrus. "I forgot to introduce him. This is Mr. Blackthorn."

"Oh, come on." Dr. Ingram glared at Shen. "Your reverence for formality is so irritating."

"I'm Cyrus Blackthorn." He extended a hand.

"Much better." Dr. Ingram reluctantly reached out for Cyrus's clawed hand. "Alexus Ingram. Well, Cyrus, as I was saying, programmable matter is a substance capable of changing its physical properties either autonomously or based on user input, hence the term 'programmable.'"

"That's pretty cool." Cyrus leaned down to take a look.

"Oh, yes, it is," said Dr. Ingram in rigorous agreement.

"What do you plan to do with it?" asked Viddur.

"We intend to do all kinds of things with it. This 'goo,' as you called it," Dr. Ingram cringed as she said the word, "is made up of sub-millimeter nanobots that have the ability to communicate with each other and move around. They can connect electrostatically to change the overall shape of the substance. This particular batch acts like a shape-shifting metal alloy. We intend to use it to create shape-shifting tools and weapons."

"Sweet," said Viddur.

"Sorry if I got a little defensive." Dr. Ingram looked from Viddur to Cyrus. "We've been working on different kinds of programmable matter in the robotics department for some time now, and I'm just a little protective. It's like one of my children."

Shen tapped his foot impatiently. "Would you please show us to the sparring bot now?"

"Oh, yes, of course, Daniel," Dr. Ingram replied. "Sorry, just don't get me started on programmable matter. I'll go on for days. This way," she said. Ingram led them to a large, blue gym mat near the back of the gigantic room. In the middle of the mat sat a human-sized object covered by a dull grey curtain.

"Here it is, the sparring bot." Dr. Ingram took hold of the curtain, prepared to pull it. "Yet another contribution of my department to the anti-vampire project." She pulled the curtain away with a flourish, revealing the most technologically advanced robot Cyrus had ever seen.

The machine was chrome-plated and consisted of a vaguely human-shaped head and torso with two sets of arms. These sat atop a chassis connected to eight segmented metal legs. It looked like a giant, metal arachnid centaur.

"Wow, that's a heck of a bot, doc," said Viddur. Dr. Shen stood behind the others, not at all taken by the machine.

"Sorry, but how am I supposed to learn to fight vampires from this?" Cyrus was skeptical. "I mean, it's cool, but it's basically just a big, metal spider."

"OK, I will pretend I didn't hear you say that." Dr. Ingram placed an open palm on her forehead. "Though I guess, since I tease Dan so much, I kind of had it coming."

"Could I not just pair up against a human?" asked Cyrus. "Or at least something more human-shaped?"

"I had considered having you spar with Viddur and Elysia." Dr. Shen cut in. "However, I didn't want to chance them being hurt. Lab assistants don't grow on trees."

"Excuse me, but if you just give me a moment, I'll explain why this bot is superior to any human sparring partner." Dr. Ingram let the curtain fall to the floor, moving behind the robot. "I'll go ahead and turn it on to demonstrate." Ingram pulled a remote from her apron pocket and pointed it at the robot, flipping the 'on' switch.

The machine came to life. Its human-like eyes glowed devilish red as the robot crawled toward them.

"Well, come on, go try it out." Dr. Ingram turned toward Cyrus, signaling him to walk toward the bot with a subtle head bob. "I'll explain everything as we go."

Cyrus shook his head, still doubtful about the machine's usefulness. He stepped onto the mat while the robot crept toward their group. The kresnik had a difficult time seeing the bot as intimidating, despite its arachnoid build. Its movements were like that of a giant, freakish crab. The bot had a childlike naïveté about it, as though it navigated the world for the first time.

When Cyrus approached, the robot halted its progression toward him, dead silent and motionless. A red laser light abruptly radiated from an apparatus off the right side of the robot's head, expanding into a square-sectioned scanning field that converged on Cyrus.

"What's it doing, doctor? Surely it's got more than that," asked the kresnik.

"It is sizing up its opponent," Dr. Ingram explained, a hand on her hip. "It is capable of imitating many different fighting styles, and right now it's determining which one to employ. This bot is highly adaptable and is capable of learning from experience. It's guaranteed to have the perfect combative solution for every adversary."

The scanning field disappeared, and the bot took on a fighting stance. It resembled an eight-legged, chrome praying mantis that was ready to strike. Several rows of razor-sharp metal fangs suddenly sprang from its jaws.

That's better, Cyrus thought. He crouched down, readying himself for the anticipated attack.

"I thought we had agreed that the bot would not be armed at this point," said Dr. Shen. "Mr. Blackthorn is not properly attired at present. He only wears the helmet to cover his face."

"I don't recall being told to leave it unarmed," said Ingram. "I was told that today was the deadline for completion, full completion, with all the bells and whistles, including full armament. Your kresnik is just going to have to watch himself."

"Be careful, Cyrus!" Elysia shouted from the edge of the mat. "Don't let it hit you!"

"Wasn't planning on it!"

"The sparring bot is capable of movements that no human could possibly duplicate," Dr. Ingram continued. "It displays a degree of athleticism on par with nearly any vampire. It will give you more than a run for your money."

"Well, that's great." Cyrus suddenly abandoned his position, frustrated with the doctor's insistence on the bot's superiority.

He turned his back to the robot while the machine continued to creep toward him.

"Looks like you got the vamps taken care of." The kresnik rubbed his palms together and began to walk away. "I'll be on my way then. It's great to be obsolete, and so early on in my career."

"Don't turn your back on it!" Dr. Ingram shouted.

Seemingly activated by her words, the bot lunged at Cyrus. The kresnik spun to meet it, quickly jumping to the side, barely avoiding its devastating strike. The robot tumbled to the ground, skidding across the mat. It climbed back onto its insectoid, spiked feet.

"I only said it was capable of movements on par with a vampire," Dr. Ingram spoke in a much calmer tone. "I never said it surpassed them. Besides, it lacks certain qualities already ingrained into the mind of an organic hunter. It can't smell, and it isn't capable of taking on several adversaries at once. We also haven't found a way to mass-produce them at the rate the vampires would likely destroy them."

The bot regained its footing and turned back toward Cyrus, scuttling after him in its crab-like fashion. Unwilling to let it surprise him again, Cyrus leaped at the machine, seeking to level it to the ground with a heavy blow to the head. The robot proved quicker than he anticipated, instantaneously blocking the hit with a spindly but strong metal arm.

Cyrus roared, wanting to beat the bot down. He lashed out with a barrage of savage blows, all rendered ineffective by the bot's lightning-quick deflections. He wished he were back at the facility hunting zombies, where the mere proximity of his prey was enough to awaken his primal instincts.

"Give it to him, Cyrus!" Viddur called from the sideline.

"What you got, Dan?" taunted Dr. Ingram. "This bot really puts you to shame, huh?"

"Oh, I wouldn't say that," his retort was immediate. "I created kresnik the whole project is built around."

"Dan, you've got to remember who's responsible for making that achievement possible." Dr. Ingram's eyes narrowed, unsurprised by Dr. Shen's answer.

"You only provided the basal technology." Shen was unwilling to give her the win she sought.

Meanwhile, the bot was on the attack, scuttling toward Cyrus at a surprisingly fast speed. It rained blow after blow upon him with its thin, spider arms. The kresnik was quick enough to dodge its strikes but remained in retreat, never with enough time to launch his own series of counterblows. He wasn't sure how much it could have learned from him in such a small amount of time, though it did successfully imitate his previous movements and at a faster rate than he could perform them.

Cyrus howled when the bot suddenly attacked with a bite, digging its many rows of teeth into the flesh of his arm. "Hey, how about a little help here?" He screamed in desperation, unable to shake the bot loose. "How do I get it off?"

"Just give it a couple of good smacks, and it will let go!" Dr. Ingram yelled back as though he had rudely interrupted her conversation.

Cyrus did as instructed, slapping the bot on the side of the head before it released him. A relatively small amount of black blood dripped from his wounds. The bite was painful, but it did far less damage than he had expected. Cyrus retreated to the edge of the mat, running backward while grasping his bloodied arm, sure to keep an eye on the approaching bot.

"Call off your bot doctor," said Dr. Shen. "We cannot allow Mr. Blackthorn to become grievously injured before he is properly equipped for practice."

"Sure thing, Dan." Dr. Ingram pulled the remote from her pocket and pointed it at the sparring bot. "I have more important things to do anyway, and without the benefit of my staff." She flipped the switch, and the bot slowly assumed its resting position, the red lights of its eyes fading.

"That's enough for today, Mr. Blackthorn," said Dr. Shen, grim as he approached Cyrus. The doctor walked sideways so he could keep an eye on the bot. "I will bandage your wounds as soon as we arrive back at your room."

"Will I spar with it up here to train, or will you move it somewhere else?" Cyrus turned around to walk toward Dr. Ingram. He clenched his injured left arm with his right hand.

"What? And risk you potentially dismantling one of our other projects?" Dr. Ingram asked with a certain degree of severity. "Besides, we already have Viddur here for all our wanton destruction needs." She smiled, her harsh attitude instantly fading.

"You know it!" Viddur gave Dr. Ingram a mischievous grin. "Hey, so whatever happened to that battle drone anyway?"

"Like you need to know," said Elysia under her breath.

"It has been moved to one of CyberGen's more secure locations." Dr. Ingram's frown returned.

"OK, well, you have seen everything I have here to show you." Dr. Ingram turned to Dr. Shen, addressing him only. "The bot will be sent to the gym in the basement. Cyrus can practice with it more tomorrow. As for now, you take this one with you." She pointed to Viddur. "And make sure he continues to stay out of my lab. Just having him in here is about to give me an anxiety attack."

"I appreciate what you have done for the kresnik project Dr. Ingram," said Dr. Shen before turning to leave. Elysia and Viddur followed close behind him.

"Not a problem," Dr. Ingram replied, her attention turning back toward the sparring bot.

Cyrus followed the others, briefly glancing back at Dr. Ingram and her bot, less than keen on another bout with his new metal   adversary.

Chapter XXI

Deceptive Appearances

Cyrus lay flat against the surface of the hanging platform, peering over the edge at the robot below.

I have you now, he thought to himself, not wanting to alert the sparring bot to his presence.

The machine stopped to scan the water hazard and surrounding area with its laser searchlight, sensing its adversary was nearby. It was the longest the bot had ever gone without finding Cyrus. It typically remained on his tail throughout their training sessions and rarely gave him a chance to hide.

It was four months since Cyrus began training with the bot. All of his exercises were constrained to CyberGen's gym. Shen had the facility laid out like an obstacle course, filled with hanging and grounded platforms, pits, and water hazards.

Cyrus had yet to win a decisive victory over the bot. His foe was unrelenting and merciless. It was always prepared for his attack and gave him few opportunities to land a blow. Dr. Ingram had created a brutal masterpiece. The machine learned as it fought and hunted him, anticipating his every move.

Crash!

Cyrus jumped from the hanging platform, falling like a black-clad raindrop and landing on top of the bot, leveling it to the ground.

"Give it to him, Cyrus!" Viddur called from the balcony overlooking the gym.

Cyrus barely heard him as he struggled with the bot, fighting to keep it pinned to the ground. The machine kicked out with its spider legs against its assailant, trying to push him off so it could rise to its feet.

Unable to keep it on the ground, Cyrus wrapped his arms around its torso, the bot's limbs constrained against its side. The machine bit at him with cruel, metallic teeth. Cyrus quickly gained his footing, straining as he hoisted the bot off the ground.

The bot hit the water with a splash as Cyrus tossed it into the hazard. The kresnik hoped the moisture would finally end its tyrannical reign.

"Very good, Mr. Blackthorn," said Dr. Shen, standing off to the side of the gym course, seeming to appear from nowhere. "I'm impressed." His voice was emotionless, as though he didn't mean what he said.

Cyrus gave the doctor a fang-filled smile, his cat eyes concealed by his helmet visor. He was proud of his victory despite Shen. He gazed up toward the balcony, finding Elysia and Viddur focused on the water hazard and drowned robot. Cyrus turned to look down at the bot.

It now swam toward the edge of the pool.

"Look out, Cyrus!" Elysia yelled down at the kresnik.

Cyrus jumped to one side as two heavy grappling hooks exploded from the robot's shoulders, tearing into the concrete underneath the mat and rapidly pulling the machine through the water. The bot shot out of the pool, landing back on the floor a few feet away from Cyrus.

The kresnik bounded for the nearest hanging platform. The machine went after him, traveling at an impossible speed that it had never displayed before. It was enraged by its venture into the water, and its eyes became a blood-lusting red. The machine leaped onto the platform and gave chase. It raced after him over the multiple hanging platforms as it sought to beat him down with its mantis-like front legs.

The bot pressed in close behind Cyrus. The kresnik jumped from platform to platform with renewed urgency, desperate to escape. He heard Elysia and Viddur yelling down at him, but he was unable to understand their words. His focus was on the chase. Cyrus glanced back at the bot, finding it right on his heels and intent on mowing him down. Running out of room in front of him, the kresnik leaped for the platform at his far right. This one hung over yet another water hazard.

Cyrus groaned when he landed chest first, banging one of his legs on the suspension chains and scrambling to rise back to his feet. The bot slowed to a stop on the last platform, adjacent to Cyrus and the water hazard. It displayed a human-like hesitance, in no hurry to return to the water.

The bot sprang from the platform, landing back on the mat. It scanned Cyrus with its red searchlight, waiting for him to move away from the water.

Cyrus suddenly felt additional eyes on him and looked across the gym to see Dr. Shen. His arms were folded across his chest, as he was eager to see how the kresnik might escape his situation.

Apprehensive, though undeterred, Cyrus turned and dashed for the platform's edge. He launched himself, clearing the distance to land atop the plateau-like structure. He then bolted left onto the nearest hanging platform. The bot's search field followed him as he moved.

Cyrus made another quick turn to the left. He bounded over platform after platform as though the bot gave chase, in an attempt to move around the machine to find a hiding place. With no more hanging platforms in front of him, the kresnik jumped to the mat, immediately changing direction to dash for the nearest grounded platform. The bot's search field was too slow to catch him.

Cyrus panted heavily, his back against the side of the raised platform, taking a moment to catch his breath. He had successfully out-distanced and confused the bot, hearing it move only slightly with his cat-like ears.

The machine anticipated his reappearance.

Cyrus needed to move. He knew the bot would wait only so long before it searched for him again. The kresnik remained flat against the side of the platform, clearing the corner to continue along its next side, taking a cautious glance in the bot's direction. He slowly peered around the corner and found the bot's back to him.

Sensing an opportunity, Cyrus bent his knees toward the ground, staying as low as possible as he made his way along the water hazards. Carefully, he moved toward the next grounded platform. The bot was oblivious and kept its back turned to him.

Cyrus reached the platform, keeping his back against it and making the corner as he prepared to bolt. He peered past the next corner, but he still heard no movement from the bot.

The machine was laying an ambush.

As Cyrus crept his way along the next group of water hazards, the bot finally began to move. It slowly scuttled, laying its search field in front. Cyrus prepared his own ambush now and jumped onto another platform that overlooked the water. The kresnik tripped as he moved onto the next platform, his knee landing on the wooden surface.

The bot let out a blaring alarm.

Cyrus's heartbeat exploded as he dropped from the platform and into the pit, hoping the bot had only heard him. He crouched, able to hear the bot's movements clearly, the machine's heavy spider steps rapidly approaching.

Just when Cyrus was sure the bot knew his position, the claw-steps suddenly stopped. The silence lasted only a moment before resuming.

The bot backed up, preparing to jump. It landed on one of the far hanging platforms, its metal claws striking the wood, the machine now searching for the kresnik from above.

His first true victory within reach, Cyrus remained unwilling to let it slip away. He continued to crouch down in the pit as the beginnings of a plan materialized in his mind.

The bot leaped onto the next platform, stopping to scan the area underneath. It moved ever closer to Cyrus. Only one platform remained between the kresnik and the bot now, hastening Cyrus's resolve. He needed to enact his plan.

Cyrus sprang from the pit, extending his arms to grasp the edge of the hanging platform above with his claws. He remained there, suspended from the platform, awaiting the bot's approach.

The bot's landing on the platform caught Cyrus by surprise. The whole apparatus swayed back and forth under the metal monster's weight. Still Cyrus waited, tightening his hold on the bottom of the platform. His black claws dug into the wood as he listened for the sound of the bot's scanning sentry light.

The bot searched first to the left and then to the right. Its red scanning field glided over the mat below, then the platform, finally stopping to search the far pit opposite Cyrus. The machine grew still. The bot acted as though it thought he should be below. It had scanned the wrong pit.

Sensing his last chance at victory, Cyrus grew tense as he prepared himself. He roared, leaping onto the platform, barreling into the bot.

The kresnik sent both into the pit below with a heavy crash.

Cyrus continued to shriek and scream, ignoring the pain of impact. His focus was on the bot's head as he tried to wrench it from its neck. The bot flailed underneath him, desperately lashing out with all its limbs. Elysia and Viddur shouted down at Cyrus, egging him on, though he was too preoccupied to understand their words.

Cyrus mercilessly beat the robot's cranium against the floor of the pit, tearing the head from its body. The red eyes went dim, and the machine died, at least until Dr. Ingram repaired it.

Cyrus threw the bot's lifeless head onto the mat and wordlessly climbed out of the pit after it. His victory after four months of training felt strangely hollow.

"You got him good, Cyrus!" Viddur yelled down at him.

Cyrus looked toward the balcony and found the siblings just where he had left them. Viddur's enthusiasm contrasted with Elysia's look of relief.

"Well done, Mr. Blackthorn." Dr. Shen applauded. He walked toward Cyrus as the kresnik rose to his feet. "Only slightly behind schedule. Though, still very good."

"What happens now?" Despite acting frustrated, Cyrus was excited to defeat the bot, but he worried that it only brought him closer to a much more dangerous assignment.

"Having completed your training with the bot, it's time to submit you to yet another test."

Cyrus sighed, shaking his head. "What's it going to be? Surely not another survivability test." He remembered the trial with dread. The ordeal was so intense that it seemed like it had taken place years ago. Cyrus was accustomed to being alone in his former life, but it never came close to his loneliness during his time in the zombie facility.

"It is another survivability test of sorts."

"Great. How long will this one last?"

"Only a single evening, Mr. Blackthorn." Shen gave him an awkward smile, offering Cyrus some relief. "In addition to that caveat, you will not be alone this time. Elysia and Viddur will be with you."

"Already sounds ten times better than the last survivability test." Cyrus put a hand behind his helmet and stretched, sore from his fight with the bot. "It will be great to have your lab assistants around for the test. But, there's just one thing." He paused as he considered his words. "Well, it's that Elysia and Viddur are your lab assistants. I mean, I know they're not your average lab assistants, abducting people from their homes as you routinely have them do. But, what exactly do they have to offer against a zombie or vampire? Well, provided that is actually what the test involves."

"We have plenty to offer!" Viddur shouted angrily. He suddenly passed through the gym doors and hastily walked toward Cyrus. Elysia followed him, frowning at his abruptness.

"I'm sorry, I didn't mean to insult you." Cyrus extended a hand to stop him. "I just don't see how a non-genetically altered organism could survive an encounter with a zombie or vampire. Heck, I had plenty of trouble with zombies. If you've seen the footage from the facility, I tend to only go after the old and sick."

"We are genetically modified!" Viddur declared. His anger gave way to a less severe demeanor.

Cyrus was unsure how to react to Viddur, though he didn't feel any surprise. It was just more information Dr. Shen had withheld from him.

"Tell him, doctor." Viddur pointed at Cyrus. "Tell him what we really are." Both Viddur and Elysia stopped behind Shen, the former shaking her head.

"Very well." Shen kept his back turned to Viddur. "Come and sit down, Mr. Blackthorn. You need a rest given your bout with the bot."

"Will do," said Cyrus as he turned to walk toward one of the grounded platforms.

"I suppose I will start at the beginning." Shen followed Cyrus while Viddur and Elysia stayed a few steps behind him. "As I've told you in the past, CyberGen works in close connection with the United States government and Legion 96."

"I remember." Cyrus sat down on the platform's bottom step and removed his helmet. He looked up at Shen with his cat eyes, no longer hairless as he was months ago. White fur covered his face, and a tufted mane grew on his scalp, all of it now wet and matted down.

"We began collaboration with Legion 96 approximately ten years ago," said Shen. "The Legion had existed for some time at that point and had recently replaced their lower caliber assault rifle for an automatic shotgun, this deemed more effective at combating vampires. Though the use of the shotgun resulted in fewer human casualties and higher rates of mortality among vampires, the Legion still needed something else. They needed something to level out the unavoidable shortcomings of human soldiers."

Shen pushed up his glasses with an index finger.

"That's when the government propositioned CyberGen with their first contract, asking that we create genetically enhanced super soldiers for the Legion. It was a simple enough contract for CyberGen to fulfill. We conceived a group of artificial humans, organisms that possessed only the most beneficial genes from the human genome. Essentially, we were to create a creature that brought humanity to the very height of its physical prowess, all in hopes that it would keep the balance in favor of the human race."

"Interesting." Cyrus saw where the conversation was going. "How did that project work out?" He wanted to hear the extended version of Shen's story.

"CyberGen fulfilled the contract exactly as requested. We created a small force of super soldiers for the Legion, each genetically superior to any naturally conceived human. There was not a single loss of function mutation between them. Both Viddur and Elysia were part of this group." Shen puffed up like a proud parent. His close relationship with his lab assistants made sense at last.

"I'm sorry. Maybe I misspoke." Cyrus stopped Shen. "How well did your superhuman soldiers do against the vampires?" He already knew the answer.

"Though I wish it were otherwise, the project was a near total disaster." Shen shook his head regretfully. "We incorporated only human genes into our soldier's genome, mistakenly believing it would be enough to combat the vampires. As a result, virtually none of our super soldiers survived the initial field tests. Granted, some of these were irresponsibly planned. Unfortunately, I was not in charge of the project."

Shen sighed. "The vampires were simply too much for our soldiers. They were always stronger, faster, and more brutal. They decimated our soldiers very early on, leaving only two survivors out of several hundred. Only the ones we never field-tested survived. These two were Elysia and Viddur."

Viddur gave Cyrus a hardy smile, and Elysia placed a supportive hand on her brother's shoulder.

Cyrus grimaced at Shen, noticing something was off. "But you said the project began ten years ago."

"That is correct, Mr. Blackthorn." Shen nodded as Elysia watched him closely. "We accelerated the growth rates of all our super soldiers. Both Viddur and Elysia are less than ten years old, though their maturation rate makes them appear to be in their early twenties. The clones were intended to mature quickly but age slowly, so they might fight for many years to come."

"Ok. I suppose it will be nice to have someone along with me for the test. I'm just a little concerned. You want Viddur and Elysia to help me face a group of vampires, even though they were part of a group of soldiers utterly destroyed by them? You said they haven't even been field-tested." Cyrus looked up at Viddur and Elysia.

The two had accusatory looks on their faces, though they made no move to correct him.

"That is correct, Mr. Blackthorn," said Shen, emotionless as usual. "The failure of the super-soldier project was the primary reason for beginning the Kresnik Project in the first place. We quickly came to realize that only a creature physically superior to any human had any hope of surviving a battle against a force of vampires. I firmly believe things will go much differently for Elysia and Viddur when they are paired with you, a kresnik."

Cyrus gazed over at Elysia. Her expression held great expectation.

Chapter XXII

A Dubious Strategy

Cyrus strained, struggling against his restraints. His strength was limited when in a sane state. All he could do was lie there, strapped to the inclined metal table, hidden within the back of the armored truck. He ceased his struggle and gazed up at the dark nothingness that was the truck's ceiling. The moon provided the only light source. Its beams flowed in through the crack below the window slit cut into the backdoor.

The darkness was only a minor inconvenience to Cyrus. His enhanced vision easily cut through it, allowing him a black and white view of his surroundings through his helmet. Still feeling uncomfortable, he tried moving his arms again, hoping to gain a small amount of relief, but to no avail. The restraints were simply too restrictive. Frustrated, he surrendered to the cold, hard, painful embrace of the table. Secure as he was, he had no trouble discerning the terrain over which they traveled.

The harsh rattling of the truck's walls and doors revealed an exceptionally rough gravel road, and they hadn't deviated from it for some time.

Cyrus was bored from staring up at the ceiling when a sweet, savory scent unexpectedly wafted into his nostrils. It was similar to the stench emitted by the 'zombies' at the quarantine facility, but it was much more pleasant, somehow cleaner, fresher, and healthier. It was arousing, like a perfect, raw steak. He felt his bloodlust awaken yet again, and there was no mistaking the source of the smell.

His prey was close and plentiful.

The kresnik's tongue involuntarily slid across his lips,

causing him to flinch when he pricked it on one of his elongated fangs. Cyrus could only lie there, flat against the table, a low, guttural gurgling sound resonating from his stomach. He was ravenously hungry, in a way he had never been before.

The truck suddenly swerved to the side, abruptly freeing Cyrus from his voracious thoughts. They had left the road, abandoning it for the grass and moderately thick brush. They drove over it for only a moment before stopping. The engine died seconds later, and Cyrus heard the front doors swing open and then slam shut. The sound of feet walking over the grass toward him followed. The covering over the door slit slid open, and the light of the crescent moon shone through as a single, broad beam.

"Hey man, how you doing back here?" Viddur peered through the slit, the moonlight illuminating his face, giving it an unintended sinister quality.

Cyrus rolled his eyes, coolly shaking his head. He was certain Viddur had been driving. He looked up to meet his gaze but could not do so as his helmet obscured his eyes.

"Can't complain," said Cyrus. "You know me, I've always loved a good restraining." He struggled against his bonds yet again, making no attempt to conceal his sarcasm. "In all seriousness, though, don't you think all this precaution is a little much?"

Viddur fell from the back step of the truck just as he opened his mouth to answer. He landed off to the side in the tall grass.

Elysia smiled at Cyrus through the darkness, the super soldier's elegant facial features bathed in moonlight. "Cyrus, you know you are only restrained to prevent you from jeopardizing the first half of the operation," she said.

"Yes, that part was pretty understandable," he spoke somewhat indignantly. "All of it together just seems like overkill." He struggled against his cumbersome metal restraints once again. "You have me strapped onto a table with restraints I obviously can't break, and to top that, Dr. Shen had the door welded shut!"

"Viddur," Elysia turned her head to her brother off to the side of the van, ignoring Cyrus's complaints. "Can you go grab the packs with the explosive charges while I talk to Cyrus?"

"Sure thing," Viddur stomped back toward the front of the truck.

Elysia turned her attention back to Cyrus. "Since this is your first operation, there are a few things Dr. Shen asked me to address. As you understand, this portion of the mission requires stealth most of all. Due to your genetic alterations, that's not something you'll be good at, at least not at this point. That's why you will be left here for this first stage."

"But…" he frowned, confused. He considered stealth to be one of his stronger points.

"Those are Dr. Shen's orders," Elysia interrupted him before he could continue. "Yes, I realize you were quite capable of sneaking around undetected when you were hunting infected zombies, but vampires are different. The doctor says you will have a more difficult time controlling your urges when you get near them. He says you won't try to hunt them at all. You'll try to kill every single one you come in contact with." She gave him an apologetic look, remorse in her brown, doe-like eyes. "It's not your fault. You were designed to behave that way. Eventually, you will find a way to better control your urges. Well, that or we might find a solution for you. Until then, you will not be able to participate in anything involving stealth and vampires together. It makes your job easier, though at the cost of making ours hard."

She gave him a weary smile.

"Anyway, all you need to do for the present is remain calm and stay in your restraints. Viddur and I will carry out the first part of the mission. We will take out the guards and lay down the explosive charges. After that, we will come back to you and wait for the Legion to arrive. They never disclosed any information regarding how they were arriving, so we'll just have to be ready for it. They're supposed to surround the slaughter plant to make sure none of the vampires can escape. We wait for them to give us the signal to move into position. It will be at that point that your involvement in the operation will take place."

"Dr. Shen already told me all of this before we left." Cyrus gave her a smug look, though only for his own benefit since his face was concealed.

"Hey, back with the charges," said Viddur.

Elysia descended from the step of the truck and took the pack he offered her.

Cyrus heard Viddur continue onward towards him, climbing onto the back of the truck.

"We'll do you the favor of leaving the window slit open, just so you can see what's going on," said the super-soldier as he peered through the slit. "Going to have to try and not make any noise, though. It could jeopardize the whole mission and make things interesting."

Viddur paused to think.

"Probably should have brought a gag or something. Oh well, too late now. Can't get back there with the doors welded shut."

Viddur's face disappeared from the slit a second time, pushed from the back of the truck yet again. He stumbled around in the grass, barely catching his balance before he fell.

"Hey, what's with the shoving?" he asked indignantly. "You're going to mess around and give me motion sickness or something."

Elysia ignored his protests and gazed through the slit at Cyrus. "I think I'm less worried about you doing something to expose us than I am about Viddur." She gave her brother a severe look.

"What?" Viddur squawked.

"Remember, this is a stealth mission." Elysia stepped off the ledge. She stomped toward Viddur, poking him in the chest with her finger. "Nobody cares about what you can do with a knife!"

"Whatever do you mean, dear sister?" Though Cyrus couldn't see it, he was sure Viddur had given her a mirthful smirk. "I would never do anything to jeopardize the mission. My knife-throwing skills are beyond superb. Even Cyrus says so. Besides, there's nothing wrong with giving the enemy a show. It'll be the last one they'll ever see."

"Viddur." Elysia sounded agitated. "That's exactly what I'm talking about. Keep it up, and one day it might get us killed in probably the worst possible way!"

"Hey, don't get loud. You'll jeopardize the mission," Viddur mocked.

Elysia continued to glare at him, her face hard as stone. Cyrus grew weary of their bickering and wished Viddur had left the slit closed.

"Keep the knives in your hands," Elysia growled at Viddur through gritted teeth. "There is no need to throw anything."

"Whatever you say." Viddur put his hands in the air in exasperation. "Just stay off my case."

The argument came to an abrupt stop, and an awkward silence resulted.

Cyrus heard them head toward the plant, their sneakered feet moving covertly through the grass. The footsteps quickly died away, enveloped by the constant chirping of insects and the occasional cry of a coyote.

* * *

Elysia followed Viddur into the bush, seeking concealment against the chain-link fence as they waited to make their next move. They remained on the left side of the fence, crouched amongst the thorny foliage, positioned adjacent to the guard booth.

Viddur gazed intently to the right, Elysia's side against his back as she looked to the front. She waited for just the right moment to strike, at a time when the guards had their backs to them. Their quarry was staggeringly easy to spot, their armor-clad, insectoid forms revealed by the moon's ghostly light, assault weapons at the ready.

Elysia counted only three guards, all human, on the fence's far left. Their movements gave them away, their gaits slow and clumsy compared to the innate balance and grace displayed by their overlords. Elysia's eyes shifted to the slaughterhouse roof, relieved when she spied a total lack of guards atop the vantage point. The vampires of the organization seemed considerably complacent to her, keeping the plant so understaffed. Assuming there was an average of three guards on each side and at least two in the booth, there was a total of no more than fourteen guards watching over the facility's exterior.

Everything agreed with the gathered intel.

Bright, though the moon was, it put them at a disadvantage by increasing the guards' ability to spot them. They would have to be swift and silent, but also patient and careful while moving their bodies, all while remaining unseen. The task was doable, so long as they didn't run into any true bloodsuckers.

Viddur waved the back of his hand in Elysia's face, three

fingers stretched out, indicating that there were three visible guards on his side of the fence. Three more guards to spot her should she miss her timing. They remained in the bush, Elysia nearly breathless as she waited for the signal.

Viddur nudged her in the ribs at last, indicating he was ready to dispatch the guard in the booth. He moved out of the bush away from her, crouching to search for a rock amongst the grass.

The rock slammed against the side of the booth, striking harder than intended, sending Elysia's heart racing. The noise from the blow threatened to reveal their position.

Elysia managed to maintain her composure, keeping one eye on the guards in front of her while watching Viddur with the other. A slip up at this point would not end in their deaths, but rather a potential mission failure. They could double back and try again, with a significantly reduced likelihood of success.

The guard remained in the booth, oblivious as Viddur dug around for another rock.

This rock hit the booth at an even higher velocity, threatening to reveal them once again.

Elysia tensed, her heart rate increasing still more, feeling as though it could burst. If the guard didn't move soon, the whole facility would know of their presence.

Elysia let out a silent sigh when the door to the booth finally swung open. The guard stepped outside, his form concealed behind the open door, thrash metal riffs following him. Viddur quickly positioned himself, crawling underneath the boom barrier to reach the other side of the door, careful to step lightly.

"Hey!" one of the guards on the other side of the booth yelled. "Do something about that noise!"

"Just give me a moment!" the first guard yelled back, stepping back inside the booth to turn off the music. Suspicions remained high, and the man stepped outside the door once again, swinging it shut as he investigated the source of the thrown rocks.

Viddur lashed out like a viper, slapping a cupped hand over the guard's mouth, silencing him before he could lay eyes on his attacker. The cold steel of a dagger glistened in the moonlight as Viddur jabbed the point of the blade into the side of the man's neck, slicing through his artery, the blood spurting onto the asphalt.

The man struggled for only a few seconds before the light faded from his eyes. Viddur held him in his arms as he bled out, pulling the man's slackened body back to the booth. He carefully removed his blade, thick blood flowing through his fingers as he did so.

Elysia had difficulty keeping an eye on her sector of the fence from the bushes, the violent scene before her a distraction.

Viddur slowly re-opened the door while holding onto the guard. He dragged the man into the booth and placed him back in his seat to ensure the other guards remained unaware of their presence. The super-soldier slunk back out the doorway, careful to close the door without a sound, sliding back underneath the boom barrier. Viddur concealed himself against the other side of the booth outside the fence perimeter, his back pressed against the chain links.

Elysia's gaze returned to the guards on her side of the fence. Viddur looked back at her, awaiting her signal to proceed.

Elysia's gloved hand shot up from the bush when all three of the guards turned away from them.

Viddur moved back to peer around the booth, gazing through the fence before disappearing into the night. Elysia remained in the bush, still ever watchful of the guard's movements, waiting for Viddur's signal to move over the fence.

A screech owl cried out after what seemed like an eternity to Elysia. The sound came from a device engineered by CyberGen, the sound imitator capable of creating a variety of animal calls.

Elysia's legs had grown sore as time passed. The stress and anticipation felt as though they could kill her. She waited for the guards to turn toward the source of the call, surprised when none of them noticed. Elysia rolled her eyes. The organization apparently did not possess observant human employees.

As though on cue, all the guards in front of her finally turned their backs to her.

Elysia burst from the bush, treading lightly through the grass before reaching the fence. She leaped onto the metal railing, a creature of deadly silence and grace intent on her unsuspecting prey. Elysia pivoted on the bar and then glanced off to her right as she assessed Viddur's handiwork.

Her fellow soldier had successfully eliminated all three guards. He had piled the bodies up near the middle of the fence just beyond the vision of the others. The asphalt lay covered in blood, both in pools and smeared across the surface in trails.

Content that Viddur's side was clear, Elysia turned her attention back to her side of the fence. She carefully descended to the ground before the guards had a chance to spot her. Elysia sprang from the fence, rushing her listless, sauntering target before he could turn to see her. She quickly closed in on the guard, savagely slapping her hand over the man's mouth to suppress his screams.

The man flailed and thrashed about as he tried to twist away from her.

Elysia put an end to the man's struggle, thrusting her knife into the side of his neck, just as Viddur did to the guard from earlier. The man's body went limp as Elysia caught him in her arms. She gently laid him down on the ground in a pool of blood, darkening the asphalt.

Elysia repeated the procedure with the second man, abruptly dropping the body as the third man turned around. She ran for him, barely concealing the noise of her steps, the need to reach him outweighing all. Elysia dropped to the ground, sliding behind him just as he changed direction, somehow remaining unseen.

The super-soldier was back on her feet in a heartbeat, barreling towards the guard from behind, cupping her hand to his mouth as she leveled him to the ground. She jammed her dagger into the man's neck, his body convulsing as he died, the blood splattering the fence.

Elysia tucked her arms under the dead man's shoulders as she pulled him back around. She dragged him back in the direction she had come, concealing his body under the shadow of the plant. Content the body would remain unseen, the super-soldier jumped back onto the fence railing and descended to the grass below.

Elysia sighed, suddenly worn by the now nearly completed task, so preoccupied she hadn't even bothered to glance over at Viddur's progress. It was just as well, as she preferred not to watch his antics, never having taken to killing the way he had. This was far from the first operation that called for the elimination of a target, but Elysia still found killing unsavory. She had grown immune to it over time, realizing it was a necessary task done only for the greater good. Viddur's attitude towards it was different. He saw it as an art form, always looking for new and different ways to dispense it. Her brother found a small pleasure from killing with a variety of weapons and combative techniques.

Elysia continued to move along the outside of the fence, ducking down among the foliage to remain unseen by the last few guards. She took her final position behind a massive rose bush near the corner, setting her pack down to remove her sound-mimicking device.

The massive hangar lay at Elysia's side now, illuminated in the moonlight. It loomed over the various small planes, a flock of misshapen pterosaurs nestled near a barn-shaped volcano. They were to leave it untouched, something for the Legion to take care of later.

Elysia toggled her device, pressing down until she saw the word 'bullfrog' appear on the display screen.

The croaking call went out into the night.

Elysia checked the position of the guards on the other side of the fence, waiting for the answer. She heard the screech owl nearly a minute later, her anxiety slowly rising to the point of panic. She was sure Viddur had purposefully made her wait, not wanting the guards to catch onto their calls. Ready for their task to be over, Elysia shoved her sound device back into her pack, zipping it up and putting it back on.

The super-soldier wheeled around the rose bush on her way to the fence, nearly clearing it entirely as she bounded toward the next guard. Elysia was unworried about the noise now, knowing she needed to quickly catch the first guard, forcing the second to turn toward her and not Viddur. She grabbed the man with a cupped hand, sliding her dagger across his throat, blood spraying from both arteries.

Elysia looked up from her dying target to see the second guard's assault rifle pointed directly at her head. Her muscles stiffened as she glared down at the ground, frustrated that her death should come so quickly. She waited, ready for the barrage of gunfire, confused when all remained silent.

Elysia gazed back up just as the guard fell, face to the ground with blood flowing from his back.

The moon shone upon Viddur's dagger, the steel shimmering in the night, the blade seeming to wink at her.

Elysia saw Viddur standing some distance in front of her, holding his thumb up to the sky, an idiotic grin wiped across his face. She shook her head, frustrated by his actions, yet relieved that he picked the right moment to employ them.

Wasting no time, Elysia removed her pack, carrying it toward the plant. She set it upright upon the ground some twenty yards away from the edge of the wall. The charges weren't lethal, but they were loud, placed there to help scare the vampiric butchers from their posts, hopefully right out the front doors.

Elysia glanced toward the adjacent corner of the plant, giving Viddur a thumb's up once he set his own pack down, which was the signal to return to the truck. Phase one complete, Elysia sprinted back toward her side of the fence, Viddur following close behind.

The serene chirping of insects made the night appear calm and uneventful despite what had just occurred. It was how they wanted it, silent due to the lack of life, a fortress ready for the taking.

* * *

The heavily armored, black-clad battalion marched down the wide, concrete corridor en route to the base garage. One thousand human terminators hell-bent on destruction were out on orders given by high command.

They would eliminate another human slaughter facility, reportedly the largest in their sector. Successful execution of the operation would result in a crippling blow to vampire society, a major hub of food distribution and transport destroyed. Crucial though it was, destruction of the facility was only secondary to the primary objective: the evaluation of yet another new weapon.

Asher gripped his shotgun tightly with both hands, trying to retain a hold on his anxiety.

Though the orders were clear, he considered the operations briefing to be more than dubious. The plan presented to them was utterly irrational, so much so even a child could see through it. It simply put far too many of them at risk. Asher realized how important it was to have as many weapons as possible to bring down the vampire menace, but he felt there were better ways to do so.

The black-armored battalion abruptly ceased its marching as

the soldiers prepared to exit the door to the garage. Asher nearly crashed into those in front of him, so preoccupied with orders that he hadn't realized he was looking down the whole time.

Marching resumed as soon as Captain Kilgore opened the large, upward sliding door at the end of the hall, allowing the battalion to filter through the exit-way.

Asher continued to have difficulty keeping pace with the group. He looked at Milo and Driscoll and then to his right at Aaron, expecting any one of them to protest the high commander's orders.

"Captain!" yelled Asher as he crossed through the door, breaking rank and sprinting toward Kilgore.

Aaron shook his head as Asher moved away from him, extending a hand to catch him by the shoulder. He recoiled at the last moment, deciding to avoid a potential reprimand by the captain. He briefly turned to Milo and Driscoll, both of whom shrugged in response, expressions masked by the visors of their helmets.

"What is it, Private?" asked Kilgore. He jerked around to meet Asher, his angry facial expressions concealed by his helmet. "Whatever it is, it better be a good one. I could write you up for stalling an operation as important as this one!"

The rest of the battalion passed through the door behind them, the soldiers marching toward their designated transport vehicles.

"We're not actually going through with this, are we, sir?" Asher asked, his look of concern and frustration concealed by his helmet. He could hold it in no longer.

"We are indeed, Blackthorn," Kilgore replied, his rage giving way to simple irritation. "Why do you think we've spent so much time going over the attack plan? I hope you're not insinuating that the commander willfully wastes time explaining things just to hear the sound of his own voice."

"Sir, that is not my intention," Asher retorted. "I just think the plan is a little... Well, it's kind of..." He had difficulty finding the exact and least offensive words.

"Blackthorn, just spit it out." Kilgore's answer came as an order.

"Sir, the plan is questionable at best," Aaron said abruptly, appearing behind Asher. Milo and Driscoll stood right behind him, though offered no additional words of aid.

"Pritchett, I assure you everything will make sense as soon as we get going. As long as you do what you've been ordered to do, there is nothing to worry about."

"Sorry, sir, I just think it is a terrible plan," Asher interrupted. "Most of it's kind of insane when I think about it."

"Enlighten me, Private," said Kilgore, arms crossed. "What is so insane about it?"

"Well, nearly all of it, sir. It goes against all standard procedure."

"How so?"

"I believe the situation demands that we remain as hands-off as possible," Asher explained. "I know you said it earlier, but aren't we attacking what is really just a vampire feeding grounds? One where the enemy's number cannot be precisely ascertained?"

"That is correct, Private," the captain nodded.

"Why can't we just blow the whole place to heck like we normally do?" Asher grew frustrated. "It's the most rational way to go about it and would take a significantly smaller force."

"I believe you are missing the point, Blackthorn." Kilgore's frown was apparent even through his helmet. "The whole purpose of the operation is to test a new weapon, one so important it overrides any potential losses."

"Why couldn't this weapon be tested in a lab somewhere? Why are we even involved at all?"

"I suppose it could." Kilgore placed a cupped hand thoughtfully below his helmet's mouth vent, lowering it from his face a second later. "I don't know why we're involved. It's just how the high commander wants it done. Anyway, it doesn't matter what you think. You will follow the orders you have been given."

"Sir, I agree with Blackthorn and Pritchett," said Ito, the sergeant appearing out of absolutely nowhere.

Asher was dumbfounded, this being the first time he had ever observed the sergeant question anyone's authority. Ito practically worshiped the ground her superiors walked on and obeyed orders to the letter.

The whole battalion congregated around them now, all eyes on the potential spectacle occurring just in front of the garage door.

"Sir," Ito continued in a softer but still assertive tone, "I think they're right, though I don't believe I agree with some of the phrasing. It might be the worst plan ever drawn up. Essentially all we are doing is charging in there, guns blazing, all the while hoping that the enemy will come for us. We'll be unnecessarily exposing ourselves to attack. On top of that, we're engaging a large group at night. It all sounds like you plan on using us, your own soldiers, as blood bait."

Asher was sure the sergeant was nervous, though she maintained her usual temperament without faltering in the least. He stood there, waiting for what the captain would say next.

Before Kilgore could answer, the doors of the garage swung open. A fully armored Commander Greaves stepped in among the crowd.

"What's the problem, Captain?" Greaves asked. "Why aren't the troops loaded up and ready to go?" He turned to Kilgore, his confusion and brewing rage revealed by his stiff posture.

"We are just having a slight disagreement over the orders, sir," Kilgore explained.

"Oh, that all?" The commander maintained his composure surprisingly well, a broad grin appearing on his face. Maybe he would hear them out.

"Everyone!" Greaves roared, losing control. "Get in your designated transport now! One more mention of the plan, and I'll send you all down to the range to be my personal practice target! Shoot, the next one of you who utters even a single word before we roll out will be used for target practice right here!"

The commander took aim with his weapon.

The battalion scattered, fleeing from him like a group of ants from a booted foot, finding shelter within the confines of the various armored vehicles parked in the garage.

Asher ran after the rest of his squad and sought shelter from Greaves in the back of their armored truck. He took his seat last behind the others, slamming the door shut. He anxiously peered through the back window, hoping the commander hadn't singled him out as the one responsible for the delay.

Chapter XXIII

The Predator, Now the Prey

The Legion convoy of a dozen armored personnel carriers and a multitude of trucks made its way down the gravel road as the crescent moon disappeared behind a growing wall of clouds. The vehicles revealed the Legion's intentions, their refurbished Strykers armed with M-2 Browning machine guns. They were unapologetic intruders into the landscape. They invaded as a stream of metal-plated insects, creeping through the shadowed woodlands as they descended upon their unsuspecting victim. The convoy raced over the rough gravel, bounding through the heavily foliaged forest and over uneven terrain.

Asher peered through the transport truck's rear window, careful to hold onto the front of his seat as he gazed up at the gathering thunderhead above. It seemed strange to him to arrive anywhere so far past the twilight hour, at a time when their quarry tended to be much more active. Asher found the presence of clouds unsettling, certain whatever rain they might produce would only complicate things. A feeling of eerie foreboding washed over him, and the hair on his forearms stood on end.

We shouldn't be out now, he thought, mouthing the words.

"Nervous?" asked Aaron. He leaned in towards Asher from where he sat on the other side of the truck, keeping his voice down so the others couldn't hear.

Asher took glanced to his left, certain if anyone listened in on them it would be Driscoll. He found his corporal sitting near the front of the truck, engaged in a mostly one-sided conversation with Salvo. He was trying to flirt with her, though by the look on Salvo's face, he was failing.

"Hard not to be when you're about to bring down the vamps." Asher turned to Aaron, his voice on low volume as well. His helmet concealed his look of confusion.

"You know that's not what I mean. You're more tense than usual. Still hung up about our standoff with the captain?"

"Uh, yeah, I suppose you could say that. This whole stupid plan is just suspect."

"Those are the orders, though." Aaron shook his head, his helmet preventing Asher from seeing the look on his face. "Just between you and me, I think I'd rather take my chances with the vamps than deal with Greaves. I mean, what are the bloodsuckers gonna do? Bite you? Kill you? Anything like that will be over in a second. Greaves could mess you up for life. Who knows what he could do to you, or worse, make you do. Dude's a freakin' psycho sometimes."

Asher suddenly felt eyes on them. He looked up to see Sergeant Ito glance at him through her visor from where she sat at the front of the truck. He doubted she had heard anything, though he knew she wouldn't care for the way they spoke about their superiors.

Asher turned his head to the side to find Milo staring at him. The medic was intently interested in their conversation, holding his arms crossed over his chest as he listened in.

Asher suddenly grabbed the side of his seat. He nearly fell to the floor when the truck abruptly swerved to the side, narrowly missing a large object parked in the middle of the road. As they passed in front of it, Asher glanced out the window to see an armored truck. It was clearly not one of the Legion's, its paint job reminiscent of an ambulance. He couldn't fully make out the green lettering through the darkness. He thought it said Cyber something.

"Sorry to butt in." Milo leaned in toward them, speaking as though nothing had happened. "But you're not saying anything no one's said before. I think we can probably all agree, Greaves might be and probably is, a controlling sociopath."

Bam!

One of the Strykers in the front of the line slammed into some kind of small metal construction outside the slaughter plant perimeter, shutting down their conversation. Asher couldn't see it from where he sat, but the sound of Stryker treads rolling over thin metal was unmistakable. Whatever it hit likely was reduced to nothing more than a pile of tattered debris.

The Strykers behind the first ran through the plant's chain-link fence, just as Captain Kilgore said they would, turning it into a snake-like line of scrap as they skidded onto the asphalt parking lot. Their transport vehicles followed, pulling around to form a line behind them, parking horizontally to create a fallback point should they need it.

The driver of their transport truck slammed on the brakes, jolting all inside forward, swerving to a stop atop the wrecked fence.

Asher shook his head, unsure of the Legion's driver selection process.

"Take up your positions in front of the trucks!" Greaves called out to his battalion through their helmets.

Asher opened the door and jumped from the back of the truck, running around their line of vehicles to the designated spot. Several more Strykers rolled around the outside perimeter, moving farther down each side before turning to crash into the fence as they took their positions at the other edge of the parking lot.

Asher stood nearly 100 yards away from the front of the plant, his comrades filing in beside him. Though a mass of clouds masked the moon, the target remained visible. The yellow-orange glow of the streetlights interspersed across the parking lot helped the situation.

The soldiers made their line just a few yards behind the plant's irregular formation of parked cars, unable to prevent the creation of several large gaps as they took the best vantage points. A second line formed behind the first, ready to file past them when it came time to reload.

Asher assumed his shooting stance, his shotgun nearly at his hip, the need for accuracy lessened because of the line. He looked to both sides, finding Aaron to his left and Milo to his right, having to turn his head to see Driscoll just off in his peripheral vision. He couldn't see Sergeant Ito from his position, though he was sure she was somewhere nearby in the second line. They held their weapons, keeping to their orders and remaining silent as they waited for Kilgore to arrive.

"Hold your fire until given the order!" Captain Kilgore leaped onto the hood of the red Firebird in front of them, shouting at them directly. "The commander wants to give us a show first!"

Asher tightened his grip around his firearm, his limbs tense as he waited for the commander to ignite the explosives.

"Detonating the charges now!" Greaves called into their helmets, the man himself somewhere behind their line.

The charges placed behind the plant exploded. The deafening sound was so loud it felt as though it might crack the sky. Noisy as they were, the explosives produced only sound, not damage, as they were placed too far back to have any effect on the plant's back wall. Greaves wanted to cause the enemy to flee the plant and run out into the open.

"Hit 'em from the back!" roared Commander Greaves, his voice barely registering over the ringing in Asher's ears.

The six Strykers behind the plant fired their M2 Browning machine guns. The .50 caliber rounds sliced through the thin tin walls, the shots pointed toward the ground so as not to hit the line of soldiers out front. The guns sounded much less intimidating from a distance, but Asher knew how powerful they were. Without adequate shelter, nothing living could stand against them once they began to fire.

The guns ceased shooting and dead silence held sway once again. No one had left the plant.

"Hit 'em with the second round!" Greaves commanded without hesitation, giving the signal for the Strykers out front to fire.

Bang! Bang! Bang!

The six Strykers parked behind the line answered with their M2s, drowning out his words. The stream of fire started only a few yards in front of their line, moving through the parking lot up to the plant. The slugs tore into the vehicles, exploding windshields, tearing through metal bodies with unrelenting, destructive ferocity. They continued up to the plant wall, the rounds punishing the thin tin with round after round.

They ceased to fire when their guns grew hot, smoke flowing into the air from the barrels.

The plant's walls stood riddled with holes, a great metal block of Swiss cheese under the yellow-orange glow of the streetlamps.

"Grenades!" screamed Greaves, undeterred, the enemy refusing to rear its head. "Tear up the place!"

The battalion's grenadiers stepped forward through the line, the barrels of their launchers pointed toward the plant. The grenades burst forth, striking parked cars and the slaughter plant walls. Several cars exploded, sending metal debris flying, causing some of the soldiers to step back. The vehicles were set ablaze, further lighting up the lot. A few of the grenades hit the plant's wall, leaving tattered holes in the metal. They reduced the area into a smoldering wreck, yet no one ran from the plant.

Asher was beginning to believe the place was empty.

The grenadiers continuously pummeled the ground, firing off round after round. Cars exploded, the wall was further punctured, and yet no one exited the plant. They ceased fire moments later, the smoke clearing to allow Asher a better view of the destruction.

The parking lot was decimated, a graveyard of twisted, smoldering metal wrecks, precisely what the commander had prescribed. The silence returned, even more eerie and awkward than before, more deafening than the thunder of guns. A menacing red light now flowed out from the tattered holes blasted into the building. The front door was gone entirely, reduced to a gaping, bloody portal into a house of damnation. The wall of clouds above had gone from grey to a furious black, ready to burst.

The hair on the back of Asher's neck stood up. Something was wrong.

"Still no sign of the enemy, sir," Kilgore said through his helmet.

"Do you think we have been given faulty intel, sir?" Tarango asked from near the other side of the line.

A thunderbolt punctuated his question as lightning streaked across the sky. The gathered clouds above unleashed a torrent of rain, the heavy drops racing toward and then engulfing them. The soldiers had no choice but to let the water rush over them, nailed to the ground by Greaves' orders.

A giant shadow suddenly filled the doorway, turning the blood-red light to darkness. A towering man dressed in black-plated armor lumbered out, laboriously dragging a colossal, bloody meat cleaver behind him. Multiple large and identically clad figures followed him, each of them carrying an impossibly large shield and a vaguely stick-shaped implement.

Asher squinted at the objects in their hands, instantaneously recognizing them yet not believing what he saw.

They carried fully automatic assault rifles.

The plant soldiers poured out, nearly two hundred strong as they formed their own single line.

"They are armed, sir!" screamed Tarango.

"Keep your shirt on, Lieutenant!" Kilgore scolded. "We're a thousand strong, and we got all the big guns!"

The giant man let out a hateful roar, flourishing his great cleaver and pointing the blade toward them, his eyes glowing red beneath his helmet. His voice held no hint of humanity. His black-plated troops responded to his call, slamming their heavy shields into the ground. They drove them down deep into the asphalt, creating a barrier between themselves and the Legion's line.

The slaughter plant soldiers took cover behind their shields, having no need to crouch. Only the muzzles of their assault rifles remained visible through the gaps in their barrier.

"Grenadiers, fall back! The rest of you keep your positions!" Greaves commanded with unease. "Hold until I tell you to fire!"

The line remained in place, the grenadiers moving back behind the rest of the soldiers.

"Fire all we got up front!" Greaves roared. "There's no way to know what those shields are made of! Hit 'em with all you got!"

The sound of the firing shotguns and M2s intertwined, and the second line stepped in between the gaps in the first, their gun blasts creating a symphony of destruction. Their fire was relentless and unending, continuing until they spent all their rounds. Asher removed his double drum magazine as the smoke cleared, revealing the virtually untouched enemy line.

"Move to fall back positions!" Greaves' frustration was apparent. "We're not penetrating those shields!"

Their line had slowly fallen apart before the commander gave the order and now dissolved completely. The Legion personnel turned and dashed for the trucks like a panicked colony of ants. The enemy's guns called after the battalion as they fled, instantly killing several of their number on the spot. The shots were accurate and well placed, hitting their victims in the neck where they had less armor.

Asher ran for the truck directly behind him, dropping to the ground to slide across the slick asphalt and underneath the bed. Pushing through to the other side, he took up a position crouched behind the front tire. Several of his comrades did the same.

"Got room for two, Ash?" asked Aaron. He emerged from underneath the truck to crouch beside him. Milo followed him, remaining silent and leaning his back up against the side of the truck beside them.

Asher looked past Aaron, finding Driscoll standing near the back of the truck. The enemy had them pinned down, and he couldn't recognize anyone else.

"Grenadiers!" called the commander. "Fire from the fallback position!"

One of the grenadiers, a slightly built woman, moved past Asher and the other huddled soldiers, stepping between the front of their truck and the back of another. She fully exposed herself to enemy fire as she aimed her launcher.

"Intel is obviously faulty!" Driscoll moved toward them, yelling over the gunfire. "They were ready for us!"

"We're gonna have a heck of a time pulling out of this one!" Aaron called back, somehow remaining positive.

The grenadier at the front of the truck fired her launcher.

Asher slowly rose from where he squatted and cautiously peered over the truck's hood to view the assault through the heavy rain. Surveying the devastated battlefield, he caught a glint of movement off to his peripheral left. He turned to see an abandoned armored truck, the one they had nearly run into earlier, slowly rolling backward into the parking lot.

"Sir, our guns aren't doing the job!" yelled Kilgore. "We need to try something else or start a full-on retreat!"

"Release the hounds!" Greaves screamed into his microphone.

Asher's eyes darted toward the right, their pack of dogs appearing atop the hills surrounding them, charging down the slopes toward the parking lot.

The pack had almost doubled in size, with nearly fifty animals racing for their quarry. They crossed over the edge of the crumpled chain-link fence in seconds. Several of the vampire gunmen turned to face the hounds, their shots bringing down several of them. The rest of the pack hurtled toward them, bounding over their fallen comrades, their lust for vampire flesh unquenchable. Only a well-placed shot to the head could bring down a hellhound.

Asher's eyes darted back through the heavy rain, focusing on the truck. Something stirred in the back, slamming itself against the walls, the sound distant and soft compared to the fire of their guns.

"The weapon has arrived, sir!" Kilgore yelled at the commander.

It took Asher a moment to realize what the captain meant, too preoccupied with everything going on around him. Greaves gave little information about the test weapon.

The pounding intensified as the truck ceased to roll, gently stopping against one of the metal wreck piles.

The vampire commander howled, indicating the truck with his cleaver. The vampire soldiers not preoccupied with hounds shifted their attention from the Legion's line to the vehicle's doors. The enemy personnel at the peripherals of the line remained focused on the attacking beasts, pelting them with gunfire as the animals crashed into either side of their line.

The doors to the armored truck burst open. A black-clad creature sprang forth, charging toward the vampire soldiers so rapidly that its feet barely touched the ground.

The commander howled yet again, his soldiers opening fire on the creature.

Two knives materialized in the giant's raised sword arm, one in the elbow and the other in the wrist. The monster let out a surprisingly high-pitched shriek and dropped his cleaver. The weapon hit the asphalt with a heavy, metallic thud and slid across the slick ground in front of the shield barrier.

The test subject was at the vampire line now, suddenly joined by two dark-cloaked, dagger-wielding figures running close behind, bounding over the piles of wreckage. The vampire soldiers fully shifted their focus to the three black-clad enemies rushing toward them, issuing forth a barrage of relentless fire.

The three charged their line, unaffected by the endless volley. The test subject hit the ground, gliding across the asphalt on its backside, feet first, taking hold of the vampire commander's dropped cleaver as it went. It jumped to its feet as it slid on toward the vampire shield line. The test subject leaped up onto the edge of one of the massive metal shields, using its momentum to propel itself above the vampire commander.

It raised the cleaver to strike.

The vampire screamed his last as the test subject slammed the weapon down through the center of his helmet and descended back to the ground. It left the blade embedded deep in the monster's skull.

The test subject's companions followed him, leaping over the shield barrier, unleashing a hail of daggers into the vampires' ranks. The vampire commander fell backward, landing prostrate on the ground with a mighty crash, blood flowing from his grievous head wound, his intimidating howls forever silenced.

The hounds tore through both sides of the vampire line now, downing soldier after soldier, ripping them apart where they fell. The test subject and his companions joined forces with the beasts. Daggers flew, claws and fangs slashed, vampire limbs and heads littered the ground in a relentless scene of blood and horror only slightly concealed behind the shields.

Asher couldn't take his eyes from the battle before him, ceasing to watch when he felt a hand touch his shoulder. Sergeant Ito stood beside him. Aaron and Milo looked in their direction with idiotic smiles on their faces.

The routed enemy shrieked, and the survivors dropped their weapons as they attempted to escape from their own line of shields. Some of them slipped upon the blood and rainwater slicked asphalt as they fled, falling to the ground to be torn asunder by the hounds.

"Kilgore!" Greaves shouted. "Move your company out to keep those bloodsuckers from escaping!"

"You heard him!" Kilgore cried out from behind. "Move out before they get away! We're gonna have to go in close to hit them!"

Asher sped around the hood of the truck, weapon raised, trained on the escaping enemy. He quickly regained his former position, his comrades filing in beside him, his concentration focused solely on what was going on around him. He stared down his gun sights, having some difficulty taking aim on the fast-moving enemy through the slowly slackening rain. The new line was in place now, and the Legion's soldiers stood locked in a firing stance as they waited for the enemy to come within range.

"Forward!" screamed Kilgore, seeing his line was too far back, allowing the enemy to escape off to the side.

The company obliged, rapidly moving forward, stepping over and around parts of wrecked cars, occasionally causing significant gaps in the line. Several of the surviving enemy had already fled, escaping to the surrounding hills, never coming within the effective range. Nearly two dozen of the fleeing enemy soldiers rushed toward them, insanity the only force driving them to charge the line.

Asher aimed at the vampire nearest him, waiting for it to draw in closer so he could hit it with the full force of his fire.

The vampire suddenly ceased its charge and pointed a wet, dirty finger in his direction. It lowered its head and ran straight for him, covering ground quickly, leaping over debris and smoking wrecks to reach him. Asher held his ground, staring down his sights, his weapon trained on its head. The creature was oddly large.

"They're coming right for our line, sir!" cried Tarango.

"Shut up, Lieutenant!" Kilgore shouted. "We got 'em right where we want 'em! Fire!"

The blast of nearly one hundred shotguns hit the crazed, charging enemy. The attacking pack of vampires continued toward the company line, only slightly slowed by the repeated gunfire.

Asher pelted his target with shot after shot, nearly every one striking it in the head, his fragmentation rounds somehow unable to penetrate its strange helmet.

"That armor is killing us, sir!" Tarango yelled with renewed concern.

"Keep up the fire!" Kilgore grew enraged. "We can't let them escape!"

Asher continued to fire on the vampire, never letting up, suddenly finding a ragged hole in the armor resting against its forehead. He immediately focused solely on that spot. A grin appeared on his face when he saw a fountain of blood and brains explode from the vampire's exposed skull.

The monster screamed as it staggered to the ground, falling at Asher's feet, its dirty clawed hand outstretched, grasping for his leg. Aaron stood near him, giving him a thumb's up, his booted foot resting on a dead vampire's ruined, pulpy head.

"Driscoll!"

Asher heard Ito scream through the gunfire. He jerked his firearm around, nearly pointing the muzzle at his fellows. He was a substantial distance from the sergeant's position, unable to see what was occurring on that side through the rain.

"Retain your positions and hold the line!" Kilgore called in response, seeing several other soldiers turn toward the sergeant.

Asher remained in place, unable to fully comply with his orders. He could only assume one of the vampires had killed his assault group leader.

"Sergeant!" Kilgore cried out. "What's your status?"

"I'm fine, sir!" Ito nearly screamed into her helmet, her voice shrill. "They got Corporal Driscoll! It was a big one! It just grabbed him and ran!"

"Fall back!" Greaves' voice bellowed into their heads, drowning out the sergeant's cries. "We're gonna give the test subject and the hounds time to leave the field before we start clearing the place! Witchburn wants no contact with either of them at this point in the operation!"

Asher gazed back over toward the vampire line, the test subject and his friends already vanished, vampire bodies littering the ground, all of the enemy dead or fleeing. Only the hounds remained, returned to their more pleasant selves, many of them laying on the ground to gnaw on discarded body parts.

"What about our dead and wounded, sir?" asked Tarango.

"Pull your people back!" Greaves commanded, ignoring Tarango's plea. "We will regroup and catch our breath! I will send someone else out for our dead and wounded!"

"What about Driscoll?" Asher turned and yelled. He hoped one of the officers would hear him. Both Aaron and Milo remained on either side of Asher, the same look of concern scrawled across their faces.

Orders prohibited all personnel below lieutenant from using their microphones during the assault. The higher-ranking officers wanted to prevent the flood of input. Asher couldn't say he had grown close to the bossy, narcissistic assault group leader, but he still didn't relish losing him.

"Move to the fallback position, Private!"

Asher found Lieutenant Tarango standing off toward his right, rainwater flowing over his body armor.

"Those are your orders!" The lieutenant motioned with his shotgun. "It would be a good idea to follow them!" He held the weapon at his hip, and though he hadn't pointed it directly at them, the stiffness of his body language suggested he might use it.

"I saw Corporal Driscoll fall!" Tarango's posture softened. "One of those filthy bloodsuckers got him! Just carried him off! He's a dead man!"

Asher remained where he stood, looking over at Aaron and then Milo, the three of them stunned by Driscoll's disappearance and the lieutenant's brazen attitude.

"Fall back!" Tarango roared. He broke through their mental haze, the severe grip on his weapon returned.

The three of them instantly ran for the line of trucks, the barrels of their weapons pointed toward the ground as they sprinted around and away from Tarango. Asher looked back for just a moment, finding the enraged lieutenant right on their heels.

Chapter XXIV

Excruciating Extraction

Asher took his eyes from his gun sights and looked to see who stood next to him. Unable to place the man, he returned his attention to his weapon, intent on what lay in front of him. He and the rest of his company formed a line in front of a light pole on the plant's perimeter, all with their weapons trained on their captive.

The vampire stood in front of him, bound securely to the pole, a cloth gag stuffed into his mouth. The Legion had apprehended him sometime earlier, finding him hiding in a small corner office within the hanger cowering under his desk, too cowardly to attempt an escape. The Legion remained on the premise of the slaughter plant, ordered to complete the operation by thoroughly clearing the area.

Once given the signal, Asher's company made sure no escaped enemy soldiers remained near the destroyed fences. Kilgore had called them into position where they now stood after receiving word of the prisoner's capture. Commander Greaves was convinced this particular vampire was the one responsible for overseeing all operations at the plant. It was a viable theory given the expensive-looking blue suit the vampire wore. It was far from appropriate attire for someone who worked on the ground floor of a slaughter plant.

In addition to the suit, the vampire's physical appearance was significantly different from any other Asher had seen thus far. He wasn't sure if he was of African descent and also happened to be albino or had some other skin condition.

Asher yawned, wondering if Greaves would arrive at all. His doubt ceased when he heard the sound of boots on asphalt. He turned from the vampire to spot the commander walking toward the firing line, pale moonlight glistening upon his bald head.

Greaves had ditched his usual dark tank top and jeans and opted for black body armor and a military trench coat, only keeping his boots and signature sunglasses. He puffed out his chest out as he swaggered toward the line of personnel like a conquering emperor. Greaves continued over the asphalt until he reached Captain Kilgore, who stood off to the side of the line.

"You got him to say anything yet?" asked Greaves.

"Not at all, sir," Kilgore answered.

"What have you tried so far?"

"We've threatened to blow his freakin' brains out several times already, sir. He just won't give us anything."

"Well, no wonder he won't say nothin'," Greaves chuckled. "You can't just point a gun at somebody and expect them to spill it. Yuh gotta use finesse when yuh interrogate someone."

Greaves left the captain standing there as he made his way through the line toward the captive.

"You best start talking soon, vamp, or it's just gonna keep gettin' worse for yuh." Greaves pulled the gag from the captive's mouth, stepping back when he did so, expecting the vampire to lash out at him with a torrent of screams.

"I already told your captain!" Desmond shrieked in desperation. "I know nothing!"

"Ah, come on now," Greaves coaxed. "Yuh oughta know those ain't the answers we're looking for. Yuh have to know something."

"I have no information to give you!" The vampire screamed as though he might start sobbing.-

"I just don't believe all that. I mean, we catch you in what looks like your own private office, wearing that fancy pants suit of yours, and somehow you're not the neck-biter in charge?"

"I know nothing!"

"Well, I guess if death threats and guns ain't gonna do the trick, we better try somethin' else." Greaves put a hand to his chin.

"Looks like the filthy bloodsucker has gone and made his choice!" Greaves turned to the gathered personnel, raising a gloved fist toward the sky for punctuation. "Thinks he ain't gonna tell me nothing!" Greaves taunted.

His words elicited jeers from the soldiers, all directed at the bound vampire.

"We can't have that, sir!" shouted one of the men over the others. The speaker was Captain Kilgore.

"Don't go a' worryin' about it, though!" the commander called back to them. "I'm fixin' to teach 'im the error of his ways! Bring me my interrogation tools, Captain!" Greaves motioned toward Kilgore.

"Yes, sir!" said Kilgore, sprinting across the asphalt toward their fleet of Strykers now resting nearby.

The captain returned some minutes later carrying a rather unassuming briefcase. He passed through their line of personnel to reach the commander, stopping to hold the case out flat in front of him.

Greaves stepped toward the captain, unlatching the lid of the briefcase, as Kilgore held it open. The commander then methodically removed his leather gloves and placed them in the case before taking out a pair of small objects, a metallic gleam briefly shining in Asher's eyes. Greaves closed the case and motioned the captain away.

Desmond strained his neck to see what the commander now held in his hands.

"Suppose I don't need to tell you what these are." Greaves turned back around to face Desmond.

He held up his right hand, showing him the particularly gruesome-looking pair of spiked brass knuckles he wore.

"These are custom. Solid titanium. Tough as heck, but hardly weigh a thing." Greaves opened his hand to reveal a second pair of knuckles, bouncing them around in his palm before slipping them over the fingers of his left hand. "The spikes were purely my idea. Makes it easier to turn yuh into a bloody pulp."

The commander stepped closer to Desmond.

"These are illegal in nearly every state, even Texas. Absolutely not supposed to have 'em. Witchburn would throw a fit if she ever found out. Problem is, they're just too useful to go givin' up. Perfect for beatin' the snot out of even the stubbornest of bloodsuckers!"

"Could you possibly cease this mindless dribble?" Desmond gave Greaves a look of defiance, mustering up at least an ounce of courage.

Asher frowned, feeling any display of bravery was ill-advised when bound and confronted by a man like the commander.

"All you've done is talk and shown me a rather brutish piece of jewelry," Desmond returned the commander's mockery. "Do you really think a worthless blood bag like you is going to convince me to speak?"

"I like to think I'm pretty good with 'em." Greaves continued to admire his knuckles, paying little heed to Desmond's words. "Can break whatever bone I hit," he remarked, his voice distant.

"You can torture me all you want!" Desmond growled with fervor. "It's an entirely useless tactic! I will give you nothing!"

"You got one last chance to tell me what I need to know before things have to get painful," Greaves threatened. He stepped ever closer, glaring at Desmond through his sunglasses. "Heck, even if you won't give us anything, I reckon it'll stop all your back sass!"

"Burn in Hell blood bag!" Desmond howled.

Greaves dealt Desmond a quick but heavy blow to the ribs.

Desmond screamed on impact. A face twisted in pain replaced his defiance.

Asher cringed, hearing the vampire's bones crack and break even from where he stood.

Desmond remained motionless, occasionally wincing due to the pain, a small amount of blood staining his expensive suit. Greaves stepped back and stood for a moment, pausing to allow the vampire additional time to answer the question.

"You're gonna have to say somethin'!" Greaves drove his fist into the opposite side of the vampire's ribcage.

Desmond howled, his face contorting, the sound of bones breaking once again reverberating through the air. Blood stained the other side of the vampire's suit when Greaves pulled his fist from the newly formed wound.

"Yuh sure you don't have somethin' yuh wanna share?" Greaves asked, waiting for the vampire's answer. "The next ones will be to the face, and it's only going to keep gettin' worse from there!"

"Hmm... " Desmond paused, sarcasm in his voice. "You'll have to excuse the lewdness of my language, but go drop dead, you swine!"

Asher shook his head. Desmond was either tougher or more stupid than he thought.

"One to the head coming up!" Greaves dealt Desmond a hardy blow to the forehead, the spikes of his brass knuckles puncturing the skin.

Blood flowed from the wounds, running down the vampire's face when the commander pulled his fist away. Desmond didn't scream this time, dazed by the strike.

"Now that one was just me being nice. The next is to your jaw, and I intend on breaking it. Ain't gonna be no fun being a bloodsucker with a broke jaw."

"My bosses never go by their real names!" Desmond shrieked, sounding like a dying cat. "Nobody within our organization does!"

"Well, that's good to know, but how does that help us? You're going to have to do better than that if yuh want all this to stop."

"The Master is the head of our organization, but I have no idea where he could be found! No one does! He constantly moves! He has to because we can't risk his discovery by people like you!"

"Once again, good to know, but it does us no good. Just out of curiosity, how does your organization run if you have no idea where the boss man is?"

"We meet with him by appointment only," Desmond explained. "We send word to his selected couriers and exchange information that way. If it's an especially urgent message, we send it over the dark web. It's the only way we can communicate without risking discovery."

"You got any other names or aliases you might want to share with us?" There was an aggressive edge to Greaves's voice. "Your boss's alias ain't gonna cut it if you want to stop all this."

"Our head of research and development calls himself The Surgeon," Desmond spoke without hesitation.

"Hmm... that's interesting..." Greaves spoke to himself now, his interest suddenly diverted. "That's the first I've ever heard about something like that. Had no idea y'all was that involved or went that deep. Thought you were just messin' in traffickin' food mostly. Now, can you tell me exactly where we can find this Surgeon feller?" Greaves pulled back his fist as though he were preparing to strike Desmond again.

"He has a big lab in the San Gabriel Mountains in California!" Desmond screamed, reacting to the commander's movements. "It's off of Highway 39, right off of the closed portion! It's built right into the mountain! If you bring me a map, I can show you exactly where he is!"

"Wow, you got way more goin' than I ever thought!" Greaves grinned. "Sinkin' some serious money into this organization of yours, up and buildin' laboratories right into mountains. Who does that? That sure is seclusion for yuh."

"Yes, I was told the site was selected purely for secrecy," Desmond stopped the commander.

"Do yuh know what kind of research he does?" Greaves returned to a more somber tone.

"No, not exactly." Desmond shook his head. "All of his experiments seem to be biological in nature. He has had us provide him with specific human specimens in the past, usually individuals with certain blood-related diseases. It all has something to do with creating a more reliable food supply."

"Um... Hmm..." Greaves took a moment to think. "Yeah, that's not much. You see much of what he's got in there?"

"I have seen a few things." Desmond nodded. "Lots of living human and primate specimens, lots of dogs and rats. Some things I didn't recognize. He was keeping something big in there too. Some kind of giant animal. It seemed rather dangerous. I suppose there could have even been more than one. Whatever it was, I certainly never want to go near it."

"And I don't suppose you know any other names?" Greaves crossed his arms, his frustration visible in the pulsating vein in his neck. "Not even of your immediate superiors?"

"Sorry," said Desmond, his confidence fading. "I don't have any more names that might help you."

"Ha!" Greaves chuckled. "Do you expect me to believe that's everything you know?" He paused, ready for Desmond to act up yet again. "Doesn't matter, though," Greaves continued. "You'll be giving us plenty to work with just by spilling your guts about this Surgeon."

"You're... You're not going to kill me now, are you?" Desmond's tone was sorrowful. The vampire closed his eyes and turned his head away from the commander.

"Well, normally we would." Greaves slouched as though he were disappointed. "You're kind of a special case seeing as you are so willing to speak to us. You're easily the most talkative vampire I've ever met."

"What are you going to do to me?" Desmond was wide-eyed, more worried now that he knew he would live.

"We're gonna drag you back to HQ and give you over to High Commander Witchburn." A wicked grin slowly appeared on the commander's face. "She would love to have a neck-biting rat like you. Be the best captive yet, that is so long as you keep toeing the line." Greaves turned to walk away from the captured vampire.

"How are you going to know what I say is true?" Desmond screamed, defiance suddenly returning. "For all you dimwitted blood bags know, I could be leading you into a trap! Surely even a buffoon like you would know better than to just trust me! That's what makes torture such a useless tactic!" He accepted his fate and now only sought to ridicule the commander.

Greaves turned back toward the prisoner.

"I knew we had us a smart one," he said with a smirk. Greaves humored Desmond despite his insolence as he stepped in close. "Here's the thing about the Legion." He whispered into the vampire's ear. "The moment yuh join, your life ain't ever gonna be the same. Huntin' n' killin' bloodsuckers is dangerous business, and death rates are always high, as you might imagine. We always expect to be taken out by you vamps one day. It's all just part of the job. That's one of the reasons why they sometimes call us the Phantom Legion. Death means nothing to us!"

"Aren't you concerned about the welfare of your men?" Desmond was undeterred by Greaves's words. "You can say what you want about vampires, but at least we take care of our own!"

"Oh, trust me, there will be consequences for you if you've been a' lyin' to us bloodsucker!" Greaves' anger brewed up anew, his voice sounding as though he might consider taking Desmond's life after all.

One of the hellhound handlers passed by the line of soldiers with one of the hounds in tow as the commander spoke. Asher turned his head to see it was Garm. It was difficult to miss his pitch-black coloration, bright, haunting eyes, and multiple scars. The pupils of the hound's yellow-green eyes dilated, and his nostrils flared the instant he caught the scent of his mortal enemy.

The dog lunged sideways toward the vampire, violently dragging his handler along with him.

"Hold it, boy!" yelled the handler. He dug his heels into the asphalt just to keep the colossal animal at bay, only slowing Garm down for all his effort.

The hound continued to move forward, though at a crawl. Asher wasn't sure how much longer the handler could maintain his hold until the dog broke free and went for the Desmond.

"Oh, I suppose you haven't met Garm." Greaves chuckled. "He's one of our new vampire huntin' hellhounds. We're pretty proud of this one. Just been racking up the kills since his first operation. So good at it I'm thinkin' we might have to give him an official rank. Sure loves runnin' you vamps down and then ripping you all apart!"

Desmond had no retort for the commander this time. He was preoccupied with Garm, fear plastered all over his face as the hound struggled against the leash, continuing toward him.

The massive beast had worked himself into a frenzy, foamy saliva dripping from his mouth between rabid snarls, repeatedly lunging forward as he pulled his handler along through the line of personnel. Several soldiers quickly moved out of the way, allowing the hound to cross through their line as he drew closer to the vampire. No one wanted to be between such a massive, enraged animal and his intended victim.

"Ah, and here I go a' ramblin' on about the dang dogs!" exclaimed Greaves, putting an open palm up to his forehead for exaggerated effect. "It's just so great to have 'em. Really reduces the workload. Anyway, I think before I go take my men out to see this Surgeon feller, I'm gonna recommend to High Commander Witchburn that she hands yuh over to Garm to be his own personal chew toy!"

"Would you like that, boy!" Greaves walked toward Garm, squatting to address the hound, though at a safe distance away. "Oh, I just knew you would! Now, who's Daddy's bloodthirsty little puppy?"

Garm's snarls only grew louder due to the commander's taunts, the rage in his eyes directed at Desmond. Asher was sure the hound might have bitten the commander if he were any closer

"So, ah, yuh think yuh might need to make some changes to the information yuh gave us?" Greaves rose to his feet and walked back towards Desmond, placing a hand on the vampire's shoulder. "Any changes at all?" he asked again, nearly at a whisper.

Desmond wordlessly shook his head no, somehow able to remain calm despite his fear of the approaching, heavily enraged hound.

"Well, for your sake, I hope you are," said Greaves. "Make it so much easier on yuh when it comes time to kill you!"

Desmond remained silent, ignoring the commander's attempt to unnerve him. Asher was sure it took all the vampire had not to react to Greaves' comment.

"Oh, I forgot, we'll be takin' you with us on the operation." Greaves paused for dramatic effect.

Desmond's pupils dilated as he opened his mouth to protest.

Greaves turned and slapped a gloved hand over the vampire's mouth, careful to mind his fangs, before continuing. "That way, we can get our intel straight from the vamp's filthy mouth and in real-time. Be right under my direction with Garm there the whole time. Just one false or misremembered direction, and we'll be feeding you to him!" Greaves removed his hand from the vampire's face.

Desmond remained silent, rendered incapable of any further protest. Instead, he gave Greaves a highly agitated and flabbergasted look.

The commander turned away from the captured vampire and brought his attention back to Garm, who continued to drag his handler toward the intended prey.

The hound appeared demon-possessed, his eyes alive with red-hot rage and bloodlust, saliva frothing from his mouth as he snarled and howled. Asher was grateful the hounds only had eyes for non-human prey.

"Call off your beast!" Desmond screamed, his fear renewed. He sounded as though he were in danger of wetting himself.

"Ah, yuh 'sure yuh don't wanna meet him?" Greaves teased.

"Call him off!" Desmond shrieked. "I may be a filthy bloodsucker, but I don't deserve to be eaten alive!"

"Hmm… That's funny. I really thought yuh'd get along just fine, yuh know, being kindred spirits and all. I suppose I really ought to humor you, now that you're gonna be the high commander's new pet rat."

Greaves turned around to face the line of soldiers, his eyes resting on Asher.

"Blackthorn! Come over here and help 'em with this hound! We don't want 'em a' tearing apart our new most valuable commodity before we're through with 'em"

"Yes, sir!" said Asher. He slung his weapon around his back as he sprinted after the animal and handler.

"Don't yuh worry none." Greaves turned back to Desmond. "We'll take good care of you."

His sinister grin made Desmond wince.

Chapter XXV

Life's Greatest Illusion

Imani placed a hand over her growling stomach, hesitant to open her eyes, as she awoke back into a world of tortured howls, snarls, and screams, back in the crimson-lit holding tank. She remained there on the ground, ignoring her hunger and the horrors around her. She knew her jailers would likely come back soon.

Imani reached out, finding her brother, Isaac, lying beside her, still asleep, still safe. She pulled her hand back slowly, not wanting to chance waking him. Sleep offered them a rare respite from reality, granting them a period of liberation from their waking nightmare.

Eyes still closed, Imani wrinkled her nose, finding the stench of the cavern as repulsive as ever. The smell of excrement wafted through the air. Some of the less intelligent animals relieved themselves right on the bare ground. The rest had their own toilets, which amounted to plastic waste buckets in the corner. Regardless, the floors were always filthy, and the waste receptacles only occasionally dumped.

Imani sat up, sore from the hard floor, unable to lie there any longer. She rubbed her eyes, keeping them closed as long as she could before finally opening them. The red light overpowered her vision.

Imani frowned. The smell and the floor didn't lie. They were still in the holding area, still in their pen, kept there like livestock. It didn't matter how much she wished otherwise. Imani had no idea how long she slept. The unchanging light conditions and sedatives horrendously distorted her perception of time.

Imani looked to her right, into the pen where they kept the lab dogs. She found the barking culprit immediately. The specimen was similar to a German shepherd in build but lacked hair, displaying bone-white skin and light, marble-blue eyes.

The dog barked again, trotting toward the fence away from the large group of dogs in the pen, tail wagging. The animal would have seemed horrifying to anyone new to the holding area. His hairless skin and sickly appearance outweighed his friendly attitude.

Imani was happy for the lane between their pen and the dogs. She smirked and looked back toward Isaac's sleeping form. She remembered how much he wanted to pet the dogs in the beginning. Imani had reminded him numerous times that it was unwise to pet any animal they did not know, especially one from the holding area. Their mother always told them to be careful around strange dogs.

Mother.

Imani had had a brief glance at her parents' corpses that night. She saw their mutilated bodies through the darkness, and the gruesome images seared into her memory. This was the first time she had thought, or even dreamed, about her parents since the abduction due to the effects of the frequently administered sedatives.

A feeling of immense sadness rushed over her now, drowning out all other thoughts, causing her to begin sobbing. She was careful to keep the noise down. The keepers would eventually be back to give them their next round of sedatives, and she did not want to hasten their return.

Tears rolled from Imani's eyes like thick, globular raindrops, saturating the front of her examination gown as she cried into her lap. Her murdered parents and the hopelessness of her situation bore down on her like a great stone block. She was alone with her pain, her sleeping brother her only comfort.

Imani looked up from her lap some time later, unsure how long she had cried. She sobbed until she was no longer able, depleting her supply of tears. The searing, nauseating agony was reduced to a throbbing ache, one absorbed back inside for the moment.

Imani turned to her left, toward the other pens, desperate to find anything that might take her mind from her grief. It was an impossible task in this wretched place. She smiled, wiping her tears, delighted by what she found.

The pen across the lane, moved overnight, now sat directly against theirs. Several hundred woven-wire cages, stacked nearly to the ceiling, filled the place. Each contained a single white rabbit, the crimson light coloring the animals pink.

Imani sighed, trying not to giggle, finding how the rabbits wrinkled their noses and bounced around in their cages amusing. She slowly rose to her feet, cautiously venturing over to the corner of her pen to take a closer look. She stood at the edge, her arms folded upon the top of their pen as she peered into the cage of a particular rabbit. Imani put what her mother had told her into the back of her mind.

The rabbit gazed at her through calm, black eyes as it chewed a bit of celery. Surely, no harm would come from touching such a gentle creature.

Imani reached through the bars of the pen and into the cage, straining as she tried to touch the animal.

"I wouldn't pet him."

A pale, clawed hand grabbed her wrist.

"I'm sure he bites."

Imani looked up to see a porcelain-skinned, shorthaired woman clutch her hand, pulling it away from the cage.

The rabbit, if that was even what it was, opened its mouth to reveal a shark-like maw with row after row of tiny, razor-sharp teeth. The miniature horror screamed, lunging at the side of the cage, biting at the bars. Saliva fell from its mouth in large globs as it tried in vain to attack.

"That's gross."

Another woman appeared, disgusted by the predatory rabbit. She stood back near the edge of Imani and Isaac's pen. She had long hair but was otherwise identical in appearance to the first, both pale-skinned and dark-haired, dressed in black leather clothing.

"Just another freakin' day in this crap-soaked place," said the male vampire following behind. He rolled a large flatbed trolley past the second woman, two human-sized carriers placed on the transport bed. His physical appearance and clothing were similar to that of the first two vampires, so much so that he could be their brother.

"Those things are freakin' nasty. What does the boss want

with them anyway?" The man stopped to frown at the rabbits, forgetting his previous complaint.

"I have no idea," said the second woman, shaking her head.

"We finally found the carriers, Anoura." The man spoke to the first woman, taking a last look at the rabbit. "The boss needs to do something about that supply room. It's a wreck in there." He turned back around and grinned awkwardly at Anoura.

She glared back at him, expecting him to do something other than stand there. "What are you doing?" Anoura asked impatiently. "Stop gawking around and get in that pen."

"Here we are." The man stepped around the trolley and picked up one of the carriers, casually throwing it into the pen. The large container landed only a couple of feet from where Isaac slept.

"And here we are." He tossed the second carrier into the pen, hitting the woven metal fence.

"What are you doing tossing them in there like that, Luther?" the longhaired woman asked. "We need to keep them on the cart." She stepped down the lane at the right, leaning over as she unlocked the gate.

"The Surgeon will be displeased if we hurt his specimens." Mara frowned up at Luther. "Don't you remember? We had to get them special for him a few months ago, when we started here."

"Be careful with that gate," Luther mocked, leaning on the trolley's handle to look over at her. "They might try to make a run for it. We wouldn't want something so precious escaping, now would we?"

"And if they do, we will have no trouble catching them." The woman's eyes narrowed as her voice took on an edge. "They are only children."

"Whatever you say, Mara," Luther spoke through gritted teeth.

"Let's end the bickering now," Anoura hissed. "Set those carriers back onto the trolley."

"Yes, Anoura." Luther gave her an apologetic grin as he pulled the trolley backward and toward the right.

Mara held the gate open, following Luther into the pen after he pushed the trolley through. She handed the gate off to Anoura, who entered and made a b-line for Imani.

"What's your name?" Anoura smiled as she squatted down to look her in the eye, displaying a set of gleaming white fangs.

Mara and Luther picked up the large carriers and placed them back on the trolley before beginning the unnecessarily long process of opening the wire doors.

"My name's Imani," she responded, though without understanding what the vampire's angle could be. She didn't want to talk to her any longer than was necessary.

"Hello, Imani. My name is Anoura." She put a pale, clawed hand on her shoulder. "Is that your brother over there?" She pointed toward the sleeping boy.

"Yes, ma'am." Imani's voice was bland. She tired of them asking her that question.

"Ooh, what lovely manners." The woman smiled at her again, her demeanor overly pleasant and fake. "What's your brother's name?"

"Isaac." Imani wished Anoura would just read the names printed on their hospital bracelets.

"Lovely." Anoura removed her hand and stood up. "Can you please wake Issac up for us?"

"Why?" asked Imani. She didn't understand why they couldn't just pick her brother up and shove him in the carrier. They tended to be very forceful in everything else they did.

"We need you to get into the carriers," Anoura explained. "We need to take you someplace else. Someplace better, where nasty rabbits won't bite you."

"Yes, ma'am." A hint of enthusiasm entered Imani's voice. Few places could be worse than the holding area.

She turned away from Anoura and rushed to where Isaac slept.

"Isaac, wake up!" She grabbed her brother by the arm and shook him.

"What?" He sounded tired and was unwilling to open his eyes.

"Wake up." She continued to shake him. "They're taking us somewhere else! Someplace better! Come on. We just have to get in the carrier."

"Ahh… I don't wanna get in there." He batted her away.

"Come on! The lady promised it would be better!" Imani shouted. "You can go back to sleep there!"

"Well, OK." Isaac balled his hands into fists and rubbed his eyes, then rose to his feet at last. Imani was relieved that he had decided to comply.

"Hurry it up, kiddies!" Luther stood beside the trolley and snarled, showing his fangs. "We don't have all day, and I'm beginning to get the munchies!"

Mara remained on the other side of the trolley, angst and frustration written across her face.

"Come on, Isaac, let's go!" Imani shouted before running for the trolley and jumping inside her carrier.

Isaac followed her and quickly climbed into the carrier beside her. They both knew how their jailers could react when they didn't comply.

"That's better," said Luther, slamming the carrier doors shut. "You might want to be more compliant in the future!" He leaped in front of the cages, fangs and claws prominently displayed, a look of crazed hunger in his eyes.

"Ahhhhh!" Imani shrieked.

"Cut it out, Luther!" Anoura slapped him on the shoulder and pulled him back up. "There is no need to scare them like that!"

"Oh, sorry, Anoura." Luther held his hand up to his forehead. "You know how slim the rations are in this place. I just started to lose it. I feel so hungry."

"You only have to stick it out a little longer," Anoura reassured him. "As soon as we bring The Surgeon his specimens, we can take our daily rations."

"Better get a move on," said Mara as she moved to reopen the gate. "I'm beginning to get hungry myself."

"Here we go." Luther took hold of the trolley handle and pushed it back through the gate.

* * *

The trio of black-clad individuals made their way down the craggy, stone-sided hallway, bathed in blood-red light, on their way to The Surgeon's office. Luther continued to push the trolley, and the children remained silent in their carriers, both put off by how often their keepers spoke of their hunger.

"I don't understand what he intends to do with them," Luther whined. "They've been sitting in the holding tank for two months, just taking up space. Blood disease carriers or not, they're food. Couldn't they just be rations?"

"Whatever their purpose is, I'm sure it's an important one." Mara glanced back at Luther. "The Surgeon doesn't deal in the mundane. Why else would he put out a special order? I'm sure we'll get them back as rations when he is through."

"Would you both shut up?" Anoura turned to hiss at them. "The sooner we deliver the children, the sooner we get our rations, so let's stop all the whining!"

Luther and Mara went silent, not wanting to aggravate their superior further.

"Are we there yet?" asked Isaac. He looked at Imani through the slits in the side of his carrier, careful to keep his voice down.

"I don't know," Imani whispered. "Just be quiet. You know how they don't like us to talk."

"Hey!" Luther slapped the side of Imani's carrier. "Keep it down in there!"

The group continued down the hallway. Luther answered Isaac's question moments later, the vampire parking the trolley beside a plain-looking wooden door.

"Sir!" Anoura rapped on the door. "We are here with the children!"

They waited as The Surgeon rushed to the door. The trio patiently stood by as he quickly unlatched the many locks barring it.

"Ah, never can be too careful these days." He pulled the door open wide, holding it and allowing them to pass through. "I have quite a few valuable things in here."

"Here are the children, sir, just as requested," said Anoura, passing through the door.

Mara followed, and then Luther entered with the trolley. Each of them stopped when they entered The Surgeon's office, finding it filled with many strange things.

Sharp-bladed objects and torture devices hung from the walls along with several shelves full of a multitude of specimen jars. The body parts of various creatures or whole organisms themselves were encapsulated within. Piles of junk sat upon several tables and file cabinets. Several dried skins, both human and otherwise, were scattered in the stacks. The rest was a grotesque, jumbled mess, full of even more strange and horrifying objects piled up in such a way that they were difficult to identify. The Surgeon had all kinds of staff under his heel, but a maid wasn't one of them.

"Just park the trolley over there." The Surgeon pointed to the cleared corner near a wooden desk marred with what looked like knife marks. "You can leave it in here. I'll have somebody else run it back later."

Luther parked the trolley in the specified spot, releasing the handle as his attention turned to what hung above The Surgeon's desk.

Imani gazed up at the wall through the slits in her carrier, curious to see what kept the vampire so enthralled. The bulky metal knife handles that hung on the wall caught her eye. Above those was a single, elongated object that appeared to be a metal cricket bat. They weren't very interesting at first glance. Their only appeal was that they didn't seem to fit in with the rest of The Surgeon's collection.

"Will there be anything else, sir?" asked Anoura, ready to leave. She was not at all taken by any of the strange things she saw.

"That should be all for the moment," said The Surgeon, giving Luther a suspicious look.

"Come on, Luther," said Anoura, digging her claws into his arm to pull him away. He was as immobile as a statue.

Anoura continued to pull, not understanding his fascination with the objects. They looked useless to her.

"I see you're admiring my weapons, uh..." The Surgeon regarded Luther thoughtfully, as though he needed help.

"Luther," he frowned, wondering how The Surgeon could forget his name.

"Yes, Luther. Try not to be so forgettable in the future," The Surgeon advised. "I see you're admiring my weapons."

"I don't know if I would use the word 'admiring,' sir." Luther shrugged. "I just want to know what they are and why they're up on the wall like that. To be honest, they don't look like weapons to me. You'd probably be better off with a baseball bat."

"Huh." The Surgeon stepped behind the desk to take one of

the smaller objects from the wall. "Yes, I suppose if you just go by appearances, no, they don't look dangerous enough to be weapons. Your assumption would be wrong, though." He held the object in his hand the way one might hold a knife, turning around so they could all see. "All of these were created in our labs in the east and are gifts from The Master." The Surgeon flipped a switch on the side.

The object emitted a flash of light, a red laser beam erupting from the end. The beam was nearly a foot long and glowed like the arc from a welding torch, blazing a fiery red even against the red lighting in the room.

"Why would The Master give these to you?" asked Luther, forgetting his place.

Anoura glared at him, irritated, wishing he could keep his mouth shut.

"I don't know," said The Surgeon, pressing the pointer finger of his free hand to his chin. "She just wanted to get rid of them, I suppose, though I can't imagine why."

His eyes fell back on the object in his hand. "This is a plasma knife."

He waved it around dramatically.

"Not significantly different from the plasma torches the blood bags use for welding. The main difference is that the beam is much more powerful and burns much hotter. The power source is condensed, so that the user no longer plugs anything in or must lug around some clunky machine. It easily cuts through flesh as well as body armor, even the more advanced sets. Best used for thrusting or stabbing."

The Surgeon made several thrusting motions with the beam blade before spinning it around, jamming it down into the top of his desk. He flipped the switch once more, causing the beam to disappear.

"This long one up here is a plasma sword." The Surgeon placed the knife back on the wall, taking the sword down to show them. He flipped the switch, causing a long red light to run down the length of the blade, from filament to filament.

"A little more complicated than the knife, but the same basic technology has been applied." He took the handle in both hands, holding it like a samurai's katana. "Once again, extremely powerful with a condensed power source, though with a longer plasma stream. Slices through flesh like butter."

He swung the blade around several times, his last strike nearly hitting the desk.

"It's just too bad I have nothing to demonstrate on." The Surgeon looked suggestively toward Luther, causing him to take a step back. He continued to stare at him, as though he might test the sword out on his underling.

"Oh, well, I suppose you get the idea." The Surgeon shrugged, switching the weapon off, the bright red beam disappearing immediately. He moved to place it back on the wall.

"Will there be anything else, sir?" asked Anoura, growing impatient.

"Oh, yes, I nearly forgot." The Surgeon turned away from the wall, reaching over his desk for a piece of paper.

Finding it, he walked around his desk and presented the paper to Anoura. She frowned down at it, as she found The Surgeon's scribbled handwriting difficult to read.

"I need you to pick up a specimen at the address listed," he said.

"You're sending us out for a specimen pick-up in the middle of the day?" Luther finally lost his cool.

The Surgeon shrugged. "I didn't say it would be easy. I used to go out in the daylight all the time before The Master transferred me down here. Wear some sunglasses, and you'll be fine. You won't melt!"

"Any specifics other than what is written here, sir?" asked Anoura, hoping to stop Luther before he flew into a rant.

"Not at all." The Surgeon gave her a knowing, though somehow inappropriate grin. "Just go to the location and pick up the specimen. It's all written there."

"Can we have our daily rations before we make the pick-up?" asked Luther, a hint of worry to his voice.

"Of course," said The Surgeon. "I'm already sending you out in the daylight. I won't have you starve as well."

"Yes, sir." Luther smiled like an idiot before turning to rush out the door. Mara followed close behind.

"We will be back with your specimen as soon as possible,

sir," said Anoura. She kicked up the stopper and closing the door behind her.

"That woman." The Surgeon clasped his hands together, grinning fondly at the closed door. "One of my best delivery people. One of my best personnel, really." He stood for a moment longer before walking toward the children.

"Hello, children." The Surgeon squatted in front of the carriers. "Would you like some candy?"

His smile was friendly and genuine despite his fangs, but Imani still found something off about him.

"Candy!" Isaac's eyes lit up for the first time in months. "I wanna piece!" he shouted, crawling to the door of his carrier, excited. He stuck his hands through the bars, quivering with anticipation.

"Ah-ha! That's more like it." The Surgeon took a large bag of Skittles from the corner of his desk. "Just one piece? Pfft..." The Surgeon scoffed. "I think I can do better than that. Hold out your hands." He dumped half the bag into Isaac's hands, sending candy rolling onto both the floor and the bottom of the carrier.

"Oh, boy!" Isaac exclaimed before shoving a whole handful in his mouth.

"Would you like some candy, little girl?" asked The Surgeon, his cold eyes meeting Imani's as he looked down at her.

"Uh..." she hesitated, afraid to say yes.

"Ur not 'ungry 'moni?" Isaac asked through a mouth full of Skittles.

"Yes! Please!" Imani couldn't contain herself any longer. She eagerly put her hands through the door of the carrier, not wanting to miss out. She didn't like taking candy from the man, but she was too hungry to resist.

"Ready? Here you go." The Surgeon dumped the rest of the bag into Imani's hands, not at all concerned by the mess he made.

Imani shoved her face into her Skittle-filled hands, greedily devouring the candies.

Isaac was on his second handful, ravenously shoving it all into his mouth. Hands free, he picked up the dropped candy from the bottom of the carrier.

"Yes, eat it quickly, children." The Surgeon dropped the

empty candy bag into the trashcan beside his desk. "I will administer your shots as soon as you are finished." He walked over to a junk-laden table, pulled a small metal case from under the wreckage, and placed it down on his desk.

"No! Not a shot!" Isaac protested, candy spewing from his mouth. "All they give us are shots!" He hastily scraped candy off the floor, sticking his hand through the bars of his carrier to reach it.

"Nonsense," said The Surgeon dismissively. He pulled a pair of rubber gloves from the pocket of his lab coat and began to put them on. "Shots never hurt when I give them."

Imani swallowed, immediately shoving her second handful of candy into her mouth.

The Surgeon opened the case, revealing multiple drug-filled vials and syringes. Taking two syringes from the case, he placed one in his coat pocket and used the other to draw fluid from one of the vials as he held it up in the red light. "Give me your arm." The Surgeon leaned down beside Isaac's carrier.

The boy clenched his wrist, a worried look on his face.

"Give him your arm, Isaac," said Imani, swallowing the last of her candy. She didn't know how The Surgeon might react if they didn't follow his instructions. "It's going to be OK. I know it will," she whispered, wishing she could believe it.

"Your name is Isaac?" asked The Surgeon, reading the boy's armband.

"Uh-huh," said Isaac, still scared.

"Just hold your arm out through the bars," coaxed The Surgeon. "I promise it won't hurt." He smiled at Isaac, his pointed fangs betraying his sincerity.

Isaac begrudgingly put his arm through the bars.

The Surgeon took him by the wrist, clenching Isaac's arm in his clawed, bone-white hand. He moved to prick the boy with the needle. Isaac turned away, closing his eyes and gritting his teeth, preparing for pain.

"Look over there, Isaac." The Surgeon pointed to a spot on the wall.

"Over where?" Isaac opened his eyes, turning his head to see what The Surgeon indicated.

The Surgeon gently stuck the needle through Isaac's skin,

pushing down the plunger to administer the drug.

"Are you going to give me a shot?" Isaac asked.

"I already have." The Surgeon threw the used needle at the trashcan, missing it entirely. "My apologies, children." The Surgeon unwrapped a Band-Aid and stuck it on Isaac's arm. "I do not have any Band-Aids with cartoon characters on them."

Isaac groaned, looking down at the plain pink Band-Aid.

The Surgeon rose onto his feet and walked back to the desk, taking a second vial from the case. He drew out the fluid with the syringe he had been saving in his pocket.

"OK, now it's your turn." The Surgeon squatted beside Imani's carrier. "What's your name?"

"Imani," she said halfheartedly, not buying his antics.

"Hold out your arm, Imani." He grinned once more.

Imani shoved her arm through the bars, tired of the man's unnecessary insistence on pleasantries. He would administer shots regardless of whether they cooperated or not.

"Good girl," said The Surgeon, grasping her wrist.

Imani looked away. She didn't like watching the needle penetrate the skin.

"And there we go," said The Surgeon. He flung the needle at the trashcan, successfully landing the shot this time.

"Are you going to let us out?" asked Isaac, having no more candy to keep him occupied.

"I will eventually, but only after you take a nap." The Surgeon walked back toward his desk, pulling out a rolling chair to sit down. "You children are going to help me with my research."

"A nap?" Isaac asked in protest. "We just woke up!"

"Aren't you tired?" asked The Surgeon.

"No!"

"I'm sure your attitude will be changing very soon." The Surgeon gazed back toward the carriers from where he sat. His cold, blue eyes were the very picture of serenity.

"I don't feel tired." Imani yawned, however, and leaned against the side of her carrier. She yawned for a few more moments before looking through the slits at her side.

She found Isaac sprawled out on the floor of his carrier, already asleep. With no way to prevent it, Imani closed her eyes, drifting   into   unconsciousness.

Chapter XXVI

Immunity

"Man, the weight bench is for, you know, lifting weights. What are you doing sleeping on it?"

Asher opened his eyes to find Aaron staring down at him, his face upside down, both his hands resting on the barbell of the 310-pound weight.

The gym was nearly silent this morning, all but void of Legion personnel. It was one of the places on the base the Legion had bothered to furnish or decorate. Workout equipment filled the space, TVs hung from the ceiling, and pictures of cartoon people exercising were painted on the walls. A full-sized track encircled the area.

"I don't know." Asher sat back up on the weight bench, his voice echoing across the room. Nearly the whole Legion was still in bed, sleeping off last night's operation. "I didn't sleep very well last night."

Asher had spent most of his evening staring up at the ceiling from his bunk, too restless for sleep. He occasionally looked over at Driscoll's empty bed only to feel a sickly, depressive shock wash over him each time. Though he had never grown close to the corporal, the sense of loss clawed at him. Driscoll was yet another corpse on Asher's pile of the dead.

"Driscoll?" Aaron asked, stopping Asher before he closed his eyes again.

Asher swung his legs over the side of the bench and leaned down to pick up his water bottle. "Who else?" he asked before taking a drink. The loss of the corporal put him in mind of his own family. He missed his brothers greatly, but there was nothing to do about it. They were dead. He tried not to dwell on them.

Asher had put in for leave as soon as the option was available, hoping to visit his mother at the asylum soon. He called her several times throughout his duty, though he couldn't tell her anything about the Legion. Most of their conversations consisted of convoluted stories concerning his past work as a police officer. Asher was sure she knew something was up.

"Yeah. I hear you." Aaron shook his head. He took a seat at the arm press machine across from Asher. "Training with the guy kind of sucked, but he ended up being a better group leader than I thought he would. Never really grew on me as a person, though. Kind of a jerk and hard to get along with."

"Yeah, I never really cared for him either." Asher sat his bottle back down. "Loss itself is pretty rough, though."

"You heard anything else about what happened to him?"

"I haven't heard anything other than what Tarango told us." Asher leaned up to talk to him.

"Yeah, I haven't heard anything either." Aaron shook his head again before looking down at the floor, his depression unmistakable by his posture. "Don't know why they couldn't have said something last night. Maybe they think that since we didn't find a body that the vampire ran off with and…" He paused and gazed up at Asher. "Uh… took care of him…"

"Pretty likely, the vamps being what they are." Asher stared down at his socks, suddenly realizing they didn't match. "I've been trying to find Ito for most of the morning. You know…" he stopped, feeling he had missed something. "Come to think of it, I haven't seen any officers this morning." He frowned back up at Aaron.

"Where is everybody?" asked Aaron, raising his voice and looking around the nearly empty room.

The few soldiers present gave him dirty looks.

"I mean, I can understand wanting to sleep in for a bit, you know, since there aren't any assignments this morning, but what gives?" Aaron glanced down at his watch, returned to his normal volume. "It's kind of getting late."

"Well, anyway, it would be nice if we could find Ito. She was right beside him when he was grabbed, and I figure, if anyone knows anything, the sergeant would be the one most likely to tell us."

"Guess she went wherever the heck the rest of the officers went."

"Hear any word about all our final losses and kill counts?" Asher asked, trying to move away from the topic of Driscoll. He hoped to glean as much information from Aaron as possible.

"Only secondhand stuff," said Aaron. "I heard Kilgore and Roth talking about it when I passed by them at the plant. Said we lost something like twenty personnel and a few hounds. Killed more than a hundred or so vamps, though. Guess we ended up not doing too bad, especially when you consider how bad things were going there for a while. They'll probably give us the final numbers later today."

Asher shook his head, knowing how much worse the operation might have gone if the test subject and the hounds hadn't been there. It was a tactical loss. The Legion itself had failed to kill all but a handful of vampires.

"Have you seen Milo this morning?" Asher asked, finding a way to talk about something not involving death.

"No, I haven't seen a sign of him since last night after we all went to bed." Aaron rose from his seat to stand beside the arm press.

"Must have slipped out real early, maybe even right after I finally fell asleep," said Asher. "I suppose I'm not surprised. He seems to have taken the loss pretty hard. Makes sense. He's had a lot of it."

"Not sure where he would have gone. He does like to run to deal with his stress." Aaron looked around the track but found no one walking or jogging along it. "Guess he's just been dodging us all morning."

"My company, briefing room, now!" Captain Kilgore commanded. He suddenly appeared in the gym, catching them off guard.

Kilgore was already suited up in tactical gear, his firearm hanging from his shoulder. Though he yelled at them, he wasn't angry, just merely in a hurry for their compliance. He turned from them and ran back toward the entrance.

"Wonder what he's so excited about." Asher rose to his feet, unsure when he would have time to suit up.

"Suppose we'll find out," said Aaron. He turned toward the open gym doors right behind him.

* * *

Asher crossed through the doorway into the briefing room, Aaron still on his heels. Moving to take a seat, he saw several officers standing against the back wall.

Captain Kilgore was near the door, and was the only one decked out in body armor. The rest of the officers appeared grave-faced and tired. They spoke little or not at all.

Asher's eyes darted to Ito, who stood in the far corner.

She smiled at him when he looked at her.

Asher returned her expression with a frown. As Driscoll's immediate superior, he wasn't sure why she couldn't tell the corporal's assault group anything about his disappearance.

Both Asher and Aaron took seats near the front. The room filled with the rest of their company as they waited. The noise level slowly rose to a normal volume thanks to the privates who were less affected by last night's events than the officers.

Asher noticed Milo sitting behind them in the corner, absentmindedly staring off into space. He couldn't read the medic's mood, but his best guess was that Milo was in shock over Driscoll's disappearance.

Asher faced the front of the room, increasingly irritated by the long wait after Kilgore's call for quick action.

"Quiet down," said Commander Greaves. He strode through the doorway and turned off the lights.

Greaves approached the stand beside the front desk and opened one of the top drawers to remove the remote. He pointed the device at the gigantic monitor screen in front of them. The light at the edge flickered green as the machine came to life, the screen itself glowing blue, lighting the dark room. Greaves kept his sunglasses on, even in the low light. The blue glow from the screen made his bald, shiny head all the more apparent.

"Before we get started, I'm going to go over the numbers from last night." The commander hit the remote, revealing a screen resembling a scoreboard. "This company is the last to see them since I decided to wait to show them to you."

He paused as the numbers appeared.

"Here it is," Greaves continued. "We lost eighteen. All of them fine soldiers. They will be missed, but unfortunately, that's just the Legion for you. Death's always an occupational hazard. Ended up losing nine hellhounds, which are harder to replace than any soldier. Each of 'em costs I don't know how many millions of dollars to create. They did save our butts from being annihilated, so that's somethin'. The result of all our loss was one hundred and twenty-four dead vamps and one demolished human flesh traffickin' center. Was it all worth it?"

The commander looked around the room, trying to find someone to answer the question.

"I don't know." Greaves shook his head after answering his own question. "On the positive side, though the operation was not a tactical success, the test was. We pulled the vamps out of the plant, and the test subject and his friends successfully took care of most of 'em, just as promised."

"Exactly what kind of creature is the test subject, sir?" Lieutenant Tarango stepped forward, hand raised. "I mean, it was shaped like a man, but it moved like a cat."

"CyberGen, that's the folks with the contract to make us new weapons, calls him a kresnik," said Greaves. "That is all the information I can give you on our new weapon and his pals. Most of it is highly classified, and even I don't have the clearance to know it."

The commander gazed into the crowd. His sunglasses concealed the intensity in his eyes as he dared someone to question him.

"Now onto the briefing," Greaves continued before his personnel could raise any more questions.

The death toll tally on the screen disappeared and gave way to a blue blankness.

"This company has been selected for a special mission out in District X, in collaboration with the battalion out there. I won't lie, this particular operation will be a real dangerous one. A big reason for that relates to the source of our lead. Most of the intel was taken from that coward bloodsucker we grabbed last night. Could end up being a real good recipe for disaster."

Greaves waited for some retort from his captains.

"And yes, we do take intel from filthy neck-biters, so long as it's good." The commander spoke to the privates now. "If what he's tellin' us is anywhere close to true, we need to get out there and take care of it as soon as we possibly can. We need to bring 'em down and do away with all this vamp experimentin' goin' on there. Maybe we can even save some captured folks."

A few of the soldiers let out audible yawns, still exhausted from the night before.

"I will turn you over to High Commander Witchburn now," said Greaves. The screen behind him flashed on, revealing a live video shot of what Asher assumed to be High Commander Witchburn's office.

He nearly jumped out of his seat when a woman with long, dark hair, translucent skin, and ghostly eyes, one eerie blue and the other sightless grey, appeared on the screen.

Asher wasn't the only one startled by the high commander's appearance. A number of the newer recruits let out loud gasps. The realization struck Asher like a freight train. He had thought he was fighting the forces of darkness when he had only been a pawn in some kind of sick vampire scheme.

"Try to stay calm, everyone." Greaves waved a large hand downwards, motioning for everyone to remain seated. "There's no reason to lose your drawers. I had forgotten most of you hadn't met High Commander Witchburn yet."

"And just how the heck do you expect us to calm down, sir?" Asher shouted, jumping up onto his feet, joined by several of his peers. "Does she have you under some kind of spell? She's one of them! This whole time…"

"Dang it! Private, sit down!" Greaves threateningly stepped forward, roaring Asher into submission.

"Sit down, Greaves!" the woman shouted. "It seems you didn't properly prepare your people to meet me."

Greaves reluctantly moved around his desk and took a seat, his shaded eyes intent on Asher.

"How do we know you're not one of them?" Asher continued to shout. He balled his hands into fists, ready to face all opposition. The room was mainly full of privates, and he was sure that between their numbers and youth, they could overwhelm the officers.

"Does this help?" The woman looked at Asher through the screen. She smiled at him, revealing normal human canines.

Asher's heart continued to hammer away as he stood there, his rage still smoldering. He was willing to let the vampire speak for only so long.

"If that doesn't work, I also have this." Witchburn raised her right arm in front of the monitor.

The limb was no longer flesh and bone but a robotic prosthesis, the arm of a skeleton, composed of chromed, metal bones.

"And I don't know if you noticed the scars." The high commander put down her prosthesis, pointing to several very obvious, pink, jagged scars, most of them focused around the ghostly-grey, blind eye, several running down onto her neck.

Asher had missed them due to his shock at seeing her. His comrades returned to their seats, leaving only Aaron and himself still standing.

"What does that prove?" Asher remained unconvinced. "You could have had those scars before you were bitten! Your arm might have been amputated earlier! And... and..." his rage caused him to lose his train of thought. "You could have filed your teeth!" he pointed up toward the screen.

"Boy, you best return to your seat right this second!" Greaves jumped back onto his feet, removing his sunglasses, hanging them from his shirt collar, his eyes ablaze. "If you don't take a seat, I will be forced to seat you!"

Asher glared at Greaves, gritting his teeth, wanting to strike his commander.

"Greaves, sit down before I write you up for insubordination," Witchburn said, calm but cold. "It will be an easy task since I'll be the one who both writes and reviews the paperwork."

Greaves' anger waned as she went on, the fire in his eyes vanishing. He reluctantly took a seat.

"Private, would you sit down as well?" Witchburn asked politely.

"Come on, man, sit down," Aaron spoke to him in a calm, low tone. "Maybe if we just give her a moment to better explain..."

Aaron slumped back in his seat, his arms folded, a frown across his face.

"There is no call for this degree of aggression," said Witchbun.

Asher gave the camera at the edge of the screen a hostile look, his rage still simmering as he took a seat. He supposed he could try to hear her out.

"Now, let's see…" High Commander Witchburn placed her good hand thoughtfully beneath her chin. "Oh, here we are." She reached across her desk, grasping for something just out of frame.

Witchburn brought out a bright red apple, holding it up so they could see.

"So, as I hope you have learned in our classes, vampires are obligate cannibals. This means they can't metabolize anything that is not human flesh and blood. Therefore, whenever they eat normal human food, they become violently ill."

Witchburn bit a large chunk out of the apple.

"Now, if I can eat this whole apple," she spoke out of the corner of her mouth as she chewed. "And not get sick after, it should prove, without a doubt, I am not a vampire."

Asher felt his rage finally subside, his mind now at ease. He doubted a real vampire would even attempt to eat normal food.

"Maybe you should tell them the story, ma'am," said Greaves.

The room was silent like a crypt.

"Looks like I will have to." High Commander Witchburn swallowed and then smiled again, rolling her good eye.

Asher couldn't help but stare at her teeth once more, just to remind himself that they weren't sharp.

Well, anyway," Witchburn began, taking another bite out of her apple, quickly chewing it up and swallowing. "A long time ago, when the Legion was first formed, myself and Commander Greaves were part of the same assault group."

"Matilda was the group leader." A broad grin appeared on Greaves's face. "She ordered me around just like she does now."

"Who's telling the story, Commander Greaves?" Witchburn's tone was severe, though with a hint of mirth.

"Sorry for the interruption, ma'am." Greaves apologized as

though he were speaking to his mother.

"Oh, that's OK, you can tell them your part when I get to it." The high commander laughed, and the smile returned to her face. "Just try to keep it professional. We still used assault rifles then, and those just didn't have the same stopping power." Her voice grew muffled as she chewed. "You could run through round after round just to bring down one or two vampires. As you would expect, casualty rates tended to be high."

"Uh, I remember." Greaves leaned his chair back, placing his giant hands behind his head.

"This operation started out just like any other." Witchburn gave up on keeping Greaves quiet. "We got the call, and we went out. We only traveled as assault groups in those days, so there were only four of us. We weren't even a literal Legion then. We ran way, way less than one thousand personnel, all scattered across the country. Still had the ten bases, but each was only occupied by a single company. Still had our smaller outposts."

"It was hard to catch a vampire then," Witchburn reflected. "Actually had people that specialized in tracking the things but didn't have nationwide informants or drones. These vampires, they were involved in meat trafficking, like so many of them now, and our squad was out to bring down this particular group for good. We went into this house and cleared the living room. Caught the two vamps unaware and blew them away. We thought we killed every one of the perps, even though we had yet to clear the place."

Witchburn swept her robotic hand across the bottom of the screen.

"We had thought wrong. A whole pack of the bloodsuckers ran out of the next room just as we were stacking up by the kitchen door. They ran right into us and cut through two of my men right there. It was just Greaves and me against six or so vamps, our chances of survival minimal

"Dang right," Greaves muttered where the high commander couldn't hear.

Witchburn belched, finished with her apple. "Oh, well, excuse me," she said, reaching under her desk for the trashcan to throw away the core.

"Now." She turned in her seat to look at the clock on the

wall. "If I can keep from vomiting in the next few minutes, it should prove to all of you that I am, indeed, human. OK, back to the story."

Witchburn turned back toward the camera. "We fired on the vampires, but the spray of bullets from our rifles had little effect on them. They were so close to us and moved so quickly that only a few of our shots hit their targets. It was just enough to keep them off us, and they continued out the front door, out of the house. One of them knocked me down as he went by, jumped on top of me, slashed up my face. He latched onto my arm, tearing into it with claws and fangs. I suppose he just wanted a snack for the road. He might have killed me if Commander Greaves wasn't there."

Greaves's broad grin returned to his face.

"Somehow, this big lummox kept his wits and attacked the vampire with his hatchet." Witchburn shook her head as she remembered.

"I had run out of bullets," Greaves explained, rising to his feet to stand beside his desk. "When I saw that filthy bloodsucker on top of my leader, I all but lost it. I pulled out my hatchet and gave that dirty vamp a few good whacks to the back of the neck until his head went bouncin' onto the floor." He turned and looked right up at the camera on the lower corner of the screen, his grin now so wide that it threatened to break his face. "Saved your life, didn't I?"

"Only after that bloodsucker filth nearly had his way with me. I'm not convinced that vampire was actually trying to kill me. As I said, he seemed to only want my arm as a quick snack. You know how beastly they can be."

"Saved your life," Greaves mumbled under his breath as he took his seat.

"Anyway, regardless of what this vampire's intentions really were, he had bitten through my body armor, infecting me." Witchburn ignored her commander. "There being no cure for vampirism, my options were limited. I would either be turned or, preferably, be disposed of via beheading." She grimaced. "As you can imagine, I didn't care for either of those. I took my hatchet from my belt and…"

"Cut her own arm off!" Greaves interrupted again, unable to wait until the end. "I was there, and even I couldn't believe it! Did it so quick, I couldn't stop her."

"Well, thanks for that, Commander." Witchburn's face turned red in embarrassment.

"Welcome, High Commander." Greaves' voice was grim.

"Anyway, as if on reflex, I yanked off my arm guard, pulled out my hatchet, and with one heavy swift swing, I chopped off my own arm."

Witchburn's face returned to stark, colorless white.

"It's a good thing it was sharp." The high commander's grin returned. "I started screaming and sobbing like a lunatic, as you can imagine, the blood spewing from the stump. Greaves, still somehow un-phased by all this, took off his belt, put a tourniquet around my arm, and rushed me back to the base for medical treatment."

"Just doin' what I had to, ma'am." Greaves leaned back in his seat once more. This time he put his feet up on the desk with not a semblance of humility.

"And now here is the funny part." Witchburn placed her mechanical hand against the side of her mouth as though she were telling a secret. "We get to the hospital wing, and they tell me it was completely pointless to amputate my arm! They said there was no way I could have cut it off quickly enough to keep the infection from spreading! Told Greaves he should have just killed me right there."

Asher thought she might start to laugh, the only one to find such a situation humorous. The high commander's audience stared at the screen, silent and stone-faced.

"They decided they wanted to keep me for observation. Wanted to see what happens when someone turns."

Witchburn's smile vanished when she observed the lack of laughter.

"They didn't even try to re-attach my arm. Said it was pointless since I would be euthanized afterward. They were certain I would go vamp on them. They patched up my wounds so I wouldn't bleed out and threw me into what was essentially solitary confinement. Kept me locked in a dark room for days, feeding me through a slot in the door. They finally let me out a week later when I didn't turn like they thought I would. It came as a surprise to everyone."

"Why didn't you turn, ma'am?" Asher raised his hand to be recognized.

"They told me I must have an immunity to the virus. One of the few."

"What about your appearance, though?" asked Asher. "Why did that change?"

"Nobody really knows. It's just a side-effect of being exposed to the virus. Instead of turning, I was left with this permanently youthful, though vampiric, appearance. Unfortunately for me, I was not granted the same healing capacity, so I was left with these scars, a blind right eye and an amputated arm. To be clear, even a vampire can't regenerate those last two, at least not naturally anyway. It's not all bad, though. I haven't seemed to age a day since I was bitten."

High Commander Witchburn leaned forward in her chair and looked toward the camera so they could better see her face.

"I'm much older than I look. It's kind of like having both the worst and the best plastic surgery at once."

Asher felt embarrassed by his actions earlier. Witchburn's story both impressed and shamed him.

"Well, it looks like I haven't thrown up that apple," Witchburn declared, her good eye widening with recollection. "Finally convinced that I'm not a vampire?" She raised both hands in the air in frustrated emphasis.

"Yes, ma'am," said Asher as several of his comrades nodded along.

"Well, now that that's out of the way..." Witchburn reached over her desk, producing a remote. "Let's get on with this briefing." She pressed a button, and a continental map of the United States replaced the camera feed of her office.

"The intel given to us by this vampire, Desmond, is accurate but very incomplete," said her disembodied voice through the speaker. "Here is the approximate location he gave us."

The map's crosshair cursor zoomed in over California, continuing downward toward one mountain range to the south. It then zoomed in even further, showing a mountain pass through which ran a mundane-looking highway. The cursor continued to move until it reached a closed portion of the road, the closure made apparent by the bright orange barrier blocking the way.

"Now, according to our captured friend, the laboratory

should be located somewhere over here, adjacent to the closed portion of the highway."

The cursor moved up, away from the highway, and through two adjoined mountain peaks, continuing along until it reached an almost invisible gravel road. A large red circle encompassed the target area.

"How have you confirmed the location, ma'am?" Lieutenant Tarango moved away from where he stood against the wall, stepping out to where the camera could see him.

Captain Kilgore groaned and shook his head, irritated by the lieutenant's need for further questioning.

"Oh, nice to see you, Lieutenant Tarango." Witchburn acknowledged him. "We have confirmed this location through drone surveillance. It's been on our radar for quite a while now. That's how we worked through the vampire's intel so quickly. There has been a substantial increase in vehicles passing through the closed section of highway, fewer government agency vehicles, more civilians, some even unmarked. Most of those traveling through the closed section turn off toward the east, disappear for a while, and somehow appear back on the road. It's always been suspicious. After receiving your captured vampire's intel, we decided to really investigate what was going on. Here are a few of the pictures taken last night."

A photo showing a closer view of the gravel road appeared on the left-handed side of the screen, shrouded in the night, glowing green through the drone's night vision camera.

"And as we move along the road..." Witchburn trailed off, several more pictures of the road appearing on the screen. "And here's where we knew we had something."

A picture of a tunnel entrance appeared on the screen, mysterious and menacing.

"Looks a little out of place, don't you think?"

"That's a heck of a hole," said Greaves. He rose from his seat to view the picture, scratching his bald head. "Little hard to find when yuh don't know what you're looking for, but awful obvious when yuh do."

"Precisely," said Witchburn. "We decided not to probe any deeper as we did not want to disturb what's there. We haven't found any kind of record of there ever having been a tunnel built in the area, and it's pretty obvious that it shouldn't be there. We also haven't been able to find any geographical record of a cavern or cave in the area, meaning that if there is a structure built somewhere inside the mountain, it is wholly human, or rather vampire-made. Quite a feat of engineering either way."

"Sure would be," Greaves spoke nearly in a whisper.

"Anyway, as far as we know, there shouldn't be any kind of underground anything there at all," Witchburn continued. "That's where you come in. We need to send in an armed group of soldiers to ensure the area is clear."

"Can't you send the battalion from District X to investigate and clear the area, ma'am?" Tarango chimed in. "This isn't our jurisdiction."

"Half of District X's forces will join you. You are being sent out because your company is to escort the vampire, Desmond, to the area to assist during the operation."

"But why this company specifically?" asked Tarango.

"Your company has recently been rebuilt. It just felt like the best choice. I anticipate that this operation will be difficult and could potentially lead to a disproportionately high death toll. That's why we're sending out six companies and most of our hellhound forces. We want to be prepared for anything. All we have to go on is the information given to us by Desmond and a few aerial photos taken by our drones. Not enough intel for the full picture, but it's all we have. You will be accompanied by our new weapon prototype, the kresnik, as well. Hopefully, that will take at least some of the sting out of it."

"When are we supposed to fly out, ma'am?" asked Greaves. He leaned on his desk, steadied by one of his giant hands.

"At approximately 1300 hours," said the high commander. "That will allow enough time for you to properly prepare yourselves for the operation. You will rendezvous with the force from District X at 1600 and then head up into the mountains immediately, avoiding the mountain pass at night."

"Yes, ma'am." Greaves stood up straight, saluting the camera.

"Very well, commander," said Witchburn. "That concludes

our briefing."

"Well, you heard the high commander." Greaves addressed the company, the screen now a blank blue. "We only got to 1300. Get a move on!" His voice steadily rose until he was nearly shouting.

The company sprung from their seats and filtered out of the door, only slightly hastened by the commander's words.

As Asher stood to leave, he felt a hand on his shoulder. "Well, I hope you're ready." Aaron gave him a reassuring pat. "This is going to be one heck of an operation!"

Chapter XXVII

Prototypes

Anoura slammed the door behind her, nearly breaking into a sprint as she strode down the craggy, unfinished hallway toward The Surgeon's laboratory. She came from the loading bay, leaving Luther and Mara to finish up with their delivery.

Anoura was seeing to more pressing matters.

Typically The Surgeon's lab was off-limits to all unauthorized personnel; all procurement staff forbade entry. She knew he would be less than thrilled over her appearing unannounced, but this was an emergency.

Anoura was halfway down the hallway, her shadow revealed in the red light, rapidly passing over the stone surface. The wall had remained untouched since the construction of The Surgeon's facility. The man was involved with his research and paid little attention to anything else.

Anoura approached the laboratory, stopping in front of the armed guard who blocked the door.

"I need to speak with The Surgeon immediately." Anoura glared at the guard, arms folded in impatience. "It's an emergency."

"Sorry, but I can't allow you to proceed past this point." The guard tightened his grip on his assault rifle. "I don't care what the problem is. You don't have the clearance for entry into The Surgeon's private laboratory."

Anoura couldn't read his expression through his helmet, his eyes concealed by his visor.

The man gave her an awkward smile, his elongated canines visible.

"I assure you, he will make an exception this time!" Anoura spoke through gritted teeth, tensed with rage. "There is a battalion of Legion soldiers headed this way!"

"Huh," the guard chuckled, his posture slackening. "Well, that may be," he said, mockery in his voice. "You know how he feels about being interrupted while he's working. I mean, if you were one of his lab assistants, things would be different, but you're not. If you go in there, you may never come back out."

"Does the phrase 'battalion of Legion soldiers headed this way' mean nothing to you?" Anoura stomped her foot in anger.

"Orders are orders." The guard's words had an edge. "Assuming they actually know the way to our facility, there's plenty of deterrents. Even if they have found the door, you know how difficult that entry tunnel can be. The Surgeon has taken all necessary defensive precautions. Trust me. It's a very bad idea to go in there."

"Thanks for the warning, but I think I can handle him just fine." Anoura's tone remained foul. She began to rethink how she felt about human personnel. Humans were much easier to intimidate, much easier to control in many respects. The Surgeon refused to use any human personnel, and most of his strictly vampiric staff followed his orders only.

"I cannot let you pass." The guard gripped his weapon. "If I allow you to pass through this door, I will be punished as well. If you want to get yourself killed, that's fine by me, but I refuse to be held responsible for letting you in."

Anoura stepped backward, startled by the guard's insolence. "You absolutely will let me pass." Her temper flared. "I told you, this is an emergency. I need access to The Surgeon!" She took an intimidating step forward, ready to attack.

"That's unfortunate," the guard smirked. "You can tell it to The Surgeon when he finishes. He's been in there a while, so it shouldn't be long now. What…"

Anoura tore the firearm from the guard and struck him in the jaw with it, swinging the weapon like a baseball bat. It broke like a flimsy toy, all but shattering on contact, unable to withstand the force produced by the blow.

The guard staggered to the side and maintained his balance,

remaining unharmed.

"Uh, yeah, I'm a vampire too," he said, regaining his footing. "You'll have to do a little better than that! Oof..." he groaned.

Anoura responded with a right hook to the man's chin. The first punch led into a flurry of blows, which she then followed up with a left to the jaw. She alternated fists as she struck him repeatedly, never allowing him a chance to fight back. Anoura knocked the guard to the ground and kicked him in the face with a booted foot, continuing until he stopped moving.

The guard lay there, stationary, appearing to be unconscious or worse.

Anoura stepped over his body and approached the door to knock.

"You make a compelling argument," said the guard, coughing up blood, delirious. "Feel free to enter."

"That's more like it." Anoura glared down at the guard maliciously.

The man lay his head down on the ground once more, in no hurry to stand back up.

"Sir!" Anoura turned back to the door and pounded on the solid metal with her fist. "Sir! Open up! We have an emergency! Legion soldiers are approaching the facility!" Frustrated by the lack of response, she tried the handle. Finding it unlocked, she pushed her way into The Surgeon's laboratory.

Anoura let the door close behind her, awe-struck by the sheer vastness of the lab.

Giant red gymnasium lights hung overhead to illuminate the massive room. Its high walls, craggy and barely finished like the hallway, were a reminder of the facility's subterranean location. To Anoura's left stood several metal-framed, glass-covered shelves that extended across the whole length of the wall and disappeared into the darkness at the back of the lab. The lowest of them rose ten feet above the ground, reachable only with the rolling ladder setting off to one side.

Below the shelves hung a variety of surgical implements, mostly saws and other cutting tools. Many of these were exceptionally large and murderous-looking, most of them meant for thick-boned animals. A line of metal tool tables followed the shelves along the wall, upon which smaller tools, mostly scalpels, scissors, and saws, sat. These were the implements necessary to cut through delicate human flesh.

Anoura cringed, startled by the man-shaped creature to her left. One of the researchers struggled to shove a gag in its mouth, failing to silence its orangutan-like cries.

It was a strange creature, looking something like an ape but hairless, its skin bright red and so thin that Anoura could see the blood through it. More of the animals filled the laboratory floor and on surgical examination tables. Those still alive were restrained and gagged. The dead lay in pieces with various organs spread out. Buckets of blood rested underneath the tables.

Around the creatures gathered the vampiric lab staff, all kept busy, a hive of activity around the tables as they tended to their subjects. Many restrained the animals, while others were farther along in the surgical process. The latter cut long, deep sutures into the creature's limbs with various tools. Some lab workers stitched up the resulting wounds or dissected the dead.

Anoura drifted toward the tables, catching a whiff of the surrounding air, surprised she hadn't noticed the stench earlier. A stale, putridly pungent odor hung about the place, a mix of blood, excrement, and fear, barely masked by air fresheners and floor cleaners.

Remembering her purpose, Anoura searched for The Surgeon, finding him challenging to spot since all personnel wore white lab coats. She stepped closer to the tables and looked over those gathered around them. None of The Surgeon's staff acknowledged her presence, too involved with their work to notice one of the lowly 'delivery' people.

"Excuse me, but do you have a death wish?" Anoura heard a voice come from across the room, though she couldn't discern the man's location within the ample space.

"If so, it can be facilitated," said the voice.

Anoura walked toward it, passing by a gathering of computer monitors at the center of the room. DNA double helixes scrawled across the screens, listing base pairs and other data written in a language she was incapable of reading.

Anoura found The Surgeon sitting on a stool beside one of

the closer exam tables, bent over one of his test subjects, apparently in the middle of vivisection. She never saw The Surgeon perform one of his procedures, but she had been around long enough to know that his primary research area was wound healing. Vivisection was a necessity in such pursuits.

The test subject snarled through its gag, violently thrashing and twisting around in its restraints. It was unwilling to let The Surgeon stitch up the wound he had just inflicted with his scalpel. A disproportionately large amount of its blood drenched the floor and the exam table

The Surgeon didn't believe in sedation except in extreme cases, or so Anoura had heard. All operations performed in his labs involved restraints and gags. Anoura wasn't sure if this was because he didn't want to spend the money or if he just took sadistic pleasure in inflicting pain.

The red, thin-skinned creature continued to struggle, leaving The Surgeon sitting, needle in mouth, unable to stitch up the wound. One of Anoura's most treasured past-times was inflicting pain on others, yet she even found the lack of sedation maladaptive to surgical proficiency.

The creature let out an all too human scream, suddenly spitting out the gag, making Anoura take a step backward. She was the only one to react to the noise that the rest of The Surgeon's staff ignored.

"OK, that's it, I have had enough of you, subject... Ah..." The Surgeon gritted his teeth, speaking with the stitching needle in his mouth. He leaned down to look at the numbers printed on the creature's identification bracelet. "That's enough, Subject 22753. It's sedation for you now." He jammed the needle into the creature's arm, pushing down on the plunger to administer the drug.

"Such a waste of money." The Surgeon shook his head as the doomed animal went slack, its screams subsiding. He tossed the needle into the trashcan by his foot, irritated by the waste.

"Sir, sorry to interrupt, but there's an emergency," said Anoura, her sense of urgency reawakened. "A battalion of Legion soldiers is headed this way!"

"Did the guard not tell you?" The Surgeon looked up at her with a frown, showing his annoyance. "No one is allowed in my private laboratory without my consent, under penalty of death."

"Yes, he did, sir." Anoura wanted to lie and have the guard removed, death being the preferred method of doing so. "I felt that in this instance, such an entry would have to be permitted." She frowned, even more frustrated than before. "Sir, I don't understand. Why is no one at all concerned with the approaching Legion presence? They'll be knocking on our front door in less than an hour!"

"You're not part of the security detail." The Surgeon spoke absent-mindedly, piercing the red-skinned creature's forearm with his sewing needle to begin his stitch. "Why are you the one providing me with this information?"

"We spotted the convoy on our way back from our retrieval assignment, just as we turned onto the highway." Anoura grew tired of being the only one concerned.

"How did you confirm that they were Legion men?" The Surgeon's attention remained on his stitching. "Isn't it possible they could be regular military who just happen to be passing through?"

"Sir, it was just an assumption," Anoura explained, a feeling of dread seeping into her mind.

Would he really dispose of one of his most loyal servants over such a minor infraction?

"Sir, it was a very large convoy." Anoura attempted to conceal her fear. "It was a line of military-looking vehicles, armored trucks, transport vehicles, a few of those tank-looking things. It was impossible to miss."

"Still doesn't rule out regular military." The Surgeon tied off his stitch and bit through the string. Finished, he looked back up at her, still skeptical.

"A regular military convoy just seems too coincidental, sir." Anoura's muscles became taunt as she waited for his reaction.

"Anoura." The Surgeon rose from his stool and stepped over to her. He reached out to stroke her face with the back of his hand, causing her to tense up even more. "You are one of the most efficient, and I dare say one of my favorite, servants."

He caressed Anoura before withdrawing his cold hand, much to her relief. If anyone else touched her the way The Surgeon had, they would receive much more than a punch to the nose.

"Regardless, I do hate it when unauthorized personnel enter this room without permission." Severity returned to his voice. "It is true, I have had assistants, good ones too, disemboweled for less, but I think I can make an exception for you just this once."

The Surgeon turned and stepped away from her. "Let us take care of this battalion."

"What is our plan of attack, sir?" asked Anoura, relieved, though uncomfortable.

She went over their defenses in her head, counting very few. The guard had insinuated that The Surgeon's lab possessed other weapons she didn't know about, though she wasn't sure if they were sufficient to deal with what looked like a whole battalion.

"Surely you don't plan on fleeing, sir." Anoura feared she had severely misjudged The Surgeon from the start.

"Flee! Ha!" The Surgeon turned back toward her, glee in his usually emotionless eyes. "And leave all of my research and life's work out here for those vultures to just take? Not to mention that we'll be the laughing stock of the organization and all vampire society. We'll be a joke to even the filthiest and most uncouth feral should they find out. Haha! That's a good one!" He hit the exam table with his fist, causing the test subject to struggle in its restraints.

"Yes, I was sure that you would never do that, sir. It is a sad day when vampires flee from humans, no matter how well armed they may be. Though in all sincerity, sir, if you don't act soon, they will likely trash the lab and kill most of us, even if they are just a bunch of pathetic blood bags."

"No need to worry, Anoura." The Surgeon gave her a wicked, malevolent grin. "I have anticipated a visit from the Legion for some time."

"Why is that, sir?" Anoura frowned.

"Oh, it's nothing really." The Surgeon's evil smile looked more insane and idiotic by the moment. "The arrival of those little soldier boys on our humble mountainside has presented a fabulous opportunity."

"What opportunity is that, sir?" Anoura felt she was trying to coax a small child into telling her where they hid their Halloween candy.

"I suppose there is no point in keeping it a secret now. The day has finally come at long last."

"Sir, could you please just tell me what you are talking about?" Anoura's mild frustration grew into anger.

"Come with me. I'll show them to you," said The Surgeon, walking away.

Anoura followed him as her rage subsided.

"So, I'm sure you, and everybody else around here, are rather curious about all the strange noises you hear around this place. You know the ones." The Surgeon led her through the maze of exam tables, weaving around lab personnel as they worked on their specimens.

"Yes, sir, they are difficult to forget, especially given the way you deal with anyone who asks. As I recall, the last time someone asked about all the noise, you stabbed them in the eye with a rusty pair of scissors."

"When I said not to ask, I meant it." The Surgeon's voice was grim.

They neared the edge of the lab, this side much less brightly illuminated. Cages made of perforated metal lined the walls, most of them empty, though the red-skinned creatures occupied a few of them.

"Back to those noises." The Surgeon's tone lightened. "They are caused by certain biotech side projects I have been working on. All under The Master's nose, of course. I wouldn't want her to take them from me. I know she would love to have them, as they are some of my loveliest creations."

They crossed into the darkest part of the lab now, approaching a door Anoura hadn't noticed earlier.

"I suppose it could be termed a 'prototype' at this point," The Surgeon elaborated. "Several prototypes, actually. I would like very much to release them now and let them have their way with the 'play' soldiers down there. It isn't right to keep such beautiful things cooped up."

"Whatever they are, sir, you might want to release them soon. Those soldiers will be in here with their guns, blasting your laboratory to pieces and stealing everything they can grab."

"Ah, here we are," The Surgeon pulled a key card from his pocket, sliding it into the door's electronic lock. "Right this way."

He turned the handle and pushed through the door, holding it open for Anoura to pass through. They entered another red-lit room, this one substantially smaller than the private lab, though still encompassing a considerable amount of space.

The Surgeon continued toward a giant, metallic door, the apparatus rising to the ceiling. He stood off to the side, resting a clawed hand against the wall beside a big, flamboyantly red button.

"Try not to be too terribly shocked or scared when you see them." The Surgeon's grin returned. "They're a sight for the unprepared."

"I think I can handle it, sir." Genuine fear was something Anoura had all but forgotten.

"Very well," said The Surgeon as he pushed the button. "Here they are."

The giant garage door slowly slid open, revealing another large room. This one was dark, separated from the lighter room by a considerably thick, heavy pane of glass.

The Surgeon's prototypes rested in the middle of the room. Massive metal restraints held them against enormous, upright display tables.

"Impressive." Anoura's jaw went slack. Shock was an emotion to which she was unaccustomed. "What do you call them?"

"Do   they   need   a   name?"

Chapter XXVIII

The Revelation

Asher slapped the side of his helmet, having lost the card game he was playing on his visor screen. Frustrated, he leaned against the SUV door to pick it up and paused to look through the window at the scenery. He found the sky was turning from blue to orange, and the sun crept ever closer to the horizon. Shadow already masked some of the low-lying areas. The night would soon be upon them.

Their Legion convoy had made its way up the mountainside for some time now, crawling forth like some great, green serpent. Their precession carried what amounted to a few hundred more than half a battalion, all of them crammed into various dark military green vehicles.

They moved at a leisurely pace, their momentum halted by the highway's heavy curvature and rough surface. The terrain was hazardous. The San Gabriel Mountains were prone to rock slides, the most recent one cleared poorly and not long ago. In addition, an endless multitude of coniferous trees dotted the slopes. This offered a tremendous amount of cover to all creatures upon the mountain.

Asher's eyes left the window as he took a quick survey of the rest of his immediate surroundings, his gaze drifting toward the driver's side window.

Sergeant Ito drove, her arms taut upon the steering wheel. With Driscoll missing in action, she served as their temporary group leader and fulfilled his role while she carried out her duties as a sergeant. Their assault group occupied their own SUV due to Ito's dual stations, making their trip quieter and more comfortable than usual, though it did little to ease their restlessness.

Sergeant Ito had been wordless for a while now, focused on the road, as fed up with the trip as Asher was. Time dribbled away from them ever since the early morning, the day marred by delays. The most significant of these was an unexpectedly slow travel rate due to all the hairpin loops in the highway and the hazards on the mountain road. Their superiors couldn't account for everything.

Aaron and Milo sat behind Asher, both deeply involved with their helmet visors, desperate to find any way to make their trip up the mountains seem shorter.

"Are you ever going to tell us exactly what happened to Driscoll?" Asher asked abruptly. He was sick of the hesitation displayed by his fellow privates. None of them dared to ask Ito, and her silence during the trip suggested she wasn't ready to tell them. Asher couldn't wait any longer.

"What do you mean?" asked the sergeant, her voice remaining level. "You were there," she said, unwilling to elaborate.

"Yeah, I guess you told us enough already." Asher decided to leave it, prepared to bide his time until she was ready.

For a paramilitary group accustomed to death, they sure are touchy, Asher thought to himself.

"Do you have any idea how much longer it will take to reach our destination, Sergeant?" Milo inquired. "I've looked, and I know we're nearly finished with the highway, but with our slow speed around these turns, it's kind of difficult to determine how much longer things will take."

"We should be approaching the barrier shortly, Private. I can't give you a precise amount of time."

"Can't we turn on the radio or something?" Aaron asked. "We've been driving for a while, and I'm getting tired of the silence." He leaned up from where he sat behind the sergeant and reached for the radio knob.

"Absolutely not, Private." Ito gently pushed Aaron's arm away. "We need to keep things quiet in here so we can hear whatever orders arise. This pass is dangerous, and we don't know what might be up here."

"Whatever you say, Sergeant." Aaron moved his arm back, exasperated. "Though I think I might lose it if we don't get there soon."

Silence returned to the vehicle's cabin, giving way only to the hum of vehicles upon the highway and the distant sounds of nature from outside. Asher let out an audible yawn.

"Approaching the road barrier now." Asher heard an unfamiliar voice say into his helmet. It was the commander from District X.

"About time," Sergeant Ito murmured.

Asher looked over at the clock display on the SUV's radio, taken aback when he saw it read 6:37 PM.

"Looks like we'll have to snap that chain," said the voice. "The barrier is locked."

Ito pressed down on the brakes, and they slowed to a stop, a line of red lights in front of them. The other vehicles in the convoy stalled as well.

A noise came from over the ridge above, a faint, distant howl like that of a wolf.

Asher perked up when he heard it, looking over his shoulder in the direction of the sound.

"Do you hear that?" Asher asked no one in particular, feeling as though he were the only one to hear the noise.

"Well, yeah," said Aaron, still frustrated. "Kind of hard to miss something like that."

A howl came again, different from the first, this one belonging to another individual.

"You have any idea what it is?" Asher asked.

"I don't know." Aaron shrugged. "A coyote? A wolf, maybe? You ought to know. You're the one from Hickville, Missouri."

"I thought it might be a coyote, but I kinda doubt it." Asher scratched his chin. "Sounds way too big."

"You think it might be a wolf, Sergeant?" Aaron leaned up toward Ito's seat once again.

"I have no idea, Pritchett. Sorry, but I don't know much about animal calls."

"This is southern California," Milo chimed in. "Wolves aren't native to the area."

"Think it might be a bear?" asked Aaron.

"What kind of bear howls?" Milo chuckled, barely

suppressing his laughter.

One of the howls grew louder as the creature drew closer. Asher glanced past Ito and back through the window, trying to determine the direction of the noise.

"It sounds closer now," Aaron held his weapon in his hands, gripping it tightly. "You think the commander is hearing this? Maybe you should say something, Sergeant."

An enormous creature suddenly burst through the trees, charging down the hill like a kamikaze locomotive. The thing slammed into the truck in front of them, sending it flying from the road. Both beast and vehicle plummeted down the ravine, leaving nothing but dark skid marks on the highway.

"What was that?" Asher jumped in his seat, nearly hitting his head on the ceiling. It all happened so quickly that it gave him little time to react. The beast was massive, as big as a grizzly bear, and he could have sworn it was wearing some kind of armor.

"Commander, are you hearing this?" Ito shrieked into her speaker, her composure gone. She slapped the side of her helmet but received nothing but static. "Everyone out of the van!" she shouted, turning the keys in the ignition and scrambling for her door latch.

"Why would you want to be out with that thing?" Milo shouted back at her. "You saw what it did to that truck!"

"It beats just sitting in here waiting to be thrown down the mountain!" the sergeant shouted back, dismissing Milo's concerns as nonsense.

Asher already had his door open and climbed out of the vehicle. He sensed the need for urgency. Many soldiers behind them climbed out of their vehicles as well, mortified by what just transpired. Ito slammed her driver's side door and joined Asher and Aaron on the other side of the SUV. Milo appeared moments later, going around the back of the vehicle to stand beside the back tire.

Asher looked over the SUV toward the line of coniferous trees near the road. He felt eyes watching him.

The howling sounded yet again, coming from the trees on the upward side of the mountain. The soldiers turned in that direction, expecting the creature to burst through the line of trees at any moment.

"What are you doing?" Greaves bellowed at them, emerging

from one of the trucks near the front of the convoy.

The soldiers turned toward the commander, no longer watching the forest.

"You're supposed to stay in your vehicle until we reach the destination!" Greaves thundered, oblivious to the missing vehicle and unable to see much from where he stood atop the step of his own truck.

"Commander, one of our trucks was just sent over the edge by some giant animal!" Ito shouted at Greaves.

"Can't you hear that howling, Commander?" Asher heard someone closer to the front of the convoy yell. Whatever else was out there, it knew exactly where to find them.

"What are you talking about?" the commander roared. "Get back in your vehicles! We got the boom barrier open now!"

"Keep your voices down!" Asher shouted at the commander, disregarding rank, certain his shouting would just make things worse. "There's more than one of them!"

Asher's words didn't reach the commander before another massive creature emerged from the forest. The beast lumbered out of the woods above them on the mountainside, its eyes resting on Greaves. It was just as big as the first but stood upright, rising nearly eight feet from the ground. It was fitted with a preposterously heavy set of black plated armor, covered in such a way that Asher couldn't discern exactly what manner of beast it was. He guessed it was some kind of giant bipedal wolf, equipped with mercilessly sharp fangs and claws, predator and weapon fused into one.

The giant creature made for the commander, steadily accelerating toward him on its hind legs. Greaves remained oblivious, his attention remaining on his personnel.

"Commander!" Asher yelled, sprinting for Greaves on reflex, running past his comrades to reach him.

"Commander Greaves!" Sergeant Ito shouted, joined by Aaron and Milo as they raced after Asher. The beast crashed through the boom barrier, oblivious to the metal bars crushed beneath its massive bulk, still intent on Greaves. The thing roared, dropping to all fours, barreling across the highway as it charged toward the commander.

"We got company!" Greaves shouted. He jumped off the

truck step and onto the road, his firearm strapped to his back. "Looks like the fight's come to us!" He scrambled up onto the hood of the truck and then onto the roof, aiming his weapon at the beast.

"Fire 'em if yuh got 'em!" commanded Greaves. He pulled the pin out of a grenade with his teeth and tossed it at the beast before opening fire.

The grenade was off target, landing behind the improbably quick monster, throwing up dust and shrapnel upon the mountainside.

"Why won't you die?" Greaves shouted. He sprayed the raging creature down with round after round, failing to penetrate its armor, the gunfire doing little to slow its attack. The commander was lost, his weapons useless and his support minimal, while most of his soldiers were still in their vehicles.

The beast plowed through the convoy, intent on tearing Greaves into a bloody pulp, oblivious to the gunfire. It ran for the front of his truck at full gallop, wolf-like maw opened wide, ready to have its prey.

A small mass of soldiers gathered near the boom barrier, weapons raised as they fired on the beast. They had a difficult time hitting their target, firing toward the end of the convoy. The soldiers were all too late.

"Commander!" yelled Asher. He raced toward Greaves, still multiple vehicles away, the rest of his assault group close behind.

They wouldn't reach him in time.

Greaves continued to fire upon the creature, but neither his rounds nor those of his comrades had any effect.

Asher gritted his teeth. They didn't have the weapons to stop the beast.

A human-sized, black streak suddenly burst from the cover of the trees, dashing headlong at the charging beast. It slammed into the giant creature's side just before it reached the truck, shoving the beast through the line of parked vehicles, launching both off the highway and down the mountainside. They plummeted down the ravine in a jaw-snapping, claw thrashing storm.

Asher slowed his pace, taken aback, though continuing toward the truck.

"Wow, that thing nearly got me," said Greaves. He lowered

his weapon and pulled out a handkerchief from his pocket, wiping the sweat from his brow. "Kresnik's in for one heck of a fight," he muttered. Greaves remained atop the truck cab, taking a moment to catch his breath before turning toward the approaching assault group.

"Sergeant Ito," said the commander, finding her assault group below. "Take your group down the ravine and see if you can't find that wrecked truck."

"Lieutenant Tarango," Greaves spoke into his helmet. "Gather up the rest of your platoon and follow after them. There's no tellin' how many soldiers it may take to bring that thing down. I'm hoping our kresnik can take care of himself, but I'll have you go after him just in case." They heard a brief spurt of static as the commander switched frequencies.

"Follow me!" Sergeant Ito commanded, moving around the rest of the group and sprinting back down the highway. Her assault group dashed after her, weapons still at the ready, hurrying to fulfill Greaves's order.

A shrill scream sounded over the mountainside as the assault group raced toward the forest, knowing their extra effort was a waste. It was the cry of a woman in distress, the beast likely tearing into her.

"I have gathered up the rest of the platoon," said Lieutenant Tarango into their helmets. "We are proceeding toward your position now. Do not engage that monster unless it forces you!"

"Yes, sir!" they said, nearly in unison.

Asher wondered if the rest of the platoon would arrive in time. Greaves had sent them on what amounted to a suicide mission. Their backup lagged behind, and the four of them were unlikely to survive an encounter with the beast on their own.

"This way!" said Ito. She took a sharp turn away from the highway and onto the mountain's forested slope.

Asher moved quickly but cautiously after her, careful to keep his footing as he descended the mountainside. Milo remained close to his side and Aaron behind him.

The sound of savage, bestial combat exploded from the trees below. The battle sounded surprisingly close, the roars and howls of the giant wolf-thing interlaced with the leopard-like shrieks and snarls of the kresnik. The great noise produced by the relentless death match reverberated across the mountainside, causing several large groups of birds to abandon their perches.

"Move," Sergeant Ito's command came as a whisper, keeping their position concealed.

The assault group's progress down the mountain slackened considerably as Asher and his comrades darted between trees, taking cover should the first beast come back up. The wrecked truck lay below, crashed over on its side against a tree.

Only the bottom of the vehicle was visible to Asher. He saw no evidence of the creature as he continued downward, crouching against the trunk of a tree. The roars of the second wolf-thing quieted and turned to long, low bellows, all conveying a sense of helplessness and defeat. The beast was dying.

Asher cautiously peered around the edge of the tree, his weapon at the ready. He expected the first beast to reappear at any moment to lung at him through the hail of useless bullets. The private looked down the slope toward the wreck, his heart's rapid beating slackening when he saw no sign of the creature. He saw the ruined vehicle lying undisturbed.

"Proceed," Ito's voice drove them forward from their cover. "Let's take a look behind the truck."

The battle to their left had reached its conclusion, the cries of both warring creatures now silenced, and the forest returned to its natural volume.

Asher took a deep breath, quickly moving from cover toward the back of the overturned truck, leaning against its closed double doors, still finding no evidence of the creature's presence. He glanced over his shoulder, seeing Ito and then Milo and Aaron stacked up behind him.

Ito reached over and grabbed the back of his arm, silently instructing him to search around the truck.

Asher slowly made the corner, prepared to fire, feeling as though the whole procedure was ridiculous. Four soldiers wouldn't be enough to stop the beast. Their rounds would be rendered useless by its massive bulk and armored hide.

"Uhh." Asher grimaced, caught off guard by the horror show before him.

The top side of the truck was ripped open, the metal hull

shredded like a tin can by the beast's giant claws. The bodies of the Legions soldiers lay thrown across the mountainside, limbs and heads scattered everywhere, pools of blood soaking into the rocky ground. Despite the gore, none of the bodies looked even partially eaten. The beast had killed out of bloodlust alone.

There was still no sign of the monster as far as Asher could see. Perhaps the creature had run off after the kresnik or doubled back toward the Legion convoy.

A shiver ran down Asher's spine as a sense of unease swept over him.

They needed to leave before it was too late.

Asher finished with the corner and moved toward the nearest whole body. He rolled it over to find the man's stomach a bloody, juicy mess, slashed open by the beast.

The rest of the group followed Asher, all four searching over their fallen comrades, finding their bodies desecrated, bloodied, mangled, and torn asunder. They looked over the destruction for nearly five minutes but found no survivors.

Asher moved down the ridge, pushing the last body over with his foot, finding the man bloodied and lifeless, his brains protruding from his skull.

"Looks like that's all of them," he said as he walked back up to where the rest of his group now stood near the overturned truck.

"No need to rush down here, Lieutenant," Ito said into her microphone, a tinge of hopelessness in her voice. "The monster is gone, and there are no survivors."

Asher jumped as the beast reappeared several yards below, bearing its teeth as it crashed through the trees toward them on its hind legs.

"Way to call it too soon, Sergeant." Aaron's voice went cold. "And here I thought we might make it until sundown."

Asher took a grenade from his pack, pulled the pin, and let it cook before he hurled it at the monster. It struck the beast directly in the head, exploding on impact, sending shrapnel into its eyes.

The beast roared, thoroughly enraged, dropping to all fours to charge them.

Their group opened fire, all of their rounds landing squarely on target, but they could not damage the beast's armor. This was it.

They would all die here, naught but fodder against this bloodthirsty monster.

Asher took a deep breath, hoping the monster killed quickly.

The beast was nearly upon them when a black streak fell from the treetops, landing atop its back, tearing into its exposed neck with deadly fangs.

The beast screamed in pain, rearing up as it tried to throw off its attacker.

The kresnik dug into its neck, fighting desperately to cut through its bulk to reach its spine. The blood was black and viscous, flowing from its victim's wounds like syrup.

The monster roared for the last time and staggered, then fell to the ground, landing with a thud less than ten feet in front of them.

The kresnik shrieked and leaped to one side of the beast, jumping unnecessarily high before plummeting back down to land on its feet, crouching to catch itself. It stood up and turned to look at them, acting as if it was surprised to find them there.

The kresnik was dressed in full black body armor, complete with helmet, all of it more advanced than their own. Only the lower portion of its face was visible. Stark white fur grew upon its chin, and a pair of large fangs protruded from its mouth. It walked toward them, its focus resting solely on Asher as it stopped to remove its helmet.

Asher stood, both amazed and terrified, unable to move or speak.

The kresnik gritted its teeth at him, making him think it might suddenly attack.

It took Asher a second to realize the creature was smiling.

The kresnik pulled its helmet from its face, causing all of them to jump a little. It looked like a cat, complete with large, pointy ears and enormous, yellow-green glowing eyes, a tufted, white mane crowning its head.

"What... What are you?" Asher stuttered, unsure if the creature would be able to answer him.

"Asher, it's me!" it proclaimed, its voice deep and rumbling, sounding so familiar yet completely alien. "It's me, Cyrus!"

"What?" Asher nearly fell to the ground. "But that can't be," he continued, unable to find the words. "You're dead!" he said at last.

The creature continued toward him, slouching down toward the ground. It cautiously circled him, sniffing the surrounding air.

"I'm dead no more," it said, rising to its feet when it did so.

Asher could only stare, speech completely lost to him once again.

A third beast howled from some distance away, its cries coming from back over the ridge to their right. The kresnik's green-yellow eyes went wide, like a cat catching sight of a mouse.

Asher raised his weapon, startled by the sudden change in behavior.

The kresnik turned to pick up its helmet, shoving it back over its head before it darted past him. The urge to kill seemed to carry it back up the mountainside.

"What's going on?" asked Lieutenant Tarango, appearing off to their left side. He pushed his way through the trees toward them, forty or so soldiers in toe behind him.

"That monster killed everyone from the truck, sir," said Ito, lowering her weapon. "It was waiting for us. It would have killed all of us easily, but the test subject, the kresnik, killed the monster."

Asher was grateful when she left it to only that.

"Well, now that we have established that there are no survivors, let's head back up," said Tarango. He placed a booted foot atop the dead beast's head, its tongue rolling out of its wolf-like jaws. "I'm sure you heard all the howls from up over the ridge. Let's not wait around for a fourth monster to join these first three. You heard her!"

The lieutenant moved away from the enormous dead creature to address his personnel. "There's nothing to see down here! Back up to the convoy!" He waved the gathered soldiers back up the ridge, following them as they made their ascent.

Aaron and Milo followed the rest of the departing soldiers.

Asher remained in place, nearly sliding to the ground as he leaned against the back of the truck, still too shocked to move.

Sergeant Ito began to follow the rest of their platoon but went back to find Asher still cemented to the ground.

"Come on, we can't just leave you out here in the woods," she said, putting her hand on Asher's shoulder. "You'll have plenty of time to think about all this later, so long as we survive the operation, that is." She extended her hand, waiting to help him back onto his feet.

"Better start heading back," said Asher at last. He took her hand in his, the capacity to stand returned to him. "It's already getting dark."

Ito continued to hold onto his hand, gripping it in hers for a prolonged amount of time as she stared up at him. "Oh… sorry." Ito released his hand, embarrassed.

Asher's feet remained rooted to the ground as he watched her leave. He found the sergeant's actions awkward yet comforting. Slowly coming to his senses, Asher followed her, overwhelmed by all that had occurred in such a short amount of time.

Chapter XXIX

Into the Mouth of Hell

"Sanders, what's your status?" asked Sergeant Ito, beginning another round of pointless status checks. She was temporarily back to her original duties serving as sergeant over a squad of fifteen.

The convoy had regrouped after the ambush and now made its way up the road and over the ridge to rest near the lab's tunnel entrance. Night had set in fast, and menacing darkness had replaced the delicate orange and purple pastels of evening. The Legion personnel remained stationed at strategic points around the mountain. Half of their number waited outside, forming defensive lines around the perimeter, while the rest remained in their vehicles, waiting to proceed into the tunnel.

Ito's assault group was the latter. Their orders confined them to their SUV until the kresnik's recapture from the wilderness was complete. Asher retained his seat up front beside the sergeant. All occupants sat with helmets on, weapons held across their chests, prepared should an unforeseen enemy suddenly appear.

The entrance to the tunnel lay in front of them, illuminated by the glowing headlights. It gaped open like the dark, toothless maw of some great Stygian worm, a dread portal to Hell. The lab's automated massive security guns loomed above the tunnel, ready to fire should an unrecognized individual approach. It was poised to tear them in half with a devastating hail of lead.

The kresnik had silenced the rage-fueled roars of the rampaging wolf beasts some time ago. The Legion waited for the return of their killing machine, expecting the retrieval team to reappear at any moment.

"Do you think that thing really is your brother?" Aaron asked Asher in a near whisper. He leaned in from behind his seat, careful not to interrupt the sergeant.

"It can't be. It's impossible," said Asher, his voice grave. "My brother is dead."

"I heard how it spoke," Milo cut in. "It seemed convinced."

"Oh, come on. You too, Milo?" Asher groaned. "Isn't the way it looks enough for you? It's not even human."

"You know how much vampires change when they turn." Milo's eyes went wide behind his visor. "Granted, the change isn't as drastic as what would have to happen to go from human to kresnik, but the same basic rules still apply. You can't say it was never human by going on looks alone."

"Cyrus died of heart failure." Asher gritted his teeth. "We had him cremated. That thing can think or say whatever it wants. My brother is dead."

"Ash, you got to admit that the possibility exists," said Aaron. "I mean, neither of us thought vampires, hellhounds, and giant werewolves existed a few months ago. All I'm saying is that it's odd that of all the people it could claim to be."

"Sorry, Aaron, there's just no way," Asher cut him off. He wished Aaron would leave it alone. "I mean, maybe they, CyberGen, the Legion, whatever, somehow looked up my family, picked a name, and told the kresnik that was its identity." Angry as he was, he felt an unsettling sickness in the pit of his stomach.

What suffering would Cyrus have had to endure to become that thing? Asher asked himself.

"Man, that makes even less sense." Aaron frowned. "I mean, I don't know how long it takes to make a kresnik and have it ready for testing, but it's got to be longer than just a few months. The Legion didn't even know you existed then."

"Both of my brothers had muscular dystrophy, and both of them are dead." Asher knew he would snap soon. "The disease is always fatal. They reached the end of their lifespans and died."

"That still doesn't eliminate the possibility," said Milo. "Who knows what they actually did with your brother's body after he died."

"Man, would you guys just drop it?" Asher nearly yelled at

them. "You're starting to make me angry. I don't want to be off my game when we go in there."

"Uh... Captain Kilgore," Ito said into her headset, effectively silencing the rest of her assault group.

Asher took several deep breaths, caging his anger. He turned on his helmet speaker, not wanting to miss what the captain had to say.

"What's our company's status?" asked the sergeant.

Our status..." the captain's voice was full of frustration. "We've been sitting here for an hour. Nothing has changed."

A burst of static followed as the captain switched between channels.

"Sir, what's the hold-up?" Captain Kilgore asked Commander Greaves. He spoke over his company's channel, allowing Asher and the others to hear. The captain was close, waiting in one of the nearby vehicles.

"We're still waiting on the District X folks to retrieve the kresnik before we proceed." Greaves stood beside the back of an armored truck, X-12 strung about his torso, impatiently kicking up gravel from the road.

Asher saw his massive form illuminated in the headlights, the commander trading in his tank top and jeans for body armor and a helmet.

"We can't have him and the vampire out at the same time," Greaves explained. "A vamp that'll talk is hard to find, and we don't want him torn to pieces just yet."

"Understood, sir," said Kilgore. "I suppose it's kind of late to gripe about the itinerary now, but we need to get a move on."

"Dang it, Captain," said Greaves, his frustration setting in ever further. "Do you think I don't know! If I had a nickel for every complaint tonight," he muttered through gritted teeth.

"Kresnik inbound," the commander from District X spoke into everyone's helmet.

"Thank you, Commander Griffin," said Greaves. "'Bout time! Sun's been gone for a while now." Greaves switched channels as he spoke, his voice now only heard by those ranked captain and above.

"Bring out the vamp!" Greaves slapped a giant gloved hand

on the side of the truck parked beside him. "We gotta get a move on!"

The sound of multiple locks unlatching met Greaves' words, the double doors swinging open. The vampire Desmond rested upright in the back of the truck, strapped to a handcart, his arms further secured by a straitjacket, a muzzle affixed to his face. Bandages adorned his forehead; the wounds inflicted upon him from the night before yet to heal completely. His face splotchy as before but no longer bruised and bloodied. He wore a black collar around his neck, this a spring-loaded guillotine-like device set to decapitate the vampire should he attempt escape.

A guard stood to either side of Desmond, each with a death grip on their weapon should the prisoner dare make a move.

"What are you waiting for?" Greaves shouted, gripping his weapon. "Unstrap him! He's the only one who can go up to those guns without gettin' tore' up."

The guards paused before hastily undoing Desmond's straps, releasing him from the handcart.

"Take his mask off! I'll need to talk to him."

Obeying the order, one of the guards took his hands from his weapon, making to remove the vampire's muzzle.

Desmond snarled at Greaves as the guard pulled off the mask, his eyes alive with a fiery hate.

"Shut it, bloodsucker!" Greaves roared, pulling a red-buttoned device from his pocket. It was the kill switch for Desmond's collar. "You only speak when spoken to!"

The vampire's eyes widened, his hateful angst turned to fear.

"The straight jacket will need to come off too," Greaves instructed, both guards turning to look at him.

Though their helmet visors shielded their eyes, it was clear the guards thought he had lost his mind.

"What's he gonna do?" Greaves waved the kill switch around in the air, giving Desmond a sinister grin as he did so.

Both of the guards stepped behind the vampire as they went to remove his jacket. They struggled with the unconventional garment for some time before finally freeing the prisoner from his bindings.

Desmond looked down over himself, grimacing in disdain,

finding his sleek blue suit replaced by a baggy gray jumpsuit.

"I hope you don't have a problem with your attire," Greaves spoke with mock sincerity. "I'm sure it's not as stylish as what you're used to."

Desmond glared at him.

"Remember our deal, scum!" Greaves snapped, jumping onto the back of the truck. He grabbed Desmond by the shirt and yanked him from the vehicle, sending him flying toward the ground, the vampire barely catching himself as he hit the gravel.

"You do what you're told, and you get to live just that much longer!" Greaves dealt Desmond a brutal blow to the ribs with his boot, causing him to roll over on the ground.

Asher winced, sensing the hardiness of the blow even from where he sat.

Desmond groaned, holding his side.

Legion soldiers formed a line on either side of the truck, their weapons trained on the vampire.

"Hey, throw me his headset!" Greaves called to the guards, catching the requested device in his free hand. He shoved one side of the headset in his chest guard pockets beside the red-buttoned remote, making sure both hands were at the ready should the vampire try anything.

"Come on, get up and quit that sniffling." Greaves walked back toward Desmond, leaning down to pull him up onto his feet by the back of his jumpsuit.

"I think you just broke a few of my ribs." Desmond winced, bent over, still holding his side.

"What did I say about talkin'?" Greaves' threatening tone softened somewhat. "I suppose I need to allow it when you have something to tell me. Better not lie to me, though!"

"Understood, sir." Desmond slowly removed his hand from his ribs.

Greaves took the headset from his pocket and slipped it on over the vampire's pointed ears. He took a step back behind Desmond, not wanting to touch him any longer than necessary.

"Get a move on, bloodsucker!" Greaves kicked Desmond toward the entrance to the tunnel, causing him to stumble. "Don't you even think to try anything! You try escapin', and I'll have your head for a bowling ball! I got the kill switch right here!" He shook the device at the vampire.

"There is always the possibility that The Surgeon has changed the codes." Desmond regained his footing, somehow still defiant despite the threats. "I haven't been here in months."

"That ain't no concern ah' mine, bloodsucker!" Greaves spat on the ground. "We'll just send you back with one of our codebreakers. It's just easier to throw you out here first."

Desmond walked toward the tunnel entrance, his shadow diminishing in the headlights as he progressed some distance away. The turreted guns mounted above turned toward him before returning to their original position, recognizing him as a friendly.

The vampire disappeared beyond the beams of light, now deep within the dark tunnel.

"The vampire is en route to the first gate," Greaves spoke over the common channel.

The six company force waited in anticipatory silence as the vampire typed in the security code. Greaves impatiently pawed the ground with a booted foot.

"Commander, they are approaching with the kresnik now," said Griffin, his voice heard by all. "I have ordered the retrieval personnel to remain at the back of the convoy until you're finished with the vampire."

"Roger that," said Greaves. "Better check on that vamp," he grumbled, switching channels once again.

"Got that door open yet, bloodsucker?" Greaves asked, his tone racked with anxiety.

"Ah... I will never get tired of all the name-calling..." Desmond's voice was barely audible.

"What was that?" asked Greaves.

"The door is opening now, sir," Desmond spoke at a higher volume.

"Did you take care of the guns? Don't do us any good to have the door unlocked if we're just gonna to be mowed down."

"I don't know how to deactivate those, Commander." Desmond failed to hide the hint of satisfaction in his voice.

"You best be figuring it out then!" the commander roared.

"My apologies, Commander." Desmond was unfettered by

Greaves' shouting. "I was only in charge of a slaughter plant. This technology is far above my pay grade."

"Uh! Dang it, come back out for the codebreaker." Greaves planted an open palm on his forehead. "Come out with your hands above your head! I don't want no funny stuff!"

"Wouldn't even think of it, sir. You threatened to beat, blow, and slice my head off plenty of times already."

"Haha. Dang, smart-aleck vamp. Get back over here before I have you blasted to smithereens! They'll be pickin' up pieces of you for months."

"He'll be needing a codebreaker!" Greaves faced the line of personnel.

A nearby soldier answered his request almost immediately, passing him the strange, tablet-shaped device. Its blue screen glowed through the darkness.

The soldiers waited as Desmond emerged from the tunnel. The vampire stepped back into the line of headlight beams with his hands raised high. He stopped several yards away from the commander, unsure what to do next.

"Get over here so he can hand it off to you." Greaves' voice was flat with impatience. "I can't chance any of my people gettin' close to those guns."

Desmond responded and walked toward the soldier with the codebreaker, reaching out to take the device. He walked back toward the tunnel, his pace slackened by the weight of the burden he now carried.

"What are you draggin' your feet for?" asked Greaves, seeing the vampire's intent. "I've never seen a vampire move that slow. You can't be that out of shape. Pick up the pace before I really lose my patience!"

Desmond straightened up and walked at a slightly faster pace, though he still saw no reason to move too quickly. His future with the Legion would be quite dim even if the commander allowed him to live.

"That's better," said Greaves, satisfied.

Desmond re-entered the tunnel, disappearing back into darkness.

Greaves continued to monitor the vampire's progress. The

commander spared the rest of the Legion from having to hear their squabbling, preferring to keep his helmet tuned only to the vampire's headset until the task was complete.

"Uh," Asher moaned, more than tired of the wait. "Are we sure it's a good idea to use a vampire for this? I know they put a guillotine collar around his neck, but he could still be leading us along."

"Have you not seen the guns, Blackthorn?" asked Ito. "He's the only one who can go in and deactivate them. It's much better to deal with him than risk our personnel. Besides, I've never known a vampire who would choose to protect his comrades over saving himself."

"Going by this particular vamp's behavior, I assume he would always take the selfish route," said Milo. "Let's just hope he doesn't suddenly experience an overwhelming surge of loyalty."

"Yeah, let's." Asher watched Greaves through the window.

The commander kept a tense hand on both his shotgun and the kill switch in his pocket.

"The third door is opening now, Commander," Desmond spoke into his headset. "It's the last one, I swear."

"What about the lights?" asked Greaves. "I don't want to send our personnel in blind."

"Commander, there are lights, but I'm not sure if I can turn them on."

"Do you know what kind of light switch it is?"

"It's just turned on with a key," said Desmond, expecting Greaves to shout at him.

"That's good," said Greaves. "The codebreaker is a multi-function tool, and you should be able to use it to turn them on. Just put the gripper up to the lock like yuh did with the keypads."

"Very well," said Desmond. "Give me a moment, Commander. The stress of the situation was creeping up on the vampire.

The tunnel lights flashed on nearly a minute later, filling the total darkness with a deep red glow.

"Congratulations, bloodsucker, you get to live to suck another day, or… night. Stay where you are, and we'll pick you up. No reason to take all six companies down that way without knowin' if it's safe."

"I believe I have opened and turned off everything," Desmond assured him.

"That's what you say. Put those dirty claws up where we can see 'em. Anything, and I mean anything, happens, and there goes your head."

"Understood, sir." It was difficult to tell if the vampire's defeated tone was genuine or fake.

"I take the red lights to mean that we are now ready to proceed to the second briefing with the high commander," said Commander Griffin over the shared channel.

"That we are," said Greaves. He climbed up into the back of the armored truck, its double doors hanging open.

Asher shifted around in his seat, nervous with anticipation.

"We are ready to proceed to the second briefing, High Commander," said Griffin.

"And only a mere two hours behind schedule," said Witchburn, her voice materializing through a static-filled haze.

"I thought you were informed about our little mishap on the way up here, ma'am," said Greaves as the doors of the truck closed behind him.

Asher watched the dark green truck lurch backward, turning around and rolling toward the tunnel entrance. Red light reflected off its metallic hide.

"Oh, yes, Griffin informed me directly," said Witchburn, the static now gone.

Asher thought he heard a sharp thumping sound carried over the speaker, suggesting High Commander Witchburn had kicked something.

"It's something that could not be helped, though it does make this operation all the more difficult. We're late, and you will not have the light outside to fall back on, as I'm sure you're aware."

"It does put us at a disadvantage, High Commander," said Griffin.

"You should all know your assignments, but I will go over them once more to minimize any confusion," said Witchburn. "First, Commander Greaves and his new vampire sidekick will exit the tunnel, careful to keep him away from the kresnik. I think we can still press our vampire for additional information, so I would like to keep him alive. Greaves, you still have my permission to execute him if it even looks like he has betrayed us."

"Whatever you say, High Commander Witchburn." Greaves sounded inappropriately gleeful. His headset picked up the sound of the truck's revving engine as it sped toward the vampire at the end of the tunnel.

"OK," Witchburn continued. "Once the tunnel is clear, 1st Company from District X will enter. They will be followed by the truck carrying the kresnik, which will then be followed by our single company from District V. The 2nd Company from District X will be behind that, guarding their six. The last three District X companies and our hellhounds will remain outside, retaining our current perimeter. The District X company inside will fan out as best they can, and then the kresnik will be released at the end of the tunnel. After that, we just play it by ear until we have searched and cleared the whole area. I hope you're ready. This could be a long operation, and the casualties will likely be high."

"Understood, ma'am," said Commander Griffin.

"Stop squirmin' so we can get 'ur jacket back on!" Greaves shouted, the sound of multiple feet striking the truck floor audible through his helmet. "You're job's over bloodsucker. Don't make me mess up and hit the switch now!"

"Commander?" asked Witchburn, sensing possible trouble.

"Sorry, ma'am," said Greaves. "Everything is still fine at this end. I was just havin' a little trouble puttin' the vamp's straitjacket back on. We'll have him loaded back up here in a moment, no problem. I'm not sure if anyone noticed, but it looks like the guns are disabled."

"Have you heard anything I've said?" asked Witchburn, ignoring the heavy sarcasm in Greave's last statement.

"Every word."

"Wouldn't it be best to pull the kresnik through first?" Griffin interrupted their exchange. "He could deal with the vamps before we enter. Keep our losses to a minimum."

"Yes, I suppose that's the most rational way to do it, but that's not how I would like it done. Let's not forget who's operation this is." Witchburn sounded testy. "Surely you can appreciate the hazards involved. We simply do not have enough information to verify what is contained in this laboratory. We don't want to subject one of our newest weapons to an enemy onslaught at initial contact. High casualties are to be expected, and we can't afford to lose the kresnik."

"Yes, ma'am." Griffin didn't argue the point further.

"We have the bloodsucker secured," Greaves informed them. "Proceeding toward the entrance now."

"Outstanding, Commander," said Witchburn. "We will keep the lines of communication open from now until the operation is complete." She switched between channels, no longer needing to speak to all of them at once.

Asher jumped in his seat as his assault group's SUV roared back to life. Greaves' truck became visible within the tunnel, rapidly speeding toward them as it exited, turning off the gravel road to jet down the side of the ridge.

"District X, 1st Company, proceed," said Commander Griffin, seeing Greaves exit.

Asher watched as the vehicles nearest the entrance rolled forward. A line of red taillights glowed brightly against the tunnel's red backdrop. His muscles tensed as his anticipation at entering the foreboding tunnel renewed.

"You ready to do this?" Aaron slapped Asher on the shoulder and shook him. "Better get psyched."

"About as ready as I'll ever be." Asher gripped his weapon.

"I know I'm ready," said Milo sarcastically. "Gonna go down a creepy tunnel with who knows how many vampires at the end, and in the middle of the night, too."

"I hear that," said Asher in agreement. "So long as we can get in and out without getting too messed up, that's good enough for me.

"We should be in the safest place within the procession, right with the kresnik," Ito assured them. "Probably not as safe as remaining out here, but it is what it is."

Their SUV crept forward behind the rest as the last vehicle of District X's 1st Company made its way into the tunnel.

"Proceed forward with the kresnik," Commander Griffin's voice resonated within their helmets.

A black armored truck with a green cardiac line down either side appeared from out of the trees, coming from the opposite direction Greaves had gone. It sped down the ridge, bounding over the rocky, uneven terrain, sending gravel flying as it turned down the dirt road and continued into the tunnel.

"District V, proceed," said Captain Kilgore just as the CyberGen truck crossed the threshold.

The four in the SUV waited as the other vehicles lurched forward and entered the tunnel. The heavy guns hung above them, the motionless death machines rendered powerless, seemingly enraged by their deactivation.

"Whoa, the anticipation is killing me!" proclaimed Milo.

Asher glanced toward the backseat to see the medic sitting with his weapon at the ready, a smile across his face. He had changed his tune, the soldier now strangely content during what would likely be one of the Legion's more dangerous operations.

Their vehicle slowly accelerated as they left the open air on the mountain ridge for the red-lit, claustrophobic entry tunnel.

Asher gazed up at the tunnel ceiling through his window, seeing the turreted guns hanging above them. They were the same size as those out front, placed ten feet apart, their barrels pointed straight down at them. The Legion's vampire informant had come through for them, thus far keeping them from unnecessary exposure to gunfire.

"District X, 2nd Company, proceed," said Commander Griffin, sending the last group of vehicles in after them.

The line of vehicles approached the end of the tunnel now, several of them already stopped, parking off to either side to allow passage for the CyberGen truck.

The black vehicle made its way through the line, traveling onward toward what looked like a semi-circular hanger door, illuminated by yet more red light. The truck turned around and then backed up toward the opening, allowing plenty of space for the Legion soldiers to pass by.

Seeing that the kresnik was now in position, the soldiers from 1st Company emerged from their vehicles, a flurry of doors opening and then slamming shut as they made for the circular door.

"1st Company, form up!" A single soldier, obviously their

captain, stood in front of the others, fist raised the air to signal them. Upon hearing the order, the company hastily arranged themselves into a four-person wide column.

Ito veered their SUV off to the side now, filing behind an already parked transport truck. "Let's do this!" she commanded.

The whoosh of released seat belts answered her enthusiastic order.

Ito closed her door and trotted toward the end of the tunnel. Asher, Aaron, and Milo followed close behind, joined by a second mass of black-clad soldiers.

Asher felt his heart rate increasing as excitement and a heavy dose of fear flowed through his veins.

"My company!" Captain Kilgore appeared in front of them, weapon at his side, hand raised to be recognized. "Form up! And prepare for entry!"

The company scrambled into position, forming a column four soldiers across.

"No sign of the enemy!" roared a captain from District X into their headsets. The news conveyed a bit of relief to all, the looming battle yet to begin.

"Proceed to stage two!" Commander Griffin shouted. "The kresnik will remain in reserve. Spread out and retain your position until District V is there to support."

"You heard him," Greaves responded to Commander Griffin's orders. "It's go time!"

"Proceed!" Kilgore commanded through his helmet. His soldiers responded by marching forward, continuing toward the opening, past the CyberGen truck.

Asher passed through the entryway, cold sweat forming on his hands as he followed Ito to the left. They entered into a vast, red-lit room, immediately met by a multitude of stacked cages and crates lined up near the jagged, stone walls. The containers extended into multiple columns and filled most of the space.

A massive wall was visible at the other side of the giant room, this one smooth, made of concrete. A metal mesh bridge, approximately ten feet above the ground, spanned the length of the wall. Its multiple tributaries jutted out from it and hung above the soldiers' heads, allowing onlookers from above an aerial view. Asher saw a single door on that side, which gave the only suggestion that anything else was buried under the mountain.

"Keep close to those walls!" Kilgore wasn't intimidated by the vastness of the cargo bay. "We don't want any surprises."

Asher's group followed the captain's orders, continuing to walk along the wall until Ito raised a fist for them to stop.

Asher clinched his weapon in an iron grasp, ready for the enemy to rush forth at any moment. Their force could spread no further. They stood in front of a pile of crates, no longer able to see the far wall.

Asher peered into the crate nearest him, certain he heard breathing. He found a hairless, deathly pale monkey-like creature with rage-filled, ghostly blue eyes resting within.

The creature shrieked and launched itself at him, bearing a surprisingly large set of fangs.

Asher jumped away while the monkey thing reached for him with its claws, unable to touch him confined to the crate as it was.

"Stay calm, man," Aaron waved him back toward the wall.

The area was never quiet after their entry. The plethora of animal-containing crates inside prevented it. However, the cargo bay was more tranquil than it should be, with still no sign of the enemy.

Asher turned toward a noise, finding it came from within the green-lined vehicle. The vehicle shook like a washing machine. Jagged slash marks appeared in the back doors. The beast inside screamed, exploding into a blood-lusting rage.

"Commander!" roared Kilgore. "The kresnik is losing it!"

The words barely left the captain's mouth when a blaring alarm sounded. The far wall detached itself from the bridge, sliding upward toward the ceiling as it opened.

Another of The Surgeon's giant wolf-beasts bellowed in rage, pulling itself out from under the door.

"We got company!" Kilgore's voice rang in Asher's head. "We can't face that thing as a line! Find cover!"

The door slid up further, revealing an onslaught of black-armored, heavily armed vampiric soldiers, the enemy over 500 hundred strong.

"Release   the   kresnik!"   Witchburn   howled.

Chapter XXX

The Nature of the Beast

Cyrus shrieked, tearing at the truck doors with his claws. His humanity had entirely vanished from his mind.

Blood! I want their blood! I will have it! He screamed inside his head, his ability to speak overridden by relentless hunger and rage. Cyrus slashed and clawed at the doors in a bloodlust-fueled frenzy, shredding jagged holes into the metal.

"Let him out!" Cyrus heard a voice cry out, his comprehension of human vocalizations limited. "We need him now! They're tearing into us!"

Cyrus halted, his ears perking up as the door latch screeched open.

A deep red line appeared between the opening doors.

Cyrus pushed through, springing out of the opening, the light embracing his dark form. He bounded across the floor, his bloodlust driving him down the lanes between the crate piles. The kresnik's prey was everywhere. Black-clad figures rushed around the vast room. Their smells called to him. The air was so saturated with the scent that it was impossible to determine who was most vulnerable.

Cyrus stopped, scratching the concrete floor as he skidded to a halt. He turned his nose skyward, taking another whiff of air into his nostrils, deciding whom he might attack first. One of the savory smelling creatures had a stronger, more pungent scent.

The giant wolf beast stood on its hind legs and roared, drawing Cyrus's attention. The monster dropped back down on all fours, charging headlong through a pile of crates and into a group of Legion soldiers, sending wood and debris flying. It tore into the soldiers with deadly claws and monstrous jaws, dispatching them one after the other, the blood pooling thick.

"2nd Company! Grenades!" Someone yelled from a distance away.

The explosives careened through the air, each erupting into a devastating fireball when they struck the beast. Wood flew everywhere as the containers exploded. Some of the luckier lab animals survived the blasts, breaking free from their crates. They ran around the cargo bay in a frenzied panic as they searched for the exit.

The beast howled in pain, though it wasn't significantly injured, protected by its heavy armor. It charged toward another line of soldiers, attacking with even greater ferocity.

Seeking a better vantage point, Cyrus jumped up onto a pile of crates.

"Hit it again!" The same voice screamed once more.

Another onslaught of grenades hit the creature, fire and shrapnel sent flying. It continued its blood-drenched rampage, not at all hindered by the explosion, ripping apart Legion soldiers in a storm of blood, severed limbs, and heads.

Cyrus had little time to view the second grenade blast before an enemy sniper shot him off the crate pile. He careened toward the ground, landing safely on his feet.

Cyrus glanced back at the attacking beast, his mind still in a frenzied state, his instincts pulling him toward it. Though enthralled by bloodlust, he knew his choices were limited, an aerial attack made impossible.

Still, Cyrus moved toward the monster, not running but stealthily creeping toward it. He approached from behind, the beast crushing a Legion soldier's head between its jaws, oblivious to the imminent threat.

Quickly within a few feet of its hindquarters, Cyrus poised to pounce. The kresnik screamed, leaping onto the beast's back. He dealt it a savage bite to the back of its exposed neck, digging and tearing through flesh, biting and clawing at its spine.

The monster howled one last time, charging through crate pile after crate pile, finally dropping dead right before it reached the left wall.

Cyrus sprang from the wretched monster's back, its black blood flowing from his mouth, his bloodlust only beginning to be satiated. He wouldn't rest until all his prey lay dead, leaving him an insurmountable feast.

The kresnik raced toward the nearest group of vampire soldiers, the need for caution no longer necessary. He flung himself into them as they turned to fire on him, their bullets rendered near useless by his rapid speed and superior armor. Though they were swift and strong in their own right, Cyrus was always faster and more brutal.

A relentless Cyrus dispatched all in a mad, bloody slaughter, ripping through throats, slashing through abdomens, tearing off limbs, crushing vertebrae in his powerful jaws. He feasted while he fought, the kresnik tearing off chunks of flesh, swallowing between victims.

More and more of the enemy zigzagged between crate piles as they advanced on the Legion soldiers. The enemy force was considerable now, much larger than that of the Legion's, and threatened to overrun them. Cyrus's devastating rampage served as the only thing keeping them from it. Despite his speed and power, even he would eventually grow tired of killing them.

"We need all outside companies!" The voice from earlier sounded once more. "There's too many!"

"You will not take my lab!" A white-coated man roared.

Cyrus looked up as he choked down the ragged trachea of his latest victim.

The man stood at the other side of the vast space underneath the bridge, holding a strange, sword-like object against his shoulder. Three leather-clad individuals stood behind him, one man and two women, all carrying short, cylindrical, metal devices in their hands.

"You will all die here!" The white-coated vampire ranted. "Make them suffer!" He raised his sword and pointed it toward the concentration of Legion soldiers hiding behind the crates at the other side of the room.

Cyrus saw several flashes of light as the three charged past their master, laser knife blades exploding from the metal devices as they raced toward the soldiers. He was immediately enthralled. Their mesmerizing laser lights called to him through a haze of thick but desensitizing vampire stench. Cyrus turned away from the group of vampire soldiers and slowly crept around the piles of stacked crates toward them.

A barrage of flying daggers met the three, catching them off guard, the vampires barely dodging the blades before they hit their targets. Two black-cloaked figures followed the storm of daggers, both with a long-bladed knife in each hand. They ran at the three, intent on quickly cutting them to pieces before they had a chance to reach the Legion soldiers.

The male vampire made for the figure to his left, not at all intimidated by the knives. The females took his lead, one joining him in his attack and the other rushing to the right to confront the remaining figure, both intent on deadly assault.

Plasma laser struck metal blade when the combatants met, joining in a furious dance of death, a flurry of stabbing and slashing intermixed with the dodging of incoming attacks. None of the strikes hit their mark despite the battle's intensity. The skill of the fighters and the deadliness of their weapons was so great that any wound would be lethal.

Cyrus continued toward them, taking no notice of the combatants, still taken by the red lasers. He had lost his lust for the kill, intent on his new desire, the lights simply too alluring to ignore.

One black cloak fought against two, its movements both intricate and elegant, its strikes relentless and brutal. The two vampires had taken on more than they could handle, barely moving out of the way before the cloaked figure's blades found flesh.

One of the female vampires snarled as the figure sprang at her, driving a metal blade beneath her ribs. The figure followed up with a brutal slash to its victim's neck with its second blade.

Blood flowed like a fountain onto the ground. The head fell from the body as the dead vampire slumped to the floor.

"Mara!" yelled the male vampire, rushing toward the black cloak. Seizing the opportunity, he jammed his laser knife into his foe's chest.

The black-cloaked figure moaned with a male voice. He looked down to find the vampire's blade burning through his ribcage, running him through.

The figure collapsed, faltering down onto the floor in a heap.

"Viddur!" The remaining black cloak screamed with a woman's voice. She was unable to reach him, still occupied by her quick-paced fight with the remaining female vampire.

She sounds so familiar, Cyrus thought. A little bit of forgotten humanity slipped in while his attention remained on the laser knives.

The male vampire was upon his victim now, taking a knee as he drove his weapon right through the man's skull. Satisfied, he rose back to his feet, rushing over to his remaining comrade to help her dispatch the remaining cloaked woman.

"I will not have you make a mess of my lab!" a man shouted, catching Cyrus by surprise.

Cyrus screamed, receiving a booted kick to the back, turning to see the white-coated vampire upon him. He lunged to attack, skidding to a stop when the man flipped the switch on the handle of his blunt sword.

The blade's whole edge became an intense light, bright even in the red-lit room. Cyrus's eyes widened, taken in by it, the largest, most beautiful laser light of all.

"Oh, I see." the white-coated vampire smirked.

He looked at Cyrus and then back at his plasma blade.

The vampire turned and then viciously spun back around, raising his weapon in the air to bring it back down on Cyrus's right arm.

Cyrus let out a very human scream, his primal urges instantly gone. He staggered backward to collapse onto his knees, overcome by the mind-numbingly searing pain, grasping at the cauterized stub below his elbow. The severed limb lay some feet in front of him, the end of his forearm blackened and steaming.

"Cyrus!" Elysia screamed, still in a furious fight with the remaining two vampires, unable to reach him.

"This is it, wretch!" The white-coated vampire raised his sword high, ready to bring it down on Cyrus's neck.

Cyrus heard the distant sound of another wolf-bear beast, forgetting his pain, the call coming from the far left wall. There was something different about this howl. It sounded somehow... Mechanical.

The ground shook as the thing ran toward them, causing the white-coated vampire to turn away from Cyrus, his face intense with fear.

The thing burst through the stony left wall, sending rocks and debris flying everywhere. Once through, the creature stood as the dust cleared, a strange green light emitted by one of its eyes.

Cyrus gazed upward, amazed by the new creature.

It was tall but not as massive as the wolf monsters, spindly where they were bulky, its limbs long and disproportionate to its body. It wasn't entirely biological, machine parts implanted at various areas of its body, especially at the joints. It was covered in a layer of white hair where it had skin, its ears pointy, the one biological eye yellow, slit down the middle by the pupil.

All soldiers, both Legion and vampire, ceased to fire their weapons, all eyes on the creature.

The beast continued to stand there, looking around the loading area, scanning the room with its single cybernetic eye, the green field it projected passing over Cyrus before finally resting on the white-coated vampire.

It walked toward the white coat, gaining speed as it went, the ground shaking with its surprisingly heavy steps. It charged through the body of vampiric forces near the wall, tearing through their line, bodies flying everywhere as it made for the white coat.

"No! No! No!" screamed the vampire, dropping his weapon as he turned to run.

The creature bounded after him with considerable speed, murder in both eyes. It rushed past Cyrus, causing him to wince as it stepped down upon his severed arm, crushing it, the bones cracking under its weight.

Cyrus kept a firm hold on his still steaming stump, only able to stare at the creature as it moved past, catching a brief glimpse of the beast's wristband. He went slack with disbelief as he read it, the name TALON BLACKTHORN glaring back at him in big black letters.

The white coat screamed as the machine creature yanked him off the ground, taking him up in its massive paws, raising him high above its head.

The vampire let out one last blood-curdling howl, the creature stretching his spine and tearing him in half, a torrent of blood rushing forth, the white coat's intestines exposed and tattered.

The creature slammed the two halves of the broken body onto the ground, the vampire's face twisted in terror, the calm eyes now lifeless.

The vampire leader dead, the firefight began anew. The Legion soldiers took the opportunity to weave between the crate piles, advancing toward the enemy.

The cybernetic beast roared, turning to face the two vampires engaged in combat with Elysia. It charged for them, Elysia barely weaving past it as it made for its prey.

The female vampire screamed as the beast brutally slung her into the nearest wall, where she landed in a heap. The raging machine creature grabbed the male off the ground, making him scream when it threw him down, crushing his skull under its foot.

"Cyrus!" Elysia screamed. She rushed toward him, watchful of the beast as she tried to pull him behind the nearest pile of crates.

The creature turned toward them.

Cyrus's heart beat rapidly as he regained his senses, fearful the beast would attack.

The machine creature regarded them for a moment more before raising its nose in the air, catching a whiff of something. It stomped away from them, heading toward the nearest gathering of vampire soldiers.

"Get to the walls!" ordered one of the Legion's commanders. "That thing will take care of the enemy for us so long as we stay out of the way!"

The Legion forces staggered to either wall, some remaining behind the crate piles to give their comrades cover. The maneuver was hazardous, and enemy fire felled a few of the soldiers as they attempted the move.

"Get up, Cyrus," said Elysia, helping Cyrus to his feet. "We can't stay out in the open like this. We need to get you to a medic."

The kresnik wordlessly let her lead him between the crate piles toward the left wall, hoping to sneak back behind friendly forces.

The beast continued its rampage, tearing the vampire forces apart en masse, leaving piles of body parts and pools of blood in its wake.

The vampire soldiers turned away from the Legion, focusing their fire on the beast.

The creature dropped a partially eaten body from its mouth, swatting at the bullets as though they were gnats. It turned and bolted toward the tunnel, the shots painful due to its lack of armor, lumber, and bodies flying as it made its escape.

The enemy force lay decimated. More than half of their soldiers were now either dead or wounded.

"Stay against the walls!" The commander ordered, blending in with the rest of them. "Just let it go out the tunnel! We can deal with it later!"

The beast quickly closed the space, charging through the rounded door into the tunnel. It left wrecked vehicles and twisted metal frames in its wake as it ran for the outside.

Elysia kept Cyrus moving along the left wall, leading him behind the soldiers that stood there, still locked in combat with the vampiric forces.

"You got 'em on the run now!" yelled another unseen commander, his voice fuzzy as it proceeded from the Legion soldiers' helmets. "High Commander Witchburn wants this place cleared of vamps!"

"You heard him!" yelled the officer from before. "Just got to take care of a few more of them, and this place is ours!"

"Almost there," said Elysia. She took Cyrus past the truck he had arrived in, now wrecked and turned over on its side.

An influx of newly arrived black-clad Legion forces swarmed past them as they made their way through the tunnel door, the soldiers called in from guard duty outside.

Cyrus groaned, still clutching his stub, the skin blackened but no longer steaming, the pain extraordinary.

"Medic!" Elysia removed her hood. "We need a medic!"

A handful of soldiers stayed behind as their comrades moved on, surrounding Cyrus and Elysia.

"Let's go over to the tunnel wall," said one of them.

Elysia led Cyrus away from the circle of soldiers and through the Legion's line of vehicles, the medic who gave the order following beside them.

"Go back to your assignments!" The medic waved her companions away. "I know it looks bad, but we really won't be needing your help!"

"I'll have him sit down against the wall." The medic turned to Elysia. "The flesh looks to be completely cauterized, so blood loss should be minimal. Since he's been taken out of the fight, I'll hit him with a sedative. Keep him asleep until something more can be done."

Elysia released Cyrus, allowing him to sit against the wall.

The medic pulled a vial from the pack at her waist, assembling the syringe as she knelt beside him. "OK, here we go," she said, jamming the needle into Cyrus's neck administering the medication.

"That's it!" The commander was so loud that his voice rang down the tunnel. "We got 'em! It's time to break into assault groups and clear out the place!"

Cyrus barely heard his cries, the light giving way to darkness as he slipped into unconsciousness.

Chapter XXXI

Fall Prey

Ding!

The elevator rang, the doors sliding open to reveal a dark, hulking shape. The thing lumbered through the open doorway, lugging its human-shaped burden along behind. It held onto the man with a vice-grip, a pale, clawed hand wrapped around his ankles, the back of the man's head dragging the floor.

Driscoll groaned, unprepared for the change in terrain. His head no longer slid over the smooth tile in the elevator, the floor becoming hard, stony ground. Stuffy, cool, and dank, he felt the atmosphere change dramatically as the doors opened. Though Driscoll could not see through the black bag pulled over his face, he knew they had entered a cave.

"Ow! Watch it!" the corporal protested, his head striking a rock. "You'll crack my skull on these rocks!"

"Shut up, blood bag!" The vampire growled, letting Driscoll's legs fall to the ground. He tore into the sides of the corporal's already ruined body armor with deadly claws, hoisting him up to remove the black bag from his face. "One more word out of you, and I'll tear your head clean off!" The beast snarled, drawing Driscoll in close, revealing its visage in the darkness.

The thing was grotesque, the similarities between the creature and the typical vampire stopping at the pale skin. This creature was a beast, its ears large and pointy like a bat's, its jaw jutting outward like a bulldog's, prominently displaying its bottom fangs and teeth. The eyes were worst of all, the irises bloody red, full of hostility and void of mercy. The vampire called himself

FALL PREY: THE ATTACK

Bloodbath, a testament both to his capacity for violence and lack of intelligence.

Bloodbath stared into his quarry's eyes in an almost desperate attempt at intimidation.

Driscoll returned his gaze with a blank stare. He had traveled with the vampire for several days, continually pushed and dragged around, Bloodbath's numerous unfulfilled threats quickly desensitizing him.

"Yes, but then you will have nothing to give The Master," said Driscoll, confidently. "Then you can say goodbye to that promotion. Can you even get out of here alive without me? I wonder."

The vampire roared, trying to force his silence yet again.

"Maybe a breath mint?"

Bloodbath muffled Driscoll's words as he shoved the bag back over his head, the vampire pulling the drawstring tight.

"Walk!" Bloodbath commanded, planting Driscoll on his feet and pushing him forward.

The corporal fell, just catching himself before his head hit the ground.

"Probably not a good idea," said Driscoll, on all fours as he struggled to stand back up. "Not walking for a couple days will do that to you. Help if I could see."

Bloodbath growled and yanked Driscoll up off the ground, violently slinging him over his shoulder.

Driscoll remained silent despite his rough handling, not wanting to press his luck further.

Burden secure, Bloodbath descended deeper into the cave, the loose, stony ground crunching underneath his clawed, shoeless feet. His pace increased significantly as Driscoll's words weighed on the vampire's fear of his master.

Bloodbath continued on his trek for only a moment before a single figure became visible in the distance. The surrounding darkness and the black cloak and wrappings it wore concealed its identity.

The dark form stood in the space between a small table and throne, both made of shining black stone. While the table was plain and simple, the throne was ornate. The black obsidian displayed

387

intricate carvings of bats, snakes, and skulls with deep red rubies set in the top of its high backrest.

Bloodbath's step slackened as he stood to meet the figure.

"Ah, Bloodbath is it?" The figure had a woman's voice, sickly-sweet yet menacing as it echoed through the dark cavern. She was dressed all in black, wearing both a robe and a cloak, her hands, arms, and feet wrapped in black linens, her face obscured in the darkness.

"Yes, Master." Bloodbath bowed to the figure, nearly dropping Driscoll when he dipped down and rose back up again.

"I've been told you have a present for me." The woman took a blood-filled goblet from the black stone table and drank. "It had better be a good one for your sake! I despise being disturbed while in my throne room."

"Master, I bring you something most appeasing!" Bloodbath proclaimed. He yanked Driscoll from his shoulder and stood him up, spinning him around to face the figure. "I present you with this blood bag!" He pulled the bag off Driscoll's head with a flourish, the soldier frowning, finding the need for the dramatic unnecessary.

Eyes having no time to adjust, Driscoll squinted through the darkness to view The Master. He saw very little of her in the darkness, her face masked by a black cloth and her head covered by her dark hood. Only the bottom portion of her visage was visible, revealing bone-white skin and full, red lips.

"Oh, a man," The Master's sarcasm was undeniable. "Do you mean to mock me, Bloodbath? I'm perfectly capable of procuring my own snacks."

"This one is from the Legion." Bloodbath sounded worried, fearful of The Master's judgment. "His mind is weak! He can be turned to our cause!"

"Hey…" Driscoll started, his protests met with a sharp slap to the back of the head.

"Hmm… Yes, I can see the insignia." The Master mused, placing her goblet back down on the stone table.

"I am rarely presented with Legion soldiers. Most of them simply don't make it through transit." She looked at Driscoll through her cloth. "I can't imagine why," she said, revealing a pair of fangs.

She walked toward them, her steps soft but assertive as she

strode over the cave's rough floor. The Master circled Driscoll, pushing Bloodbath to the side to better view him, regarding the Legion soldier as though she were a spider and he was a fly.

"I won't tell you a thing!" Driscoll suddenly lost his composure, sweat gathering on his forehead. "You should just kill me now. I'll never talk!"

"Legion soldiers..." The Master sighed, her voice cold. "Always thinking they are so incorruptible." She stroked the side of his face with her hand, revealing her sharp, uncovered claws.

They were painted red, though not from polish.

"You will be broken," The Master whispered in his ear.

* * *

Cyrus blinked, awoken by the unforgivingly bright lights glaring down upon him. The effects of whatever sedative they gave him began to wear off. He was in a pure white room again, strapped down flat on a cold metal table, a thin hospital gown the only barrier between his skin and the open air. He stirred as the beeping of the machines helped him to come out of his fog. His right arm felt strangely numb.

Cyrus looked down at his side, the absence of his limb causing him to flinch only a little, his outburst prevented by the drug's effects.

"Hey, where's my arm?" he tried to ask, but he couldn't speak in his current state. Frustrated, he gazed upward, realizing people stood over him.

"Well, doctor, what do you plan on doing with him now?" asked Elysia. She remained off to Cyrus's left, appearing to be an angel under the lights. She spoke to Dr. Shen, who stood on the opposite side.

"Mr. Blackthorn is salvageable," said Dr. Shen, sure of his words.

It was difficult for Cyrus to see his expression through the light's glare.

"As important as it is, it's still just a limb," Shen continued. "We will have the Robotics Department make a prosthesis. I would have liked to have at least attempted a replantation, but, unfortunately, given the severity of the damage to the limb, such a procedure would not be successful."

"But, doesn't he have a higher regenerative capacity?" Elysia asked, the gravity of the doctor's answer going unregistered.

"His regenerative capabilities are enormous, but they still have their limits." Shen shook his head. "No mammal, kresnik, vampire or otherwise, has the ability to completely regenerate a limb."

The double doors on the right side of the room swung open, causing Elysia and the doctor to look up. A black-suited, middle-aged man walked into the room, his hair dark, his skin bronzed by an artificial tan. He stood off to the side, out of Cyrus's line of vision.

"Oh, hello, Mr. Dolore," said Dr. Shen, the tone of his voice revealing he was not excited to see the man. "What brings you down here to grace us with your presence?"

"Hello, doctor," said Mr. Dolore, his voice severe. "I am here to discuss the future of your test subject."

"I would suspect as much." Dr. Shen's careful smile showed his unease. "I would never take you as one prone to visit purely for a social call."

"I was told the test subject had his right arm amputated during battle and in such a way that it cannot be reattached." Dolore ignored the doctor's slight.

"That is correct."

"It's just my opinion, but I believe euthanasia is the best way to go." The black-suited man's tone was emotionless and cold.

"Euthanasia?" Dr. Shen instantly lost his composure, his eyes wide. "Are you insane? What about all the money we have invested in him? The board would have our heads! He has only lost an arm."

Elysia remained silent, not wanting to speak out of turn, though great concern and worry were plastered all over her youthful face.

"Well, excuse me, Dr. Shen." Mr. Dolore placed a hand on his chest, looking as though he was the one who had been offended. "We're dealing with much more than just the loss of a limb. You know the only reason he had it sliced off in the first place was because he goes totally berserk when in the presence of vampires. He's just too difficult to control."

"But, you know how long it takes to create, test, and train just one kresnik!" Dr. Shen continued his tirade. "Months of work and preparation just thrown away! Not to mention everything we've put him through. Tests and trials he wasn't even ready for. Aren't you even at all concerned about the money we have invested?"

"Yeah, probably no way around the monetary waste, substantial though it was." Dolore was unaffected by the doctor's rare display of empathy. "The government wants more anyway. Our profits will be huge once we come through with more product, much more than enough to cover this loss."

"I was granted full control over this project." Dr. Shen spoke through gritted teeth. "It doesn't matter what you think or want. If I say we will continue the project with this particular specimen, then that is precisely what we will do."

"Yeah, I think the board will see it differently." Dolore's jaw tightened. "Previous decisions can always be overridden. As CEO, I won't press them toward euthanasia, but I won't keep them from it either."

Dr. Shen tensed, angered by the man's words. His skin was now bright red, making him look like a stick of dynamite about to explode, too agitated to speak.

Cyrus moaned, stirred by Dolore's words, the mellowing effects of the sedative subsiding. He had a few things to say to the man.

Seeing Cyrus's distress, Elysia placed a comforting hand on his shoulder.

"We can always try a clone, maybe even several at once, each of them with all four limbs," said Dolore. "You'll be able to control their development from the very beginning. We'll prevent a lot of problems that way. No more test subjects taken off the street who may not even survive the initial procedure."

"It always takes time for the board to come to any kind of decision." Dr. Shen's rage faded due to the thought. "Until then, I will retain control over the project. Mr. Blackthorn will remain alive so long as I have the final say."

"What's the deal, Shen?" Mr. Dolore's eyes were hostile yet full of inquiry. "Why are you so protective of this particular test subject? Now is not the time to suddenly grow a conscience."

"Sorry to interrupt," said Dr. Ingram as she burst through the double doors. She walked around Cyrus's bed to stand beside Elysia.

"I rushed over here as soon as I heard. Shen, you can still move on with the project using Cyrus as the test specimen."

"How nice of you to join us, Dr. Ingram," said Shen. The tension in his voice decreased due to her arrival, though his face remained red and taut.

"I believe you may have been poorly informed," said Dolore, unconvinced. "The project absolutely cannot continue with the current test subject. His injuries are simply too extensive."

"Come on, Dolore, he's only missing an arm." Dr. Ingram blew him off. "We'll give him a prosthesis. Not just any prosthesis either. We'll give him one made of programmable matter."

"But how can that work?" asked Elysia. A mixture of confusion and hope filled her eyes.

"Cyrus will need to undergo osseointegration for permanent attachment of the prosthesis," said Ingram. "First, titanium bolts will be inserted into what remains of the ulna and radius. It normally takes a substantial amount of time for the bone to heal and adhere to the bolts in the typical human patient. Since Cyrus is a kresnik, I think the healing process would only take a few days at most. After that, abutments will be attached to the bolts. So far that's all standard procedure for direct bone attachment of a prosthesis."

Ingram paused to make sure they all still followed her.

Dolore had a smug look on his face, his doubt about the whole process unmistakable.

Dr. Shen and Elysia remained intently focused on Dr. Ingram, ready for her to move on.

"The prosthesis will then be attached to the abutments," Ingram continued. "The prosthesis itself will be made up of most of the usual parts found in a myoelectric prosthetic, complete with controller, the necessary shock absorbers, etc."

"What about the nanobots?" Dolore interrupted, his interest suddenly spiking. "The technology will need to be new and dynamic to keep the project going."

"I was coming to that," said Dr. Ingram. "The mass of nanobots, i.e., the programmable matter, will float around the end of the controller, or rather the controller will float within the mass. We will inject him with nanobotic biosensors targeted to specific areas in his brain. Once there, these nanobots will interface with Cyrus directly, relaying the electrical impulses created in his brain to the nanobots making up his prosthesis, essentially allowing him to control them with his mind. When he thinks to tighten the remainder of the muscles in his forearm, the mass will become solid and rigid, whereas when he relaxes, it will become less so."

"Sounds great if you don't listen to what is being said." Dolore rolled his eyes. "Exactly how does this solve any problems? For all your techno talk, none of this sounds much more technologically advanced than what is already available. Myoelectric limbs are dated these days, and this seems to have fewer practical applications. What is he going to end up with? A mass of nanobots that transitions between a liquid pool and a solid structure?"

"That's more or less what we're going for," said Dr. Ingram. "I assure you, this will in no way be a traditional prosthesis. The outer structure of each nanobot is composed of alloyed metal, allowing the overall structure of the prosthesis to become like that of a blade or other metal implement while in a solid state. Since we have opted for direct cranial innervation, Cyrus will be capable of instantly changing the shape of his prosthesis with a mere thought. He will be able to transform and configure his prosthesis into all matter of melee weapons and defensive implements, swords, axes, hammers, bulletproof shields, whatever. He will be limited only by his imagination. If this device works like I believe it will, he will be even stronger than before. His only possible equal will be the beast that escaped from the mountain lab. We have been given a great opportunity. Cyrus's kresnik healing ability allows him to withstand the mechanical stress of using such a device in a way no ordinary human could ever hope for."

Dolore frowned, still not caring for what he was hearing.

Dr. Shen's frustration died away, replaced by hope. Both he and Elysia hung on Dr. Ingram's every word.

Cyrus groaned again, barely understanding what he heard.

"Looks like we have you, Dolore," said Dr. Shen. He smiled, confident of his victory over the CEO.

"It does sound impressive." Dolore was unwilling to accept defeat. "The board will likely proceed with the project using the current test subject so long as this procedure is successful. It absolutely has to work, or else will be forced to move on with a different test subject."

"Oh, believe me, it will work." Dr. Ingram gave him a smug look. "We will increase his killing efficiency to such an extent that we'll be wondering why we didn't replace his arm with a prosthesis before Dr. Shen even began his gene-altering procedure."

"We'll see," said Dolore as another unsavory thought entered his head. "But what about the test subject's hyper-aggression? He will remain in danger of further injury if he continues to display such behavior. How do you plan to deal with that?"

"Simple," said Dr. Ingram. "Additional nanobots will be injected into his brain. We have created bots capable of suppressing the activities of certain areas of the brain that increase aggression, such as the amygdala, and act to increase the activities of certain areas of the brain that act to decrease it, like the prefrontal cortex. This will substantially reduce Cyrus's aggression when confronted by a vampire such that he will remain capable of rational thinking."

"Did somebody call for a surgeon?"

A man in green scrubs burst through the double doors. A group of similarly dressed nurses followed him, some of whom pushed metal, rolling trays.

Most of the trays carried the traditional instruments of surgery, scalpels, saws, and the like, whereas strange objects lay atop the others. These were the parts of Cyrus's soon-to-be prosthesis. All that was missing was the metallic mass of nanobots.

"Hello, Dr. Smith," said Ingram, smiling. "Yes, I absolutely called for a surgeon."

"I suppose you had this planned the whole time." Dolore groaned with frustration. "Whatever. Since Dr. Shen still has absolute say over the project, his word is all that matters. Things may change soon. Catch you guys later." He smirked at Dr. Shen and turned for the door, leisurely strolling away.

"Well, as you've heard Dolore say plenty of times," said Ingram. "You're in charge, Danny boy. Would you like Dr. Smith to proceed?"

"Yes, of course," said Shen, turning to speak to Dr. Smith, "You are free to proceed."

"Here we go." Dr. Smith rubbed his rubber-gloved hands together in anticipation.

He stepped toward Cyrus's bed as Shen, Ingram, and Elysia backed away.

"Hello, Cyrus." Smith looked down at him, his face hard for Cyrus to see through the light. He had dressed for surgery, his face concealed by a mask, and a surgical cap covered his head. "I'm Dr. Smith. I don't believe we've met. Are you ready for us to fix you up?"

Cyrus attempted to say 'yes' but instead nodded his head to convey the answer.

"That's what I wanted to hear," said Smith. "Nurse!" he called over to his staff. "The patient needs more anesthetic stat!"

The nurse strode across the floor, a giant needle full of anesthetic nanobots in her hands. She looked down at Cyrus as she prepared to inject him.

"I will try to be gentle," said the nurse. "This will only sting a little." She gently jabbed the needle into his neck, pushing down on the plunger.

"Goodnight, Cyrus," said Elysia. She stood beside his bed, her beautiful brown eyes full of hope.

"When you wake up, you will be even better than before," said Dr. Ingram, standing at Cyrus's feet. Dr. Shen stood beside her.

Cyrus could only stare at them now, expecting the nanobots to take effect soon.

"I'm going to have to ask you guys to leave the room now," said Dr. Smith, his demeanor still friendly. "Space is at a premium in here."

"Goodbye," said Dr. Ingram as the three of them all turned toward the doors.

Cyrus tried to say something yet again, but the already bright lights above him grew intense as he fell back into unconsciousness.

* * *

Cyrus blinked, awoken by the intense lights, the anesthetic effects of the nanobots dying off.

"It's magnificent, isn't it?"

He looked up to find Dr. Ingram with her hand on his right shoulder. She was staring down at his arm, repressed pleasure in her voice.

"I call it the TAPSAW, a *Transformative Alloy Prosthetic*

Shape-Altering Weapon."

Ingram ran her hand over Cyrus's head, petting him as though he were a cat.

"You will be unstoppable. The vampire's reign as apex predator will soon be over. All will fall prey to you now."

Cyrus tried to flex his arm, wishing it could somehow be whole again. He trembled, straining to see what had become of it.

Instead of a limb of flesh and bone, it was a mass of hardware connected to what looked like a pool of metallic, obsidian-black tar.

The   dark   pool   began   to   ripple...

About the Author

Dallas Massey

 Dallas Massey is from Seymour, Missouri, and has always fostered a love of both reading and biology. He received his Master's in Cell and Molecular Biology from Missouri State University in 2014. He returned to the same university as an online adjunct professor, teaching Concepts/Issues in Life Science. Dallas likes to incorporate his scientific knowledge into his writing wherever possible, adding a dose of authenticity to his fictional works. Though he loves writing, it was never his first career choice as his initial ambition was to become a successful genetic engineer. Unfortunately, Dallas was born with Duchenne's muscular dystrophy, a degenerative muscle disease that grants him only limited use of his limbs, his disorder keeping him from his dream occupation. He turned to writing after the loss of his younger brother, finding it provided him a constructive way to cope.

.

Made in the USA
Middletown, DE
10 June 2022

66909763R00246